In Spite of All
—JP Ishaq—

JP Ishaq

In Spite of All
Copyright © 2012 by JP Ishaq

ISBN 978-0615745329

To Steven Hinshaw, Teacher,
Who all those years ago took this seriously
Enough that I did the same

Protocol Additional to the Geneva Conventions of 12 August 1949

Article 47. Mercenaries

1. A mercenary shall not have the right to be a combatant or a prisoner of war.

2. A mercenary is any person who:

(a) is specially recruited locally or abroad in order to fight in an armed conflict;

(b) does, in fact, take a direct part in the hostilities;

(c) is motivated to take part in the hostilities essentially by the desire for private gain and, in fact, is promised, by or on behalf of a Party to the conflict, material compensation substantially in excess of that promised or paid to combatants of similar ranks and functions in the armed forces of that Party;

(d) is neither a national of a Party to the conflict nor a resident of territory controlled by a Party to the conflict;

(e) is not a member of the armed forces of a Party to the conflict; and

(f) has not been sent by a State which is not a Party to the conflict on official duty as a member of its armed forces.

—International Committee of the Red Cross, *Protocol Additional to the Geneva Conventions of 12 August 1949, and relating to the Protection of Victims of International Armed Conflicts*

Contents

Overture: Regret

It began with a dream of mushroom clouds. It haunted him less frequently than it once had, when his nights had been plagued by fire. In his vision a city nestled amid rolling hills, with broad boulevards and orderly blocks of towers marching toward the horizon. Inviting and gleaming, it was the ideal city a child might draw, an amalgamation, a pastiche.

It vanished in a flash as the dreamer watched, in a roar of fury such as only atomic weapons could make. The watercolor city was erased in a heartbeat as the clouds above parted and fled, leaving a hole in the sky. Spindly and terrible, the mushroom clouds climbed upward, flowers reaching for the sun.

The shadows of the bombs that had flattened the city twisted and swayed, looming over the hot panorama of ruin. Gods of carnage played among them, winding through the pillars of smoke and ash. Terrible and beautiful they were, dancing and frolicking as the world ended.

The dreamer stood on a hill, overlooking the destruction with eyes like slate, gray and unflinching. His young face was carved from indifference: remote, haughty, and angelic. In his mind's eye he saw the buildings crumble, blown away on the murder wind, stone edifices scattering like piles of leaves as trees disintegrated in fiery plumes.

Onward and upward the clouds went, laughing, crying out their booming anthem of chaos. What was left of the metropolis looked like a broken toy, hardly real. It was some city planner's little model, knocked off a table by the careless swing of an arm.

Walls of flame rose, obscuring the buildings as they continued to collapse. A massive bronze statue, grand and beautiful, melted like butter, flowed like liquid gold.

Trapped in a hall of mirrors, the dreamer saw the same painted Armageddon wherever he turned. He cried, but the tears evaporated on his cheeks. *What have I done?* he wondered, as he always did.

At the base of the hill, broad, multi-armed shapes shambled out of the inferno, their voices keening harshly as they fled the fires. In his mind's eye he saw this thing, this burning landscape in all its hellish beauty. Unable to move, he stood rooted to the spot as his boots melted, fusing with the soil.

The shapes below held out their many arms to him, their wailing increasing in pitch as the roaring, cruel laugh of the clouds split the sky. The dreamer saw the hot, hot wind scour away their shells and ignite the tender flesh beneath, cooking them even as they stumbled up the hill. The dreamer felt his own skin burn away, exposing surprised bone and muscle. He screamed, and the noise that escaped his ravaged throat was both the cry of the dying creatures struggling up the hill and the cruel, mirthless laughter of the wreckage.

A shockwave slammed into him, wiping away the hill, the creatures, the walls of fire, the clouds so tall they looked ready to topple.

Leon Victor's eyes snapped open, and he came awake in near-darkness. At first he thought his body was shaking, but as he oriented himself, he realized it was the ship. The chartered caravel, bound for Korinthe, trembled and seemed to slide laterally as though slipping on ice. Through the portholes he could see the purple walls of the conduit swirling past. Something was wrong, though, and the purple was cut with flashes of red as though the ship were being jerked to a stop by an anchor thrown out of the gravitational tunnel.

Was he still dreaming? His mind, still torn between sleep and wakefulness, conjured momentary images of the great wyrms that ancient spacefarers had believed lurked in the conduits. Were it not for the lingering effects of his nightmare he would have laughed out loud at such a foolish idea. He sat up, rubbing his shoulder. While the couch he had been dozing on was comfortable, it was no bed; his muscles had been tensed for as long as that horrible dream had lasted. Grimacing, tasting bile in his throat, Leon pushed the memory away and reached for the intercom. The ship continued to shake, and he could see his equipment sliding back and forth in the corner, kept from tumbling by cargo webbing.

"Is something wrong?" he asked, trying to control his breathing, to get himself under control.

He had to wait for a response, and for a moment he was certain that the crew was dead, that he was trapped in another horrible nightmare, one from which he could not escape. And then, strained but reassuring, a voice said, "Just a gravitational fluctuation. It will pass in a moment." There was a pause, and then, "Sorry for the inconvenience, sir."

"It's no problem. Thanks." Leon's hand fell away from the intercom button, and he settled back into his seat.

The flight attendant came to check on him, looking as though she, too, had been shaken from sleep. "We're sorry for the turbulence, sir. Is there anything I can get you?" she asked, groggy but with a note of concern in her voice.

"I'm fine, thanks. This happen often?"

"Not in my experience. We've flown this route close to a dozen times. Maybe they drifted too close to a binary star pair." The attendant left, walking gingerly across the swaying deck.

Leon Victor slid back down in his seat, looking around the small cabin. His deadly companions still dozed on their own couches, bathed in the ghostly light, looking like angry, restlessly sleeping wraiths. After a few moments the shaking subsided, and the movement became a gentle rocking, almost soothing. But sleep would not come again.

First Aria: Something Wicked This Way Comes

The patrol was routine, just like every patrol was routine. It boggled the mind that people would gamble their lives on a few empty cubic kilometers of space. Then again, the people who tallied cubic meters of space typically weren't the ones gambling. No, they had men like Major Darrel Kingston to do it for them. Kingston kept such thoughts to himself: voicing them would get him in hot water with the Valinata political advisor aboard *Proximo*, the light carrier that served as his squadron's base of operations. Then again, hot water was a luxury he would have gladly paid for.

As far as Kingston was concerned, there was nothing out here worth fighting for, certainly not dying for. He yawned inside his helmet, a long, jaw-stretching yawn, and shifted his arm away from the flight yoke just long enough to glance at his watch. No standard-issue pilot's chronometer, it was a gift from his wife. Set to their town's time back home on Lilliheim, it gave him an idea of what she was doing. Right now she would be helping the children with their homework or maybe preparing dinner. He found the normalcy of it thrilling, voyeuristic.

Two more hours, then he and his squadron could return to the bay of *Proximo*. He would get a hot meal and a hot shower (more likely a cold meal and a cold shower), followed by eight hours of rack time. Kingston glanced at the carrier as it drifted into view. Gleaming silver and dark green, she made the dull-brown planet below look even shabbier than it would normally. He didn't even remember the world's name, and he really didn't care. Just routine. Get through the patrol and back to the ship, to sleep until the next patrol. *Vital interest, my ass*, he thought as he beheld the unimpressive ball of rock. Allegedly there was a mining colony down there, one which hadn't had anything to mine in over a decade. The real prize was a large bundle of major conduits out in the open Deeps adjacent to the system, a cluster of the great gravitational highways that made interstellar travel possible. *We should just let the Coalition have this place, if they want to spend the time and money patrolling it.*

For twenty years Kingston had flown for the Valinata Space Force, the strong right arm of the Valinata Enclave's leadership. Five of those years had been spent as the commanding officer of the VSF Hydra Combat Aerospace Wing; in that time they had been at a standoff with the Coalition that sat on the other side of the border some ten or twelve times. It seemed like a waste of effort and paper to him. Politicians came and went, empires rose and fell, and the people got shit on every time. At least he got to fly, never mind that it was because two kingdoms were looking for trouble— anything to stir flagging patriotic zeal.

"Hey, chief, did you hear the one about Empress Kra'al and the cargo barge?" asked his wingman, Lieutenant William Tucker. Tucker, who was always searching for jokes and never seemed to find any worth telling; Tucker, who tried endlessly and fruitlessly to get into Ensign Kelly Fadara's bunk. "It's a good one."

"Go ahead." In fact, Kingston had heard the joke numerous times in all its variations over the years, but he let Tucker go ahead. It was easier than putting up with his sulking for the rest of the patrol. Who knew, maybe some of those Coalition assholes were listening in. Hell, they'd probably think it was funny, too, even if it was at their own monarch's expense.

As the lieutenant began reciting the joke to the grudging but otherwise bored-to-tears squadron, Kingston scanned the sector. Off at the edge of his field of vision, the silver-and-green ovoid form of the *Proxima* drifted along her route, looking like a giant turtle withdrawn into its shell. The ship's cannon turrets lazily scanned the bleak expanse; Kingston was sure the gunners were just as bored as he was.

Kingston remembered a time when the VSF's fighter instrumentation was second-rate at best, and he had learned to trust his eyes and his instincts. When he saw a glimmer, a flicker of movement off to port, he paused and checked his sensors. Nothing. Still, the political advisors had assured them all that the Coalition might try something to stoke the fire.

The pilots groaned as Tucker reached—and butchered—the lackluster punch line of his second-hand joke, wherein the Coalition head of state was confused with the head of the cargo barge, resulting in her being even more full of shit than usual. Kingston's eyes drifted back to that empty patch of space. Something *had* moved, but his scanners weren't registering anything bigger than a soup can. Maybe it was time for another physical, to have his eyes swapped. Was he getting that old?

He was about to discount it as fatigue when his sensors picked up a momentary contact and he caught another flicker at the periphery of his vision. *Damn these eyes of mine. Maybe my next ones should be green. That'll surprise the kids.* It could have been anything: a Coalition Royal Defense Force spy probe (the CRDF seemed to have an overabundance of spy probes), a deactivated mine left over from the Cincon Insurrection, or one of their own rusted communications relays, catching the light as it revolved. Kingston flipped up his visor and wiped a gloved hand across his forehead.

Somehow, over the grousing of Tucker and the other pilots, Kingston picked out a sound, little more than a snatch of an echo. He frowned. "Tucker, shut up for a minute. Did anyone else hear that?"

"Negative, Major."

Still frowning, Kingston played with the gain on his comm receiver, trying to retrieve the signal. A moment later he had it, just as the *Proximo*'s coordinator announced a distress call on the Whisper, picked up by the cruiser's more powerful comm tranceivers. It was coming from the *Nadine*, part of a patrol one system adjacent. Kingston listened to the fragmented transmission and felt his heart rate increase.

Proximo and her attendant fighters came about and merged with a nearby minor conduit. It was as simple as finding the channel of gravitational energy linking their solar system to the next one and amplifying it. As part of the Lightspeed Initiative, every task force was required to have one gravdrive-equipped squadron per carrier, and Hydra jumped hard. It was only the third time Kingston had used the fighter's built-in drive in the field, and it was far more jarring than it would have been aboard a larger vessel with dedicated inertial regulators. His brain felt as though it rattled around in his skull, his bones partially liquefied. They arrived at the *Nadine*'s position in a standard staggered combat formation, finding only empty space. Well, that wasn't entirely accurate. A few thousand kilometers away, a cloud of drifting wreckage marked the patrol cruiser's last known position, an emergency flight recorder beeping out an automated distress signal. Kingston felt a lump rise in his throat. Immediately he scanned his board, looking for energy signatures, heat registers, anything that might indicate an enemy ship.

"Reactor meltdown?" suggested Tucker.

"Quiet!" Kingston snapped. It was true that *Athens*-class cruisers like the *Nadine* were more prone to meltdowns than their leaders in the Tête would have them believe, but it didn't seem right.

Gradually Kingston became aware of a peculiar tugging sensation, pulling him to the right. No sooner had he noticed it than he realized that his fighter was likewise drifting to starboard. He looked over, and his eyes widened.

Only a few dozen kilometers away, a circular patch of space about a kilometer in diameter appeared to condense, the edges peeling inward. It was a bizarre sight, unlike anything he had seen in all his years of space travel. "What the hell?" he whispered. The comm was alive with chatter; so focused was he that he didn't bother with a reprimand. The stars had disappeared behind the shimmering curtain of black, as though oil had been poured on the motionless canvas of space. It was to that ... hole ... that Kingston and his squadron were being dragged. Slowly the rift began to close, and Kingston realized that it was an enormous conduit entry point, a messy one, the aperture somehow lingering after a ship or ships had already gone through it.

There was a flash to port, and *Proximo* appeared, bristling with weapons. Bay doors slid open, and the rest of the fighters began emerging. "Hydra, this is *Proximo*. We are detecting gravitational anomalies indicating multiple vessels in conduit. Outbound vector unknown."

Hit and run, Kingston thought, frowning. It could only be the Coalition. Suddenly Tucker's joke had lost its humor. There was no way *Nadine*'s position could have been misinterpreted: the ship was more than a hundred million kilometers from the Coalition's side of the demarcation line. Kingston's mind was racing through possibilities and tactical options as he herded his squadron into a defensive patrol while *Proximo* unloaded her other three squadrons.

Nadine had been completely obliterated, Kingston saw, the largest fragment of hull no more than ten meters long and charred by blast marks. He was in the process of ordering another flyby when a new signal came through loud and clear. This time it was coming from the colony they had just left. *Holy shit, we're at war.*

"*Proximo, Proximo*, this is Calama Territorial Command, we are registering multiple unknown contacts in our vicinity and gravity well disturbances consistent with capital ships. Please advise." The voice sounded frightened and with good reason. Until a few months ago, Hydra and *Proximo* had been attached to the 31st Dragon Valia Armada, when the Coalition had insisted on a mutual stand-down to ease the border dispute. The de-escalation had seemed reasonable to Kingston at the time. Still, it had left their navies spread thinly across a fairly unruly sector of space, with little more than pickets to hold the line. Now he saw that it had been a savvy ruse to lighten the Valinata's presence in the region, opening the way for a CRDF invasion.

"Hydra, this is Captain Vissek," announced *Proximo*'s commander gravely. "Return to Calama-446 *immediately* and intercept. We still have to retrieve the rest of the fighters. Will follow, ETA ten minutes."

Hydra Squadron realigned with Calama and jerked across space once again. Kingston glanced at his watch: the total time elapsed was twenty minutes since the first distress signal had come through.

They reverted into the Calama-446 system less than five minutes later, and Kingston saw that their quarry had already taken up position over the planet, a black dot standing out in sharp contrast against Calama's clouds.

Kingston was running a broad-spectrum scan when an alarm chirped in his ear. The intruding ship, perched over Calama's horizon, had opened fire. Green bursts of plasma discharge rained into the atmosphere.

"Contact ahead," he announced to his squad. "Fix...." His voice trailed off as he looked at his sensor readout for a detailed profile. It was taking longer than usual.

"Do we wait for *Proximo*, chief?" inquired Tucker, voice leaden.

"Negative, Lieutenant." They couldn't just let it burn the colony from orbit. "Form up into three wings. B Flight, stay on Ensign Fadara. Skip the horizon; they should lose you in the background clutter. C Flight with Ensign Bruno: take the scenic route, flank them. A Flight with me: direct approach. We'll hit from their starboard side to draw their fire."

A chorus of affirmation crackled over the speakers, and Kingston breathed a sigh of relief. They were good pilots. If they couldn't scare the enemy away, they would need every bit of their skill.

The distance to the target was dropping, with the ship less than a thousand kilometers away. Kingston couldn't quite see it, and his instruments were still having trouble locking on. This was unusual.

Another alarm alerted him to *Proximo*'s return, and Captain Vissek took control of the situation. He allowed Kingston to continue his run as the sensors indicated that the intruder had abandoned its attack on the colony in favor of the VSF carrier.

Kingston was studying the sensor readout when a cacophony of sirens went off. Suddenly red lights were blinking on his console. More contacts.

Proximo's tactical coordinator was barking instructions. "Hydra, withdraw to screening range to cover *Proximo*. We have three, four incoming bandits, four hundred kilometers off the bow!" Gone was the boredom in his voice, replaced with surprise and more than a little excitement. "Unknown signatures, dropping conduit! Drive readings don't match VSR or CROS entries." If the Valinata Ships Registry and Coalition Registry of Ships both failed to identify it, it could only be a clandestine vessel.

"This is Hydra Lead, acknowledging," Kingston said. "Arming sequence initiated. Standing by for orders." He flipped the safeties off his weapons systems and steeled himself to fire a shot in anger. He swung his fighter hard to port and monitored the sensors to make sure that B Flight was following suit. C Flight had gone far afield and was struggling to catch up.

A moment later three mammoth shapes materialized in his field of vision, close enough for the onboard cameras to construct a grainy image. Kingston froze, his eyes locked on the enhancement: floating before them, almost serene in their stillness, were monsters. He couldn't believe his eyes. The smallest of them dwarfed the *Proximo* by nearly three hundred meters in length at least.

Kingston glanced again at his targeting readout and frowned. They didn't show up as anything more than intermittent blips and temperature spikes. "Visual and thermal acquisition only. Requesting telemetry."

"Negative, Hydra Lead," the tactical coordinator replied. "Attempting to boost scan resolution. Stand by."

"For how long?" demanded Tucker, his voice a volatile mixture of excitement and fear.

Kingston fought his own rising panic, forced himself to think, to be rational. There were no space monsters, no demons of the conduit. These might look the part, but they were ships, had to be, painted and designed to be fearsome. It was an old tactic, one of the oldest. Outwardly they resembled giant black squids, with an oblong hull which appeared to be cast in mottled tones of black and brown, almost fleshlike. Along the hull he spotted moving, puckered nozzles, puffing out clouds of incandescent gas as the things maneuvered. At the bow of each one, four long and gently curving protrusions—stabilizers, perhaps—projected from the tapering hull, giving the impression of immense, probing tentacles.

The *Proximo*, still several hundred kilometers away, began her approach, coming about in a confrontational posture, weapons and shields charging as she turned to offer her flank to the enemy in order to fire a broadside—if it came to that. The commander transmitted an open hail, standard for unauthorized contacts, and Kingston got himself back under control, reassured by the mundaneness of the protocol: "Unidentified vessels, this is the carrier *Proximo* of the Valinata Space Force. You are in violation of Valinata territorial sovereignty. Cease fire immediately. Any further hostile action will be met with force. Stand down for boarding...." Kingston tuned out the rest, focusing on the unusual ships. Whoever they were, they were moving fast and showed no signs of halting their advance. His hands began darting about the cockpit, repeating his weapons-check, making sure everything was ready if the need arose.

He dialed over to his squadron's channel. "Okay, Hydras, tighten it up. Safeties off, defense grids to full power. Stay alert, and stand by to initiate flyby and scan. If they try anything, we use the can openers."

With coordination that made Kingston proud, his pilots fired their ventral bow thrusters, and the fighters abruptly reversed direction, looped back around, and angled toward the nearest unidentified cruiser. There were only a few hundred kilometers between them and the intruders now, practically the distance of a kiss among the stars, less than a second's travel for a plasma beam.

Minutes passed. The fighters flew on in tense silence, watching as the kilometers counted down, as they closed with black shapes that looked as though they had been molded from the fabric of space itself. The contact protocol went out over the comm once again in an attempt to hail the intruders. By now the commander of *Proximo* had also hailed reinforcements, or so Kingston hoped.

Their hails were met with silence, the exact opposite of a friendly apology as far as Kingston was concerned. He shivered despite the carefully controlled climate of the cockpit.

The dark ships came about, turning their own flanks toward the patrol group in perfect unison. Kingston knew hostile intent when he saw it. Without warning, a volley of fiery green energy tore through the space between the ships, glowing amorphous masses flashing right through the fighter formation and slamming full-on into the *Proximo*'s flank. Burning embers quickly went dark in the vacuum around the scorched hull of the carrier, and the first salvo was followed by another. Soon fire was raining upon *Proximo*'s hull, most of it thankfully dissipated by the defensive grid. *Credible intent established*, Kingston's rational mind announced. *Time to fight.*

The comm came alive with chatter, but Kingston didn't wait for orders. "All hands move to attack position and lock targets!" He pushed his throttle up and angled his sleek, silver-and-green leopard-class fighter toward the formation of enemy vessels, aiming to attack their dorsal hulls while B Flight broke off to hit them from below. C Flight had caught up and was angling to hit the enemy from astern.

He commed the carrier. "Scramble the rest of the fighters!" They would need all the help they could get. The tactical coordinator quickly replied in the affirmative, and the bays on *Proximo*'s port side began to open. Not soon enough, for the fourth great leviathan had drifted in from the planet, well behind the fighter screen, too late to intercept. It hammered the carrier at close range, green fire splashing against the hull. Its bulk temporarily blocked *Proximo* from the broadsides of its fellows, and for a moment the two cruisers faced each other one-on-one. The barrage smashed down the port grid and ruptured the hull. The lights in the bays went dark, and telltale jets of air and debris marked a number of breaches along the carrier's flank.

The few fighters that had managed to limp out of the carrier's bays were quickly picked off, leaving the solitary squadron to defend the now-crippled ship. A distress signal was blaring across the bands in earnest. The turrets on the *Proximo* were no longer scanning lazily for targets: they were wheeling about and raking the hull of the enemy cruiser. Some of the turrets appeared to be firing indiscriminately into space. Were they malfunctioning? It took Kingston a moment to realize that what he was seeing in the camera feed wasn't debris breaking off the enemy ship but little fighters swarming out of her belly. Flitting here and there almost too fast to see, he couldn't have made them out at all without the camera's enhancement.

Bright lances of energy tore out of *Proximo*'s particle cannons, and missiles left streaking contrails of compressed gases as they poured out of the wounded carrier and into the incoming ships. The fourth unidentified vessel, off *Proximo*'s port side, took the brunt of the broadsides, and tears appeared in its hull, venting its own atmospheric gasses.

Kingston and his squadron were now near enough to the approaching enemy fighter screen for him to make out some details, only there weren't any. No insignia, no markings of any kind. *Who flies without insignia? Only pirates and military units that don't want to be identified. Is it the thrice-damned Coalition, after all?* The little craft were painted in the same mottled pattern as the capital ships, making them nearly invisible. Looking into the gulf between their closing screens, Kingston saw that his own squadron was hopelessly outnumbered. With no transponders, the enemy fighters were difficult to track, but the sensors had gradually constructed a composite image and profile. There wasn't much to lock onto other than heat; these fighters had masked the electronic portraits for which most sensor systems looked.

The distress signal from *Proximo* was still blaring on the broadband, desperate; it was silenced as a blast from one of the black ships hit the bridge tower. It detonated in a ball of fire which quickly collapsed on itself in the vacuum. Debris spun away from the wrecked ship, glittering like confetti in the starlight.

Still the wounded carrier's turrets fired on the slowly advancing black cruisers, sending missiles corkscrewing through space to slam into the battleships' hulls. It was obvious that the *Proximo* was lost. Kingston thought he had seen it all, but he was stunned by the sudden ferocity of this unprovoked raid by the CRDF. What did they stand to gain by exterminating two VSF patrol groups? And how would they have developed such ships without anyone knowing? *Are we nothing more than a weapons test to them?*

The time for such thoughts was curtailed as the enemy fighter screen had reached firing range. Kingston waited for a target lock confirmation and smiled when the onboard computer beeped. His smile faded as the beep grew intermittent. That was when he realized that the ship's computer was still having difficulty holding a signature from the enemy ships. "Open fire at will," he ordered grimly, launching a pair of missiles which arrowed toward their target. He just hoped they could maintain a target lock long enough to impact.

Without waiting for a hit confirmation, the major jammed his thumb down on the firing stud of his flight yoke. His ship vibrated as the dual, wing-mounted, independently tracking Gatling guns opened up, unleashing thousands of rounds on the arrowheaded enemy craft. Operated by internal combustion of the pre-oxidized propellant within each shell, the Gatling was a fearsome weapon in space. With no friction and no deceleration, the big projectiles could shred through just about anything. Space all around him was alight as emerald streaks of fire and bright tracer rounds passed each other in the dark and tore into their targets with dispassionate devastation.

Explosions lit up the enemy formations. One of the enemy fighters directly in front of Kingston cracked in half, spewing flames and debris into space as the larger sections spun away. Then his ships were through the enemy formation, and both groups came about. It would be a brutal dogfight. *This is what we were made for.*

"Tucker, stay close." Kingston banked hard, maneuvering thrusters along the hull hissing as they fired.

"You got it, boss." Tucker's fighter mirrored the maneuver perfectly. It was just like training, only now they weren't facing simulated foes.

Green fire was flashing by from behind them, and Kingston thought fast. "Tucker, break to port and pull an inversion...." He steadied his hand. "Now!" The two leopards split apart, firing their bow-mounted braking thrusters simultaneously with the ventral maneuvering jets to reverse direction and face their pursuers head-on. The leopard was a worthy fighter: lightly armored but well armed, it was an able dogfighter, hard-hitting and very maneuverable, designed to wreak havoc among an enemy's heavy bombers. But when the two fighters came back around, their adversaries—who should have been settled nicely in their crosshairs—had eluded them.

"Who the hell are these bastards?" demanded Tucker, his voice angry but quaking, scared. The leopard was the most advanced fighter in the Valinata Space Force, far more agile than anything in the Coalition arsenal, and they had just been outmaneuvered. Easily.

They didn't have long to reflect on this turn of events: more enemy fire streaked in around them, and a siren screamed in Kingston's ear that he had been hit. It wasn't bad, but it certainly wasn't good. The defensive grid had deflected most of the hit, but the enemy ordnance had released so much energy that the grid had nearly shorted out.

As Kingston spun his fighter in a tight dive to avoid the incoming fire, he saw the enemy cruisers finish off the *Proximo*. The dying carrier's guns had gone silent, and she was listing to starboard, propelled in a lazy spin brought on by the atmospheric gasses venting from dozens of hull breaches. Still the black ships fired. There was a bright flash from the cruiser as her engines exploded, and Kingston had to look away. A jagged husk was all that remained when the explosion faded. The ship that had been his home for nearly six years was gone, and so was everyone aboard.

There was a scream over the comm, and a corresponding explosion in front of him as one of his squadmates was blown apart. He grimaced as the shredded remains of a fighter's wing tumbled past his cockpit, and microdebris crackled against the defensive grid. It didn't seem right that his pilot should pass in the heartless silence of the void.

"Sound off!" Kingston ordered. His squadron replied, short three voices. He couldn't grieve now as he had a job to do: get the nine remaining fighters back home alive. *Proximo* was gone, rapidly cooling wreckage drifting off into eternity. Luckily the upgraded leopards were capable of reaching the nearest sector garrison, if nowhere else.

"B-flight, disengage and provide long-range support for a retreat!"

"Not gonna happen, Major," bit back Lieutenant Fadara. "It's too thick in here."

"Tucker, get back in formation! I need you on my wing!"

"Chief, I've taken serious damage! Controls are fucked!" Tucker's voice was desolate, the anger and excitement long drained from it. "I can't maneuver for shit!" Kingston tried to break off from his own pursuer long enough to cover his wingman, but these enemy pilots were too good, their craft too nimble. Kingston's Hydras had been good enough to pass muster for border patrol, good enough to hold the line after the stand-down, but they were no match for this fury. "Help me," Tucker whimpered quietly, finally. Kingston looked over to starboard, toward Tucker's fighter. It was on fire, its precious atmosphere being consumed rapidly. There was nothing Kingston could do but watch as the craft began to tumble, an easy target.

Two more blasts converged on the hull, and an instant later an expanding vapor cloud and a blinding trace image were all that were left of William Tucker.

Kingston looked at his board, and his eyes went wide. The scanners showed only four of his squadron's fighters remaining, surrounded by over two dozen enemy craft. And the two remaining enemy cruisers were closing in now, inexorable. In the distance, more were approaching. "Pull back! Pull back! *All fighters scram for home plate!*" he screamed in vain. His ship shuddered as a green burst punched through his starboard wing, leaving a ragged, melted hole. "Break engagement and jump conduit!" They hadn't been loaded out for a full fight, had no antimatter warheads for destroying cruisers, no hyper-velocity torpedoes ... couldn't even get their damned guns to lock on. They had never had a chance out here.

Kingston's pleas did no good. The fighters were stuck fast in a trap that had been sprung well. He watched, grief-stricken, as Kelly Fadara's fighter was blasted into debris by the enemy's perfectly coordinated fighter screen. The others soon followed her into oblivion. Ensign Bruno was the last of them, fighting in silence as he tried to evade his pursuers. He brought down two before his port wing was sheared off by a blast. "*Bon chance*, Major," he said quietly before he exploded.

Not even the best Coalition squadrons moved with such single-minded synchronization. Only Kingston, flying overwatch at the edge of the engagement and dodging fire, had a chance at escaping. With all hope of victory gone, his obligation was to warn the nearest base in case *Proximo*'s hails had been jammed.

He called up the conduit map, trying to identify the quickest way out. With the enemy fighters so much faster than his, he would have to pass right across the bow of one of the cruisers to reach the nearest conduit. Taking a deep breath, Kingston picked his exit vector and lit the afterburners. His damaged fighter groaned with the effort, the engines thrumming in time to the rapid beat of his heart.

For a few moments he was in the clear. The enemy fighters receded behind him, and the nearby cruiser's plasma seemed to move in slow motion. He dodged the blasts easily, dipping his port wing to avoid one. *Just a few more seconds.* He glanced to the right as he shot past the enemy cruiser. The bow stabilizers looked as though they were reaching out to grab him. And at the join of those booms was ... *no, that's impossible.*

Dead-center between the four protrusions was a giant, bloodshot eye, roving hungrily across space, protected by a translucent membrane.

Kingston's childhood came rushing back to him, tales of ghosts in the conduits of space, the Great Dragon that guarded the Valinata while her people slept. The legends—fairy tales, really—couldn't be true. That sort of shit wasn't real; he had known that since he was eight years old!

He was facing the Great Dragon now; it was no metaphor emblazoned on the crests of ships. It was real, and it was breathing fire down upon them. *No, they're just ships!*

Kingston cursed the absurdity of it all. He had always been a profoundly rational man, lacking much of an imagination. It was therefore very distressing for him to entertain such wild fears as those great things hung there in space, monstrous and unknowable, their little minions streaming forth behind him. He kept trying to tether himself to reality, to insist that what they were wasn't important, that they were just ships. And ships could be sunk.

He rested his hand on the lever that would send his ship through a gravitational conduit to safety but hesitated. Unbidden, his eyes drifted to his tactical board again. The squad indicator was dark, and his heart sank. His entire combat wing had been wiped out, his carrier and its crew massacred. In that moment of hesitation, an energy burst from one of the enemy cruisers smashed into his cockpit. Everything was light and black and ended in an instant.

Debris cooled quickly in the deep-freeze of space, embers going from white-hot to yellow to red. Finally they were as black as the void itself, slowly spiraling toward the nondescript brown planet as the dark warships set their course and began moving again.

First Movement:
Citizen of Nowhere

1: Business as Usual

Somehow, a career already characterized by damage control had not prepared Atyre Kra'al for this hammer blow. Her desk was meticulously organized and polished to perfection, reflecting a caricature of her face, her yellow stripes dulled, her tribal tattoos distorted. The reflection looked about the way she felt: dull. She leaned back in her chair, her dorsal ridge pressing against the backrest. Whereas the males of her species exhibited dorsal spines that could express emotion, the dorsal ridge made females harder to read. Kra'al had long ago learned to compensate by exaggerating her facial expressions.

In this case, though, her nervous actions gave away her strain: the restless tail tip, the clicking claws. She was the first Prross to be given the title of Archon of the Coalition, and as if the normal scrutiny wasn't bad enough, the burden of her office had recently gotten heavier. She had inherited a divided empire, and in the dead of night, when she had nothing else to distract her, she had to admit that the prospect of unifying it was probably beyond her. She had to deal with rumblings of secession from several key sectors, economic instability, the logistics of connecting hundreds of heavily populated worlds and thousands of smaller colonies and outposts.... *A fight with the Valinata is the last thing I need.*

Her private office at the top of Tagea's Crown Palace was the size of a decent apartment and was lavishly furnished. A majestic divan occupied one corner, for those increasingly frequent occasions when she had to work through the night. Lately that opulence had been far from comforting, even with the waning sunlight pouring through the great bay windows and turning gold accents to heavenly fire. Wearily, Kra'al turned her attention back to her guest.

Before her stood Grand Admiral Hakar, the Tagean member of the Star Chamber that administered the great fleets and armies of the Coalition Royal Defense Forces and the man she hoped could provide some answers. Tall, lean, and elegant, he was the picture of Tagean nobility, with a long muzzle and eyes like burning coal. He was intelligent, loyal, and resourceful, with an illustrious military career and a reputation for integrity. He was well regarded and respected by allies and enemies alike, a fact that had guaranteed his spot on the Star Chamber even after Kra'al's predecessor's fall from grace. Kra'al was dismayed to notice that although Hakar held himself high and straight, his gray-and-purple-trimmed uniform seemed somewhat hollow, caved in, a scarecrow stuffed with leaves and hung in a field. His usually soft eyes were hard, grim, and his once-brown fur was shot through with gray. "Your Majesty, I don't know what to tell you," he growled in his native tongue, Tagean Mze. "Whoever pulled off this hit-and-fade knew what they were doing. Surgical."

Kra'al's eyes narrowed to slits. "I don't need to tell you how critical our response is right now. It must be measured. The Valinata demand an explanation, and they're making all sorts of wild allegations. Do me a favor by not sounding so impressed." When the news had reached them, Kra'al's orderly had woken her in the middle of the night. She had spent the days and nights since reeling in every expert, hoping that someone could provide insight. In the wake of the attack, blame had settled squarely on the Coalition, and even their allies were making polite inquiries. It didn't help that the long, untamed stretch of border between the Coalition and the Valinata had been hotly disputed for years. What did it say about them that Kra'al's first reaction was to suspect that some rogue admiral of their own had decided to set the powder keg alight? Now Grand Admiral Hakar stood before her, the one member of her entire administration she could count on to be objective, to be honest with her, and even he was speaking in tones of admiration. "You're certain it wasn't us?" Even entertaining the possibility that they weren't in full control of their own military was distressing.

"Your Majesty, I can assure you it wasn't a CRDF sortie. Every ship of the line has been accounted for, and I checked with the sector commanders personally. No officer in their right mind would take such unilateral action, not without clear provocation. We don't want another skirmish any more than the Vali do. I just hope they know that."

"Well, they certainly got a skirmish." Kra'al clasped her clawed hands and nodded her long, graceful head up and down, a mannerism picked up from the ubiquitous Humans that had spread to every corner of the galaxy. "We're going to be guilty until proven innocent. It wasn't us, and it obviously wasn't the VSF. Any ideas?"

"The location tells us a lot," Hakar said, a little uncertainly.

"Calama? You mean the conduit bundle, don't you?" Kra'al had been fully briefed, and she understood the strategic importance of the system in question. "Whoever controls Calama can bypass the Gates of the

Arc and get direct access to the Coalition interior. They could already be here, and we wouldn't know until they struck. Or they could be trying to get the whole VSF into a war with us to leave the Valinata interior open for a coup."

"That's right. In a few days I may be able to tell you more."

"What can you tell me *now*?"

Hakar cocked his head. "Well, that whole region has been demilitarized as part of the last Engine Accord. When the distress signal reached Commodore Quen, he dispatched a carrier battle group to investigate and render assistance as per standard operating procedures. Unfortunately they were far enough away that it took some time to respond. Also as per SOP, our ships adopted a defensive formation on arrival."

"Which nearly prompted a counterattack from the responding Valinata flotilla," Kra'al interjected.

"Correct, Highness. Commodore Quen's task force arrived to find the area empty except for the wreckage. Before interception, his ships collected samples for forensic analysis. We found traces of a Valinata carrier, *Tempest*-class, and fighters, no way to tell how many. Our ships arrived within an hour of the distress signal's transmission. Whatever happened happened within a matter of minutes. Including the razing of the colony and monastery on the world below."

"What of the pilot who managed to eject?" Kra'al had heard several conflicting reports, but Hakar had debriefed Quen himself, via long-comm ansible.

"She was recovered alive, but I'm afraid she expired. There appears to have been a malfunction with her pressure suit. Corpsmen tried to revive her, but oxygen deprivation had led to catastrophic brain damage."

"A pity. Perhaps she could have told us what happened." Kra'al snorted unhappily. "The poor thing. Flight recorders?"

"If they survived, our crews didn't have time to retrieve any, Your Majesty. The wreckage was scattered across a thousand kilometers of space. We didn't identify any wreckage other than the VSF task force: all reactor signatures scanned were consistent with Vali ships. The only inconsistency...." Hakar trailed off. He closed his eyes for a moment, and when he opened them, they had a faraway look. "There was something else there, that had impacted against the carrier and lodged in the hull. A biomass, I'm told. One of the cruisers collected the fragment they found. It's being forwarded to Triatha for analysis. It might be nothing."

Kra'al didn't respond right away. This was news to her, left out or kept out of the official reports. She wondered why. "You said all signatures matched VSF emissions. Is it possible they were attacked by their own ships? A mutiny, maybe, or a rebel faction?"

"It's possible," Hakar admitted. "But that's not entirely accurate. There were gravitic distortions that defied identification."

Too many questions, not nearly enough answers. Kra'al supposed there was nothing she could do but wait for more information. "All right. Since you have such a handle on this, I want you to take the lead. Tell the Valinata that they have our word it wasn't one of our ships. Then tell them we'll give them any assistance they need in investigating this. Offer them access to our comscan networks—limited, I shouldn't have to remind you—and telemetry databases. Just don't give away the keys to my office, all right? And stand our border ships on alert. If the Valinata decide we're lying to them, I don't want them getting in here and causing trouble. And we don't need any pirates raiding Outbound Arc planets, trying to take advantage of the confusion." She ran her long tongue along sharp teeth. "Don't mention the sample you found to anyone else until you know what it is."

Hakar bowed to her and picked up his peaked officer's cap, tucking it under his arm. Turning on his heel, he went to the door. "Oh, and Hakar?"

"Yes, Highness?" he asked, pausing.

"Find out who did this, and quickly. If they can hit the Valinata like this, they can do the same to us." Her eyes had taken on a predatory aspect.

"At once." Hakar left the office, footsteps soft and getting softer as he disappeared down carpeted hallways.

Once he was gone, Kra'al leaned back in her plush chair, her tail thumping rhythmically against the tiled floor, her mind racing. It didn't sound like pirates. She frowned, loosing an involuntary growl. *It sounds worse than pirates.*

§

Inspector Peter Kimball glanced around nervously, running shaking fingers through his thinning hair. How could such a warm place feel so cold? A tropical breeze blew in the open front door, but it brought no comfort with it. They had ordered the door left open, to preserve an illusion of normalcy while they did their dangerous business.

Kimball had done the tracking, put in the countless hours of investigation to get them to this point, but raids were a little out of his comfort zone. Several of the tactical team officers, clad in dark blue and gray riot gear, were waiting behind him. They were the picture of professionalism: calm, collected, even joking, their shotguns and stubby Warthog carbines held at the ready with casual, deadly familiarity. He wished he had their confidence or could at least feign it.

The lobby of the Hotel Thescalon was ornate, harkening back to another age of marble columns and bronze statues peering out from behind outsized primeval ferns. The Terran Revival architecture and decoration were attractive, almost soothing. A nearby fountain trickled serenely, depicting two waifish maidens pouring water out of pitchers, but Kimball saw none of it. He couldn't take his mind off Suite 3034. At the end of a hallway saturated with rich carpeting, hand-cut mosaics, and soft lighting, a dozen or so of the most dangerous criminals on Korinthe waited. Kimball had dedicated the last two years of his life and what turned out to be the final year of his marriage to putting them in a Unified Commonwealth penal colony. His moment had arrived; he just wasn't ready for it.

Kimball was not a nervous man, but having the closure to his career-making and marriage-ending case within his grasp made him understandably anxious and just as jumpy. That and the serious possibility of the evening ending in bloodshed. And so he literally jumped when a gloved hand fell upon his shoulder.

"Are you all right, Inspector? You look a little sick." Captain Vivienne Olafsen was in charge of the tactical team that would ordinarily have been tasked with conducting the raid. There was little that she and Kimball agreed on in their line of work, but this evening they found themselves united.

"I am. Thank you, Captain. I'm just a little apprehensive is all."

"I know how you feel." Olafsen scowled, and her stern face tightened. "I don't like being micromanaged, and I don't like subordinating my unit to mercenaries."

"In an ideal world..." Kimball said, leaving the thought unfinished. Olafsen nodded grudgingly. "Do you know much about the Jackals?"

"I had never heard of them until our briefing. I looked into it." The tactical team captain sighed. "They do have a reputation, but this isn't justice, Kimball. I suppose the Premier has his reasons. I don't have to like them."

"No, you don't. I wouldn't say that too loudly, though." Kimball glanced over to the far end of the lobby. His eyes settled on a gaunt and rather unimpressive gentleman leaning casually against a column. The man looked nervous and expectant; with his arms clasped behind his back and his eyes roving over the assembled personnel, he gave off a distinctly bureaucratic air. Mr. Princeton may have looked like a bank manager, but he was very nearly as dangerous as the men they were hunting.

"What would you do if it was your daughter?" Kimball blurted, surprising himself.

"She just made Constable First Grade. I'd have her thrown out and jailed."

Kimball grimaced. "That's not what I meant. What I mean is, we have a rare chance to stop this before it reaches our schools, our children. I suppose that's worth going along with … this."

"I suppose it is." Olafsen looked uncomfortable. "I'm going upstairs to check on the insertion team." She withdrew, a quiet shadow in her black tactical gear.

The minutes dragged on, and Kimball felt himself grow colder. When the car pulled up outside the hotel doors, he was almost relieved. A shield dressed as a hotel valet hastily opened the rear door.

Three men stepped out: a Prross and two Humans. They wore civilian attire, but their utilitarian bags matched, and they walked with the loose, alert gait of trained sojieri. Their studied nonchalance worried Kimball nearly as much as the occupants of Suite 3034. For a moment he felt his blood run cold as the temperature seemed to drop another ten degrees. *To kill a monster, unleash another.*

The Prross in particular stood out. He might have been the only member of his species on the planet. His red patent leather bomber jacket had been patched and torn numerous times by knives, bullets, and age. He wore a battered baseball cap which fit his sloping head awkwardly; the logo on the hat was for the Hyphen Telecom Company and proudly proclaimed "We Bring Worlds Together." There was a reason that the Human colonists who had first made contact with the Prross had called them Saurians: they looked reptilian and vicious, civilized minds trapped in savage bodies.

Was this their idea of discretion? The Prross made little attempt to hide the enormous cannon he carried, and when the taller Human reached— slowly—for identification, Kimball saw that his long jacket concealed two big pistols slung low over his hips. *A cowboy*, he thought derisively.

The officers at the reception desk examined the security clearance and pointed the men toward Kimball. He swallowed, absurdly frightened of them, even as they walked through a gauntlet of dozens of armed shields in uniform or dressed as hotel staff. He wasn't afraid for his own safety, however; on this night, these men would either make or break his career.

Jackal Pack. Why mercenaries? Of course, Kimball knew why: His Eminence, Premier Dessrotano, didn't care about due process tonight, and he didn't want his own shields to do the dirty work. But *three* of them? Where were the rest?

The tall man with the gray eyes and the half-smile looked familiar, but Kimball couldn't place him until one of the tactical officers muttered behind him. "Alvarez, you know who that is? It's the Mourning Star."

"Why do they call him that?" asked the younger officer.

"Because he—"

"Both of you cut the jawing," Kimball snapped. *Leon Victor*, he thought with a shudder. They had certainly sent their best—or their worst, depending on the point of view. At least this would soon be out of his hands. He walked to greet the vicious-looking trio. "Gentlemen, I'm Inspector Peter Kimball. I suppose a welcome is in order."

When the mercenary leader spoke, his voice was low and surprisingly soft, almost soothing. "Colonel Victor, at your service. This is Parker—" he gestured at the shorter dark-skinned man "—and Raptor," indicating the hulking Prross. "What's the situation here?" He seemed distant as his eyes narrowed, fixing on a point over Kimball's shoulder. It was discomfiting, and Kimball felt as though he were beneath this man's regard.

"Why do I have a feeling this isn't where we're going to be staying?" asked the shorter Human, sounding annoyed.

The smug smiles they wore seemed a little too put-on, but they also looked exhausted. "Jackals," one of the officers spat as they passed. The mercenaries didn't react, but Kimball thought he saw the smiles flicker for just the briefest moment.

They stopped by the lobby's central fountain as they waited for their other bags. The taller man with the close-cropped goatee—*Leon Victor, can you believe it?*—spoke quickly, and Kimball noticed that his eyes never settled, flicking quickly about the lobby as though photographing every detail.

Affecting the same air of calm, the detective arched an eyebrow and stuffed his hands in his pockets. He knew people well enough to know that these three were as nervous as everyone else; they just concealed it much better. He supposed the attitude was a form of marketing for them. Now they looked almost bored, on the verge of stifling yawns. "We've located the targets; they're in this building." Kimball's nagging doubts got to him. "I'm sorry, but you're all Jackal Pack sent? I thought there were four horsemen of the Apocalypse."

"One slept in," quipped the shorter man, Parker.

"You wanted specialists, you got us," replied Victor, clearly annoyed by his companion's remark. "We were given to understand that time was short, but we didn't expect to begin operations for at least another week. This is ... unorthodox." He was maintaining his composure, but it was clearly a struggle. "We were contracted to carry out sanctioned interdictions with shield support. This is a full-on raid, isn't it?"

Kimball nodded quickly, noting that Victor's companions seemed unhappy with how quickly things had escalated, more than his casual tone and cool demeanor let on. But Kimball was eager not to let the opportunity slip past, not with Keegan and his crew so close to justice. "We never expected a chance like this, with them all in one place. My men would have moved already, but we were told to wait. Orders from upstairs, you understand. If all goes well, you could be out of here tomorrow." *If all goes poorly, you'll be leaving in boxes.* "Shall we go upstairs? We have a room where you can change into your gear."

Victor's eyes stopped moving for a moment. The sudden stillness was unnerving. "Well, I suppose we're not being paid by the hour."

Kimball led them to the heavily guarded bank of lifts. They squeezed into the single operating lift, and Kimball hit the button that would take them to the thirtieth floor. A Banshee Gatling gun dangled from the Prross's right shoulder, poorly concealed in an olive-green duffel bag.

Another bag was slung over his left shoulder. There was barely room for the others in the lift. Kimball stood pressed against the wall, watching his companions in silence, trying to figure them out. It didn't seem appropriate to make small talk.

Upstairs, the suites had all been evacuated, their occupants quietly replaced by armed response teams. Down a side hallway, the pretense at subtlety ended. Hastily erected steel barriers had turned the corridor into a makeshift fort, and tactical shield officers from Olafsen's team guarded the door to a large double suite.

Inside, the furniture had been piled against one wall, and support personnel were manning surveillance computers and monitoring communications channels. Kimball turned to one of the officers. "Could you run upstairs and find Captain Olafsen? Tell her the Ronin have arrived." The officer left quickly.

The Jackals were fast, shedding their civilian attire and pulling on black fatigues and combat boots. Kimball couldn't help noticing the crimson tiger stripes running down the left side of their fatigues, like bloody tear drops.

Captain Olafsen returned. "Everything is ready," she said gruffly. Then she saw the mercenaries, and her eyebrows shot up. Mr. Princeton was on her heels, having taken the next lift. He appraised the trio of newcomers clinically, while Kimball made introductions.

The Jackals continued to empty their packs, sliding knives into sheaths and ammo pouches into their pockets and belts. Parker spoke up, voice smooth and quiet. "How long have they been holed up in here?" He clipped a stun grenade to the webbing on his fatigues.

"Two days. We had a hell of a time tracking them down, but they got sloppy and put themselves up in the Chancellor Suite, down the hall from where we came up." Kimball could hear the excitement in his own voice. "They don't usually stay in one place for long, but it seems there's a big exchange of some kind tomorrow," he added by way of explanation.

"You said they move around a lot. Is this deviation from that mode suspicious?" asked Parker. "They could be expecting something."

Princeton spoke now, his voice nasal but authoritative. "They won't be expecting this." Kimball looked away, trying to keep his distaste from showing.

Princeton kept on talking. "Inspector Kimball has been instrumental in putting all this together. For the past few years he's been chasing down every lead, and we've gotten this opportunity thanks to him. We need to move quickly." He narrowed his dark eyes. "We anticipated more of you."

Victor scratched his stubble. "To be honest, Mr. Princeton, this was only supposed to be a tactical assessment. As I said to the inspector, we didn't expect operations to commence for another week at the earliest. The packet only included a destination, a bounty, and Inspector Kimball's files on the cartel." Victor couldn't have helped noticing Kimball's reaction to that. *Did Princeton forward my files to these people without even asking?* He supposed it didn't matter. Victor was still talking. "Ordinarily, with this kind of operation, we qualify the job before diving in. But because it came from a head of state, General Rockmore scrambled our team to lay the groundwork." He looked at his companions as though counting them, hoping there would be more. "We were going to bring the rest of the crew in separately."

"Will that be a problem?"

"If we get the support we need, no."

Princeton puffed with pride. "Captain Olafsen's team is the best on Korinthe. They competed in a sector-wide inter-service competition and came in first in almost every event."

Victor looked at them quizzically. "I'm sure any holographic targets in there will be suitably terrified." He turned to Olafsen. "How are they with actual field work?"

"I think you'll find our operational record adequate," Olafsen said in a reassuring, no-nonsense way.

"And what's your role here?" Victor asked Princeton, who stiffened noticeably. Kimball took a little pleasure from that, for Princeton was likely not a man accustomed to being questioned.

"As far as you're concerned? I disburse your funds, and I clear any ... barriers you might come across."

"Funny, you don't look like a demolitions man," Parker said.

"Could you be quiet for once?" Victor snapped under his breath.

"Do the subjects know we're out here?" asked the Prross. He was kneeling on the floor tending to his weapon, a Gatling laser nearly four feet long. A long claw stroked the barrels in a strangely affectionate manner.

Kimball shook his head. "I don't think so. We intercepted one of them coming out on an errand a little under an hour ago. We got most of our information from him, but he wasn't too helpful. We don't know if he was supposed to call in or when he might be missed. These men are professionals, though, and they'll have posted armed guards. In fact, they'll all likely be armed."

"They may have had a lookout on the street below. Any unusual vehicles or loiterers? How's your perimeter?"

"I wouldn't worry about the perimeter," Princeton put in. "It won't be a problem. And before you ask, all comm frequencies in the area are being relayed through this room, just in case. Plus, the suite has an ocean view, doesn't look out on the street."

Parker looked up at Victor. "I think we still have to assume they're ready for us, huh?" The taller man nodded and moved on.

There were only three of them. That kept nagging at Kimball. How in God's name were three men going to collar this whole operation? At least the tactical team was on standby. Despite his misgivings, Kimball wanted to allay any reluctance they might be feeling. The last thing he needed was for them to walk away from the job. After all, this was his cause, not theirs, and for them nothing but money was on the line. He may have desired recognition, glory, possibly a promotion, and something to throw in the face of his ex-wife, but he didn't think his men could do it alone, not without it getting very messy. He certainly didn't want to be the first one through *that* door. And if mercs got killed in there, so what? Better them than good, loyal officers. Right now all that mattered was putting these thugs behind bars or underground. In a few years they could be pushing on his son.

The thought filled Kimball with cold dread and implacable hatred. "There's no reason to suspect that we've been compromised. We've never come close to them before so I doubt they're looking out for us now. You have to understand, these bastards have practically owned the streets for quite some time. Their arrogance is working against them. I don't need to tell you we won't get this chance again." Kimball looked to Princeton for approval and got a nod. "We also have a source inside, who can get a signal out to us if anything changes."

"Unless your informant's been compromised." Victor's eyes locked onto Kimball, his voice as cold and clinical as his gaze. "How many targets are we talking about here?"

"Ah," Kimball began, hesitantly, "She told us to expect sixteen, and the detainee confirmed it. We have reason to believe there may be more." For all they knew, there was a whole battalion in there having a drink, with every petty street dealer and enforcer in attendance.

"Oh, is that all?" remarked the Prross with a malicious grin.

"Sixteen's a lot for the three of us," Parker said. Kimble detected real concern in his voice for the first time. "We should wait for the armor or call it off."

Olafsen shook her head vehemently. "We can't call it off. We have our orders, and we go in tonight, with or without you."

Victor's eyebrows went up as his eyes flicked over Olafsen's rank insignia. "Thank you for the professional courtesy, Captain." He turned back to his colleagues. "We need to confer."

Princeton stepped forward. "Wait, Colonel. There may be a … I can authorize a personal disbursement should you seize certain persons of interest. To each of you." Victor didn't react right away. "To the tune of five hundred thousand apiece."

"It doesn't work like that," Victor replied sharply, but something in his manner had changed. He lingered. "It's only sixteen junkies, not crack troops," he said to his companions.

Kimball felt the sweat trickling down his back. He cleared his throat. "Some of them are ex-military."

Parker snorted but said nothing.

Kimball wanted to be as helpful as possible, whatever his personal feelings about these men. "You mentioned armor? Anything we can do?"

"Not unless you've got a spare EMMA lying around," Victor said distractedly. "Mine got held up in customs, along with our Jackhammer autorifles. They let the Banshee in but not the rest of it." He smiled grimly. "Your men at the port said it wouldn't be a problem." *Well, here we are, and it's a problem,* his eyes seemed to say.

"I'm sorry, I wasn't told. Cybernetics are illegal on Korinthe, and I'm afraid the neural links on powered armor systems fall under Category Three," Princeton explained.

So much for clearing barriers, Kimball thought. Somehow he suspected that their autorifles had been shipped with armor-piercing ammunition, which was likewise prohibited. He understood their concern: Enclosed Mechanized Main Armor granted its wearer incredible strength and protection ... and was well out of his budget. "I'm sorry, Colonel, we don't have anything like that, but we can spare a few Warthog carbines."

"That'll have to do," Victor conceded, disappointed.

"Captain Olafsen is right about one thing: the premier wants this over tonight."

Parker shook his head, and Victor ignored it. "What did these guys do?" asked the colonel. "Must have been something special."

Kimball shrugged and again looked to Princeton for permission to elaborate. Ostensibly it may have been his operation, but he could just about feel the marionette strings tugging at his limbs, and he knew who was on the other end. Princeton nodded dismissively and strolled away. Kimball let his professional mask fall for just a moment, but it was enough.

Victor looked at Kimball with concern. "Inspector, I hope this isn't a problem. It seems like you've put a lot of work into this, and I don't want you to feel like we're here to undo it."

"If it were up to me, this would be a shield operation all the way." He crossed his arms, brushing his right thumb across his badge to remind himself why he was here. "I'm doing my best to divorce my ego from the situation. The most important thing is getting these animals off the street permanently."

"I'm glad we're in agreement. They must not be your average criminal enterprise, to warrant an interdiction on this scale. I take it there's a political component?" Victor was perceptive, at least.

"It's messier than that. Our premier has a vested interest in the fate of these men. They're suspected Burn dealers." Seeing the blank looks on the mercenaries' faces, he elaborated. "Burn is a highly addictive and potentially lethal designer drug. The men in there were the first pipeline onto our world. The premier's daughter was an addict; Lord knows where she got it. She died of an overdose a few weeks ago. She was much loved." *Unlike her father.* "It was highly publicized, a huge scandal. But you haven't been on-planet long, have you? I don't suppose Korinthe's problems rate the galactic news."

Three heads shook no. *Surprise, surprise.* Kimball continued: "The dealer who provided the dose that killed her is allegedly inside, but it doesn't matter what piece of shit on the street she bought it from, because every pusher on the planet gets their Burn from these men. I've been hunting them for the last two years, but now Premier Dessrotano wants an example made, and as you can imagine, that's opened some new doors for me. We can't be seen to botch the operation. I can't let them get away again."

Victor's response was detached and disturbing, but there was a flicker of real anger in his eyes. Perhaps he did care. "Huh. Princeton left that part out of the file. It would have taken weeks to track them down one by one, I suppose." He nodded to himself, tallying points.

Princeton had returned; he coughed politely and reached into his linen suit jacket. Kimball's distrust of the man ran deep: he was no less dangerous than Victor or the men in the Chancellor suite. But where they were bombs, he was poison, insidious and silent. "There's one more thing. I understand that in certain situations, you will accept a waiver of responsibility for civil violations."

For a moment Kimball didn't understand what Princeton was saying, but then he saw the signed documents the bureaucrat was pulling from his pocket.

"I thought we were here for an interdiction. No one said anything about—" Victor began.

Kimball cut him off and inserted himself between Princeton and the mercenary. "This isn't what we agreed on, Princeton! I was told this would be treated with the utmost professionalism."

Princeton's disdainful response was like a kick to the groin. "It is. Professionalism proportionate to that of our prey. Make no mistake, Inspector, you are here as a courtesy. Your official involvement ended when you located our ... targets."

Warily Victor took the papers from Princeton. "This is a kill order," he said tiredly.

"Wow, I could use a drink right now," Parker said casually. Kimball shrugged it off as mercenary bravado, but Victor was clearly seething, his grey eyes narrowing.

"Dammit, Buzz. Shut *up*." He turned to Kimball. "Do you have a room where we can talk?" he asked. Wordlessly the inspector pointed to the bathroom. He couldn't believe what was going on here.

§

"Buzz is right," Raptor growled over the sound of running water. "You should listen to him for once." Raptor Merikii—Raptor was only his nom de guerre, but it had been earned in blood a hundred times over—knew that would get Leon's attention. "What happened to OAP?"

"It's off the table, clearly," Leon snapped back. He was concerned, too. Their mandate had been to conduct OAP—Jackal Pack's standard Observe, Assess, Plan qualification for a major contract—not dive into a firefight on their first day. "And you know what? I do listen. But it wears a little thin sometimes. You both know it's hard enough to get contracts outside the Arc. We need to prove that we can deploy quickly and efficiently. And not get cold feet at the altar." The sink had nearly filled. Leon turned off the tap and plunged his face into the water.

When he came up, he felt a little better. He reached for a towel, glancing at his reflection in the mirror. He sighed. The soft light and scented soaps couldn't hide the signs of aging. Gray hairs had invaded his temples and seemed poised to expand their little empire into his goatee, as well. "Son of a bitch," he muttered, raking damp fingers through his hair. He half-listened while Raptor continued complaining from beside the door. The droplets running down his neck were cool.

Leon was tall for a Human, but he felt small beside the thickly muscled and hulking Prross. Before she had left, Rachel had told him that his eyes were the color of soft moss over hard stone. Usually inquisitive and mirthful, they were now grim and unfocused, staring blearily back at him. He planted his palms on the cold marble counter and hung his head, trying to clear his headache.

"Do they really expect us to go in there like this? I don't even know what time it is in Tesa right now. I feel like I just went through a blender." Buzz Parker was leaning against the tiled wall of the bathroom, thumbs hooked in his pockets. "What are these assholes thinking?"

Leon had been trying not to think about his own biological clock. They had been traveling more than twenty-four hours with little rest. Most of the time aboard the caravel had been spent studying Keegan's cartel and their modus operandi, information that had been rendered largely useless.

His attempt to get some sleep had been rudely interrupted by turbulent dreams. "Who knows?"

"The pricks who picked us up at the cosmodrome certainly didn't."

It was true. The two serious-looking defense ministry officials who had met them at the spaceport had told them little and probably didn't know much more than Leon and his companions. They had simply piled them into a car for the hour-long drive to the Oceanside District of Port Veshoth. The vehicle's hard edges had been softened by opulence, but there was no masking the fact that it was, at its heart, a military transport, likely bullet-, bomb-, and beam-proof.

The hotel to which they had been delivered was likewise dripping with luxury, but here it served only to cover up more decadence. To say Leon was thrown by this turn of events would be an understatement. It was strange enough to make the journey in a chartered commercial shuttle rather than one of their company dropships, but discretion had been emphasized in the suspiciously cursory contract. Now, instead of a cold shower, a warm meal, and a good night's sleep before beginning their investigation, they were being told to kill everyone. There were no answers here, only targets.

Leon felt nauseous, paranoid. He told himself it was fatigue, the same fatigue Raptor had been muttering about, that they had come straight here from the spaceport without so much as a cup of Kaf. The shields had done what they could to secure this place, but it would soon be shot to splinters.

Raptor patted his pockets. "Shit, I think I forgot my gum."

Leon smiled wanly. "Both of you just stay cool," he said quietly to them. "We stand to make a lot of money from this." *Enough that I could retire.*

"Is that what this is about?" Buzz's eyes narrowed to slits. "That asshole got to you with that talk of a bonus." Dark-skinned, dark-eyed, and dark-haired, Buzz was slim, agile, and deadly accurate with a pistol. A former criminal himself, he had never been comfortable in the presence of shields. Leon needed him to control himself.

"He didn't get to me, Buzz. You know why we're doing this. A reference from the Premier of Korinthe would open new business channels. And don't tell me you don't like the idea of wiping scum like these off the streets."

"Not like this, and not running on empty." Buzz looked to Raptor, but the Prross was silent. "Come on, are we really going to go through with a kill-order without due diligence?"

"I'm making an executive decision," Leon said softly, but he put authority into his voice. "The client is pre-qualified. We'll go through with it, and take what live prisoners we can."

Raptor shrugged his massive shoulders. "I suppose Leon is right. The odds are against us, but we are not going in alone. The shields will be behind us. And we've faced worse. But you should know, I'm not going in first this time." His scarred and torn red bomber jacket, folded neatly with the rest of their clothes, stood in testimony of what happened when he led the way. Betraying his anxiety, Raptor's dorsal spines rose and fell, pressing against the lining of his fatigues. "Teach you to fucking leave *me* hanging."

"Were we not pinned down? Besides, what are you complaining about? You're still alive." Buzz was smirking, but there was a tremor in his voice. They were desensitized by their close brushes with death, but they also knew the consequences—and the likelihood—of failure.

"We'll go in together," Leon said evenly, fixing his gaze on each of his companions. They seemed to stand straighter when he looked them in the eyes, their confidence returning. "Now let's put on our game faces and get this over with."

"Seconded," Buzz muttered.

Leon moved to the door with a confidence he didn't quite feel. As he passed Buzz, the shorter man pushed off the wall and turned to follow. Still grumbling, Raptor brought up the rear, squeezing his broad frame through the doorway.

2: Into the Breach

Leon approached Kimball and Princeton, who stood with a wall of silence between them. Leon cleared his throat. "We'll oblige you and serve the subjects on ice, but the bonus situation has to be addressed. Last-minute changes are expensive. Six million on top."

Princeton snorted a laugh, but his eyes were flinty, cold. "There are only three of you. Three million."

"This is not a negotiation. If you're willing to pay three, you can afford six."

Princeton looked the mercenary over quizzically. "Very well, six."

Kimball's jaw was clenched so hard that Leon half-expected to hear his teeth break. He seemed like an honest, hard-working shield, but his hands were clearly tied. Leon didn't care for Princeton at all, and though the live interdiction presented substantially greater challenge with cornered criminals, Leon would have preferred to side with Kimball. Nevertheless, it was Princeton who would be signing the paychecks, and Princeton who would be making such decisions.

Still, it couldn't hurt to try and mollify the inspector. "We'll give all subjects the opportunity to surrender. Standard procedure," Leon said unequivocally.

It didn't have the intended effect. Princeton cocked his head and smiled benignly, but Kimball seemed to glare even harder. "His Eminence wants to send a message to Korinthe's criminal element," Princeton said, wringing his hands. "You are free to do whatever you wish. The majority of them are low-level thugs and muscle. They probably won't be thinking beyond getting out of the room once you go in." Princeton seemed to be weighing the value of lives and finding that they were very cheap indeed. Who was this man, who could so easily sentence people to death? *Probably the head of the premier's secret police. More importantly, he's a paying customer.*

"These six are your principals." Princeton laid out a series of folders containing detailed files on the cartel leaders and key personnel whom Leon had studied earlier. Each file contained surveillance photos of the men presumably inside the hotel suite. The majority were nondescript, bland-looking individuals. In short, they were the perfect types to mastermind an illegal operation. Raptor commented on the fact.

Kimball took over. "Most of these men run the business end of things, but they'll have bodyguards, and they'll be well armed. Dugo Ganch is one of their main chemists, brought in from off-world. We think he's responsible for refining the Burn formula and figuring out how to get it through customs. We've never been able to intercept even a single shipment."

The sixth man stood out from the others as a clear anomaly and raised a red flag for Leon immediately. "This is Marcus Keegan, their chief coordinator and enforcer. He's an accomplished fighter. He served in the UCA for ten years, four in the counterespionage corps. As a result, he's an expert in guerrilla tactics, specifically clandestine supply lines. You should exercise extreme caution in engaging him. Eight years ago he arrived on Korinthe and began making inroads against the other cartels. Violent, ruthless stuff. We think he picked up a number of his contacts in—"

"I read the file, Inspector," Leon reminded Kimball gently. The man's picture was grainy, but the facial tattoo was distinctive. His cold, dead eyes were familiar: Leon had met scores of men and women with the same gaze. Behind the blank stare would be a dangerous intellect; Leon didn't doubt that he was as deadly as Kimball claimed.

"I want these people alive, Colonel Victor," Kimball said firmly. He had a paunch, jowls, thinning hair, and a cheap suit beneath his bulletproof vest, but Kimball commanded far more respect for his integrity than Princeton did with his rank. Leon felt a twinge of remorse. "Keegan and the others must stand trial. They have a lot to answer for, and they're our only hope of getting information on the rest of their network."

Leon was about to answer when Princeton interjected, "All things considered, I think a trial is the last thing on Mr. Victor's mind. Let him do his job, Inspector, and afterwards the Adjudicators can pick over what's left."

"Dammit, Princeton, I need them alive. For the sake of justice, if that means anything to you." When Princeton said nothing, Kimball stormed off.

"I'm sorry," Princeton said, turning his palms up in surrender. He wore an inappropriate smirk that gave the lie to his words. "The inspector is under a lot of stress."

"He's not wrong," Leon said carefully.

Princeton bristled, and the placid demeanor pulled taut against his cold, hard core. "Our customs and our laws are none of your concern right now, Mr. Victor. I have provided you with a license to kill every man and woman in that suite. I expect you to do as you're paid to."

Beside Leon, Raptor and Buzz stiffened but said nothing. Kimball chose that moment to return, sparing Leon the need to reply.

"I'm glad you decided to rejoin us," Leon said gratefully. "I'm sure you have a lot of valuable insight."

"Spare me. It's bad enough these people are going to die without the three of you throwing your lives away in the bargain." Kimball held up a hand in a gesture of warning. "I think you should know what wasn't in the file: Keegan has been treated with metabolic enhancers, getting gene therapy for years. We think his Caloric intake is somewhere up around eight thousand, daily. He's a killing machine."

It was never easy, but adding an overclocked enforcer with a military background increased the potential for a disaster. That was why Rockmore had sent Leon's team. The plan had been to take them down on the streets, one crew at a time, and only after a comprehensive investigation. In close quarters there would be no shortage of targets, but their heavy support would be impractical and messy. Raptor would certainly have to ditch the Banshee. It was hardly a precise weapon, and they couldn't afford the collateral damage. They were likely to need mobility over intimidation anyway.

Princeton seemed to mistake Leon's silence for reluctance. "I can provide combat cocktails, if you want."

"Huh?" The offer took Leon by surprise. "No, thank you. We have a strict no-augmentation policy." Known by a variety of nicknames including Rage, Berserk, and Apathy, combat cocktails were a poorly kept secret among sojieri. Mixtures of stimulants and narcotics were injected into the muscles or spine, temporarily boosting metabolism and reflexes while flooding the body with painkillers to keep a person fighting despite grievous injury. Side effects included dulled thought processes and heightened aggression; the last thing Leon wanted was for his men to go in there out of control.

"Plenty of merc outfits use them." Princeton seemed disappointed by Leon's refusal.

"Jackal Pack is not one of them. Enhancers are no substitute for training," Leon countered.

"Keegan has both. Don't forget that," Kimball cautioned.

"We won't. Thank you, Inspector." Leon pulled his companions aside. Out of earshot, Leon made his feelings known. "This Princeton motherfucker isn't giving us much to go on. I have a feeling he's sitting on a lot more information."

"Here I thought I was the only one picking up the warning signs," Buzz muttered. "We can't count on the element of surprise. No matter how careful these shields have been, and no matter how stupid these pushers are, there's no way they could have failed to notice the entire local constabulary occupying their hotel. And this Keegan doesn't sound like an idiot." Buzz narrowed his eyes, gauging his companions, and took a breath. "I'm for taking the cocktails."

Leon didn't bother to hide his anger. "I'm going to pretend you didn't say that. What if there are civilians in there with them and you can't tell the difference?"

"Better if I fall asleep, you think?"

"Hey, I'm not kidding."

"Neither am I," Buzz snapped back. "We're not all ex-special forces, man. I'm hurting here."

"Leon's right," Raptor put in, his voice a low growl. "Something goes wrong in there because we're stoned, our sanctions go up. You want to risk a rerating?"

"Are you two serious?" Buzz blurted, not bothering to keep his voice low. "You're talking about monthly fees. I'm talking about getting *killed* in there. I'm taking the cocktail."

"Go in clean or not at all, Buzz. You can sit this one out if it's that big an issue."

"And face the rest of the Pack when you two idiots get shot to pieces?" He looked at the floor, his dark eyes furious. "Goddammit, all right. Fuck you for putting me in this position."

"Thanks, man." Leon put his hand on Buzz's shoulder, but his friend shook it off. His voice hardened again, all business. "How do we breach?"

"Let's take a look at the floor plan," Raptor suggested, and the three of them turned back to their hosts.

The mercenaries gathered around a large horizontal panel screen, accompanied by Kimball, Princeton, and the tactical team captain. Leon placed his fingers on the screen, moving them to manipulate the image and familiarize himself with the layout and angles of approach. "Big place," observed Buzz. "How much does a suite like this run?"

Princeton's eyebrows went up. "If you have to ask, you can't afford it."

"Oh. How aristocratic. Do these specs say twenty-five feet high? Must be a bitch to heat in the winter."

"Shut up, Buzz." Leon chewed his lip thoughtfully. "Any ideas?"

Buzz gave the plans a onceover, memorizing everything through eyes like camera shutters. "Hardly designed to be defensible. Still, if these guys have any sense they can cover everything from that raised loft area and have a few guys in the side wings to keep us penned in the central corridor. Ventilation system is segmented and the ducts are too small.... Can't go in through the windows. Too open. Front door's a major bottleneck. Either way they can bring a lot of guns to bear on us very quickly. We should wait for the armor."

Leon resisted the urge to strangle his friend. After all, Buzz was right. Though it was ripe for an ambush, the front door also provided the only ready cover, in the form of easily accessible side rooms. Coming through the oceanfront bay windows, on the other hand, would leave them stranded in an open dining and living area where they could be picked off in an instant. It left a lot to be desired.

"What's this here?" Raptor asked, pointing. "It looks like a door."

Olafsen cocked her head to get a better look. "It's a service entrance for the kitchen staff. The hotel offers full chef service, so there's an express elevator to bring wait staff, cooks, and food from the hotel's main kitchens."

Raptor's deep brows creased and he looked up at the blank inner wall of the suite they were standing in. "Presumably that elevator is on the other side of this wall, then?"

Olafsen took over, manipulating the image. She looked around, getting her bearings. "That's right, the hallway runs between all the rooms on this side of the building."

"Then we breach from there," Leon said, straightening up. "Captain, we'll storm the suite from the kitchen and sweep across. I want one of your teams to breach simultaneously through the front door."

"We'll come in from the bay windows, as well."

"No, hold that second team in reserve. They'll still be too exposed if they come through before we secure the main level with a base of fire."

"You expect them to retreat to the loft area."

"If they have any brains, it's the only place to mount a defense. I'm sure the open floor plan is aesthetically very nice, but it turns the place into a shooting gallery. And that works both ways."

Olafsen nodded. "Very well. I'll hold the second squad in reserve until we receive a signal from you."

"Okay then." Leon could feel his heartbeat pick up. They could only delay so long before the inevitable breach. The calm had to end and the storm had to erupt. "One last question. Should we expect civilians?"

"I'm not sure I understand," Princeton said coyly.

"Prostitutes or clients."

"We won't hold you responsible for any collateral damage."

"That's wonderful, but we have a record we're proud of. The question remains." Leon appreciated that Princeton was in the unenviable position of trying to expedite the slaughter, but his team had a perfect operational record. He didn't intend to compromise it for this bastard, and when the bodies were stacked, he didn't want anyone among them who shouldn't have been.

"Yes, we suspect there may be noncombatants in there, but we couldn't get a look without our thermal scanners. They're still hours away. Ordinarily we would gas the whole place with Cendol-121, but it reacts explosively with Burn."

"What about stun grenades?"

"No problems of which I am aware. Does it matter? I was told your sanction covers civilian casualties."

"Call it a personal rule," Leon said defensively.

"Clock's still ticking," muttered Buzz unhappily. "Do we wait for the scanners?"

Leon shook his head. "No. We can't let them dig in any longer." Leon looked from Raptor to Buzz, each nodding in turn. They couldn't afford to let fatigue make them sloppy, not on such a high-profile case. If they did it right, they could leave quietly. If they did it wrong, they'd be swamped by a media circus for weeks. Or they'd be dead.

"What if the civilians fire on *us*?" Buzz didn't like the prospect of utilizing fire control. Neither did Leon, but as team leader and representative of the Pack, he didn't have the luxury of saying so. For them, combat was nearly instinctual, reflex. The added variable of civilians meant they had to second-guess themselves before every pull of the trigger. Every action involved a hesitation, one their opponents might exploit.

Leon smiled. "Then they're not civilians. Hope their aim is even worse than yours." Then he turned serious. "Look, we've trained for this. Treat it like a hostage rescue. You spot anyone using a human shield, don't get fancy. Let them through, the officers will deal with them." He turned once more to Princeton. "You said you detained a subject earlier. Any chance we could have a word?"

Princeton shrugged. "That might be a little difficult. Some of our men were a little ... enthusiastic in his interrogation. He's been hospitalized."

Just great, Leon thought angrily.

"I'll be right back," Olafsen said. She stalked off.

"So? What do you think?" Buzz asked Raptor.

"I think I need some gum," answered the Prross absently, and he wandered away to introduce himself to the tactical officers waiting nearby with skeptical looks on their faces.

Olafsen returned, holding a case. "If one of your boys is wounded, we'll pull him out like one of our own." She nodded, and the gas-mask pulled up on her forehead bobbed in a parody of the gesture. "And make sure you're clear when you give the signal. When my reserve team comes swinging in, they aren't going to hold their fire. Anything in there is going to go down fast."

She opened the case. "Take these blue-tags, so we can see you on our tactical goggles. Wear 'em, eat 'em, I don't care. Just keep them on you at all times, or I can't guarantee we won't shoot you in the exchange." She held out the open case, and each mercenary retrieved a small metal cylinder. Buzz clipped his to his dogtags.

Leon slipped his into a breast pocket of his fatigues. "Thanks. Look, we're not here to step on toes; we're just here to lend our particular expertise. We're in it for the money, not the credit, so I want us to work together on this. You get the collars, we get the cash, everyone walks away happy." He snapped his fingers at Raptor, who came back over with a young tactical officer at his side. The Prross took a tag and slipped it into a pocket.

"What's your name, kid?" he growled, offering his hand in the Human gesture.

"Alvarez," the man said, shaking it firmly. He was nervous, Leon could tell, and what was clearly meant to be a whisper came out loud and clear. "That's really the Mourning Star?" Leon pretended not to hear him.

"Would you like an autograph or something?" Raptor asked mockingly.

"Uh, no. What can I do for you?"

"Do you have any cinnamon gum?"

The young officer looked surprised, but he dipped his shaking hand into his pocket, pulling it out a moment later and handing a stick of gum to the Prross.

"I knew I smelled it on you." Raptor cleared his throat, a sound more like the buzz of a circular saw than a cough. "I have a big mouth." For emphasis, he snapped jaws which could have taken off the shield's hand in one bite.

Alvarez looked irritated, but he wasn't about to argue with a scarred and heavily armed Prross. He handed over the rest of the gum. "Keep the pack." Smiling, Raptor unwrapped each piece and stuffed the whole stack in his mouth.

"Would you at least try to be quiet?" hissed Leon. "It's a miracle they haven't called the front desk to tell us to keep it down."

Buzz rolled his eyes. "What's the verdict? We greenlit?"

"Get on your armor. No point in wasting time." Their fatigues were lined with thin pouches of TacGel, a non-Newtonian fluid that hardened on impact, protecting them from shrapnel and some small-arms fire. Even so, they were likely to go up against heavier artillery, and standard flak vests were also advisable.

Leon pulled a vest out of one of the duffels Raptor had been carrying. He tossed it to Buzz. The next he put on himself, buckling its catches across his sides and adjusting the shoulder holster containing his backup sidearm, a standard-issue Coalition service pistol. The vest wouldn't stop a close-range hit, but it was lightweight, and that was more important to him. He offered a third vest to Raptor.

"No, I can't stand those," said the Prross, bravado masking fear. "No honor."

"Then don't come crying to me when you get clipped."

"Yeah, I always wanted a belly button," Raptor snapped back. Suddenly he turned somber. "Listen, though, bullet-proof I'm not. Make sure you're right behind me."

The two locked eyes for a moment. "Right behind you," Leon promised, nodding.

"Man, I hate this tropical heat," Buzz said, plucking at the sleeves of his fatigues. "Thank God for this air conditioning. Otherwise I might pass out in this brain-catcher." He slipped his helmet on, adjusting the chinstrap. The others likewise donned their own. Buzz tapped the helmet-mounted camera. "For quality assurance purposes, your gunfight may be recorded."

Leon didn't say anything, but he was cold, his hands clammy before the fight. It was queer that the police hadn't even suggested asking the subjects to surrender. There was no guarantee they wouldn't. A chill ran down his spine when he thought about it. They hadn't even referred to them as suspects, merely *targets*. The government didn't want them alive at all, did they? *They want to send a message, and they want it written in red ink.* Only Kimball had a problem with the plan to shoot everyone.

Buzz drew a scattergun from his own pack. The powerful shotgun, nicknamed a "room-broom," fired a wide spread of kinetic bursts which were very effective at clearing enemies out of concealed areas, demolishing doors, cover, and just about everything else. It wasn't very accurate at range, but in a hotel room, that wouldn't be much of a drawback. "Better or worse than the CSF?" Buzz asked, as much a part of their ritual as putting a round in the chamber.

Leon smiled thinly as he familiarized himself with the stubby Warthog carbine. His time with the Coalition Special Forces detachment known alternately as the Switchblades and the Harlequins, first as a sojier and then as an officer, was a bittersweet memory. "Well, we did have the advantage of preliminary reconnaissance and adequate time to plan. We also had powered armor. This is nice, too, though." He checked the safety on the carbine and nodded to Raptor, who had slung his own weapon over his shoulder. None of them liked going into battle with untested weapons, but the situation was far from ideal.

In the service hallway, Raptor sniffed the air carefully.

Buzz peered around the corner before following Raptor into the hall and taking up a covering position in an alcove behind a food cart. "Tell me, why are we doing this again?" he whispered.

Leon sighed and adjusted his bulky Sprawler pistols. "What's the Jackal Pack motto, buddy?"

"In Spite of All," chimed in the other two, rolling their eyes.

Leon nodded happily. "Right. So don't ask. We're getting paid pretty damn well to do this." He moved quickly across the hallway to take up a position beside the door to 3034's kitchen. Two shields had fixed breaching charges to the hinges and frame and were now crouched behind a portable barricade. More shields waited to advance behind them. Their eyes were wide behind their bulletproof visors. "Make sure no one slips past us," Leon said. He and Raptor flattened themselves against the wall on either side of the door.

The Prross peered at the wood-paneled door, sniffing it and running a long, clawed finger along the surface. It appeared to be one piece of wood with a deep red grain. Just because it was wood on the outside, though, didn't mean there wasn't a steel security door under the surface. Cautiously Raptor dug a claw into the paneling and twisted it around and around, boring into the wood, under the curious gazes of the nearby shields. "I don't want to slam into another blast-door," he muttered, irritated.

"Should come right off the hinges," Leon opined.

The other mercenary tilted his head, unsure. His yellow, almond-shaped eyes blinked once as he looked at the door. "I think it's just wood."

"Do you smell anything unusual?" When Raptor took a deep breath and shook his head, Leon was much relieved.

"Cheap cologne, expensive perfume. Alcohol. A lot of Humans … and something else. It might be Burn."

"Is it a problem?" The last thing Leon needed was for this drug to be weaponized and used against them. Who knew how it might interact with Raptor's respiratory system if he inhaled it?

"I don't think so, but there's no way to tell."

That would have to do. Leon's mind was racing as he ran over his attack route one more time. If all went perfectly…. He cast that thought aside. It never went perfectly. The best he could do was the best he could do. For many people, a firefight became a wild red blur of adrenaline, sound, and light. Leon and his friends had trained themselves to remain detached from the bloody proceedings, to catalogue every detail, because a single misstep could mean death. He felt that cold, familiar mantle of awareness settling upon him now.

Leon's hand drifted to the grip of the Sprawler on his left hip, finding it oddly comforting. The Crye-Locke SAK-233 "Sprawler" was more than just a weapon: it was a tool for redirecting fate, both his own and that of others. Its form followed its function: it was angular, menacing, and cold. Leon took a deep breath, and then it was time.

He received a nod from Buzz, a wink from Raptor. The three of them lowered the faceplates of their helmets and were transformed into anonymous, expressionless killers in death's-head masks. Because of his elongated snout, Raptor's helmet looked almost birdlike; he was a raven, a harbinger of doom. Leon held up his hand with three fingers out. He pulled in one, then another, before making a fist and drawing it down in a quick motion. "Follow me this time," growled Raptor before he drew a deep breath.

Behind them, one of the shield officers triggered the detonator, and the hallway seemed to come apart in a cloud of smoke and debris. At such close range, the concussion felt like a punch in the ribs. The door and frame vanished inwards in splinters. Raptor rolled a stun grenade through the smoking hole and heaved himself through as it went off.

Leon followed.

3: Sending a Message

Inside, a small knot of men in casual wear were still reeling from the blast and subsequent stun grenade. Shattered wood and dust caked the countertops, tables, and floor.

From the front hallway came the muffled crash of the shield team breaching. The staccato rattle of automatic weapons-fire started up immediately, and Leon frowned. No restraint, no opportunity to surrender … was this how they were supposed to play it?

"Weapons, down, *now!*" Leon shouted at the stunned subjects. Two appeared to be unarmed; another had knocked his gun off the table and was groping blindly for it, his ears bleeding, while the fourth was stumbling toward one of the short hallway jogs that would lead back to the front hallway.

At least one of the men looked as though he might comply when more gunfire erupted from their left. Two men with submachine guns had taken up position in the doorway that led to the guest suites. Leon and Buzz returned fire methodically while Raptor rushed forward out of the field of fire.

The textbook breach had already fallen apart. Forced to improvise, Raptor shot the subject running for the door, and the man's momentum took him crashing into a countertop. Dishes shattered on the tiles as the man slid off, hitting the floor in a heap. Raptor sent a booted foot into the next subject's face, slamming his head upward into the table. The Prross was a flurry of movement as he incapacitated the other two stunned criminals and tied their hands with trap-cuffs. He took a moment to roll them over as he took cover from the incoming fire.

"No principals," Leon heard Raptor growl over his radio. To an eavesdropper, it would have sounded like a garbled, encrypted message. Raptor wasn't speaking Prross Kev, his native tongue and one of the Charter Tongues which could be understood by anyone who had undergone childhood FLASH imprinting. He was speaking Xhosa, a Terran language spoken by fewer than a billion people in the whole galaxy. Leon and his team had learned it as an added measure of security in case their encryption was breached. Their accents and grammar were horrible, but they understood one another.

The two subjects in the doorway emptied their clips at the same time. Smarter men would have fired one at a time to provide cover during reloads, but these were thugs used to spraying indiscriminately. Leon could forgive them for not having a keen grasp of tactics. "Guns down now, dammit!"

They made a move to bolt, so he and Buzz cut them down. The doorframe they had taken cover behind splintered, and their blood painted the hallway into which they had tried to flee.

"Buzz, check that approach," Leon said, pointing to the left, toward the downed gunmen. He went right, slipping behind Raptor to check the parlor adjoining the front hallway. The man Raptor had shot lay by the doorway amidst the blood and shattered ceramic. Leon prodded him with his boot, but there was no sign of life. Raptor's shots had been clean, between the shoulder blades.

Leon's head snapped around when one of the prisoners began thrashing and knocked over a chair. He glanced at Buzz and blanched. "Buzz, door, *left!*" Buzz, stepping over the bodies of the subjects they had neutralized, didn't see the slatted door to his left.

Shots rang out, the loud flat crack of a large-caliber handgun, and the louvers of the door exploded outward. Buzz threw himself backwards, stumbling over one of the corpses. He regained his footing and fired two retaliatory blasts from his scattergun. "God, who takes a gun to the toilet?" he said breathlessly.

"Get your damn head on straight!" Leon snapped in Xhosa. He advanced with Raptor close behind. There was no time to be angry, no time to worry.

More subjects were waiting for them in the parlor; trapped between the mercenaries and the shield team holding the front door, they had nowhere to go.

Leon and Raptor traded fire with them from the doorway until Leon unhooked a stun grenade from his belt and threw it over the couch. The subjects saw it and reflexively scrambled away, exposing themselves to the mercenaries' fire. Leon kept firing even as his visor automatically darkened in response to the blinding flash of the grenade. When the dust settled, one of the men had toppled into a coat closet. The other two had fallen beside the couch, a cloud of stuffing fluttering down around them like snowflakes. From farther inside the suite Leon could hear shouted commands and the sounds of people scrambling to react. *Well, if they didn't know we were here before, they do now.*

"Raptor, you take the east wing. Buzz and I will keep them penned up in the main room."

The Prross nodded wordlessly and swept through the parlor. The shields in the front hall let him pass, and he proceeded into the lounge area.

Leon couldn't afford to let their targets mount any sort of defense or rally to shoot their way out. There was no way they could fight their way past all the tactical officers in the corridors, but in such close quarters it would be hard to miss. It would be a bloodbath.

The trident of the entrance hallway and the two wings housing the guest bedrooms, salons, swimming pool, and kitchen all converged on the main domicile. A large open hall that more closely resembled a corporate tower lobby than a traditional hotel room, the hall was decorated in a sort of stripped-down baroque style that evoked a number of eras of Human design.

A set of French doors led onto a wide veranda where a banquet table flanked by ranks of lounge chairs was set for a feast. The master loft perched over the rest of the suite, reached by freestanding steps that jutted from the wall. It was all very chic, in a trying-too-hard sort of way.

The doors and the huge bay windows overlooked the dazzling ocean vista where rich vacationers obliviously sailed their boats and grav-boarded over waves. Across the bay, gleaming white sands lay at the feet of magnificent hotels and corporate towers, each trying to outdo the others in lavish architecture.

Their targets were still clustered in the center of the open hall. They appeared to have been preparing for lunch or dinner; the sun was still hanging brightly over the horizon, and Leon had no idea what the local time was. They weren't stupid: the bodyguards and enforcers had formed a rough defensive perimeter as their leaders were shepherded up the stairs to the upstairs bedrooms. Leon could see a lot of movement through the glass bay windows on the second level.

The rest of the subjects were in varying states of readiness, scrambling among the leather couches and expensive-looking carpets that added color to the white-tiled expanse. Some were grabbing for weapons which had been stacked on a table while others simply bolted for the stairs or the east wing. There was obvious panic and confusion on all the faces

Leon could see. These fools had thought themselves above the law, ahead of their pursuers, and safe. Buzz was already firing steadily at them from the door to the west wing guest suites, but his scattergun was less effective at this range. The bodyguards returned a hail of gunfire as they fled.

Leon and Buzz fell back to plan their next move. What did these people hope to accomplish by fighting back? Did they think they could win free? Did they have an escape route the shields didn't know about, possibly a chopper on the way to pick them up from the veranda or the roof? Perhaps they thought they could negotiate terms if they made the raid untenable. If that was the case, Leon suspected they were in for a rude awakening: the look in Princeton's eyes suggested he would burn the whole suite down before letting them get away.

"That's a lot of artillery," Buzz said as he peered around the corner. They had taken cover by the guest suites, and the barrage of incoming gunfire was chewing up the walls and doorway.

"Colonel Victor, are we clear to breach?" It was Olafsen's voice in Leon's ear.

"Negative, Captain, negative! The targets are dug in and putting up substantial resistance."

"Acknowledged," was Olafsen's reluctant reply.

Pinned down as they were, Leon had to put his hopes on Raptor. Using the keypad on his wrist, he brought up his comrade's helmet camera feed on his own visor's heads-up-display. The Prross was making swift and steady progress. Leon could see bright paintings hung on the wall of a short hallway that jogged between the indoor pool and one of the entertainment lounges. There was a jerky movement and the view shifted. "Breaching room one," Raptor growled. A bright flash on the feed signaled the detonation of a stun grenade, and the tinny rattle of gunfire over his headset echoed the distant *bratt-bratt* that Leon could hear from across the suite.

The view whirled, disorienting, as Raptor threw himself into the room. The mottled light reflecting off the pool threw the image into a surprising mix of illumination and shadow. A humanoid shape fell into the pool with a splash. There was a high-pitched scream, and the view shifted again as Raptor bulled forward. "Drop it and let her go!" Leon heard him snarl. The camera settled on a man taking cover, arm tight around the neck of a woman in a slinky dress, a gun in his free hand.

Even through the tiny low-resolution feed Leon could see the fear in the man's eyes as he faced down the towering, heavily muscled mercenary. Few people outside of the Coalition Parliament had likely seen a Prross in person, and their reputation as fighters was fearsome, almost mythic. The thug did the sensible thing and pushed the woman at Raptor before opening fire.

Leon tensed as the camera feed jerked and shuddered. He heard the roar both in his earpiece and bellowing across the apartment, and then the thug reappeared in the camera feed, battered and bloody. There was a snapping sound, and the man's eyes rolled up as he dropped to the floor.

"Three subjects neutralized, one civilian alive but injured," came Raptor's breathless report in Xhosa. He started moving again, and Leon allowed himself a sigh of relief.

"Shit, am I hit?" Buzz exclaimed suddenly, snapping Leon back to their present situation. Leon moved forward to help his friend as the other mercenary checked himself for injuries. There was dampness on Buzz's fatigues, slick against the black fabric. His hands came away wet but not red.

Leon paused, puzzled, then laughed. "I think a ricochet hit the waterbed next to you, hotshot."

Buzz started to laugh nervously, too, and Leon could imagine the look of chagrined relief beneath his friend's helmet faceplate. Their reprieve ended when the gunfire across the suite intensified. "That's not incoming," Buzz said soberly.

"It is for me," Raptor snarled. "I'm pinned. These gentlemen are pouring it on, and they're dug in deep."

Leon swore and tightened his grip on the Warthog, thinking quickly. No time to be angry, no time to worry.... "We can't let these assholes fortify that loft, or we'll never be able to slug it out with them." He turned to Buzz and switched to English. "Cover me, everything you've got."

"We've got you, Colonel," chimed in the leader of the shield breach team that was holding the front entry foyer.

Taking a deep breath, Leon bolted from cover. The volume of fire directed at him crescendoed, bullets and beams punching through walls, doors, furniture. A shot glanced off his helmet, and another hit his vest, staggering him. He made for the stout wooden bar along the near wall, charging headlong through the bullets, smoke, dust, and settling flakes of plaster. He was nearly there when a bullet smacked into his shoulder. Losing his balance, he sprawled face-first, sliding behind the bar and crashing into a crate of empty wine bottles. He was back on his feet in an instant, shoulder throbbing but his vest intact. He brushed off the broken glass and risked a glance over the bartop.

With Raptor and Buzz guarding the east and west wings, respectively, and the shields holding the front entry, there was no way for the targets to flank them. That left all the firepower in front of them. The mercenaries were outnumbered and outgunned; it would have been an even match if not for the tactical team's mandate to provide rear support and not engage directly. Olafsen had not repeated her offer to bring the second team in.

It was Leon's job to hold the main room while his companions ensured that there was no one in the other wings to ambush them. He could feel the familiar calm, the heightened awareness of going to war. Staying clear-headed was crucial; the people he was fighting were ruled by fear and fueled by greed. He knew both those things too well.

§

Some assholes had gotten the bright idea to try and flank Leon. There were three of them coming on quickly, armed with bulky autorifles that were great for open street battles but cumbersome in the tight confines of this hotel suite. Buzz let them come, falling back to the hallway where the kitchen and guest suites intersected as they entered the west wing.

As they blundered into his sights, Buzz stepped out of the guest room doorway. "Guns down, now! Hands on heads."

"Shit! Kill him!" shouted one of the enforcers, swinging his big rifle around. Buzz fired first: at such close range, the shot took the man's face off. The other two dashed for the kitchen, and Buzz gave chase.

His quarry opened fire as he reached the doorway; what was left of the kitchen door and frame was reduced to splinters, peppering him with wood and bits of decorative molding. Buzz drew back, waiting for a lull in the shooting. "Drop your weapons and face the wall with your hands on your heads, and I promise you walk out of here alive."

"Come and get us, fucker!"

"We have a clear shot," declared one of the shield officers from the hallway.

"Negative, we can take them alive." Buzz scowled and plucked a stun grenade from his belt. He clicked the fuse and lobbed it inside. Once more the kitchen erupted with light and sound. Buzz lunged through the doorway and found one target on the ground, blood pouring down his face from his ruined eyes. He must have been right next to it when it went off. The second shooter had gotten clear, though, and was raising his weapon to fire. Disoriented, his shots went wide. Buzz dropped his scattergun and yanked his sidearm from its holster. He put a round in each of the thug's shoulders and waved the shields forward. They emerged from their positions in the service hallway, cuffing the two before dragging them out. "Two down," Buzz reported tiredly.

He could still hear the steady *crack-crack* of Leon's Warthog as the colonel carefully chased his targets from cover. Somewhere else Raptor was no doubt wreaking havoc.

He was annoyed by the shields and the way they lingered like timid schoolchildren at the periphery of the fight. He was annoyed by Leon, that he had allowed himself to be talked into going in cold with less than half of the personnel they had allocated to this mission. He was annoyed with the Burn dealers for putting up a fight, with Raptor for loving it, and with himself for going along with it.

His forehead was soaked in sweat, his hair matted beneath the helmet. Sound was muffled, his peripheral vision was compromised, and he was sweltering in the tropical heat despite the air conditioning. Buzz gritted his teeth and forced himself to think clearly, but his doubts continued to gnaw at him.

Here the potential for failure seemed so great. They were split up, supported by officers they didn't know they could trust, and armed with borrowed weapons. They were up against an enemy of unknown strength and training, and they were exhausted from their journey. Buzz didn't share Raptor's bluster or his love of combat. Nor did he share Leon's conviction and drive. For Buzz Parker, what he did was a job and little else.

He picked up one of the dropped autorifles to supplement his scattergun and rallied himself for the fight to come as he stalked back toward the main hall. When he heard the steady rhythm of Leon's Warthog change to a full-auto roar, he knew something was wrong, and he started running, urged on by the sounds of shattering glass and screaming people.

At the doorway that adjoined the main hall, Buzz came upon a scene of utter pandemonium as Leon and the shields traded fire with their prey. One shooter was going for a better angle on Leon, who had burned through the fifty-round clip in a matter of seconds and was rushing to load another. Buzz took aim and dispatched the subject with a carefully placed shot to the torso. He collapsed to the floor, slumping against the wall and clutching at his chest as his life slowly pulsed out of him.

Leon was cornered, though. He had left the cover of the bar, killing two more of the bodyguards as he pushed toward the stairs. There was a lot of open ground to cover, however, and he had gotten barely halfway from the bar; he had flipped over a heavy wood and metal-inlaid banquet table and was crouched behind it.

The initial shock of the attack had worn off, and their targets had realized that they were only facing three men while the shields remained on the sidelines. More of them were pouring down the stairs to rejoin the fight. The table was filling with holes, and it didn't look like it would last long.

Leon was giving it his all, firing blindly but intelligently in the general direction of his assailants while the shield officers in the entry foyer provided sporadic covering fire. One of the bodyguards jerked as he was hit, toppled over the railing, and crashed to the floor. When Buzz unloaded with the autorifle, the defenders faltered in the crossfire. Leon exploited the lull, popping out from behind the table and firing judiciously. Another thug fell and rolled down a few steps, crumpled on the stairs like a pile of discarded clothing.

More defenders had come streaming in through the French doors from the veranda. Buzz raked them with fire from the autorifle until the clip was empty, then tossed it aside and pulled out his sidearm. He took his time, hitting each subject center-mass. The men dropped to the floor, their weapons clattering as they hit the tiles. The subjects were brave and well armed, but they were gangsters, used to dealing with junkies and people who feared them. They weren't sojieri, and so they were woefully outclassed. But they still had the numbers, rapidly dwindling though they might be.

With the element of surprise lost and the attack bogging down, the Jackals were suddenly in an uncertain position. The Burn dealers might not have been as well trained as the shields or his team, but they were far from disorganized. *If we don't gut them now, we're going to be here all night. And they have more ammunition.* Where was Raptor?

A stray shot shattered one of the bay windows, showering everyone with glittering shards of glass that blew in like hail on the warm wind. Buzz cut down another bodyguard as he dashed from behind a column. The man half-jumped, half-fell over the back of a couch where he lay screaming.

Another subject turned his attention to Leon, opening fire with an autorifle from the head of the stairs, and the wood of the table began to splinter under the force of the large-caliber shells. Leon's vest would do little good if one of those shells found him. Buzz was compelled to leave the safety of the doorframe for a better angle on the shooter. He made for the same bar behind which Leon had taken cover, firing as he moved. Even at a distance of nearly twenty meters, several shots hit home, and the man tumbled down the stairs and rolled over his dead comrade, coming to rest on the floor. Buzz traded his clip for a fresh one.

Emboldened, Leon rose from cover, his Warthog tucked tight against his shoulder. He fired steadily, accurately, and several more targets fell. Buzz moved toward the now-abandoned main living and dining area. The tiling was broken and chipped by stray weapons fire, and each footfall sent debris and shell casings rattling across the floor. Buzz wouldn't have expected their targets to have access to so many automatic weapons, but there was no point in dwelling on that.

There was a shout from his right, one of the shields calling out a warning. Buzz's reflexes took over, and he spun and fired two quick shots from his sidearm. One bullet took the running man out at the knees, his legs sliding out from under him. A grenade slipped from his grip, rolling astray, fuse pressed. "*Down!*" shrieked Buzz, throwing himself to the floor. The blast was deafening in the enclosed space, blowing out the remaining windows and sending an avalanche of glass over the veranda. Shrapnel skittered around the floor and dug into walls. Buzz felt a piece slice into his calf, white-hot, and he scrambled to pry it out.

With the smoke still thick in the room, six more shield officers in blue and gray tactical gear swung in on rappelling cords, coming right through the shattered window. They took up positions in the main hall, and most of the subjects quickly realized the futility of their resistance and threw down their weapons. Those who didn't fled upstairs or were killed with brutal efficiency. Buzz, for his part, crouched behind a pulverized couch and checked his gear. His ammunition was plentiful, but he had no more grenades. To be safe, he exchanged the power cell in his scattergun for a fresh one from his satchel, popping the cold cylinder into the slot in the handgrip.

He took a chocolate bar out of his inside jacket pocket, unwrapped it, lifted the faceplate of his helmet, and took a bite. It was melted but delicious, and he could feel some of his energy returning. Quietly, heedless of the bloody corpses lying just a few feet away, Buzz chewed and swallowed, taking a moment to relax and collect his thoughts as he waited for his hearing to return.

He tried to tally all the targets they had killed or incapacitated so far and realized that they had indeed faced more than sixteen men. Quite a few more than sixteen, in fact, and from the sounds of it there were a dozen more upstairs. The tactical officers were swarming around the apartment now, more of them storming in through the front door, checking the dead and handcuffing the living. After all the prisoners were rounded up and taken into the hallway—with the chemist, Dugo Ganch, led before them like a trophy—the tactical squad returned to the large room. "We'll hold position here," said the captain, looking around the hall, in awe of the devastation.

Leon looked annoyed as he approached the shields. Judging by his heavy breathing, he was winded by the exchange. Buzz felt much the same way—he had already been hot when they arrived due to the tropical weather, but thanks to the exertion and the tension, his clothes were soaked with sweat which seemed to suck his bullet-proof vest against him uncomfortably. "You decided to join us," the colonel observed, deadpan.

"We thought the explosion was a signal. You gentlemen certainly don't do things by halves." There was something biting and sarcastic about the way Olafsen said it, but she was clearly impressed.

"We're not done yet, I'm afraid."

"Any sign of Keegan?"

"No, I didn't see him, but it's possible he ran upstairs with the others." Leon turned away from the shields as a familiar growl sounded from the east wing. Raptor emerged from the door to one of the living rooms, dragging three unconscious criminals behind him.

Two women were timidly following in Raptor's wake. The shields immediately cuffed them all and took them out. The Prross was bleeding from a cut to his face, but all in all he seemed to be all right, Buzz noted with relief. "You done screwing around?" he asked with a smirk.

Raptor was still chewing his nearly unmanageable wad of cinnamon gum and did not deign to reply.

The trio proceeded to the staircase, Leon leading with the other two close behind. They crept cautiously up the floating marble steps, broken glass crunching underfoot. They were keenly aware of how exposed they were as they gingerly stepped over the dead body lying across several of the steps. At the top they fanned out. The master living room was empty, a large viewer dark but the speakers still hissing. In their haste to hide, one of the pushers had spilled a drink, red wine soaking into pristine white carpeting beside a crystal glass. Some drug paraphernalia, beer bottles, and wine bottles stood on the coffee table, and an absurdly yellow jacket was neatly folded on the couch. Two smaller staircases led to the raised master suite's bedchamber. The doors were closed.

"They're in there," Raptor growled, sniffing.

Leon only nodded. A strange look had passed over his features, and Buzz was unsettled when he identified it. It was arrogance. They had managed to progress this far without taking casualties, and Leon seemed to mistake that for success. Buzz wanted to tell him that it was too early to start celebrating.

Raptor looked at the two doors. What lay behind them? How many men, how many bullets in how many clips? "What do you want us to do?"

Leon looked from Buzz to Raptor and back again. "Raptor, cover the doors with me. Buzz, go get backup. Bring more stun grenades. There may be civilians in there." The colonel lowered his faceplate again. "I'm going to try and open negotiations."

Buzz nodded sharply and went for the stairs, taking them two at a time.

§

Leon and Raptor waited while Buzz went for assistance. Leon's heart was pounding in his chest, and he could feel the adrenaline coursing through him, an electric charge pulsing along his limbs. Every detail stood out clear and crisp, nothing missed, nothing ignored. They had routed the subjects, he was proud to note, but he had to remind himself that it didn't mean the people holed up in the bedrooms would simply relinquish their weapons and give up. Few had even attempted to surrender, and he had the sneaking suspicion that the shields of Korinthe had a reputation for ignoring raised hands. It would be a foolish mistake to charge in, guns blazing, when there could be innocent bystanders in there: some of the pushers had already attempted to use Human shields.

Beside him, the Prross was breathing slowly, evenly, and seemed barely winded. Raptor was a true predator, standing still as though waiting for his prey to show itself. There was a cold gleam in his eyes that Leon found simultaneously reassuring and unsettling.

He was about to approach the door to open a dialogue when the Prross's long head abruptly swung around, nostrils flaring as he detected an unfamiliar scent.

Leon was about to ask what he smelled when the first stuttering roar reverberated through the suite. It was unmistakable, that sound. Leon had first heard it long ago; it was alien in this setting but no less recognizable. *Someone thinks this is a warzone, after all,* he thought to himself as he and Raptor dropped to the carpet. It was a machine gun, a Gladiator. Quickly, keeping flat on their stomachs, they made their way to the stairs. As they drew nearer, the stink of blood wafted up to them, mingled with vomit, urine, and cordite.

Leon's eyes widened in surprise before narrowing in concentration. Half a dozen men had emerged from the west wing his team had already cleared, all heavily armed. A number of them wore light armor, and he found himself wondering how this could have happened. Could they have come up via the service elevator? If so, what had happened to the shield officers holding that approach?

At the center of the group walked a man who looked more Minotauri than Human, at least seven feet tall and three wide across the chest. He was the one wielding the machine gun, laying down a shimmering veil of fire. The shields scattered, and Leon could see two lying, wounded or dead, upon the ground. He could not see Buzz.

What they hadn't destroyed taking the main level, the machine gunner was tearing to pieces. Leon's heart leapt into his throat at this disastrous turn of events.

"Get that fucker!" Leon shouted, tugging Raptor's sleeve. He could barely hear himself over the roar of that gun.

"What about you?"

Leon hooked his thumb over his shoulder, toward the closed bedroom doors. "I'll keep these kids pinned. Now get him, before the shields decide to write the whole thing off and burn us all out!"

Raptor seemed to see the wisdom in this and vanished quickly, rolling off the ledge with a fluidity that was almost snakelike. *Bad to worse*, Leon thought grimly as he listened to the machine gun sing its reaver's song.

He was so intent on hunting for a target downstairs that he nearly missed the flash of movement from the bedroom on the left. Leon turned, rising in a crouch, and fired a rapid flurry of shots. Hearing a wounded shout, he advanced quickly with the Warthog leading the way. As someone moved to close the door from inside, Leon threw out a foot and kicked it open, hard. The door slammed against the face of the man inside, and a gun fell to the floor. Without thinking, Leon plunged ahead.

He could have waited, *should* have waited, until the shields had finished downstairs. Frustration and the desire to get this over quickly and get the bonus got the better of him. With the impact of the kick still shuddering up his leg, Leon entered the room, firing.

It was his fury in entering that saved him. Half a dozen men and two women stood in the room in shock, looking at him as though he were a madman. *Perhaps I am.* Ignoring the terrified and logical voice in his head calling for him to retreat, Leon raked the room with fire. In truth, he had hoped most of the bodyguards had been taken care of downstairs. In truth, he had assumed only the cowardly leaders of the cartel remained. In truth, he was dead wrong. He found himself framed in the doorway, having blundered into the sights of a half-dozen armed men.

Long years honing his reflexes and his instincts had taught Leon to trust them, and he picked his targets with startling precision. The man in front of him had dropped his weapon when Leon slammed the door into his face, breaking his nose and cheekbone; Leon ignored him for the time being. Instead he turned his sights on a man with a scattergun, partially concealed behind a decorative screen partition. Partition and man were torn apart by a burst from the Warthog, and Leon was already turning as his target collapsed. Another man was struggling to raise a submachine gun which had gotten tangled in his jacket, and Leon shot him before the stubby little weapon could be brought to bear. Then the subjects were returning fire, and Leon moved along the wall, shooting. The people became vague shapes, obscured by the shower of plaster and the blinding muzzle flashes. Leon relied on his memory to guide his hands, to keep him from hitting the women who huddled, screaming, beside the bed.

The man by the door was regaining his senses, but before he could regain his weapon, Leon shot him twice in the chest. A fountain of blood sprayed out his back as the burst punched clean through him; he writhed against the wall, his mouth open in a silent scream. The Warthog was empty; instead of trying to reload, Leon dropped it and drew a Sprawler from the holster on his right hip.

That gave the others the moment they needed, and several bullets hit home. One punched through the TacGel protecting his right biceps, and he lost his grip on the Sprawler. The others slammed into his chest, and he heard his own ribs crack loudly. Without the vest he would have been a dead man. As it was, his breath was knocked out of him and he stumbled back, his helmeted head crashing into the mirror of the vanity behind him. Another bullet hit him in the leg, but the TacGel did its job and absorbed the force. *Where are Raptor and Buzz? I'm not playing around here!* He drew his second Sprawler and returned fire.

There was more movement to his right as a man threw open the door to the master bathroom. Still engaged with the others across from him, Leon could only watch as the newcomer took aim. One of the women on the floor had picked up a gun; instead of turning it on Leon, she shot the gangster in the bathroom before emptying the clip at the others. As the last of the defenders slid to the floor in a wash of blood, she threw the pistol aside and closed her eyes, shaking.

"Thanks," was all Leon could say. The woman said nothing. Her companion was staring at him, open-mouthed, her eyes vacant. They would have been beautiful if addiction and hard living had not crushed the life from them. Leon turned away and returned to the living room. "Stay ... here," he croaked. He wondered if the woman who had helped him was the informant they had been told to look for. Whoever she was, he was in her debt.

Leon's arm burned, and blood poured down to his elbow and dripped off onto the carpet. His head was pounding, and he blinked his eyes hard to rid himself of the spots he was seeing. His ears were still ringing from the grenade that had gone off downstairs, not to mention the close-quarters firefight he had just left. Wheezing, he stumbled back into the living area, his wounded arm wrapped tight around his chest. He squeezed his eyes shut as his vision began to blur, and when he opened them again they were clear. He could still hear the machine gun downstairs. How long had it been? Ten seconds? Twenty? He didn't know.

Two shell-shocked shield officers were waiting for him. One was taking potshots at the thugs downstairs. "Colonel," said the other, stopping himself before saluting, "we were told to assist you in ... oh, *shit!*" He and his comrade raised their weapons as the remaining closed door burst open. Caught between them, Leon could only dive out of the way.

It was over in a bloody, chaotic instant. Warthogs, submachine guns, and pistols erupted in fire. By the time Leon regained his feet, the two shields were dead as were four more of the gangsters. Only one man was still standing, and he was holding a large-caliber magnum.

As luck would have it, Leon was standing to the man's right. He raised his Sprawler, pointing it at the man's heart. "Don't move a fucking muscle!" he barked over the continuing roar of the Gladiator downstairs.

Marcus Keegan's mouth twitched bitterly. His finger was on the trigger, but he stayed still. Keegan was tall and muscular, a head taller than Leon. His scarred face and bald, tattooed head testified to the fact that he hadn't started his criminal career by tax evasion, and his veins stood out, pulsing visibly. One of his eyes was blank, a milky white; the other was a piercing blue, wild and furious.

"You're no shield," Keegan observed flatly.

"Nope."

For a moment neither man moved. They weighed their options, realizing at the same instant that they didn't have many. *I'm not waiting around for this asshole to shoot me.* "I want out," Keegan said in a low voice.

"Not going to happen," Leon replied. If this man was hoping to use him as a hostage to get free, he was badly mistaken. It was almost funny: even if Leon were foolish enough to give up his weapon, the shields would simply shoot through him to get to Keegan. *What's one Jackal to them?* "Put your piece down and I guarantee you walk out of here alive."

"We had a deal," Keegan said, sounding bitter and puzzled.

"Not with me, you didn't," Leon responded, confused. "Just put it down and take a knee."

Keegan was looking at the shields he had killed, a strange expression on his face. After what seemed like an eternity, he dropped the pistol and stiffly sank to his knees. Leon approached cautiously, the barrel of his Sprawler level with the back of Keegan's head. He was reaching for a trap-cuff hanging from his belt when Keegan leapt to his feet, pushing up and backwards, all lightning reflexes and spring-loaded muscles. His bald head slammed into Leon's helmet so hard it broke the faceplate. Leon heard and felt his nose break, blood gushing into his mouth.

Somehow Keegan managed to tear Leon's helmet off and get a hold of his Sprawler, pointing it directly at his face. Leon smiled weakly and held up his hand. It was gloved but for the tips of the fingers. He mimed pulling the trigger. Keegan turned the pistol so he could see the handgrip and cursed: the gun was keyed to Leon's biometrics and would respond to no touch but his own.

Keegan could have gone for his own magnum on the floor, but that might have given Leon enough time to draw his service pistol. Instead, the bald enforcer charged headlong at Leon, lifting him off the ground.

As they grappled, Leon could hear the machine gun still firing; tracer rounds, bright white, dug into walls, shattered glass, and ripped apart furniture and flesh, smoking. A flurry of them stitched across the ceiling above Leon and Keegan, and chunks of plaster pattered down around them. As he struggled to break free of Keegan's iron grip, he got a good look at the gunner downstairs and his own courage quailed.

If Keegan's enhanced metabolism was frightening, the man wielding the gun was a terror. He looked to be amped up on Burn or something else, veins popping in his neck, his eyes blazing with uncomprehending rage. He had taken several shots to his bare chest from the fleeing tactical officers but refused to go down, refused even to acknowledge his pumping wounds.

As Leon watched, another officer was riddled with bullets, but the concentrated fire of the survivors finally subdued the gunner. He dropped the smoking cannon and staggered a few steps, blood gushing from a dozen gunshot wounds. A bullet had gone through his cheek and out through his jaw; the bone hung from ragged strips of bloody flesh, turning his scream into a feral, gurgling howl. He hit the floor hard amidst the carpet of spent shell casings and didn't move. He had given his companions time to find cover, though, and they continued to pin down the shields at both ends of the suite.

"You can surrender any time now," Leon grunted. "It's over."

"For you, maybe," Keegan spat. He was incredibly quick, and it was all Leon could do to keep from being killed. He came on, pushing Leon back, the hits coming faster and harder than Leon could possibly block. It was like fighting a hurricane. Without Leon realizing it, they had neared the edge of the loft. The Sprawler was kicked aside as they went off the ledge.

For a moment, Leon could see the gunfight raging in the tiled room. All the tactical officers were down, dead or wounded. More were storming in through the foyer but they, too, were under fire, precisely what the Jackals had fought so hard to avoid.

And then they were falling, slamming down hard on the stairs. Gritting his teeth, Leon got a firm grip on Keegan's throat as they rolled over a corpse. Keegan thought to reach for the dead man's autorifle, but it slipped from his grasp and fell to the floor below.

Sliding through the railing, the two of them thudded to the ground two and a half meters below. Getting to their hands and knees, dazed, they kept fighting, scrabbling at each other while trying to reach a firearm. Keegan managed a kick to Leon's face, spinning him around and knocking him to the ground. Leon imagined he could feel every tread of the son of a bitch's boot imprinted on his cheek with the broken glass and blood. He had felt his jaw crack. He didn't think it was broken, but it sure as hell felt like a possibility.

He couldn't seem to rise. When Keegan knelt over him, he was holding a knife in his hand, a nasty-looking, curved combat knife. He began to lower it calmly, almost surgically, toward Leon's eye.

Abandoning his attempt to capture the man alive, Leon held off Keegan with his good hand while his right fumbled at a pocket flap. His fingers wrapped around the handle of a little black switchblade, no match for the killer's blade heading for his brain but deadly enough in Leon's hands. He released the smoky, gleaming trykon blade and buried it in Keegan's gut, twisting. His adversary coughed, eyes widening. For an instant, Keegan relaxed his grip, but only for an instant.

Almost contemptuously, Keegan took hold of Leon's hand and slammed it against the floor, nearly crushing his knuckles. The switchblade slid across the floor, out of reach.

Bullets whipped past them as Leon struggled to hold the knife-wielding drug lord at bay, but it was a losing battle. They had won the firefight, that much was clear, but Leon was still going to die here. Keegan planted his palm against Leon's chin, and as the mercenary's head cracked back against the floor, he saw heavy, booted feet approaching, and behind them a muscular tail swinging back and forth. He smiled through his own blood.

The blade was nearly pressed to Leon's exposed throat when Raptor's right hand fixed itself on Keegan's skull, claws raking through the flesh of his forehead and gouging bloody lines through the swirling tattoo. Keegan howled in agony as the claws of Raptor's left hand dug into the flesh between his shoulder blades. The Prross pulled him off of Leon and held him aloft for a moment before hurling him to the floor hard enough to break several tiles. And then the Prross roared, a blood-curdling bellow that frightened even his friend.

Keegan moaned and curled up to protect himself. It was over.

Raptor extended a bloody hand and Leon took it, felt himself pulled roughly to his feet. "Thanks."

"I was just in a rush. It looked like you had him."

Leon was in too much pain to laugh. He steadied himself, leaning on a standing lamp whose bulb had been shattered in the fighting. The two stood over their beaten quarry, and Leon's eyes narrowed to icy slits. "My boys and I didn't come here so some fucker like you could get away. You think you're bad, selling drugs to kids?"

"What are you ... talking about?" mumbled Keegan through his pain.

"You're not bad, my friend. You're a little gremlin in the system, chewing on the wires." Leon spat blood. "They said you were a sojier, once. Looks to me like you forgot how it works, partnering with fools like these. I served under the best, and they taught me that if you go to *war*, you make sure it's total war. We came here to erase you."

"Fuck you." Now Keegan spat blood, and it fell in a dark, glistening streak across Leon's pant leg. "You think this is over, Jackal? I know people ... everywhere. Word gets out ... you'll never be safe."

"The shields here want you alive. Too bad." Weary, the colonel stumbled over to where his Sprawler had fallen. He found his switchblade, wiping its blade on his pants leg before gently closing it. They trap-cuffed Keegan and surveyed the damage.

The suite, save for the feeble groans of the wounded tactical officers and thugs, was now quiet. Leon looked around, scanning the torn paintings, the perforated walls, the shattered bay windows, the furniture with its stuffing lying on the floor ... all the bodies. Tiredly he shook his head, trying to make sense of everything that had happened in the last few minutes. The mission had most certainly gone to hell, but they had pulled it off, barely. Had it been avoidable? Leon was too numb to think about it.

He appraised his friend. Raptor had been hit twice in the chest, the wounds like terrible glistening flowers that had blossomed on his fatigues. He was panting, but he seemed all right. What would have killed a Human had merely slowed Raptor down. Leon checked his own arm, frowned at the blood running freely from the ragged hole in the flesh. It would keep. He looked around, listening for the sounds of combat. He didn't hear any. "Buzz!"

The two waited, looking around, weapons pointed at the floor. Leon called out again. "Hey, Buzz! You dead? You can quit hiding now, they're all gone!"

Where the hell was he?

A single gunshot rang out as if in answer to the unasked question. Raptor's head swung toward the kitchen. "Someone's still shooting? Give it up already." He sniffed the air carefully, filtering scents, and his face fell. "Oh, no."

Leon didn't need to ask Raptor what he had smelled. The Prross had always been adept at identifying people by scent: hair, skin, soap, perfume, detergent ... and blood. The two ran in the direction of the kitchen. Leon gestured to the tactical officers streaming into the now-quiet suite, and a detachment broke off to guard Keegan, while others followed him and Raptor.

Skidding to a halt in the doorway, Leon stood horrified. The shields holding the door had been cut to ribbons, and it looked like Keegan's associates had stormed the adjacent suite where Princeton and his cohort had staged. In the center of the kitchen, Buzz lay on the floor, moving feebly. Three of Keegan's crew stood at the refrigerator, loading what looked like red bricks into a metal cooler. It had to be Burn. Buzz's flak vest was practically obliterated, and bloody holes were punched in his fatigues, turning them to a soggy red mess. His eyes, glazed with pain, sought out his friends imploringly. He must have been hit while trying to flank the machine gunner.

The criminals had been preoccupied, but now they looked around, understanding their mistake. They could have run, but greed and perhaps fate had kept them here. "Fools." It was only a whisper, but the hate in Raptor's voice was bone-chilling. Leon saw horror cross the face of one of the men; glaring through eyes of slate, he shot it off.

The other two bolted for the service lift, hurdling uniformed bodies. Buzz was still on the floor, breathing labored and irregular as he fought to hold on. He was bleeding to death, tears in his eyes. He moaned weakly, reaching for Leon with a red-glistening hand as his friend sprinted by.

"Leon ... wait," Buzz cried.

"I'll be right back, buddy," Leon promised, hardly pausing.

The Prross lost control in the time it took to blink. He easily outpaced the fleeing thugs. As he caught up, he pirouetted in mid-air, swinging his tail around in front of him. A metal implant in the tip of the appendage acted as a weighted club. It caught one of the men in the ribs and slammed him sideways into the wall. Raptor regained his feet and kept running without slowing. Leon stopped at the fallen, moaning man and knelt over him, punching again and again.

The spikes in Raptor's tail implant emerged with a cold, audible *click* as he reached the second man. There was a truncated scream from his victim as Raptor swung his tail upwards. It caught him in the chest, embedded in his ribs, and lifted him clear into the ceiling. There was a crunch, and he fell heavily to the floor, dead. Raptor walked back and calmly broke the neck of the man Leon had pinned to the floor, his ferocity abating like morning mist. He yanked Leon to his feet and the two returned to the kitchen.

Leon sagged against the pulverized doorjamb, exhausted physically and emotionally. A man who had been like a brother to him lay there, his hands drawn up to his chest as though he had been trying to staunch the blood pumping from so many wounds. There had never been any question of survival, no time or miracle capable of averting the inevitable. *But at least we could have been here with him.* Leon hated himself for chasing down those men and leaving Buzz to die alone.

The pool of blood was a startling crimson against the white tiles, but Leon couldn't see it as he sank to his knees beside his friend, cradling

Buzz's head gently. There was a pink froth of blood on the dead man's lips, and a thin rivulet had run down from the corner of his mouth to the back of his head. Unthinking, Leon wiped it away.

Dark brown half-lidded eyes gazed up at him without seeing, and Leon closed them. They had been filled with sadness and, Leon thought, disappointment. Raptor was silent, standing over his friends, one dead and one alive. His eyes were contemplative, his mouth open in dismay. "It's only a body now," he said finally, voice low.

Leon crouched silently in his fury, Raptor's soft-spoken words like white-hot metal under his skin. Buzz's blood soaked into his pants, before he lowered his friend's head into the red pool that had spilled from him. Raptor simmered, his own wrath a private furnace.

"Can't you pray or something?" Leon asked hoarsely.

"It doesn't work like that," Raptor said with a surprising softness in his voice. "Should we take his tags?"

"Not until after the shields are done here. I don't want them throwing him out with the garbage." Leon gave his friend one last, lingering look and struggled to his feet. When his knees buckled, Raptor's hand was there, surprisingly gentle as it lifted him. The two stumbled back out into the hall, drenched in a friend's blood and their own.

Shields were moving through the suite in force now, making sure there were no more surprises waiting for them. They stopped when they saw the two bloodied mercenaries moving purposefully out of the kitchen. They must have looked like denizens of hell, sojieri of the abyss trudging out of the inferno. Held between two shields, Keegan was being hauled to his feet, his head lolling weakly in grim defeat as he took in the ruins of his arrogant little empire.

Somehow he found the energy to headbutt one of the shield officers, crushing the man's nose. Even with his hands tied, he managed to grab the officer's combat knife and plunge it into the thigh of his partner before running for the exit, unaware that Leon and Raptor were in his path. Where was he planning on going? Leon was sick of it.

He and Raptor exchanged a look, Leon's in inquiry, the Prross's in assent. They walked toward their prey, and he turned his swollen face toward them. There was still a spark of defiance in his eye, but it was extinguished in an instant as the barrel of Leon's pistol came in line with his chest.

The shield who had been stabbed raised a hand. "Whoa, what the *fuck* are you *doing?*"

"Too dangerous to be left alive," Leon said softly, matter-of-factly, and began shooting. When the pistol was empty, he stopped and watched through the thick pall of smoke as Keegan's life drained from him and he stopped breathing. In his last moments he looked much like Buzz, eyes imploring, afraid, lips trembling. And it was then that Leon realized what he had done.

The shield officer's hand came down, no point in protesting now. He and his partner simply stared in shock, looking from the body to the smoking barrel of the gun and the battered man holding it. Keegan was dead, one eye white and glassy, the other sky-blue, both gazing sightlessly upward. Leon threw the weapon down and interlaced his fingers behind his head as the shields put him on his knees and cuffed him.

It was some minutes before he and Raptor were released by an apoplectic Inspector Kimball, who looked at Keegan's bloody corpse with regret but little in the way of pity. His expression of disgust when he saw what the mercenaries had done topped off Leon's remorse, but it was nothing in comparison to Buzz's loss.

The wreckage was total, the suite a write-off. Paramedics had arrived to cart away the wounded, followed by their grim counterparts, the coroners. The latter waited patiently, not in any particular hurry. For them time was not a factor.

Princeton entered the suite, delicately stepping over bodies and rubble. He cast one look at Keegan and shrugged. There was no revulsion on his bureaucrat's face, only clinical disinterest, and again Leon wondered who the man really was. "His Eminence will be disappointed. He was hoping especially to have a word with Marcus. Still, your performance was simply breathtaking. We caught it all on camera. And you brought us all of our priority targets but him. As agreed, the bonus will be transferred to your organization's accounts. I'm sorry our intelligence failed to account for their heavy support. Clearly they didn't trust whomever it was they were meeting." The premier's aide looked around the demolished two-level suite, glancing into the kitchen where Buzz lay. He shook his head. "My condolences." His sincerity was dubious.

"Thank you," said Leon, with equal insincerity. "I'm sorry, too. I don't think any of the officers in the way survived that attack."

"No, they didn't. I suppose this line of work is self-selecting," Princeton said cruelly. "You must be of the necessary caliber, if you'll pardon the pun."

Leon's mouth fell open, his split and bleeding lip trembling imperceptibly. Of its own accord, his right hand came up in a fist. Once he might have hit the man, might have hit him until he had swallowed all his teeth. Times changed, however, and not all the enemies were in Leon's crosshairs. He forced his fist open, and extended his hand. "I hope you'll help us make the necessary arrangements."

Princeton shook his hand. "Certainly." The bureaucrat wiped his hand on a chair and went to tend to other business.

§

Raptor lingered after Leon had gone, watching as order was gradually restored. The suite was a study in entropy, and even the shields' actions were in service of that all-powerful spiral of eventuality. Leon may have been distracted by Buzz's death, but Raptor still knew how to keep a clear head. He withdrew a small camera from a pocket of his fatigues and began taking pictures alongside the forensic analysts, a few of whom gave him strange looks. The helmet cameras had recorded everything live, but it was policy to collect forensic photographs, as well.

As he left, Raptor passed young Alvarez, who sat propped against a wall, a bullet in his leg. He clapped the tactical officer on the shoulder, and the man looked up at him through a haze of painkillers. "You made it," he said, awestruck.

"Thanks for the gum, kid. Glad to see you made it, too. Good luck."

The hallway outside the suite was bustling with activity. Paramedics were everywhere, stabilizing severely wounded officers whose blood was soaking into the rich carpet as they lay on their stretchers. *Somehow I don't think we're ever going to get a company discount from this place.* At least the building was still standing. The stretchers lined both sides of the corridor, at least ten of them. Some of the officers were being tended to. Others had sheets pulled over their heads. Captain Olafsen, bleeding profusely from her wounds, was surrounded by paramedics and worried comrades. Nearby, wounded cartel members were given only cursory care if they received any at all. It was not Raptor's place to judge.

He found Leon perched on one of the police barricades, a waist-high metal wall that would have looked more at home in the middle of the road than the middle of the hallway. Elsewhere shields were dismantling the other barriers, floating them away on grav-equipped dollies. A young paramedic was tenderly inspecting Leon's arm, simultaneous awe and disdain writ unmistakably on her features.

"The gel slowed it down some, but it's still in deep." She probed the still-bleeding hole. "I think it missed the humerus, but it's close." She picked through her kit. "We can do this quick and dirty, or you can wait for hospital staff."

Leon's face was blank. "Yeah? Do it, then," he said quietly. He didn't seem to notice the pretty young doctor or her obvious contempt for him.

With practiced speed, the medic pulled out a thin cord with a tiny ball on the end. She pushed it into the wound. Leon grimaced but held still. The medic thumbed a switch on the device's base, and he jerked. There was a metallic *ping*, and the medic withdrew the magnetic probe; there was now a slightly deformed slug clinging to the tip.

Leon's nose was already bandaged, a white brace on the bridge to straighten it. The blood had been wiped off his lips, chin, and neck, exposing the bruises and lacerations that had done the bleeding. He looked like he had been used for target practice by a blind knife thrower.

Raptor looked idly at his own chest, where the blood was still slowly pumping out. His wounds were burning, the pain radiating throughout his torso. Rather than shrink away from it, Raptor embraced it, relished it. They had won, after all, and the pain was a well-deserved reminder of the cost of victory. "Are you all right?" he asked uncomfortably.

Leon nodded, swallowing. He grimaced as the paramedic irrigated the hole in his arm. "I should have kept the two of you with me." He looked down, his eyes narrowing in a glare that settled on nothing. "For fuck's sake, he was right about the whole thing."

Raptor wanted to reach out and comfort his friend, but he didn't know how to do it any more than Leon knew how to bring Buzz back from the dead. "To be fair, it was your ass on the line," he tried.

Leon cupped his head in his hands. Raptor had apparently said the wrong thing. "Look," he tried again, unsure, "you did your best. Buzz was a sojier, just like us. Sometimes we die. It's part of the job. Buzz died with something to hold on to. That's more than a lot of people can say when it's their time."

"I'm hoping a paycheck isn't what you have in mind," said Leon, wincing as the paramedic put a needle into his arm, deftly suturing the wound.

"No, dammit. He had you, me, Jackal Pack. He had his own clan, a clan who will miss him and remember him. That's what a warrior really wants: to die that way."

"Fuck you, Raptor, that's what a Prross warrior really wants. Buzz wanted to live long enough to retire. So do I."

That was more than Raptor could take. "Then stop putting yourself in harm's way."

4: Accountability

Waiting patiently in the antechamber to Empress Kra'al's office, Grand Admiral Hakar looked through the long, curving window opposite him. Clearly there to awe visiting dignitaries, it provided an unparalleled view of the Tagean capital's skyline and helped dispel some of the anxiety he was feeling. The violet night sky was filled with glittering stars. Two moons hung over the city of Sherata, guardian lanterns themselves swept with the sparkling lights of lunar colonies. Slowly the grand admiral's gaze drifted downward to sweep over the bustling cityscape, the crown jewel of the Coalition throneworld. Sherata's skyline was all domes and spires, the tallest of which rose thousands of meters into the sky. Some of those structures were almost ten thousand years old, presiding over the city with fading majesty.

The royal palace was not nearly so old; in fact, when the first of those soaring towers had been erected, the land on which the palace stood had been little more than a swamp. Now it was the Plaza of Unity, Sherata's beating heart. The eastward side of the palace where Hakar now sat overlooked an expansive promenade dotted with meticulously pruned local trees. An ecological disaster had barely been averted some years before when, on a whim, parliament had attempted to import foreign trees for decoration. After expediting the quarantine to have them planted in time for an interplanetary conference, the Tageans found that they had unintentionally allowed parasitic organisms into the ecosystem. Tagea's biosphere was far older than its ancient civilization and stable. That stability came at the expense of adaptability, leaving the world vulnerable to outside influences. Hakar supposed the balance of power in the galaxy was much the same. The kingdoms had grown complacent with their half-hearted give-and-take, and now it seemed as though they might be getting a rude wake-up call from an unknown aggressor.

Even at this hour, people strolled along the cobbled paths between the trees, looking into the ornamental ponds and casting glances up at the domes of the palace, perhaps hoping for a glimpse of the empress on one of her balconies. Did they wonder if anyone was looking down at them? From this high up, they seemed blissfully unaware of how fragile their lives were, how tenuous the forces that connected their empire. Vehicle traffic soared at and above ground level, a revolving ballet of light around the center of the city, and the broad canals glittered like beaten silver. It was as though some of the stars had descended from the sky above in a whirlpool over Sherata. For a moment Hakar was struck by a pang of embarrassment at the realization that he, too, took it all for granted. Were he Human, he would have blushed.

He turned his attention to the doors of her majesty's office, which had opened, and he saw an intelligence officer walk out. The man nodded to Hakar, quickly averting his furtive gaze. *Are we here for the same reasons?* Hakar wondered as he picked up his cap and attaché case and walked into the office.

"Hakar. How are you?" Kra'al looked tired, her eyes red-rimmed. She had been up since before dawn and had suffered through countless briefings on the ongoing crisis in the Dias Traverse systems. She probably wanted nothing more than to rest. What Hakar had to say would likely give her another sleepless night.

"I'm fine, Your Majesty. A little on edge, perhaps. Thank you for seeing me on such short notice. How are you?"

"Well, all things considered. I apologize for my rudeness at our last meeting, Hakar. I was a little preoccupied. I had forgotten you had been to visit your family. How are they?"

"Very well, Your Majesty. They send their warmest regards."

"Your son must be nearly twelve now. He'll be celebrating his naming ceremony soon, won't he?"

Hakar couldn't help smiling, but the smile was rueful. His son was growing up so fast, becoming so precocious and mischievous, as Hakar had been. And yet he was missing almost all of this special time. "Not for a few more years but soon."

"Not too many young Tageans have the empress at their naming, I'd wager," Kra'al said with a lighthearted chuckle.

"You're too kind, Highness." Hakar retrieved a rectangular data key from his attaché case. "I hate to do this, but I have something you may want to see." He handed her the key. "This was recorded at a border station in the Zuni 2634 system, along the fringe of the Tears of Alkyra. We're still analyzing it."

Kra'al slid the key into the holographics player on her desk. A hazy image of a small dartlike ship appeared between them. It blazed through a starfield, evading incoming fire. Kra'al leaned forward, cupping her head in her clawed hands as she watched it pirouette through space, seeming to reverse direction while moving simultaneously on its original course, maneuvering thrusters firing in artful, virtuosic bursts. The camera struggled to keep the ship in view. She replayed the scene a few times before raising her eyes to him. "What am I looking at here? One of ours? Some Special Projects prototype? I've never seen a ship move like that."

"Neither have I. It's an unknown, a contact along the Valinata border. Intel has given it the coded designation 'Raven Blue.' I'll have the full workup brought to you immediately."

Kra'al's sigh was almost a growl. She was about to ask something else when a knock at her inner door interrupted them. Her orderly entered, hastily buttoning his jacket. "Good evening, Grand Admiral Hakar. May I bring you something to eat or drink? Her Majesty's chef has prepared a lovely dinner, *kerrik* simmered in wine, with buttered herbs, if it pleases you."

Startled, Hakar flattened his ears a little. "No, thank you."

"Very well. Anything for you, Your Highness?"

"Thank you, Ruush. A glass of white, please."

The orderly bowed and withdrew.

Kra'al's eyes narrowed as she popped out the data key and turned it in her fingers. "I don't like the idea of pushing matters of state to the sidelines for some mystery ship. What is it, then? Some sort of Valinata spy ship?"

Hakar flicked his ears back, *No.* "We don't think so. It's a fighter, barely eight meters long. We think it may be connected to the massacre of the Valinata carrier group in the vicinity of Calama. It seems to have been part of a larger fleet."

"Do 'we' have visuals on the fleet?"

"Unfortunately, no. The footage was obtained by a fixed gun camera from a border security ship run by the Myrmidon Company. It was...." The grand admiral cleared his throat. "It was the only part of the ship recovered. They're seeking compensation."

Kra'al went still at that. "It's not us. It's not a Valinata ship. Are you telling me it belongs to border pirates?"

"I doubt it," Hakar said hastily. "If you'll recall the biological fragment recovered from the incident near Calama?" Kra'al nodded.

"Reflective indices and spectroscopy indicate a similar density and composition."

Kra'al looked up from the data key, her golden irises barely visible through her slitted eyelids. "That ship is organic?" she asked, incredulous.

"Very possibly." He swallowed and tried a smile. He had promised her answers, but all he had were question marks. There was nothing certain out there on the hazy sweep of the border.

Kra'al didn't smile back. "You've had a week. You still don't know more than that?"

Hakar's ears flicked again. "I'm no biochemist, Your Majesty. Special Projects *has* developed a chemical and biological profile of the fragment we found. All we can say for sure is that it was made from an organic composite. Whoever built this is smart. It's not quite as strong as the standard alloys used in spaceship manufacture, but it plays hell with sensors, scatters the signals or absorbs them." It was revolutionary technology, but Hakar couldn't understand how marauders would get their hands on it or why they would risk attacking a VSF patrol or a commercial border station. Most groups like that would prey upon civilian caravans, freighters, or passenger liners. Unless they had stumbled into the Valinata carrier group by accident, what could they gain from attacking a battle fleet? *A field test of their new equipment*, he realized.

The empress appeared to come to the same conclusion. "I'd like this tracked before someone starts deploying these ships in crowded trade routes. How is the Valinata investigation coming? Any news from behind the Emerald Veil?"

Hakar flicked his ears yet again. "I'm afraid not, but we'll never get a straight answer from their mouthpieces." He watched Kra'al for a reaction. "There may be elements in the VSF leadership who are willing to sell us the data," he added to prompt her. "I'm told that our treatment of their deceased pilot was considered quite proper."

The empress thought carefully for a moment before looking up at Hakar. "I'd rather not add blatant espionage to the list of charges against us. You're aware the negotiations over Bona Ventura have stalled. I'm afraid if we keep pushing them, they'll walk away from the table. Or shove back."

"Something tells me they have their hands full, but I understand. I still recommend we develop an action plan."

"Why do you say that?"

"Comscan intercepts have been showing an unusual amount of encrypted chatter regarding a system called Tanis Ruin. You've heard of it?"

"Of course. It's a Valinata treasure."

"Well, it seems as though they've been diverting a lot of ships to Calama, as we'd expect. But they've also dedicated a substantial number of fleets to Tanis Ruin. Including two of the Dragon Valia armadas."

"Do you suspect a rebellion? It wouldn't be the first time the Valinata has Balkanized. And if that's true, the attack on Calama could have been rebels, hoping to … what?" Kra'al was a shrewd strategist as well as a skilled political negotiator. "Goddess protect us, Hakar, what if they're some hardline group with their sights on Coalition territory?"

"I wouldn't jump to conclusions, Highness. But that's precisely why I think it prudent to develop an action plan."

"Very well. I leave that to you."

"Thank you, Highness." On to the next order of business. Hakar placed his attaché case on the desk and opened it, pulling out a folder. He extracted a file and slid it across the polished wood. Kra'al picked it up. "I've taken the liberty of sketching out a few proposals."

"Let me stop you there, Hakar. Admiral Telec has just returned, and I have a meeting with him in half an hour."

"From the Dias Traverse? What does he have to report?" Hakar asked. Ordinarily the defense advisor's visit to the Dias Traverse would not have been any of his business, but his curiosity was piqued. Circumstances were hardly ordinary.

"The news isn't all bad, but we need to take a more active role or risk losing the whole region." The empress managed to say this without spelling out the disastrous consequences of such a collapse.

In the last few decades, the Dias Traverse had become the crucible for the Coalition's economic and political woes. The regional capital, Iracha, was still firmly loyal to the Coalition, but it was surrounded by planets populated by the disenfranchised, with twenty billion inhabitants below the poverty line. "The regional governor has indicated that there may be the threat of a coup, and he's requesting naval support, a show of force. Telec is inclined to grant it as a short-term solution. What do you think?"

Hakar considered his words carefully. "If we appear heavy-handed, we may only throw gas on the fire through the rest of the Dias." Before the rise of the Coalition, the Tez'Nar Empire had stretched across hundreds of systems, and the membership of those systems in the Coalition was of great cultural significance. In recent centuries, however, their planets had been pushed to the periphery despite a proportionately high rate of naval enlistment among ethnic Tez'Nar. As always, it came down to economics, and Dias was costing more than it brought in, yet none of the money seemed to be going to the right programs. And with the Dias systems' proximity to the neighboring Commonwealth, there was always the threat, however remote, of defection. "Personally, I think the threat of force is unwarranted."

Kra'al's pen moved across the paper in graceful, broad strokes, taking notes. She had an ego, but she was smart enough to listen, even to her subordinates. "I would prefer not to participate in a bombardment, it's true. But is it doable otherwise?"

"From what you told me, they're threatening a coup against the governor, not a rebellion against federal authority. I hate to undermine our own people, but if he's the problem, we should go around him and open a dialogue with the dissenting groups ourselves. Perhaps if we give them some attention, they'll see that we're not some aloof rulership raking in taxes and never listening."

"I like it, Hakar. I hope it's feasible, but if there's any way we can make ourselves friends of the Dias majority, I'll take it. We can always ask the governor to step down if it will help settle things."

"Proud to be of service, Your Majesty." The grand admiral bowed and left his empress as her orderly brought the wine. He felt sorry that her moment of quiet could not last.

§

Bosh Telec, Sanar member of the Star Chamber and Her Majesty's defense advisor, came to Hakar's office to catch up. They talked over Huus, a hot Sheff'an drink not unlike tea. "So how was your foray into diplomacy, Ambassador?"

"Please," Telec said in his native language, a bubbly assortment of consonants which were almost impossible for non-Sanar to imitate. "The Irachan Tez'Nar are a dry people from a dry world. But at least they respect decorated military officers. I daresay that my medals did far more than my position as defense advisor to Her Majesty." He swirled his Huus with a facial tentacle and sucked loudly. "The Dias Liberation Front are going to be tough to crack."

"They do have a point," Hakar said softly.

"*That* is precisely why Her Majesty didn't send *you*. They're practically terrorists. But enough about that," Telec said, a gleam in his eyes. "I hear you've been busy with this Valinata-killing organic ship."

Hakar shouldn't have been surprised that Telec had found out about the Calama Sample, as it was being called. After all, all information in the Ministry of Defense made its way across Telec's desk at some point. What surprised Hakar was that his colleague found time to read it all.

An ocean-born Sanar, Telec had to breathe through a humidifier that optimized his atmospheric mixture and maintained a high level of moisture. Although out of his element on dry land, he was quite at home in the political arena, something that Hakar had never gotten the hang of.

As a result, he was one of the most powerful of the grand admirals. Save for the high grand admiral himself, Telec was the most senior, and as defense advisor to Her Majesty, he had Kra'al's ear in a way that no one else did. As he regarded Hakar in turn, Telec's facial tentacles twitched convulsively. They were vestiges of a predatory aquatic evolution: once those tentacles had reached into rocky crevasses to pluck out prey. Nowadays Telec's prey was in the open, on the floor of the parliamentary amphitheater. "It's an interesting sample, to be sure. Nothing like it in the Coalition Registry of Ships."

"How about in the intel files?"

"You tell me, Hakar. You already checked."

"I did. We have dossiers on over seventy fighters and light ships in development by various groups. If the Valinata, Commonwealth, or the Shar'dan were working on this thing, we'd know. We'd certainly know if there were operational prototypes."

Telec leaned back in his chair, his customized uniform making a slight squishing sound, lined as it was with gel to keep him moist. "Well, we know now. Her Majesty mentioned you want an action plan." *Don't jeopardize our positions*, his eyes pleaded.

Hakar knew better than to lose his temper with Telec. Telec was far more deeply involved than he in all the goings-on of the CRDF from administration and fleet movements to choosing who got which command. The man's uniform may have been naval, but he was a born accountant and diplomat: he had dirt on everyone and he was a true chameleon, always blowing with the wind but rarely leading the charge. He and Hakar had been in the same precarious situation when Kra'al's predecessor, Telemon, had been deposed: on the verge of being indicted for war crimes. Telec had managed to get them into the new empress's good graces, and they had been granted amnesty. She had come to rely on them, but they still played a dangerous game, one to which Bosh Telec seemed better suited.

"Have you considered a Commonwealth angle?" Telec prodded.

"I have. I think it's incredibly unlikely."

"Unlikely, yes." Telec sighed, sounding to Hakar much like a kettle coming to a boil. "It may surprise you to learn that Commonwealth elements are laying groundwork in the Dias, to make defection very attractive." His round black eyes zeroed in on Hakar. It was like looking into space. "I said it may surprise you, but you're not stupid. If the Commonwealth can get us and the Valinata frothing at the mouth over Calama and the Outbound Arc, get us to marginalize Dias just a little bit more, the whole clusterfuck is off our hands, and one of our Crown Jewels belongs to them. And we can't do shit if more than half a trillion Dias citizens don't want to be ruled by us anymore. We would have to honor their defection or risk a civil war."

Hakar took a moment to think. "Allowing that sort of precedent would have its own dangers. But I doubt that's what the Commonwealth are after. They've done very well in the current climate. Better than us, most days."

"You're right. I'm just entertaining contingencies."

They may have been in Hakar's office, but he felt no home field advantage. Telec had a way of making people feel supremely uncomfortable, no matter where they were. He was often the harbinger of bad news around these parts. "Any other contingencies you'd like to share?"

"The Valinata want to provoke us into violating the terms of the Engine Accord, so they can leverage us into giving back Bona Ventura and its associated colonies." For years it had been Telec's job to anticipate every possible course of action by the various major powers. He had gotten quite good at it. "They're not above blowing up a few of their own ships just to get things cooking. This Raven Blue may be nothing more than a sleight of hand trick to stir up their own military and put us on the defensive."

There was a loud beep from Hakar's comm unit. "Sorry, I have to take this." Telec nodded his understanding and busied himself leafing through a report on ship-to-ship boarding tactics. Hakar picked up the handset for a little privacy. "This is Hakar. Go ahead."

"Admiral, this is Corporal Williams in Comms. I have an Epsilon priority signal from Admiral Shra. Shall I route it to your office?"

"Please." Hakar put down the handset and snapped his claws at Telec. "Shra is calling from Triatha."

"You sent him to safeguard your sample?"

"No, he was there on unrelated business, but I asked him to look into it." Hakar pressed a key on his desk terminal, and a Mem screen extended out of a slot. He reached over and manipulated the membranous screen, which was composed of panes of elastic conductors, stretching and curving it so that both he and Telec could view it. A few moments later, the signal came through, and Hakar's executive officer appeared before them. His image was clear and the sound was good even across thousands of light-years, the mark of Triathan direct-ansible communications.

A red-furred Tagean, Shra was a loyal and dedicated officer. He wasn't from Tagea itself but rather hailed from one of the old outlying colonies. While some home-born Tageans took a superior attitude toward cousins born away from the throneworld, it didn't make him any less of a Tagean in Hakar's eyes. He had accrued a loyal staff, something his superior officer could certainly appreciate, and he never shied away from duty, whether it was something mundane like monitoring galactic communications or something deadly such as hunting pirates through a nebula. That was why he was Hakar's executive officer and why he would be a worthy successor someday.

"Shra, good to hear from you."

"Thank you, sir. I wish I had better news to report." Shra's language was a drawling pidgin of different Tagean dialects, the result of generations of traders learning to communicate far from home.

"Go ahead. Grand Admiral Telec is here, as well."

"As requested, I've given priority logging to all Valinata communications, and the Triatha decryptors have been working overtime. They've noticed some disturbing trends."

Both Telec and Hakar sat up straighter. "Please elaborate, Admiral," Telec said abruptly. Hakar waved him down.

"It's too soon to say, but it sounds as though the Vali are considering violating the accord. Travel is being restricted, comm traffic coming out is sporadic, resources are being rationed. It's a little early to say whether it goes beyond their customary paranoia."

"Admiral, please refrain from any editorializing," Telec snapped.

Shra looked a little perturbed but he took it well. "It sounds like martial law in there, Admirals. I don't know how much more objective I can be. The sifters have logged quite a few references to Calama and Bona Ventura, up ninety-six and sixty-five percent from prior to the incident, respectively. There's been no mention of Tanis Ruin, but we suspect that the prefix 'Abaddon' may be a coded reference."

"What's their confidence in that assessment?" Hakar inquired, feeling worry gnawing at his thoughts. Were the Valinata truly considering armed action?

"They're fairly confident. The sifters are only logging encrypted comms for priority tags. There's one other thing. Long-range comscan from our auxiliaries in the Zoh Hegemony picked up a signal. It appears to be heavily encrypted. I've taken the liberty of sending you the complete analysis."

"All right, Shra, thank you." Hakar signed off and sipped his Huus. He looked over at Telec, who was dipping his tentacles delicately. "Something is happening in there."

"Well, perhaps we just need to let them sort out their own trouble," Telec countered. He said it as though he were talking about a mutual friend with a temper, not a galactic empire with a history of military aggression and an inferiority complex. He stood up. "I'll speak to High Admiral Pirsan about your action plan, but we need to be careful about reinforcing the Outbound Arc. It sounds like the Valinata are testing a new weapon out there, and they're clearly not afraid to use it on their own people."

He left Hakar alone with that vivid image.

§

The ride through the gravitational conduit was relatively smooth, with only the occasional stomach-churning lurch. Sitting in the acceleration couches of the charter shuttle, Leon and Raptor watched the vortex swirl by outside the viewport. They had the spacious cabin to themselves, and a pleasant young lady had served drinks and sandwiches earlier.

When the pilot made the announcement that they would be arriving in the Eve system in a few minutes, Leon sat up. He was happy to be back, but that did nothing to erode the pit in his stomach.

In the end they had been held on Korinthe for ten days, a full Coalition week. They had not been lounging on the beaches, they had not been sampling the world's renowned wines, they had not been buying drinks for pretty, scantily clad young women. They had been under shield observation and investigation. And in the end, as often happened when Jackal Pack operatives made a mess of things, Anika Sorensen, the mercenary legion's ever-resourceful attorney, had come and arranged their trip home. She greased the wheels with recalcitrant governments, handled bribes and payoffs, and, in some cases, expedited releases from prison. Of course, Leon and Raptor had never been under arrest as they had been engaged in government-sponsored work, but scrutiny had fallen on them, nonetheless. Apparently a media unit across the bay had captured footage of Raptor throwing a man off the balcony.

The ship lurched again, and Leon reflexively grabbed at the handrests, memories of dropship insertions on a dozen worlds springing unbidden to mind. *I never really got used to conduit travel,* he reflected. Once, he knew, gravity had been perceived as the absolute and insurmountable barrier to faster-than-light interstellar travel. As the resources of individual planets had dwindled, however, isolated species had stumbled upon similar methods of aggregate gravitic propulsion and had managed to turn gravity from impediment to enabler. Instead of fighting it, they had harnessed it. Gravity was like water, it was said, and what was ordinarily a steadily moving and stately stream—at the speed of light, granted—could provide a swift and easy ride for a ship with a sufficiently powerful method of propulsion. And so in the course of a few centuries the universe had been transformed from a vast assortment of lonely islands in a sea of darkness to an interconnected network of worlds, all tied together by the mysterious gravitational rivers of the conduits. There were eddies, rapids, and whirlpools, however, as well as disruptions that made conduit travel far from carefree. The end result was the same: where once it had taken years to traverse a single solar system, the galaxy could be crossed from the far end of the Scutum-Centaurus Arm to the trailing tip of the

Outer Arm, a distance of nearly a hundred thousand light-years, in mere months. Only at the periphery of the galaxy, where masses were insufficient to reach out to the neighboring constellations, did hyperspace travel come to a stop and the unknown resume its regency.

Although Leon had never been able to wrap his mind around the complex workings of the theory, he had a fair grasp of the fundamentals. Applied Universal Entanglement worked on the principle of twinned resonant masses: all masses in the universe exerted some small force on each other, and twinned masses—that is, masses with identical compositions and gravitic harmonics—could be induced to resonate in such a way as to exponentially magnify gravity's draw. Ships that could simulate that resonance were able to merge with conduits or even create temporary new paths to planets and stars. Astrotranslational Physics had become the new magical art in an age where nearly anything was possible, and even that was becoming gradually, inevitably commercialized. The principles had been applied to resonant mass telecommunications, allowing planets and far-flung fleets to communicate in near-real time. Even the artificial gravity aboard ships relied on it. Like the deck of any modern ship, the deck of the shuttle was laced with super-light but super-dense masses known as Rombaldt Radiant Masses which, when subjected to a current, created a localized gravitational field. Since the shuttle was an expensive one, the charge was sufficient to create a field that approximated the Terran-Tagean Standard. Negatively charged Rombaldt Masses were likewise responsible for the antigravity capability of gravcars and other hovering vehicles. Leon couldn't imagine life without a technology which would have seemed downright supernatural just a few millennia earlier.

He twirled his switchblade against his thumb, feeling the seamless perfection of the trykon crystal blade against his skin. The blue-purple light of the conduit was caught and reflected by its sharp edge, flickering in a hypnotic pattern that reminded him of light reflected on the ocean. The eyes of the inlaid trykon falcons on the knife's handle glinted brightly. He noticed a bit of dried blood at the base of the blade and picked at it with his fingernail.

Leon's body hurt. His head hurt. Thinking about Buzz's corpse, lying in a refrigerated box in the cargo hold, only made things worse. The mission had been over more quickly than anyone could have hoped, but it had not been easy, and he could hardly help reflecting on Buzz's suggestions to abort. Seventeen million for a night's work was a good deal, but seventeen million wasn't nearly the price of a good friend. Leon should have waited for more personnel, should have brought in the tactical shields sooner, should have … wishful thinking couldn't change anything now, but it was almost comforting to contemplate alternate outcomes and imagine, for a moment, that it had all played out right. At least until the reality of it all came crashing back down, pressing him into his seat.

Buzz Parker and Leon Victor had been through many things together, waging minor wars on dozens of worlds for dozens of causes, but more importantly they had shared jokes and quiet moments over drinks, becoming brothers in every sense but shared genetics. Friends were hard to come by in their line of work, and far harder to lose.

Leon Victor had idly considered retirement but now, having survived the mission when Buzz had lost his life, leaving seemed somehow inappropriate. He glanced over at Raptor, who was flipping through a magazine with surprisingly delicate movements of his long claws. The Prross was bandaged from the waist up, his shirt unbuttoned for comfort. His injuries didn't seem to distress him: to him a scar was as good as a medal, each one its own story.

The charter shuttle passenger cabin, plush and padded, consisted of a ring of couches around a central open space with two tables. As it was just the two of them, their bags, and Buzz's coffin, which was strapped like luggage down below with the equipment (including the godforsaken powered armor), they had spread out, away from one another, each alone with his own thoughts. For Leon, it had been a day and a half of ghostly recollections emerging from the tempestuous mists of his memory. Half-remembered conversations, broken promises, and the blank faces of long-lost friends. So many of the latter, a parade of martyrs before an altar of other people's causes.

"What do you think?" Raptor's voice broke the silence that had prevailed for the better part of the fifteen hours since they had last spoken. They were tired, worn out, wounded, and depressed. Hardly in the mood for conversation.

Leon continued to twirl the knife, eyes on the blade. "About?"

"What are you going to tell the general? He doesn't like bad press. He'll be upset. He may fine us." Raptor's sigh was a low growl, and he winced, his hand going to his bandaged chest. "He doesn't like it when missions go out of control. He doesn't like it when *we* go out of control."

"Out of control?" Leon closed the blade and slipped it back in his pocket. He wasn't really in the mood to discuss pecuniary matters. Not today. "The mission was a success. What is there to talk about?"

"Really, Leon? I know you better than that." Raptor put aside the magazine and sat back. He laced his claws behind his head, intertwining fingers with dorsal spines, curved quotation marks of jet-black horn that glimmered like oil in the purple light of the conduit. He was careful to keep the spines against his back so as not to tear the leather couches. Another bill for damages was the last thing they needed. "We should really be prepared. Princeton will send through a full report. This thing was high profile, and you *know* how thorough Rockmore is. He's shopping for new investors. They like reliability, not surprises."

"I know what they like: results." Leon also knew that Raptor was right, but that didn't soften the blow. He crossed his arms, felt the painful tug on his biceps, and grimaced. He looked at his scabbed knuckles, swollen from the blows he had landed on Keegan. "Next time," he said, without looking up, "you *will* wear a vest. Understand?" Raptor made no reply.

A click came over the cabin speakers. "We will be dropping conduit in ten seconds."

"Boy, they love to cut it short." Raptor glanced at his watch. He stood to secure some of his luggage that had been sitting open on the couch.

Leon looked up at him. "Sit back down. Are you crazy?"

The reversion out of the conduit was jarring, but Raptor's lightning-quick reflexes kept him on his feet, his tail snapping to maintain balance as he kept luggage from flying every which way.

The ship rolled nauseatingly, snowy pinpoints of stars whirling past. Raptor stumbled to the window to look out. "Not a bad place to be exiled," he mused.

Leon grunted. *I'm not so sure.*

As it decelerated, the shuttle rotated farther on its axis, coming into a holding pattern around Eve. The flight team was good: they had managed to penetrate deep into the system before their conduit destabilized and spat them out, and it would be a short traverse to enter the atmosphere. On the inner rim of the outer rim, as was jokingly said, Eve was a sparsely populated world far from the light thrown by the bustling cores of the empires. The planet was centrally located along the little sweep of systems that composed the trade route known as the Tears of Alkyra. More to the point, it was out of the way, at least insofar as the general public was concerned. Less oversight meant more leeway. It was the last destination of disillusioned expatriates and reluctant exiles, refugees of failed coups and criminals looking to reform. A handful of them had founded the settlements that had grown into the capital city of Tesa and the subterranean city beneath the mountain chain of Las Serras da Estrela. These enterprising associates had taken advantage of Eve's key location along the Alkyra to turn it into a self-sustaining world, a minor trade hub, and a cultural center in its own right. There was moderate space-traffic, with enough commerce to keep it thriving. There were commercial liners, freight vessels, and Jackal Pack ships on patrol.

The planet itself drifted into view, bracketed by five tiny moons, the Two Brothers which could be seen during the day and the trio of pale, nighttime satellites known as the Three Sisters. A warm, sandy savannah stretched across the equatorial belt, blending into inhospitable deserts to the north and south. Patches of green, scattered bodies of water, and some picturesque mountain ranges dotted the landscape. The planet's most distinguishing feature, however, was the striated southern hemisphere, ragged streaks running latitudanally from just north of the pole nearly to the equator, the legacy of centuries of strip mining. Eve had contained enormous deposits of aluminum, cobalt, and other valuable metals in its heyday, and entrepreneurs had torn into the crust hungrily. When veins of trykon had been discovered, all resources had been appropriated to hunt for more of the rare element. The miners and smugglers had bankrupted themselves trying to dig it out of the rock, finding that Eve had far less than those initial bountiful veins had led them to believe. That combined with the sharp drop in prices at the advent of artificial trykon, dealing a severe blow to Eve's fledgeling economy. All mining operations had shut down virtually overnight, their dispossessed miners turning to ranching and fishing. Perhaps only then did they look up and discover the natural beauty of their arid new home.

It had been a good home for the better part of a decade, and Leon felt some of the ice around his heart melt as he beheld it. *No, not a bad place to be exiled. It's the exile itself that hurts.*

And what had brought Raptor to this contested but still somehow largely ignored sector of space? His was a reclusive species with a few notable exceptions such as Empress Kra'al and Grand Admiral Najo; their homeworld was located near the warm center of the galaxy, and many Prross never left it. What was more, while most of his kind were covered from snout to tail tip in tribal tattoos and brands, Raptor had not a mark on him save for the scars he had earned in combat, of which there were many indeed. What had he done to be driven away? Leon did not know and had decided not to ask. If the Prross chose to share, he would do so in his own good time. Leon had been waiting for seven years.

Passing through a customs checkpoint that included a trio of heavy Jackal Pack fighters, the shuttle was cleared for landing and began the descent toward the commercial spaceport.

§

The boarding ramp lowered almost soundlessly, as if to remind them how expensive the charter had been. Blinding sunlight spilled across the deck, and Leon blinked, fumbling for sunglasses. He was glad for the chance to hide his red-rimmed eyes. He took a deep breath of the warm, dry, familiar air and looked around. The landing pads of the Eve Transgalactic Cosmodrome stretched to the horizon, sunbaked and thruster-blasted tarmac covered in all manner of ships. Leon saw bulky cargo barges, day-cruisers, delivery ships, dropships, and some light regional military cruisers. The control tower, an upthrust beacon marking the actual terminals, was to the south. Though Leon couldn't see them, he knew the tower was surrounded by countless other structures that sprawled out from its central spire, an undulating sea of tan brick and tinted glass. Still, though hundreds of ships stood upon the tarmac, it was sparse compared to only a few months ago. Traffic from the Valinata side of the border had dropped off considerably. From where he stood, Leon could see only a few dozen vessels emblazoned with the green and silver insignia of that kingdom, the five-headed couchant dragon against a rippling field the color of dried blood.

All sorts of explanations had been put forth: more emphasis on internal tourism, subsidies for people to avoid wasteful use of limited shipboard resources, rising fuel costs, even the seizing of civilian vessels for refitting into military vessels. It all amounted to the same thing: Eve was quieter than usual, and a substantial client base of the Pack seemed to have vanished.

Despite that, there seemed to be some sort of Valinata celebration going on, Leon noted. There were green and silver banners draped from several nearby ships, and traditional Valinata music was playing over the loudspeakers, though it was largely drowned out by the roar of engines. Eve, as an amalgamation of outcasts from different cultures and kingdoms—many of whom chose to be quite vocal about their continued devotion to the homes they had left (or been kicked out of)—presented some challenges. One of them was figuring out just which holidays were being celebrated, when, and by whom. When Leon realized it was Azat, the commemoration of the Valinata's victory over the Cincon rebels (who had wanted to defect to the Coalition), he muttered a curse under his breath. The knowledge that he had spent his early adulthood training for a war with the Valinata only to end up living among them and working for them on occasion annoyed him to no end.

Six uniformed Jackal Pack Mercenary Legion sojieri waited at the base of the ramp, standing beside a gravtruck. Like Leon, they were clad in black fatigues with red tiger stripes running down the left sleeve and pant leg. Their black berets bore the Pack crest and a diagonal red flash on the front. Like Leon's, their eyes were hidden behind black aviator sunglasses. Leon couldn't tell if they were happy to see him and Raptor.

The lieutenant at the head of the squad saluted, and Leon returned the gesture. "Welcome back, Colonel Victor, Specialist Merikii."

"Lieutenant Pintoro, good to see you. How are things here?" Leon shook the man's hand.

"Quiet with the three of you gone." Pintoro shifted uneasily and cleared his throat. "About that.... We, uh, have to pick up the ... the, uh, body. Buzz's body. Sir."

"Right. He's in the cargo hold," Leon said, amazed at the steadiness in his own voice.

He and Raptor waited patiently for the guards to enter the hold and come back out, carrying the casket like pallbearers. Leon caught sight of another gravtruck winding its way through the ships, a cloud of dust trailing behind it.

"That'd be the general," murmured Raptor quietly, watching as the coffin was loaded into the first truck.

A moment later, a well-appointed command jeep drifted to a stop, and a man in his early sixties stepped out, rough-looking yet bearing himself with a quiet dignity. General Jonathan Rockmore's face was windburned, lined with age and scars in equal measure. Close-cropped, snow-white hair and a beard like pine needles in winter covered some of the more noticeable injuries (he had famously almost lost his jaw during a battle but had kept right on fighting with his face half off). Despite a few rough edges, he had something of the gentlemanly scholar about him in his bearing and his manner. Gentleman or not, the man was a career sojier, one of those rare people who truly believed in what they were doing and would keep on doing it until it killed them.

Beneath his battered yet kindly exterior, Rockmore was a ruthless logistician with a keen grasp of the tactical and the strategic. Behind his lofty ideals resided an iron will, cold and unyielding. To those who knew him, it came as no surprise that he could take thousands of dangerous people and bend them so perfectly to that will. He was a man who hated disorder and who had turned the realignment of order into a smoothly running business. Jackal Pack resembled a special forces detachment more than it did a typical private army, boasting better discipline, training, morale, and officers than most planetary defense forces. There were other merc outfits in the galaxy; some were bigger than Jackal Pack, but none of them could match the Pack's reputation or pedigree. The legion was Rockmore's baby; he was the one who had built it and recruited the first sojieri from the ranks of the CRDF, the Unified Commonwealth Authority, planetary shield forces, anywhere he could. He took the best and the brightest and offered them money and a chance to fight.

Over the years there had been those who had tried to change the Pack into a typical, amoral, cash-at-all-costs merc outfit. Some had been officers, some had been investors, but they had all made the same mistake in failing to reckon with Rockmore and his vision. The Pack's successes differentiated it from typical bands of bounty hunters. Those thugs who did make it into Jackal Pack were promptly weeded out. The JPML was not a haven for adrenaline junkies. Jonathan Rockmore was the embodiment of his ideals, ideals which some thought were misguided at best and self-deceiving at worst. Standing before him, however, no one would dare voice such thoughts.

Leon snapped to attention, saluting. Raptor did the same. Rockmore returned the salute with a swiftness and energy that belied his advancing years. "Leon, Raptor. Good to have you back." The general's ice-blue eyes were soft as he looked over his battered sojieri. "I'm sorry about Buzz, he was...." He almost let slip the old cliché, that Buzz was a good man. But he hadn't been, had he? "He was reliable," the general settled for, and the grimace on his wind-chapped face betrayed his rueful acknowledgement of the lameness of the sentiment.

Leon nodded, not trusting himself to do more than that.

"If you aren't too tired, I'm anxious to debrief you." Rockmore cleared his throat meaningfully. "I received the full report from the premier's chief of security on Korinthe. We have some things we need to discuss, and I hope you've got some explanations for me."

Leon and Raptor exchanged a look. "Of course, sir." Victor knew that even his status as an executive officer of the legion wouldn't save him from the tongue-lashing he and Raptor were about to receive. Solemnly the three of them got into the jeep, and the driver took them north. They did not talk during the ride back, but Leon felt himself comforted by the presence of his commander, who had thought their return important enough to make the hour's journey from the Jackal Pack plateau.

5: The Island of Misfit Toys

Buzz would have been complaining about the heat, Leon knew. Eve's star beat down on the waving grasses of the savannah from a cloudless sky. But where Korinthe had been balmy and oppressive in its sopping humidity, Eve's air was crisp and dry. Being back home was energizing, even if it was more of a self-imposed prison. Still, it would take some time to reacclimate to the world's slightly lower gravity.

It was hard, but Leon watched as his friend's plain casket was hauled from the truck and taken down to the clinic where it would be put on ice until the funeral. As the honor guard and coffin entered the squat structure, he looked away, eyes raking the landscape, desperate for distraction. From the Jackal Pack base perched atop the Luxor Plateau, he could see the spaceport to the south, the capital city of Tesa to the southeast, and endless hills scattered with brush, rolling to the horizon in every direction. It was peaceful, unassuming.

After a moment Leon turned back, looking inward. Nearly thirty-five thousand people called the Luxor Plateau home full-time, including the mercenary legion's enlisted units and two thousand noncombatant support staff who kept things running. A number of the Pack's fifteen thousand specialist contractors also lived on the base, but most had homes in the city of Tesa in a district jokingly known as Jackals' Den. The base's central campus was a rough circular cluster of buildings sprawling across almost four thousand acres and arrayed around a main courtyard and assembly area. From where they stood near the center of the courtyard, Leon could see the compound of administrative buildings, the vehicle park, clinic, and the nearest barracks buildings. Perhaps most important were the mess halls and a PX Outlet, a combination general store/cinema/post office, nestled in the northwestern corner of the base. Beside the mall stood a well-stocked pub and grill, as well as the Desher Vaux, the officers' tavern. Farther away there was a flat expanse of landing pad for VIPs, with a foreign and expensive-looking shuttle resting on it. To the north was the enormous hangar that housed the Pack's mechanae, enormous war machines that rarely saw use. High above it all loomed the great leaning tower of the Pack's orbital cannon, like some lost relic of the ancient Tagean Dynasty.

Rockmore turned and led the way to the headquarters building, head down, hands clasped behind his back. A tall, trapezoidal structure with a facade of tinted glass and topped with the Jackal Pack flag, the HQ was Jackal Pack's beating heart. The coat of arms upon the flag was a quartered shield, red and blue on a crimson background. The herald's top right quadrant depicted the ancient Terran Egyptian deity Anubis, a humanoid with a jackal's head. As the god of the afterlife and funereal process, he judged the dead, weighing the worth of their souls. To the herald's left, upon a red field, was a chess queen, symbolizing the Pack's ability to fill any role on any battlefield. The lower left quarter of the shield displayed five nesting crescents representing the five moons of Eve, two facing down and three up. The lower right quarter depicted a winged hourglass on a red field: for Jackal Pack's enemies, time would run out. Above the shield was a scroll extolling the Pack motto, "IN SPITE OF ALL." The flag snapped in the brisk savannah winds. Leon followed Rockmore inside, his fingers lingering on the matched crest embroidered on his sleeve.

Inside, several staff officers welcomed the two back and expressed their condolences. Leon accepted the greetings graciously, but Raptor was more reserved, almost indifferent. The trio ascended several flights of stairs before coming to the commanders' offices. This was the floor where Leon had his office as did the other general staff. Rockmore's office suite and apartment occupied the rear third of the floor and the entire level above. The command level also contained a large conference room usually reserved for visiting investors (or potential investors), clients, and the various other guests Jackal Pack occasionally received. There was a meeting adjourning as Leon exited the stairwell, men in expensive suits and a woman in a white uniform with a commodore's bar-and-circle on her epaulets, most likely belonging to some planetary defense force. Following them out was another Jackal Pack officer clad in a naval colonel's dress uniform. A red fourragère coiled about his left shoulder, and rows of medals shone on his chest.

It was Rockmore's second XO, Irún Akida; in line with ancient Tagean custom, most leaders groomed two potential successors, one to ascend and the other to support. Where Leon was Jackal Pack's loose cannon, Akida had always been its knife in the dark. Both colonels were able front line commanders, but their tactics differed widely. Akida had served with the Pack nearly since its incorporation and had come to be recognized as Rockmore's right-hand man, though Leon was often jokingly referred to as the left foot with which Rockmore kicked ass. The two competed for contracts and the general's favor. So far it was a stalemate, though each perceived himself to be the natural candidate.

Akida was olive-skinned, with wavy, non-regulation-length black hair immaculately moussed back and to the sides. His eyes were narrow, almond-shaped, and perceptive in a way that left the people he looked at feeling somewhat stripped. The man had no shortage of self-confidence or flash.

Rockmore made his apologies to the guests for stepping out of their meeting and thanked them for making the journey as he entered the lift with them and took them downstairs. Turning to Leon, Akida raised his eyebrows, looking over the bruised visage of his counterpart.

"Victor."

"Akida." Their greetings were terse, acknowledgments rather than pleasantries.

Colonel Akida's smile was anything but friendly. "Executing captives on their knees? Must have been tough with him in handcuffs. Looking to skew your kill ratio?"

Leon twisted his right hand in the Sanar gesture for "fuck you." He would be catching flak for his failures for a while, and he supposed he deserved every bit of it. "We did our best. We did the job."

Akida crossed his arms, his eyes narrowing to judgmental slits. "Is that so? If your 'best' involves this much legal trouble, Jackal Pack can't afford you anymore. You may want to consider joining the army." He sneered. "Oh, wait, you tried that already."

Leon stiffened. Akida had hit him where it hurt and he knew it. He had served loyally once, a lifetime ago, but the shame was like a brand on his soul. It was different for Akida, who had left his post voluntarily and with an honorable discharge.

Akida wasn't done. "By the way, the Shedanese killed Operation Watchmaker, thanks to your PR stunt. They gave the contract to some corporate security firm. You're a goddamn liability. 'Leon Victor, death squad for hire.'"

Leon stood aghast. He didn't know what to say. Rockmore returned before the two could come to blows. "All right, Irún. You can cut each other to pieces after I'm retired. For now, how about you cut these two a little slack?"

Akida's face softened, just a little, and he backed off. "Sir." His demeanor softened almost imperceptibly. "Welcome back, gentlemen." With that, he edged past them and headed for the stairwell. He turned in the doorway. "I am sorry about Parker, Victor. I didn't know him well, but I'm sure he was a good guy." He disappeared from view, his footsteps ringing on the metal stairs, fading, fading.

Leon ran his suddenly dry tongue over his lips, at a loss for words. Raptor stood by uncomfortably, bemused by the Human conflict.

Rockmore only sighed. "You should know I would have preferred Colonel Akida's team for the Korinthe job, but he was already contracted for Operation Watchmaker." He paused at the door to his office. "You should also know that the reason his contract was cancelled was because he vouched for your actions. I believe he said he would have done things similarly." The general pushed open the door and ushered them inside. "Then again, better to have you there than here, getting in shootouts with the Insir Gamma Advisory Commission who were just here looking to invest."

Though Leon knew Rockmore was trying to lighten the mood, the remark still stung. "Akida's right though, General. We—I—got sloppy. No excuses."

General Rockmore's office was warm and well decorated, with vague-intentioned pieces of abstract art adding splashes of color. Leon knew that Rockmore's late wife, Theresa, had painted them all. There was a photo of her on his desk, her smile radiant, her eyes gentle. It was an office befitting a corporate CEO, which in many ways Rockmore was.

"It happens, Leon, even to the best of us. Even to you. You need to accept that." Rockmore made his way around a desk cluttered with papers and sat down, gesturing for his subordinates to do the same. He glanced momentarily at Theresa's picture, smiled wistfully, and folded his hands on the desk. "Jackal Pack is a military unit. We are trained sojieri, trained killers. The purpose of trained killers is to go up against other trained killers. You may find it hard to believe, but I would gladly be put out of a job by galaxywide peace and prosperity. That's not going to happen, gentlemen, and so we need to remember that the people we're shooting at are going to shoot back or shoot first if they get the chance." He called for some Kaf for himself and two glasses of Hais Whisky for Leon and Raptor.

Leon could feel his shame creeping over him like a blanket of insects, but the general was still right.

Rockmore pointed to the left, where the Jackal Pack standard hung from the wall. "You know what that means, yes?"

Of course, Raptor and Leon knew. *In Spite of All.* It had been ingrained in them since the day they had signed their sanctions. They nodded.

"It means we do what we have to do. Even when it's unpalatable, even when it's hard. Sometimes the things we do are unethical, illegal, even barbarous. But *we* draw the line, even in the gray areas where we work. We do what we do even when our friends are dead on the ground behind us. Parker wasn't the first man to die under your command, and he won't be the last. I cannot afford to have you dwelling on this and hesitating at a crucial moment. I need you sharp and on the ball. Both of you." Having said his piece, Rockmore leaned back, though the muscles in his neck were still taut as though he expected to spring into action at any moment. "Anyway, I have the report you uploaded from Korinthe, as well as the one written by the Justice Ministry's inquest. Your accounts agree, but it appears we have a quandary." He patted a folder on his desk. "Honestly, I don't know where to begin."

Leon forced himself to meet Rockmore's gaze. This was the moment he should have been preparing for but had instead been ignoring, like a driver passing up fuel stations despite a steadily falling gauge.

"Let's forget for a moment what this Mr.—" Rockmore flipped open the folder and scanned a few lines—"Mr. Princeton has to say. There were no civilian fatalities, which is positive. You put the bullets where they needed to go, and I appreciate that. I could care less about live capture of subjects when it's not required, but that was your decision, and I'm impressed you managed it, given the circumstances. Ultimately you did the job and fulfilled your contractual obligations to the letter. And you wrote the endings to some very unsavory lives.

"However, and this is a *big* 'however,' you went ahead with the operation even though you *knew* you were exhausted, even though you knew it could get messy. Which it did. You should have exercised your contractual discretion and refused to conduct the operation without sufficient intel and prep time. You can always waive a mission if you think it's fucked, and no client can pressure you into it with threats of litigation. They would have figured out a way to make it work, and we would still have kept the two million in down payment and consultation fees. It would have been their job to botch, and you wouldn't have been responsible. Believe me, I'd rather lose a hundred million talons than have to find and train a replacement for one of my executive officers. As it was, it got very ugly very quickly. And your conduct following the conclusion of the raid is absolutely unacceptable. If anything like that happens again, I'll be forced to take your contract under review and possibly rerate your sanctions. Our good friend Miss Sorenson is still trying to clear things up with Korinthe's judicial oversight committee. It's her job to talk us out of problems we can't shoot our way out of. Korinthe won't try to use us as scapegoats and say we went rogue mid-operation in exchange for us not downgrading their credit rating, but even Anika can't erase the memories of every person who saw Raptor throw that suspect off the balcony." He turned to the Prross. "I can't believe I had to see you in the news, dropping a subject thirty stories. You may have done irreparable damage with that little stunt."

Leon opened his mouth, but Rockmore's orderly entered with drinks before he could respond, laid down the tray, and left. The colonel sipped at his whisky, giving himself time to cool down and reflect on what Rockmore had said. The whisky, distilled on Triatha's Hais Isle, sloshed a faintly luminescent blue against the sides of the glass, lighting a welcome fire in his throat.

Raptor's glass was already empty. "There's no excuse, General. I wasn't thinking clearly."

Rockmore leaned forward, unappeased. "It's not the first time for either of you, unfortunately. If you were the types to lose your shit and fire on civilians, we'd be having this talk in front of a firing squad. As it is, you graduated from extrajudicial assassination, for which we are sanctioned, to murder. And not just vanilla murder but the murder of a subject in *shield custody*." The look of anger that crossed his features was surprising on someone who was typically so reserved. "You know as well as I do that he couldn't have gotten away. You could have incapacitated him or just let him get by so the shields could deal with him.

"Akida was right about you allowing yourselves to be used as a death squad. We come under a lot of scrutiny from legitimate government investors already. We don't need bad press deterring them from hiring us."

Rockmore sat back again, seemingly unable to find a comfortable position. Leon had never seen him so agitated, and it was humiliating to be the cause of that tension. "It goes against my better judgment to say this, but I am mightily impressed. You three went into that fight with almost no knowledge of what you were up against, no time to prep, and without your squad. You wiped out an enemy force that had you outnumbered and had the advantage of a defensive position. Oh, and at final count there were thirty-two cartel enforcers in there, not sixteen. From a technical standpoint alone, you deserve medals. Too bad Jackal Pack doesn't confer any."

"The bonus..." Leon began tentatively.

Rockmore turned his chair to look out the window for a moment. "The bonus isn't of any concern to me. Six million in the bank is six million in the bank, but Princeton shouldn't have sprung that on you. The money changed your priorities, tied your hands. In light of that, it's a miracle things went as well as they did."

Raptor's dorsal spines rose and fell like barbs of carved and polished jet, signaling his pride. "It was a big op for three guys."

"I don't think anyone else could have pulled it off," Rockmore admitted. He took a delaying sip of Kaf and sputtered, his tongue burned. "Now, this is not a fairy tale with a happy ending, as you gentlemen well know. You know what a pyrrhic victory is? First of all: murder." The general's eyes seemed to bore into Leon's, and the colonel almost flinched. "Some people would dock your commission, and some would have you shot for it. You won't get another warning, and you're too high up in this organization for me to write you off as a hotheaded trooper. Especially now, when we're fishing for investors. I've lost friends in combat myself, but you have to continue thinking clearly, no matter what happens to your team."

The two mercenaries traded worried looks.

"I get it, really I do, but you've got to learn to bury your feelings on the job. Just because you pulled those shields' asses out of the fire doesn't make you chums. You're lucky no protests have emerged directly from the premier's office, despite the best efforts of the inspector in charge of the operation."

"I understand, General. But Buzz—" Leon broke off at a gesture from Rockmore.

"Buzz Parker was a colleague and friend to a lot of us. I've spoken with his mother. She actually *thanked* me for getting him out of a life of crime. She said she always knew he would die young, but at least this way he died doing something good. I conveyed your condolences, but I left out the fact that you and Raptor murdered those people in your grief." Rockmore took another sip of Kaf and glared over the edge of the cup. "Now technically, according to the regulations that *you* coauthored, I should make some sort of pay cut for your performance and your poor judgment on this job. However, there are a number of extenuating circumstances, and I can hardly fault Raptor here for following your orders. Consider this your lucky day."

The irony and venom in the general's voice made Leon feel queasy. His head sank against the chair back. "Sir, that shouldn't be an excuse. I mean, it isn't one."

"I know, but I'm trying to give you a way out here, so do me a favor and shut up. I had Anika dig around, and what she found is really pissing me off. The whole situation on Korinthe was a mess long before you got there, and it's far from over. We didn't even know who we were after."

"Sir, if you're about to tell us they were political dissidents or something, I may lose it," Leon said, only half-joking.

"Don't worry. They were leading a drug cartel, and they deserved everything they got. I'll give you the rough cut, but you don't need to lose any more sleep over this. That girl, the premier's daughter? She was sixteen years old, dead from this drug, Burn."

"We heard," said Raptor. "Terrible."

"No, you didn't hear shit. Burn didn't come from off-world, it came from Korinthe's defense ministry. It was supposed to be the next hot cocktail for their PDF troops, only their consultant, Marcus Keegan, decided to walk out the door with the unrefined formula and take it private."

"I can see why they took it so personally," Leon muttered.

"That 'meeting' those people were there for? They were apparently going to cooperate with the Justice Ministry in return for leniency, amnesty for helping collapse their whole planetary supply network. Princeton paid for the rooms, the hookers, the food and drinks, and then set the whole thing up to be a massacre. Keegan's guard was down, but it looks like he didn't trust Princeton either, so he stashed backup downstairs. In addition to the fourteen fatalities suffered by the shields in the course of the raid, your live captures were interrogated and tortured. Half of them were executed by the premier's security forces under the watchful eye of this Princeton asshole."

"They wanted it to be a bloodbath." Leon frowned. After they had been informed that Cendol gas was out of the question, he had wondered why the shields didn't deploy screamers or other nonlethal incapacitative weapons. Now he knew.

"Makes them look like heroes and Keegan's people out to be monsters. They *needed* the targets to shoot back. It would have looked suspicious if they had gassed the suite and all the suspects had bullet holes in their heads when they came out."

Everything about the raid had been engineered to appear rushed, Leon realized. Princeton had been counting on shield casualties to deflect suspicion from his own culpability. And he had succeeded. Leon felt sick to his stomach.

"I can certainly understand a grieving father," Rockmore said sadly, "but the premier's gone off the deep end, with an army at his disposal. They're practically under martial law over there, with shields shooting first and not bothering to file the paperwork afterwards. Cleaning up the streets is a great goal, but he's headed for a coup. That or the UCA's going to forcibly remove him to prevent one." The general paused to drain his coffee and leaned back, shaking his head slowly, sadly. "They would have killed many more people with that drug, but you can't help wondering sometimes about what we do." He held up his hands in surrender. "Anyway, I want both of you to take it easy for a while. You've had a trying week. I think this is one of those jobs where I'll be happy to close the book and shelve it. With any luck, we'll never hear from Korinthe again. And listen, I know neither of you is the type to discuss these things with Doctor Vuru, and I won't force you, but maybe you should sit down with her. We keep her on retainer for a reason, and it's not a sign of weakness to seek counseling." Rockmore closed the mission dossier and slipped it into a drawer. "There are one or two other items of business, Leon. Regarding battalion command." Obligingly Raptor left the room, closing the door behind him.

Leon straightened. He had to keep himself from guessing what had gone wrong. Had Rockmore decided to strip him of command after all? Had there been another fight between his men and Akida's?

"I'm still waiting for a nomination for your command sergeant major." Leon's previous sergeant major, a big Sheff'an sojier named Trysx, had been killed on a mission in Shar'dan space. A car bomb in the staging area had killed him and three others. He had been an able officer, and the troops respected him enough to follow his orders. Finding someone to replace him had not been easy.

Rockmore was satisfied with Leon's finalists for the position, and the conversation turned to new contracts. "The Josephine Ronin took heavy losses during a slaver raid off Afura. Their survivors signed on with another outfit, but the contract's up for grabs. With Vector 9 all dead, the offer came to us. The Tilora Company wants a JPML company on retainer, under your command. I said you'd have to think it over." Rockmore tapped his chin thoughtfully. "Is Dawson up to it?"

"I don't see why not," Leon answered. "His injuries have healed, and Echo Company would follow him into the fires of Hell for hot soup if he asked them to. I'd want to send Mikaela Sommers as his second; they make a good team."

"Very well. Also, Togor Plasmatics is shopping around for a new security team for their convoys."

"Didn't they contract with Erich Russell's company?" Russell was a former Jackal officer and a good one, too, despite the way he had left the Pack.

"Yes, but for whatever reason Togor backed out of their arrangement with Zeus Security, and the paper's been passed to us. They want both of our gunships and a squadron of long-range fighters for the deal."

"Jeric would be good for that."

Rockmore cleared his throat, for the first time looking nervous himself. "I hate to do this, Leon, but we need to discuss your friend Jeric."

"God, what now?" Jeric, like Raptor, had come to Jackal Pack with Leon, and he had always been a problem child. He had beaten various drug habits only to succumb to others, and finally getting clean had done nothing to soften his volatile personality. There was no questioning his skill as a pilot, but he was generally considered unreliable, and as a result, few team leaders ever crewed with him. So he flew local patrols while also serving as

104

an assistant flight instructor and advisor for the Pack's aerospace wing, drawing a nominal salary. Leon had asked him only to stay off Rockmore's radar, and apparently he couldn't even do that.

"Some of the specialists think he's a liability."

"I think he's a liability," Leon joked.

"This is no laughing matter, son. His drinking on the job and his behavior even when he's *not* drinking on the job get noticed. That doesn't exactly inspire client confidence."

"The other fliers respect him, and if you know a better pilot—"

"True, but let me put it in terms you can't justify yourself around. One complaint and he gets his sanction downgraded from a B to a C. Nothing you or I can do about that. Maybe he can afford the additional fee. I don't know. He seems to live off you, anyway. What we can't afford is the umbrella coverage. You know as well as I do that a team's sanction rating is only as good as its lowest-rated member. If a whole team goes from a B to a C rating because of him, we're looking at a major loss out of pocket. I want you to talk to him." Rockmore looked at Leon for a long moment, and his face softened. "I hate to lay all this on you, Leon, but you didn't sign on because the job was going to be easy."

"No, General, I didn't."

"I know this is hard for you, especially since Rachel wasn't waiting here to welcome you back, but right now you don't have the luxury of wallowing in guilt. You've got another ten thousand sojieri for whom you're responsible. More of them will die. You can't hold yourself to blame for every one of them, or it'll kill you. Welcome back, son."

Slowly, deflated, Leon rose from his seat, saluted, and walked out. Buzz and Trysx would be buried on their homeworlds, near their families. A marker would be erected for each in the grove north of the plateau, alongside hundreds of others.

§

Leon forced himself to breathe deeply and evenly as the isotope was pumped into his system; the spot where the needle contacted his skin felt intensely cold. The deep breaths only intensified the pain in his ribs. Looking down at his chest, he saw an angry purple bruise peeping out from beneath the bandages. His stomach felt like it had reached absolute zero.

It didn't help that he was nervous, as he was always nervous when he came to these appointments. All those years ago, after the fallout had nearly killed him, the Coalition had flooded his dying body with macropolymerases programmed with his recruitment DNA sample. They had repaired the damage caused by the radiation, a going-away present from the kingdom he had vowed to serve, to let him live long enough in exile to wish he had been executed.

A few feet away, Doctor Koridin Reonil, Jackal Pack's Niaotl chief medical practitioner, was reviewing Leon's file. Beside him stood Corporal Alexis Thorne, a former CRDF corpswoman who handled most surgical procedures. She was a pretty redhead with beguiling eyes and a low threshold for bullshit, which made her on-again off-again romance with Leon's friend Jeric all the stranger. Lately it had been off ... again.

"Starting imaging," Alexis said, smiling at Leon. The imaging sensor hummed quietly as it traversed its armature, taking scans of Leon from various angles. Thorne leaned against the counter and crossed her arms. "So, what's your friend's problem? Six months ago we were practically married, and now he won't even say hello."

Leon grimaced. It seemed no one had a kind word for Jeric, and he hadn't even seen his friend yet. "I wish I could tell you, Alexis. It's not like it's the first time."

"That's true," she said. "But does he have to be such a *child* about the whole thing?"

Leon had to laugh, which caused him to wince with pain. "If you know anything about Jeric, you know that's a ridiculous question."

Alexis didn't seem to find it that funny. "Is scaring away good women a hobby for you assholes?"

That stung even more than the needle. Had he scared Rachel away? It wasn't as though she didn't have plenty of good reasons to leave. But they had had something special, and she hadn't even said she was going. His inquiries had been met with shrugs from the base personnel, and the one call he had dared to place to her mother had earned him a cackling, venomous laugh over the network. It had been months with no word, and he supposed he should return the engagement ring to the jeweler.

Leon was grateful when the scan completed and Alexis busied herself processing the data. His arm grew warm, then hot, tingling, as the cold subsided. Doc Reonil reviewed the scans on his computer, and Leon watched as a computer-generated image of his circulatory system was manipulated on-screen, lines of data scrolling past.

It took a few minutes before Reonil turned back to Leon, pleased. "Well, your levels are good. There's still a higher concentration of the macropolymerases in your lungs, liver, and kidneys, but that's a normal pathology, considering you were exposed to thermal, beta, and gamma radiation on Daltar. I still remember your levels when you first got here. They pumped you full of them to deal with the radiation poisoning. You must have *eaten* one of the nukes for them to give you such a dose."

Leon flashed his lopsided smile, trying to keep the mood light, despite being reminded of past horrors. "They taste best with a Hais and soda. Any sign of cell division amplification?" He looked closer at the image.

Reonil laughed. "Sometimes I forget you know as much about this stuff as I do. No, no tumors I can see, and considering the baseline of the macropols, I doubt you'll ever see any. One of the nicer side-effects of the Generation One Polymerase Swarms. Whoever did yours was an artist, if a bit heavy-handed."

"Are you saying we won't see any more drops?"

"In the polymerase counts? I doubt it. The Generation Ones were completely artificial, and they almost never degrade past a certain point. You should just be happy they worked the way they were supposed to, and your white blood cells are normal. If you'd been coding any Tez'Nar proteins when it was administered, you'd probably be dead. I doubt we'll need to have any more of these sessions unless you encounter difficulty breathing beyond the usual."

"What about the lung?"

Reonil considered for a moment. Leon had always had trouble reading the expressions of Niaotls, but the doctor was even more stoic than most of his kind, and his round, brown-furred face gave away nothing. "It could become an issue. Because it was grafted *after* you received the swarm, it has a slightly lower concentration of the macropols than your birth lung. The residual proteins could still trigger a replication cascade to try and repair the healthy tissue, thinking it's damaged."

"I was reading about an experimental therapy for that, where a second polymerase swarm could be administered to the organ in question. I'm concerned that it could spread to other tissues and we'd be back to square one."

"Yes, that's a possibility. I think your lung will be fine. Honestly, some day you may have to have it swapped out again, but that's better than being dosed with a Generation Four Polymerase Swarm and having it try to neutralize the Generation One. They still haven't elaborated on the mechanism of interaction between different generations, and no one in their right mind would administer another Generation One flood."

"Okay, Doc. I'm sold. We'll stick with your course of treatment. But if I *do* need the lung swapped, don't have Alexis do it."

The surgeon pretended to be offended. "Come on, Leon, I'm not going to carve a hate note to Jeric in your lung with a surgical laser."

"The fact that you thought of that worries me," Leon said lightly. After all, he'd just gotten some very good news, something he desperately needed at the moment. "Can I go get a drink to celebrate?" he asked.

"Oh, sure. The isotope goes inert quickly. It'll pass out of your system fully in a day or two. You'll be pissing red for a couple of days, but it's not blood, so don't worry." Reonil was absorbed in reading the scans again, and he didn't pick up on the sadness in Leon's voice.

Alexis did. She evaded the issue, however. "Hey, I heard your little sister is getting married soon. Natille, right?"

The smile on Leon's face turned genuine. He was to give her away at the ceremony. Natille was only ten years his junior, but he had trouble accepting that she had grown up, that she wasn't the same little girl who had begged and cajoled for piggy-back rides. Her wedding was scant months away, and she had been planning it for a long, long time. Since she had been begging and cajoling for piggy-back rides, in fact. "It's going to be a hell of a time. I ... expected Jeric to invite you."

The surgeon was kind enough to ignore that statement. "Maybe you should take it easy for the next couple of months. You want to be able to dance at the reception, don't you?"

"Good idea. I'll take it under advisement." He turned to leave.

"I'm ... sorry about Parker," Alexis blurted. "I always had fun at the pub quizzes with him."

Leon's grin faded. "Thanks, he always liked you. Will you be taking care of him?"

Alexis's face hardened. "Not really my department, but if it's important to you, sure, I'll get him cleaned up to be sent home." *Sent home,*

Leon thought. *It must be nice to have a real home, even if it's only a place to be buried.*

6: Before the Arch

The throne room of the royal palace was a vaulted masterpiece, a monument to an empire that had stretched across the heavens for thousands of years. Tapestries several stories tall hung from the walls, many of them predating even the Tagean Dominion. Gazing at those images, Hakar felt himself once again swept up in the grandeur. There were pastoral scenes, battles, and the pantheon of Tagean gods. Over the years people had argued that the Tageocentric art created a biased atmosphere. It was *art*, Hakar thought. It was nothing *but* atmosphere.

The triptych that had caught Hakar's eye as a child and made his heart quicken with wonder still hung behind the Jade Throne. It was a depiction of the Dawn Wars, beginning with the assassination of the would-be founding emperor of the Tagean Dominion at the hands of the Red Blade. It ended with the ratification of the Coalition Charter between Empress Kalex and a retinue of politicians and rulers whose names had largely been reclaimed by history. Between the two, the battles that had laid the foundation for the Coalition blended into an epic constellation of violence.

The rest of the hall was no less ornate, bedecked in potent reminders of the power of the Crown. Like the tapestries, most of them had been added well after the reign of the Coalition's founders, by emperors and empresses desperate to leave a mark of their passing on the Palace.

Centuries before, the Royal Family of the Tajin had ruled the Coalition they had built, presiding over an uneasy peace with charm, threats, bribery, and outright violence. The Young Wolf had inked the beginning of the Dominion with the blood of the Red Blade. He had then chosen a simple arch for his heraldry, to embody the grace with which he intended to rule the heavens, over the Rienda, the glyph that stood for Honor and Valor, the highest Tagean virtues.

Some of his descendants had lived up to that grace and some had fallen short. But during the War of the Veil, the dynasty had come to an end. Fearing the imminent invasion of Tagea and the slaughter of her family, the last blood empress, Vherax, had taken her entire bloodline aboard the great Citadel *D'morath*. They had vanished into the conduits, leaving Archon Cel, a Sanar vassal and consigliere, to rule in her place until her return. Once the invaders were repelled and hunted down, the archon sent word, and the kingdom braced for their royals' return. But the Citadel never came back. The theories surrounding the mysterious disappearance of the Tajin dynasty's entire bloodline were many. They ranged from the technical and mundane (the Citadel's grav-drives collapsed due to an envelope fault common to technology of the era) to the grand and implausible (the royals had abandoned their floundering ship and taken wing upon the great wyverns of the conduits, forgetting their kingdom in the joy of eternal flight).

Upon her deathbed, after nearly two centuries of waiting, Archon Cel commissioned an Arch of carefully sculpted trykon crystal to stand in place of the Crown and bear witness in the years to come. While the monarchy may have been hereditary, the office of archon was not, and Cel commanded the parliament to appoint a new archon as they always had.

For centuries more, the archons reigned from the seat beneath the Jade Throne, each becoming more and more an emperor in the eyes of the people, until Archon Corrthesk had chosen to sit in the throne itself rather than the seat below it. That caused a scandal but only a small one. Another century and a half passed before Archon Genethon, the White Witch, took the title of Empress for herself. By that point, the lines between archon and emperor had blurred to the point of irrelevance. The sanctity of a vanished bloodline was forgotten in the face of economic, social, and religious upheaval brought about by the explosive birth of the Valinata.

Recent emperors and empresses still technically held the title of archon but were granted the style of their absentee masters until the royals returned to claim their throne.

The centuries had, of course, brought claimants and pretenders in their thousands, and some had even made it onto the great seat of their supposed ancestors. Some were able, others incompetent, but none had demonstrated enough of a claim to wrest the throne from the parliament and reestablish a hereditary monarchy.

Hakar turned his attention to the crowd, blinking in the sunlight. It poured through the enormous windows in slanting, golden waterfalls that spilled across the ornate mosaics on the floor. The dignitaries and celebrities in attendance were likewise radiant in their finery. Hakar saw members of every species, representatives from hundreds of worlds in hundreds of varieties of dress. The line of people awaiting presentation to

Her Majesty was long, but Hakar didn't mind waiting. He had finally managed to nail down an appointment with the empress and Telec. The other grand admiral stood beside Hakar, looking bored, his facial tentacles twisting around each other out of nervous habit. Affairs of state were his daily routine.

Surrounded by her gold-clad royal guard, Kra'al looked regal in a rich, embroidered gown of purple, rings on her arms and tail glittering. She greeted each visitor warmly and heard what they had to say, listening attentively. Not once did she show any sign of boredom or derision. Not once did she lose her temper with an unreasonable guest, not even when a junior ambassador from the Valinata, looking harried, announced abruptly that his superiors were closing their mission and recalling his staff.

Hours later, when the light streaming through the windows had gone and the lamps had been lit, Kra'al dismissed the attendants and left the hall with her gown flowing behind her. Hakar and Telec followed, threading their way through the thinning crowd.

In her office, safe from judging eyes and cameras, Kra'al let her facade slip and seemed to age ten years in an instant as she flopped into her chair. Hakar stepped forward and slid a folder across her desk. She flipped through it, and a rattling sigh escaped her throat. "You always get right to the point, don't you? Do they think it's subtle, closing their embassy?" she asked tiredly. The Valinata had begun their customary saber-rattling, only this time there was more at stake than saving face.

Telec was quick to respond. "Your Majesty, you can hardly blame them. We've mobilized forces to the systems adjacent to Calama, which they see as confirmation that we have designs on the sector. If they thought these attacks were connected to us before, they're likely certain of it now." Perhaps if the Valinata had opened channels to the Coalition they could have resolved this equitably. Now it looked as though it would be settled with missiles, and the Valinata would be able to field test another weapon. The bad blood ran hot and deep, and even the most reasonable Vali leaders would be reluctant to open a dialogue. So far, Coalition sources inside the Emerald Veil hadn't yielded any information. It was anyone's guess what was really going on.

The rest of the admirals in the Star Chamber had been briefed via hypercomm and were consolidating their positions. Unfortunately, as a result of the recent Engine Accord, few of them were anywhere near where they would be needed, and moving entire fleets was no mean feat.

At the very least they needed to preserve Kra'al's credibility. She was good for the Coalition, and the last thing the kingdom needed was another disgraced monarch.

"Any news about your organic composite?" began Kra'al almost conversationally, "or have you determined it to be a remnant of whatever passes for food on VSF cruisers?"

"If Valinata navy crew can chew through that material, we should be very frightened of them indeed." Halfhearted though it was, the attempt at levity was welcome. Once more on the cusp of war, the three leaders felt isolated and exposed. For Kra'al, it would be an opportunity for detractors to claim evidence that she had never been ready to lead. For Telec and Hakar, it would amount to the final nail in their collective coffin.

Hakar briefed Her Majesty on the latest news from Admiral Shra. What little there was was very strange indeed. Was it disinformation? Overreaction? Had there been a coup, or was there one in progress?

And so they speculated, trying to build a whole truth from the various facts they had accumulated. The footage of that ship, rumored attacks and sightings even on the Coalition side of the demarcation zone, the fragmented signals they had intercepted coming out of the Valinata, all seemed to be connected.

By the time Hakar leaned back in his chair, glancing at the clock on the wall, they had been at it for hours, and they had been running in ever-tightening circles of absurdity as the hands ticked onward. "I'm not willing to rule out the possibility of a Valinata hardline group," Hakar said. "And I hate to advocate incursion, but whoever it is could do a lot of damage should they use the Calama bundle to reach our interior." The Coalition was huge, the galaxy even larger, with thousands upon thousands of worlds and quadrillions of people, millions of stars and great gulfs of unexplored space. The Valinata may have been small, and in many ways they were backwards, but they still had the capacity to bring conflict on a scale that had not been seen since the Dawn Wars.

"I think you're being melodramatic," Kra'al said less than playfully, and Telec bobbed his head beside her. "What other scenarios have you two looked at?"

Hakar grunted, too tired to play games any longer. "Scenarios? There aren't any. All we have is conjecture. At this point, information could be our greatest weapon. A well-informed navy could be the difference."

"If knowledge is our greatest weapon, then we are woefully short of ammunition, Hakar." Telec's bulbous eyes took on a different sheen as he stared his colleague down. "I agree that we need to consider seizing Calama, but doing so if it's unwarranted is political suicide. We should focus on protecting vital strategic and economic assets."

"One thing is certain," Kra'al put in. "The delay at which our data is arriving is unacceptable. Is there anything Admiral Shra can do to expedite that sample?"

Hakar glanced at Telec. Somehow he suspected that the defense advisor was feeding Kra'al her lines here. There was nothing wrong with her seeking clarification in an unfamiliar area, but if she was letting him dictate her policy....

Hakar flicked his ears in the negative. "The Calama Sample? Apparently the defense labs on Triatha had a go and couldn't figure it out. They forwarded it to a biolab under contract with Edenbridge Biotechnics. All references to Raven Blue have been redacted from the files."

"It would be nice if next time they would do us the courtesy of *asking*," Kra'al muttered. "At least pretend we're not in their pocket for billions of talons."

It hadn't pleased Hakar to learn that either, but Edenbridge Holdings had quite a few defense contracts, and he supposed they had the necessary clearance. "Hopefully we'll learn something soon. Now, what do we do about keeping a lid on Calama?"

Kra'al rose abruptly. Seeing her up on her throne from a distance or while seated at her huge desk, it was easy to forget how imposing she was. She towered over Telec and stood eyeball to eyeball with Hakar, outweighing the latter by at least twenty kilos, all of it muscle. "Walk with me," she said. Leading the way out of her office, she waved to her guards to remain behind. The two sojieri exchanged a look but stayed where they were.

The grand admirals followed their leader to a stairwell and from there to the palace roof, ending up on a terrace just beside the vaulted roof of the main audience chamber. It was a cool night with a brisk breeze.

"Sometimes I find the palace stuffy. I feel like a prisoner," Kra'al confessed.

"Surely, Your Majesty—" Telec began.

"Not now, Telec." Kra'al sighed and paced the terrace, pausing now and then to look out over her adopted city. Hakar often wondered how it felt for a Prross to live here, so far away from her home, reigning over an alien world. "I find it bracing out here, and sometimes I need it, to remind me what I'm doing. Seeing it through a window ... just isn't the same."

"Like commanding a fleet from a desk," Hakar blurted out. He knew the feeling all too well.

"Exactly like that," Kra'al said, nodding sagely. "How can I guide trillions of lives when I can't even walk down the streets of the capital without a military escort?" She sat down on the low stone wall, her back to the city, and carefully arranged the folds of her gown. "I need to get out here more often. It'll be getting cold again soon. So, how *do* we put a lid on Calama, Hakar?"

He knew he had to choose his words carefully. Kra'al was smart, and she would rip apart a bad idea, dig her claws into any contradictions and pull them wide open. "Well, we've redeployed most of our Outbound Arc forces to the Dias since the demobilization, so we don't have much along the Arc at all. What we need is a quick response force to hold position behind it, in the Yangtze, or maybe at the Amanra Crescent. And I'm not talking a picket flotilla. I'm talking a battle fleet, something that could go up against a Dragon Valia armada if it has to."

"And you don't think *that* will provoke a response?" Telec scoffed.

"That's why it goes nowhere near the Calama sector or the rest of the Valinata border. A vice-grand admiral at minimum should have command. Their mission can't be to engage, only to deter attack. Calama's conduits spill out all along the Alkyra, the Amanra, and some go as far as the Yangtze Tradeway. This fleet's purpose would be to engage any invading forces until the grand fleets can be brought to bear."

Kra'al stripped the bark from a small shrub with her claws, watching it peel in curling strips. "It has to be someone who understands discretion. Someone with a proven diplomatic track record. I want a peacekeeper, not a gunslinger. Any recommendations?"

Telec looked uncomfortable when he realized they were both looking at him. "Well, it can't be one of us. The Valinata would certainly take that as a direct threat. I think you're right about a vice-grand admiral." He thought hard, and a queer whistling sound came from his mouth, hidden by its curtain of delicate tentacles. "Winters's XO, Rodriguex, is an able commander. She's stood across the line from the VSF several times and knows how to bluff them. She won't do anything we don't want her to do, but she can make snap decisions when she needs to."

"Very well. Hakar, what do you think?"

"I think Rodriguex is an excellent choice. The Valinata know her, and they know she's not a hardliner. Am I recalling correctly that she has some Vali ancestry?"

"Could be," Telec murmured. "I'll look into it. It might be helpful if true."

In truth, Hakar had his reservations about Rodriguex. He would be happy to have trained eyes on the situation, and Rodriguex was an able commander, with one of the finest fleets in the Coalition Royal Navy. Unfortunately, she had a tendency to toe the party line, and while she wasn't exactly unpredictable, she was blunt enough that any diplomatic maneuvers would be better off without her. Hakar said so.

Kra'al ran her tongue along her teeth, and Hakar could hear the golden rings on her tail clanking on the stone. "Very well, what would you say to putting a velvet glove on this iron fist of ours?"

Hakar breathed a sigh of uneasy resignation masquerading as relief. Attaching civilians to a military task force was a risky proposition, especially if it came to violence. At the same time, he wanted to avoid a war, and taking that burden off Admiral Rodriguex would be advisable.

"Prime Minister Somerset has a rapport with the Tête," Kra'al mused. "It shouldn't be too difficult to convince him a potential warzone would be more pleasant than remaining in Parliament."

Hakar chuckled grimly at that. They worked out the details, and when their business was concluded, they adjourned and fled to their respective offices where they would spend sleepless nights alone. Time was not to be wasted. There suddenly wasn't enough.

7: Diplomacy

Getting shot down was uncommon, whereas crashing for no apparent reason happened with alarming regularity. Jeric still didn't know what had gone wrong, but he wasn't focusing on that as he wrestled the halberd-class patrol fighter for control. Flashing by beneath him and to all sides was the tarmac of Eve's cosmodrome, covered in hundreds of ships and vehicles. If he misjudged or lost his touch on the jerking flight stick, he could plow into one of them. At his current speed—which he had to estimate due to the complete failure of his boards—he would be vaporized instantly, along with whoever happened to be nearby. He didn't focus on that, either.

As he reached a cleared patch of tarmac, Jeric worked the rudder pedals and flared the braking thrusters manually. Normally the *halberds* were nimble fighters, but with no electronic assists, it was like trying to fly a fully furnished apartment. His craft jerked hard and threatened to slide out or bank right into the ground, but he reacted as though they were of one mind. Almost gently, he settled her on the tarmac.

With the thrusters still smoking, he blew the canopy and leapt onto a still-hot wing. All around him were the flashing lights of rescue vehicles. A contingent of port personnel stood watching from what they hoped was a safe distance.

Helmet still on, he glanced left, then right, as if unused to being on the ground among mere mortals. He took hold of the helmet in gloved hands and pried it loose. His blond hair tumbled out, and Jeric brushed it aside as he donned his sunglasses. Privately he admitted to himself that he liked the attention.

Looking at the ground as though he found it distasteful, he dropped off the *halberd*'s wing and leisurely walked toward the port personnel. It was hot and the wind was blowing hard across the tarmac. He had been lucky to set down so easily. A strong gust might have carried him laterally, just enough to clip another vessel or the ground. With boyish wonder, he watched a bulk freighter lumber into the cloudless blue sky on tails of fire, smoke, and dust. Its roar was the sound of a lion bellowing over its kill.

A man emerged from the group of workers and approached Jeric, meeting him between the emergency vehicles and the fighter. He wore goggles and a floppy hat, but his fine longcoat and the suit beneath were well tailored and immaculate. In his left hand was a slim databoard. He didn't fit Jeric's stereotype of a port manager at all. Instead of a balding and sweaty bureaucrat, this man was young, fit, and confident. He offered his hand and Jeric shook it. "Aiden O'Reily, Deputy Director of Cosmodrome Operations. So you're the one?" he shouted over the din of arriving and departing ships. He spoke with an Irish lilt. From the purity of the accent Jeric took him for a native Terran. There weren't too many of those wandering around these days.

Jeric nodded. "Yeah. Name's Jeric."

"Jeric what?"

The pilot smiled. "Just Jeric. I don't know what the hell happened. My instruments went dead, so did all the pilot assists. Sorry about the commotion."

"You'll be sorry when I bill your outfit for the hauler." O'Reilly shrugged. "New port regulations: we're not authorized to give you the same deal we give the CRDF garrison. We do have plenty of paying customers." To emphasize his point, the operations director showed Jeric his databoard; long lines of shipping manifest data scrolled across its thin screen.

That made Jeric a little hot under the collar. In his mind he was already formulating another request to the general for an overhaul for the fighter corps. Suddenly he felt he needed a drink. Leon and Raptor were probably getting shitfaced already; Jeric decided to join them.

§

As Jeric had expected, Leon was in the Desher Vaux, the glass of Hais at his elbow nearly empty. Across from him in the booth were Major Liam Dawson and Mikaela Sommers, two of his most trusted specialists. They were deep in conversation, but it was obvious to Jeric that Leon was drunk. The pub was nearly empty, but there were always sojieri coming off duty in need of a drink. Dawson spotted the pilot first and waved him over.

Cyma-molded wood panels rose up to a Human's waist height and faded into walls painted a dark green and covered in bric-a-brac. Once someone had framed and hung an article about Leon's dismissal from the CRDF, but it had come down quickly over that same someone's head. Now most of the paraphernalia was sports related and not framed with glass.

"Heard you crash-landed at the port," observed Leon snidely as the pilot slid into the booth beside him. Jeric could smell alcohol already on his friend's breath, at least three Hais' worth, and he supposed he couldn't blame him. "Forget to fuel again?"

"Oh, hah-hah. Welcome back, asshole." Beneath Leon's usual sarcasm Jeric detected real concern for a friend's safety. The pilot gestured for a drink.

Mara, the waitress, seemed as though she never left the bar. She walked over to them, smiling. While no one would ever call her beautiful, with her stringy brown hair and tired, worn-looking face, she had a great smile, and her charming way with the troops had defused many a potential fight. As clairvoyant as ever, Mara brought Jeric a Hais. He took a sip, glaring at his friend over the rim of the glass. "Major, Mikaela, how are you?"

"Fine, Jeric," Dawson replied with a smile. Even-tempered, amicable, professional Liam Dawson. Jeric thought he was a bit bland and a little too puppy-dog loyal to Leon, but the man was an incredible leader under fire, which was what really counted. As for Mikaela Sommers, she had been a shield in her former life. She might have been beautiful once, but a cornered suspect had taken care of that. She wore her scars proudly, defiantly, and kept her hair in a tight military Mohawk. She raised her glass to Jeric and downed the whisky in one swallow. She was a hell of a boxer and was an expert in more martial arts than he could even name.

"So listen," Leon said to the two across the table, resuming their earlier conversation. "I don't know what it is about these Tilora Company guys, but they sound like they play it close to the vest. They won't give you anything they don't have to, and asking will only get you laughed at. Just walk in like you own the place, and don't talk to anyone but the people in charge."

Dawson nodded, that trace of a smile always on his lips. "Sure, Colonel. I'm always for cutting out the middleman."

Leon nodded. "Good. Remember, you're the primary for the company, but your main job is to interface with the sector justice department, see if you can't secure a long-term intervention." He broke off as Mara approached again, and Leon looked up at her.

"What'll you have, Colonel? Another Hais?"

"Sure, on ice. Actually, no. Dawson, what are you drinking?"

The major paused and looked at his beer as though he had forgotten what it was. "Stout. The local one."

"North Bay Crude," Mara said.

"That's the one," Leon said, nodding. "One of those, please." When she brought the drink, deep black in a tall pint glass, Leon took a sip and smiled appreciatively. "Thanks, M. Anyway, Mikaela, I want you to run interference with the local shields. I don't know what the relationship between Tilora Co. and the Corda locals is like, but if you can make some contacts, use 'em."

"Will do, Colonel. Corda's pretty quiet. I don't know if we have to worry about a posse of gunslingers going off and poaching our kills, but I'll post a notice to the regional command, get them to rein them in."

"That's perfect. And remember, it's better to abort than try and fail. Something smells wrong, you walk away. Understand?"

The two looked uneasy, and Jeric pointedly distracted himself, trying to fold a napkin into a little fighter.

"Understand me?" Leon repeated emphatically. They nodded. "Okay, then, go to it."

Dawson and Sommers stood, saluted smartly, and left the bar. Jeric moved to the other side of the booth, to face Leon. His friend was a wreck, looking like he hadn't slept in weeks, and his face was a mess. The way he had been chiding Dawson and Sommers as though they were rookies made him sound as though he was coming unhinged. Unfortunately, it wasn't the first time: Leon managed to detach himself from the loss of people under his command for the most part, but occasionally the deaths got to him and stayed with him. Jeric supposed it was time to get it over with, though he hated awkward condolences. "Welcome back, Vic. Poor Buzz."

Leon sighed, rubbed his eyes. "I can't keep hearing that."

"I heard you got the bastards that killed him." Jeric's eyes were expectant.

"Yeah. You're the only one who seems to be happy about it."

"Aw, screw it." Jeric shook his head and took a stalling sip of Hais. "What's a couple of dealers, right? It's not like Rockmore docked your commission, after all. Did he?" He was excited to see Leon again, and he was chatty as a result. "Sorry, I need to shut up. So, ah, how did it … happen?"

"Shot, how else? Vest and TacGel didn't do a damn thing." Leon swallowed. "He didn't go quickly." He flicked a finger against his glass, listened to it ring. "Thought for sure it was an easy job, didn't expect to go up against an entire cartel in one shooting gallery. Fucked it up good. I should've kept him with me." He raised haunted eyes to Jeric. "Does Traxus know yet?"

Jeric averted his own eyes from that stony gaze. "Maybe. She's been out on training maneuvers since you left, but the news must have filtered down by now."

Leon sighed. "I was kind of surprised she didn't meet us at the port. I hope she's taking it all right."

"I heard you and Raptor got clipped, too."

"Yeah." Vic tapped his arm where the wound was still healing. "Nothing too bad. Raptor got two in the chest. Pissed him off, sent him into a tizzy. He's fine."

"Yeah, I'll bet. You look like hell, though. I like the nose job."

"Fuck you." Leon gingerly felt the bridge of his nose and winced.

"So ... I guess this means I'll be filling the slot."

Leon nodded and stared dejectedly into his own drink. It had to be his fourth or fifth, and it wasn't yet three o'clock in the afternoon. "Probably. With Buzz gone ... and Traxus doing in-house—"

"Is it true the grand admiral asked for her to be kept out of trouble? Seems like kind of a dick move."

Leon shrugged. "I don't know. He might have. Not our business, right? But yeah, I think after she got hurt on Mar Sai, he took an interest. Can you blame him?" He finished his drink, leaving nothing but cream-colored foam clinging to the sides of the glass. Suddenly he seemed uncomfortable, and Jeric cursed the distance that had come between them. "Well, I've got to go approve some applications. Rockmore sent Akida out on a dinner date with some clients in Tesa, so I'm pulling his paperwork. Anything you want me to expedite?"

"Nah." Jeric raised his own glass in salute. "See you tomorrow." Leon got up and walked out.

The pilot watched him leave, finished his own drink, and ordered another. Vic was a mess, that was certain. Jeric hadn't liked the look in his eyes at all.

§

The *Royal Dawn* sailed through the void with a purpose, engines burning a trail across the heavens. The ship was painted in gleaming silver with a sunburst on the bow; instantly recognizable, she was one of the

Coalition's oldest and most illustrious vessels. The Coalition Charter had been ratified on board by delegates of all eleven member species hundreds of years ago. They had stood in this very parlor, looking out over the galaxy through panoramic windows. The ship was palace, museum, and embassy in one. Countless treaties, truces, and alliances had been put to paper and database aboard the storied vessel. Her passenger manifests read like a who's who of historical leaders from all the major powers.

Admirals Hakar and Telec had been afraid that the *Royal Dawn* would prove a tempting target in the event of hostilities, but Empress Kra'al and Prime Minister Adam Somerset had calculated carefully. Even the most hardline Valinata officers were careful to extend the hand of friendship toward the *Royal Dawn*, which had a reputation of peace only partially tarnished by the disgraced Emperor Telemon, who had used it more like a personal yacht. If things went badly, the Coalition was a victim of its own good will, but if things went well, Somerset and Kra'al would be hailed as heroes, finding a gem of peace where others saw only coal for the furnace of war.

Coalition intelligence services had petitioned for surveillance devices to be installed and had been rejected. That was not to say that certain among the crew or the ship's passengers were not clandestine operatives. Many parties had a stake in the *Dawn*'s success.

Having drawn and redrawn his share of borders, Somerset was keenly aware of the very tangible effect of the artificial and somewhat pointless demarcations of the galactic map. They were impossible to patrol or defend effectively. If it came to war, dozens of planets could be razed before any fleets managed to find each other. It was Somerset's job to ensure that the situation never became that dire.

Pointless though they may have been, those borders, visible only as lines on a computer display, were treated like tripwires. Simply bumping against one without the proper documentation could be enough to bring down the wrath of a whole fleet, assuming there was anyone watching. And so the *Royal Dawn* and her escort stopped their advance several thousand kilometers short, full-stop to keep from provoking the Valinata border patrol that had been dispatched to keep an eye on the Coalition diplomats. As soon as they had arrived one of those Valinata ships had come about and burned for home, likely a courier.

Minister Somerset sat calmly on one of the lavish couches dotting the inside of *Royal Dawn*'s ballroom-like passenger cabin. His staff and several other Coalition officials—including one retired admiral who had a number of contacts within the Valinata defense council—rested tensely in their seats. For Somerset it was just another matter of state. As leader of Parliament, he was often called upon to undertake tasks that required a deft touch, and he honestly didn't think the Valinata would risk war. Like most people with routine exposure to the Vali, he had grown immune to the constant posturing, learning to look beyond it to the real issues. That did not mean he would treat the matter with anything less than his customary dedication. In fact, he was somewhat flattered that the grand admirals had seemed so enthusiastic to have him along. What had he expected? Reluctance? Hostility? The grand admirals were more politicians than military commanders these days, and they didn't want war, either.

He adjusted his position and winced as his back cramped. Where once the plush couches of the *Dawn* had been a welcome comfort, he found that with advancing age he needed something a bit firmer. He was about to ask for some more pillows when the captain piped a transmission over the speakers.

"I repeat to the Coalition vessel: this is the cruiser *Rampant* of the Valinata Space Force Outer Patrol. You are in violation of the provisions for territorial sovereignty outlined in the Yin Treaty. Turn back immediately. The Valinata are in a state of combat readiness, and we will fire on your ship if you trespass any further." The voice on the comm was deep, flat, dead-serious. Somerset didn't panic. This wasn't the first time this had happened. The Yin Treaty was old, often invoked but seldom enforced.

"Minister?" asked the captain over the intercom. As a senior diplomat, Somerset was given the authority to deal with any hurdles they might encounter.

"It's in your hands, Captain." Being a senior diplomat also meant respecting those he was working with, and the men and women responsible for keeping him safe were certainly at the top of that list.

The captain, also a veteran of the diplomatic corps, appreciated the gesture. He calmly replied, "*Rampant*, this is Coalition Diplomatic Envoy *Royal Dawn*. We are on an authorized diplomatic mission from Coalition High Command and request a conference with your regional commander.

We will lower our defensive grid and stand by for scan but request that you respect our flag of peace and make no attempt to board."

The altercation between the two captains was not over. Even Valinata officers were not usually this intractable. After a few moments, twin beams of yellow plasma seared the darkness on either side of the *Royal Dawn*, warning shots fired by the VSF cruiser. Somerset's stomach clenched, and the admiral across from him rose and walked briskly to the bridge. The door closed behind him.

The warning shots were no danger, but if the Valinata ship actually fired on *Royal Dawn* or her escorts, it would be considered an act of war, Somerset knew. He also knew that the *Dawn* could not withstand the sort of bombardment that a VSF cruiser could deliver.

He was growing concerned when there was the briefest tugging sensation in his stomach. It grew steadily until he felt almost as though the ship was tilting. As a lifelong traveler, he would have recognized the signs of an unfolding conduit anywhere. Within moments a dozen warships had appeared all around the *Royal Dawn*: gleaming, torpedo-shaped destroyers, gunships bristling with weapons, and enormous carriers that looked almost as though they were disintegrating into clouds of flitting fighters as they disgorged their lethal cargo. The CRDF markings on their flanks flooded the parlor with relief.

One of the ships was *Champion*, commanded by Vice-Grand Admiral Flora Rodriguex. Somerset did not know which, but he assumed it was the largest, a looming dreadnought that looked as though an entire fortress had taken flight.

"Prime Minister Somerset, this is Admiral Rodriguex," a woman's voice assured him in liquid, confident Spanish, echoing through *Royal Dawn*'s parlor. "Please forgive the rushed introduction, but I've asked your crew to evacuate to the adjacent system until this has been resolved."

"As you wish, Admiral," Somerset said, embarrassed that he couldn't think of anything else to say. People were counting on him, too, after all. He had found himself shaken by the VSF's aggression, and he wondered if there wasn't something to Empress Kra'al's concern after all. Relations with the Valinata had always been rocky, the smaller kingdom insisting that the Coalition was held together merely by greed, that the amalgamation of a thousand cultures had led, effectively, to an absence of culture, and that the vast, arrogant CRDF had few truly fierce fighters. It came across much like a napoleon complex: the Valinata viewed backing down or accepting the hand of charity as weakness. Adding fear to that already volatile mixture could be dangerous.

Coalition fighters buzzed *Royal Dawn*, flashing by the windows as they formed up around the diplomatic vessel. Even though they were friendly, the presence of so many warships in close proximity caused people to back toward the center of the deck.

Royal Dawn may have been unarmed, but she had a marvelous bank of engines, and the captain put them to good use. As they rumbled to life, bottles and glasses at the bar rattled. She came about, maneuvering thrusters firing, and Somerset got a look at the Coalition armada, seventy ships strong now and still growing as more tumbled out of their gravitational conduits, bearing down on the smaller and outnumbered VSF ships. It no longer seemed like a standoff, Somerset had to admit. It was an exercise in intimidation.

The stars outside the portholes elongated, stretched into infinity, then flashed into the maddening kaleidoscope of a conduit. They had jumped. The admiral returned from the bridge, looking satisfied. Somerset's lip curled. *Warmongers*, he thought venomously.

The Prime Minister was surprised to see that his own hands were shaking.

§

Love me, called an ethereal voice. Baleful yellow eyes swam out of the darkness, set in a beautiful, young face Hakar had once known. *Love me*, the voice called again, tauntingly. *You did this.*

The grand admiral awoke with a jolt of fear. He fumbled for the bedside lamp and turned it on, chasing the shadows from his room. *There is nothing to be afraid of*, he thought, but was it his voice … or hers? There wasn't anyone or anything lurking in his bedchamber, that much was immediately obvious. Away from his family, Hakar lived monastically, and there was nothing in his room for an assailant to hide behind.

There wasn't any assailant, anyway, not unless the past could rise out of memory and kill. *Perhaps*, he mused humorlessly. Throwing his feet over the side of the bed, Hakar stood and padded through his silent apartment to the kitchen, to pour himself a glass of water. Restless ghosts and too much beer the night before had left him parched, and he drained two glasses before his thirst was quenched. Still he could not shake the sense of unease, and he turned on his Memscreen viewer, flipping through the channels. It was all mindless, sound and light without thought. The news made only the barest mention of the troubles with the Valinata, and no one thought to speculate on why so many blank spots had suddenly appeared on the map.

Maybe, just maybe it's because we're too spoiled to care. And maybe this administration isn't so different from the ones that came before it. Hakar's disillusionment had grown immeasurably in the past decades. Once he had been an officer, and before that a sojier. Matters were simpler then. Moving up through the ranks brought with it complications best not thought about. Sending thousands to their deaths, using populated worlds as bargaining chips. And keeping facts from the public. That was a big one, a key part of ruling.

The justification—the ability to rationalize anything being another keystone of government—was that responding to events on the already unpredictable border would be easier if they didn't have to deal with scrutiny from the whole galaxy.

The situation would continue to deteriorate, Hakar knew. It was like the change of day to night: inevitable. Just because a person closed their eyes did not mean the change didn't happen. He was growing increasingly concerned that they were facing more than the usual Valinata games. Kra'al and Telec had both accused him of borrowing trouble, but he was almost certain that the Valinata were *not* the problem. Somehow there was another force behind the Emerald Veil, wreaking havoc. The most important question was: did the Coalition also have to worry about them or was a new faction rising to power, perhaps one the Coalition could help or at least endorse?

Hakar's cupboards were nearly empty. His adjutant kept asking if there was anything he wanted, but most of the time Hakar ate in the defense ministry's cafeteria or at his desk. His stomach rumbled, and finally he opened a box of crackers and reflected on his dilemma.

There were wolves at the gate, and no one knew whether or not they were rabid. They didn't know the extent of the conflict or how much territory was still under the control of the VSF and the Tête. The only thing worse than an uninformed decision would be no decision at all. *How to get information without starting a war?*

He almost dropped the box of crackers when he saw the solution to his problem appear on the viewer's screen, a newsfeed about some public relations scandal on a Commonwealth world. *The Valinata Space Force nearly started a war over the Calama incident, claiming that their attackers were prototype CRDF ships with no markings. Ships with no markings might be just the ticket. While we're dredging up the ghosts of the past, we might as well get some use out of them.* Hakar picked up the remote and turned up the volume.

"... and the Premier's office released an official statement to the contrary, sources within the Unified Commonwealth Department of Justice have confirmed that talks are in progress to tighten restrictions on sanctioned interdictions," the reporter was saying. "During what was to be a routine arrest of high-ranking members of a notorious drug cartel, gang members using stolen security clearances attacked the officers in an attempt to free their leaders. Supported by private security auxiliaries, the shield officers were able to fight off the criminals and affect the capture of most of their targets. Fourteen shield officers and one Jackal Pack mercenary were killed in a pitched gun battle, in addition to twenty-two cartel members."

§

Telec came without complaint, roused from a restful sleep. How Telec could sleep well at a time like this Hakar would never understand, but he had long suspected that a conscience was not among the burdens his colleague carried. They were sitting in Hakar's Spartan quarters around the small kitchen table, which was bare except for the Tagean admiral's minicomputer, its Memscreen extended between them.

"The Valinata have closed down the border like this at least once before that I can recall," Hakar said glumly. "And when they reappeared, they smashed the Aradon Dominion and captured a fifth of our space before we forced them back."

"Oh, you're not anxious for a reenactment?" Telec snapped. His tentacles convulsed and he snorted wetly. "I apologize, I'm still groggy. Why are we even still talking about the Valinata like they're responsible? Haven't we gotten past that?"

Hakar didn't let his irritation show although his ears flicked back. "We have to consider all possible angles, Bosh."

"Well, then, let's consider that mysterious signal Shra sent you. Any insight?"

Hakar brought up the snippet of transmission, less than a minute of unintelligible noise. He had listened to it again and again though it did no good, and once was enough to chill him to the bone. He tapped the screen and the recording played. The apartment was filled with a low moaning punctuated at intervals by slightly higher ululations.

Listening to it, Hakar was reminded of his dream, of the angelic face with the demon eyes, accusing. It was like a sound out of the space between nightmares, the call of some primeval predator crashing through the brush or gliding through deep, dark oceans. Initially it sounded like random noise, but the initial cryptography pattern analyses had detected different overlapping, repeating frequencies. It was a transmission of some sort but unlike any Hakar had ever heard. The VSF, or perhaps this enigmatic Raven Blue, were using heavy encryption, signals buried so deep that the codebreakers on Triatha had no clue how to even begin.

Telec's face was still. "That … sounds familiar," he said, searching his memory.

Hakar didn't answer. The codebreakers may not have been able to decrypt the signal, but it had been triangulated. The source, unsurprisingly, appeared to be Tanis Ruin. *Tanis Ruin*, Hakar reflected morosely as Telec scrutinized the pattern analysis, trying to glean some elusive nugget of wisdom. *An ancient mystery that keeps on giving.* Ruins left over from the ancient Tagean Dynasty were well documented and had been studied for centuries. Tanis Ruin, however, continued to stump scholars. The architecture was far different from that of any other ruins both in the layout of the cities and also in the style of the buildings. It seemed distinctly military in nature, and the wrecked technology seemed to have developed along different lines than that found in most Tagean ruins. And, of course, the Valinata had not allowed Coalition researchers anywhere near it for hundreds of years.

Cosmographically, there was nothing to distinguish the Tanis Ruin region other than its emptiness, which made it the perfect place for a large force to stage without attracting unwanted attention.

Telec let the recording play through again, clearly frustrated. "Well, I give up. We might as well file it under Raven Blue until more information surfaces."

"Frankly, I'm tired of waiting for comscan to turn something up," Hakar said, rising to pour himself a glass of water. "We need eyes on the problem."

"What do you suggest? Send in Rodriguex's fleet? She nearly got into a shooting war with VSF ships already, and she's far closer to the border than she should be. We need to pull her back to the Alkyra, at least for now. If we make one misstep here, we could find ourselves fighting a war against two enemies. We can't afford it."

"No, of course not. We need plausible deniability. If our forces are caught beyond the Veil, the Outbound Arc will burn."

"What do you propose? Mercenaries?" Telec burbled a derisive laugh until he saw that Hakar was considering just that. "You can't be serious. Her Majesty will never approve."

Both their comms buzzed, their morning alarms. It was time for work.

"Well, let's find out," Hakar said nervously. He folded the Mem screen and slipped the computer in his pocket. Telec preceded him to the door, gulping down the rest of his Kaf and leaving the empty cup on the counter.

Turning, the defense advisor said with a mocking gleam in his eye, "Hakar, you should really look into decorating this place. You're a grand admiral for Empress's sake, not a cadet. Personal possessions are not contraband." He stepped into the hallway.

Hakar turned off the lights and closed the door behind them.

8: Plausible Deniability for Hire

The standoff had been going on for days. Nine ships from the Valinata and seven from the Coalition drifted on opposite sides of the imaginary line that split the indefinable and indivisible void between the two empires. The fleets were extremely close, their bows less than a hundred kilometers apart, cannons and missiles trained and loaded. All crews were on general quarters alert.

From the bridge deck of Admiral Rodriguex's flagship, *Champion*, Prime Minister Adam Somerset had a great view while he tried to remain composed. He had a face that was tailor-made for politics, the sort of chiseled but kind face that inspired trust. His winning smile had adorned campaign posters, political announcements, and even shirts as he became a sort of celebrity politician for his popular policies and his flair in parliament. Right now that face was pale, drawn, and covered in a fine sheen of sweat.

He hated the idea of bearing witness to a battle, but if he had to see it, he wanted to be on the winning side. And since Admiral Rodriguex had dispersed her battle fleet to better cover vulnerable systems, the task force to which Somerset had been attached had been outnumbered. His understanding of their orders was that the fleet was to remain well behind the line to respond to threats, yet Rodriguex seemed determined to put herself in harm's way. It had all started when her battle group had approached the border to cover *Royal Dawn*'s withdrawal, and now she was stuck here until the situation calmed down.

There may have been fewer vessels from the Coalition Royal Navy, but the CRN officers assured Somerset blithely that they had their counterparts vastly outgunned. Though Somerset was not a military man, he suspected that at such close range they would all be crippled or destroyed in an exchange—no matter who opened fire first.

There was no doubt that the balance of firepower in the region had shifted after the Fifth Battle Fleet had stormed the Outbound Arc, but that provided little consolation to the men and women on the firing line.

Ultimatum after ultimatum blared across the gulf between the two facing fleets: Stand down, pull back, stand down, surrender, stand down. The pattern had grown routine, demands being issued every morning by one side or the other, and a counter-threat being transmitted by the opposing force by lunchtime. The days' festivities consisted of each battle group staring down the other and trying very hard not to blink. Somerset felt paralyzed as he watched the ranking officers butt heads.

At the moment, the focus of this test of wills was occurring between the fighter wings, which were going through strenuous maneuvers, trying to out-fly each other. Fatigued, neither side was doing a particularly impressive job.

About halfway through this particular morning, as Somerset sipped at a cup of battery acid masquerading as Kaf, a garbled transmission was routed through nearby comm satellites to the Valinata ships. While the Coalition comm technicians were struggling to decrypt the message, all nine VSF cruisers recalled their fighters and pulled back, streaking off toward the Valinata interior. The Emerald Veil dropped down again.

Somerset insisted on seeing the transcript of the decoded transmission. There were gaps, but the gist was clear: Valinata forces had been redeployed to protect the Tête as the ruling councils fled the capital. *What is happening in there?* Somerset wondered as he waited nervously. His military protectors seemed equally perplexed.

§

Leon lay prone, peering over the low rise at the hazy silhouette of his target. The stock of his Leight-Arm TK-77 Proton Rifle was tucked tight against his shoulder. He peered through the scope and adjusted his aim slightly. Gently he tightened his finger on the trigger, and the rifle jerked against his shoulder. A shimmering green dart of densely packed protons flashed out across the crater-filled field, impacting against the target. There was a bright blast and a loud crash as the projectile destabilized on impact and the wood cutout disintegrated.

Leon shifted his aim, squeezing off another burst, and the next target in the series vanished. He lost himself in the rhythm of practice. The air stank of ozone, and his shoulder ached from the kick of the rifle's recoil.

When he was done, the speaker in his protective headphones crackled. "Great job, Colonel. Twenty-one in sixty on that last time-trial," the chief range master reported. "Seven misses."

Leon stood up, wiped his brow, and stretched. Targets lay smashed all over the field, but his performance was disappointing. He didn't often come to the firing range anymore, but he tried to keep himself up to spec.

There had been a time when he could hit a target nearly every second, a time when he had never missed. Those days were gone, he admitted. It wasn't aging that upset him, it was losing his edge.

As he gathered his spent magazines and his water bottle, he saw Asar, the Pack's resident marksman, pass through the range gate with his long-range rifle, a customized Gauss coilgun. Asar kept all his records secret, and no amount of bribing would loosen the range master's lips, but it was rumored that he routinely averaged more than sixty a minute. It didn't seem possible; had anyone else made such a claim, it would have been discounted as having no basis in any reality they were a part of. Leon had seen Asar shoot, though, and the man fired a weapon the way most people breathed.

Leon returned the sharpshooter's salute as he walked by, then began disassembling his own rifle. The TK-77 was a sleek weapon, well designed and deadly. Like the Sprawler, its construction was of the highest quality; there was no tacky-looking, cheap-feeling plastic or commercial flair. The weapon had a sturdy weight, and its clean lines and angles even had a grim beauty. It was hardly a delicate weapon, and Leon rarely had call to use it on live targets, but when he did, he seldom required a second shot. The rifle had its drawbacks, however: it required constant maintenance, and because it fell into a restricted category, parts and ammunition were expensive.

The target practice was a cool-down exercise, and Leon's clothes were caked with dirt and grass, his old gray academy t-shirt dark with sweat from running and lifting weights. He dusted himself off, pulled on his black beret with its crimson flash and Pack crest, and picked up his rifle case. The weight caused a slight twinge in his shoulder, but he forced himself to carry it with his wounded arm anyway. From farther along the line, he could hear the steady *whoosh-crack* of Asar's weapon, and he shook his head. He would never pass Asar in the rankings. There wasn't even any point in trying.

At the other end of the range, a few Jackals were practicing their drives, sending golf balls deep into no man's land, while other troopers tried to shoot them out of the air. Jeric was among them, grinning as he knocked two balls in a row into one of the downrange targets. He looked like a movie star, albeit a very short one, who had wandered off his set. His service pistol was shoved carelessly in its holster, his carbine buried under a mound of balls. As a pilot, Jeric put little stock in infantry weapons, although he was a good enough shot that he could defend himself when necessary. "Interested in a drink?" he asked, pausing on his follow-through to watch another ball sail past one of the targets and bounce off the far berm.

Leon made a show of glancing at his watch. "Are you sure you can spare the time?" In fact, he felt bad for being so dismissive the other day.

Jeric packed up his clubs, and they checked their weapons with the range master, keeping their sidearms. From there they followed the path from the firing range to the main compound, pausing to watch a dropship lift off with a roar. No doubt it was ferrying mercenaries to some job, maybe the overthrow of a dictator or perhaps just an expensive lunch. The thruster wash was blinding, forcing the two to look away. There was another roar behind them, and a second dropship ascended into the atmosphere, riding pillars of fire. *It must be a big job. Or a big lunch.* They passed a squad of heavy infantry drilling in full EMMA gear. The armor made them look like metallic gorillas. They stopped to salute; Leon returned the courtesy but couldn't help feeling a pang of regret that he hadn't had his own armor for the fight on Korinthe.

The pair of mercenaries strolled into the pub, took their usual seats, and ordered their usual Hais Whisky. The pub's name was a well-loved joke, the result of an ominous mistranslation. Desher Vaux had been roughly translated from the classical Vodroshoyan to mean "Fortune's Favorite." Unfortunately, one of Leon's Vodroshoyan commandoes had informed the officers that the name actually translated to "Hostage of Chance." The mercs grumbled but had to admit that the latter name was probably more appropriate.

The Desher Vaux was usually quiet and had an excellent drink selection from across the galaxy. It was open to all, but most troopers tended to venture into the city to blow off steam. Consequently the regulars were officers and specialists who appreciated the low-key atmosphere.

Leon and Jeric sat discussing politics, and therefore business, for a while. The fate of Jackal Pack was inextricably linked to the balance of power in the galaxy, and the space between the Valinata's hammer and the Coalition's anvil would be a boomtown of lucrative contracts. Eve, though technically in Coalition space, was affiliated with the neutral trade sector between the two empires. As a result, Jackal Pack's taxes all went to the accountants on Benez, the sector's de facto capital, and the organization was legally accountable to no one. Lately the Dias systems had been the Pack's hunting grounds. Then the CRDF had stepped in, and above-board contracts had dried up overnight. Privately Leon sympathized with the Dias Liberation Front, if not their methods. They were likely only trying to get attention as a way to secure much-needed financial aid. The Dias Traverse was a vast and heavily populated region, but by and large, it was impoverished and ignored by the rest of the Coalition. People should not have been surprised that this made for a hotbed of contention and violence.

Rockmore insisted that the Pack drew boundaries, but those boundaries tended to be somewhat fluid, although even the most ruthless of Jackals had their limits. And if it was perplexing that an organization might claim to represent order while thriving on chaos, it was doubly so for Leon. He justified it the same way the general had for years, telling himself that Jackal Pack honed dangerous people into precise instruments of destruction that could effectively manage the violence inherent in their work. Ideally a few specially trained commandoes could do the work of an entire battalion and with far less collateral damage. It hadn't always worked, Leon had to admit, but it was a goal worth pursuing. And every once in a while—just once in a while—small Pack teams were dispatched to improve the legion's reputation by engaging in "cause warfare," for instance, taking up arms against small-time dictators, pirates, and slaver cartels. Most recently Jeric had spearheaded a campaign against a despot deep in Aradon Dominion territory. He had led the JPML combat aerospace wing against military targets with precision that would have eluded even the best-trained CRN bomber squadrons. Eventually his pilots shot down half of the planet's meager complement of fighters without sustaining a single loss of their own. After two weeks of nonstop bombardment, including a terrifying but harmless strafing run on the presidential residence conducted by Jeric himself, the petty dictator had agreed to recognize a minority group in the planetary parliament. The Pack contingent had stayed just long enough to oversee the ratification of the amendments and then jumped the nearest conduit before the Aradon military showed up. The action had raked in millions of talons in investments, and Jeric had been drinking his bonus ever since.

"You probably know CRDF strategy better than anyone here," Jeric ventured. "You think they'll risk a push into Vali space?" He looked curiously at Leon as he sipped his drink.

"Under Telemon I would have said it was a given. Now, though...." Leon shrugged. "After eight years I still don't know much about Empress Kra'al or the new people she put in the Chamber. Hopefully she's got a cooler head."

"What about Hakar? Traxus thinks there's no way he'd support a war."

"Maybe Traxus is right. Hakar taught me that just because the Valinata are small and poor doesn't mean they can't fight like hell. Almost half their population is in the VSF reserves, and everyone from their shock troops to their maintenance technicians and cooks will fight to the death." Leon sucked in a breath and blew it out. It was weird to talk about a war with the Valinata in anything but abstract terms. "Even if we did manage to stomp on them, our reputation in the galaxy is still shaky. We might actually lose the Dias Traverse for good, maybe even the Zoh Hegemony. Bad for business."

Jeric gave a wry grin. "Whose business, Vic?"

Leon pointed a finger at his friend. "You got me. I still think like a Coalition citizen, I guess. The Coalition's business is what I mean. Kra'al needs to solidify relations with the provinces. A decade isn't a long time to heal old wounds, and there's still a lot of mistrust after Telemon. If the CRDF starts flexing muscles again, people are going to think it's a message to them to pay up and play along. Not a spectacular idea."

"I'd say putting the Fifth Battle Fleet in the Arc is a pretty loud message," Jeric pointed out. "The Vali probably just want Bona Ventura back."

The "conquest" of Bona Ventura, as the Vali referred to it, had occurred under Telemon nearly thirty years previously but was still a point of contention. Planets and solar systems moved all the time; minor conduits were stretched, occasionally even breaking and reforming again as the links between gravitational bodies changed. Only the trade routes, kept in relative equilibrium by surrounding gravitational forces, remained stable for thousands of years; however, even those changed. The Bona Ventura system had drifted into Coalition space, and Telemon had repatriated it.

Leon leaned back in his seat, the leather cushion squeaking. "You think a fight's going to clear the air? There's no way they're getting Bona Ventura back, not with the ore deposits. Besides, I really don't think the Valinata actually want a fight. Think about it: they have a lot to offer, even if they do treat some species as second-class. What they don't have is size or resources, and the ones they do have they burn through like there's no tomorrow." It was true the Valinata had gotten the short end of the stick when it came to colonies with exploitable resources. Most worlds behind the Emerald Veil had been only nominally habitable, and massive effort had gone into making them hospitable. "In the end, the only way for the Valinata to *really* thrive is to throw in with the allies economically and make peace. I think all this hooting and banging of war drums is a way to show the Coalition and the rest of the galaxy that they won't be cowed, so they can get good terms for trade when it opens up. If they bloody the CRDF's nose or annex any of the Arc worlds, they're looking at another fifty years of embargo or even occupation. No telling if their reserves will last that long."

Jeric nodded, grudgingly accepting his friend's reasoning. The Inter-Regional Economics Organization, or IREO, was a multinational body that oversaw trade between kingdoms on an individual system level. It crossed ideological, political, and cosmographic boundaries and had often served as the only channel for communication in times of conflict. Even the Aradon Dominion systems were members. Only the Valinata and some of the innumerable small enclaves scattered among the major powers refused to participate. "All right, I see your point. But listen, even if there *is* a war, there's no way it could go bigger than a few systems, *maybe* the Amanra Crescent. And that's not a war."

"Daltar was a single planet," countered Leon curtly.

Jeric winced: he knew where this was going. "Yeah, Leon, but that was a single campaign. Calling it a war...."

Leon felt anger well up, unbidden. "It certainly felt like a fucking war to me. They stripped me of rank, Jeric, revoked my citizenship! You see these?" he asked. His beret was beside his right hand, and his index finger flicked the crown and falcon insignia that marked him as a combined-arms colonel. "These don't mean shit anywhere but here." He tilted his glass up, the Hais disappearing down his throat. Then with an effort he calmed himself. "Whether it was a 'war' or not according to your definition is immaterial. Look what happened to both sides. The Coalition staggered, thanks to the news coming out of one little planet. Telemon lost his throne in the rubble."

Jeric shifted uneasily. "Maybe we should discuss something else."

"Like what? Your drinking?" Jeric took the hint and swam into warmer conversational waters.

"Sorry, Vic. I didn't mean to piss you off."

Leon waved him away. "I'm sorry, too. With everything lately ... I couldn't focus on the range today."

"Only one cure for that." Jeric waggled his glass in front of Leon and drained it. He belched quietly. "By the way, I think Trax should be back tonight. I saw the first tanks rolling back in."

They talked for a few more minutes, ricocheting from superficial subject to superficial subject until Raptor stomped in, momentarily blocking the light coming in through the open door. "Rockmore's turning over bunks looking for you. Answer your damn comm."

Leon checked the radio clipped to his sleeve, cursed, turned it on. "I must have switched it off. What's going on?"

"He called a meeting. He wants you and the flyboy there." Leon and Jeric exchanged a puzzled look, paid Mara for the drinks, and followed the Prross out, walking briskly toward the administration building. Though the reflection of the setting sun glared blindingly off the windows, all three had a feeling that the general was watching them from his office, hands clasped behind his back, watch ticking.

§

"There you are," muttered Rockmore, nearing the end of his patience. "I've been waiting. So has Grand Admiral Hakar." He raised his voice for the benefit of the microphone. "We're all here, Admiral. Go ahead."

Also present were Colonel Akida and Captain Cheth Nysh, head of Jackal Pack's fighter corps. Akida glared at Leon and Jeric and tapped his watch as they walked in. Victor, to his credit, ignored the other colonel pointedly. He removed his cap and stood at rest in his sweat-stained workout clothes. He looked a bit embarrassed to be so underdressed.

Rockmore had shelled out for a tactical holographics projector, and the damn thing took up a whole corner of his office. An image of Grand Admiral Hakar floated before the four mercenaries, flickering and oddly skewed. Though projected three-dimensionally, the image was a frontal, two-dimensional feed, meant to be displayed on a screen. The admiral looked as though he had aged noticeably since the last time Rockmore had seen him in person, but it could have been the poor quality of the transmission. "Glad you could make it, Leon," he barked gruffly, though his tone betrayed the barest hint of mirth. He skipped the pleasantries, owing to the cost of such transmissions. "I've got a job that requires your particular skillset. I need two long-range fighter-bombers outfitted for reconnaissance work. It's a two-week job, three tops." He didn't elaborate.

"Kind of vague, isn't it, sir?" Leon asked, brow furrowing. He probably didn't realize it but he was beginning to look like Rockmore when he frowned: thoughtful, skeptical, calculating.

There was a delay as they awaited the response flung through space. Then Hakar smiled bitterly. "Sorry but circumstances aren't what they could be. We're going to outfit them with a special sensor package. The ships will have to infiltrate Valinata space. Can't have our markings on them, you understand."

So it was beginning. Somehow Rockmore had expected the posturing to be just that. Accepting a job from the CRDF would effectively decide Jackal Pack's allegiance, no matter how competitive the rates might get. And if the Valinata tracked the fighters back to Eve, the Jackals could never defend themselves against retribution, not the way the VSF fought. The way the VSF fought was to nuke the target flat and worry about the fallout when their own children started coming out of the birth canal with the wrong number of limbs.

Hakar waved a hand and flicked his ears no. The image flickered again, the speakers crackling with distortion. "It's not like that at all," he said preemptively, picking up on their reactions. "There's a sphere of quarantine in Valinata space, a restricted area. The VSF fleets are guarding it like it's their last can of beans. They're trying to contain something, and they seem to be failing miserably. We need to know what it is and how much we should start worrying."

Rockmore sighed. "Something tells me you have your suspicions, and something tells me you're not going to share them."

Hakar barked a laugh, and because it came a minute late, it seemed out of place and slightly insane. He seemed too strained for the laugh to be genuine. "You know me too well, old friend. If a Coalition ship were to make the journey, we'd be embroiled in a war by the end of the week. Until we have eyes on the situation, we have to assume the worst and prepare for it."

What's the worst? Rockmore wondered.

"Between us and whatever they're busy guarding, we think the VSF have their hands full. All we expect your ships to do is scan a few dozen systems for activity. If all goes well, they won't see a thing."

That was small consolation. Rockmore knew that Hakar wouldn't have approached them if he expected things to go well. The Coalition wasn't in the habit of hiring mercenaries, and those few times Jackal Pack troops had been seconded to Coalition units had all been off-the-books operations. How could this be anything else? "How much are you offering? I have to tell you the going rate on a job that could result in all-out galactic war is pretty steep."

"Four million."

No one made a sound. That was laughably low. The heads of a few drug dealers lately cost more than that.

The grand admiral was quick to explain. "This *is* a covert operation. Her Majesty doesn't know, and she doesn't want to. She can't, not with her position on sanctioned mercenaries."

"Jackal Pack isn't exactly flush with cash right now, Hakar" Rockmore said evenly. "We couldn't possibly do it for less than twenty million."

"That may seem like a small amount for a royal battle fleet to part with, but I assure you I'm under pretty intense scrutiny right now. Maybe I can swing eight up front. We're skirting a budgetary oversight inquiry as it is, and this is coming out of my discretionary budget. You're the only ones I would even consider for this sort of job. And I can offer you something else: right of first refusal on any contracts. I won't approach another outfit until I talk to you. Plus compensation for assets in the event something goes wrong. As much as fifty million."

"That doesn't even cover the cost of the fighters," Nysh muttered to Akida.

Rockmore had to think long and hard. This wasn't a decision to be made lightly. Leon would have taken the job out of lingering loyalty, he knew, which compromised him in Rockmore's eyes. As usual, it was hard to tell what Akida thought. Jeric and Nysh were probably going through the pilot rosters in their minds, trying to determine the best candidates for the mission. As for trust, Rockmore knew he had the admiral's word. The only problem was that a guarantee on contracts was only good if the CRDF decided to hire outside talent, and that happened rather less than rarely. "All right, Hakar. Transmit the details to our secure comms station."

"Done. Good luck, gentlemen." That was that. The image flickered and vanished.

A collective sigh rose up from those present, but it was hardly one of relief. While Hakar had never been anything but forthright with the Pack, there was no telling who was watching over his shoulder these days.

"Leon, Jeric, I want you to go down to the pad and see that the fighters are kitted. Load for bear. Irún, Cheth, pick out your most reliable flight crew. No one who likes to brag." Rockmore looked away. Outside the setting sun broke through a wall of clouds. He activated his comm and began dictating orders to his assistant. He was done with them, attention gone entirely to the job. His officers had their orders, and they left to carry them out.

§

Hours later, night was coming to Eve. Leon watched from afar as the first fighter-bomber was dragged from its hangar, covered in a white tarpaulin. Jeric stood beside him, straining for a better view. The wind whipped the tarp wildly around the hidden frame of the ship like a gown revealing fleeting glimpses of the woman beneath it.

The pilot pulled off his sunglasses. "Still kinda surprised the boss agreed to all this. We've never done a deep deployment like this, and those *guillotines* have been gathering dust for two years."

Jackal Pack was a well-run organization, but maintaining the legion's heavy equipment cost a small fortune, especially with Rockmore's pack-rat mentality and kitchen sink approach to the legion's arsenal. The agreement with Eve to provide a PDF should have kept the Pack in the black, but the planetary government was already in debt to them for nearly a billion talons. The interest on the loans was in Jackal Pack's favor, but Eve defaulted regularly. Rockmore may have been willing to accept IOUs to keep their host planet tractable, but IOUs didn't pay the Pack's own debts, which were many and large. The *Star Wolf* cruiser alone had cost six billion, and it was about as practical as using Raptor's Banshee Gatling laser for eye surgery.

"We haven't even tested any of those jets. Not to their limits, anyway. I don't know how they'll hold up under prolonged use. The reactor's prone to rapid cycling...." Jeric continued to list the ships' deficiencies.

Meanwhile, Leon's mind was preoccupied with images of Valinata ships coming across a malfunctioning Jackal Pack spy jet and immediately putting two and two together in a very violent fashion. "We don't even know where they're going." He glanced down at his diminutive friend and caught the flash of envy in Jeric's eyes. "Oh, shit. You wish you were going, don't you?"

Jeric shrugged, trying to be nonchalant. "Okay, yeah. Those jets are sleek honeys, and you know I'm the best damn pilot in the legion."

"Ego, Jeric. We have to remember that we're all part of a team." Leon shook his head in consternation. He understood the thrill of being in control of that much power, but with Jeric, it was somewhere between a love affair and a hopeless addiction. At least, it was healthier than some of his previous addictions—and love affairs, for that matter. "You're straight-up crazy, buddy."

"I guess I'd prefer something more agile anyway."

A sojier walked up to them, holding a rolled Mem with a security read-only tag glowing on one corner. Leon tried to remember the man's name but drew a blank; he sneaked a glance at his nametag. "Colonel," the trooper said, sketching a salute to Leon, who returned it. "The general wanted me to deliver this. It's the packet from the CRDF." He held out the Mem.

"Thanks." Leon took the Mem and waited for the man to leave before turning his attention to its contents. He glanced through the documents, frowning, skimmed through them again. "Someone certainly lit a fire under Hakar's ass. Or maybe it's the other way around. They expect the fighters to rendezvous with the Fifth Battle Fleet at Iris tomorrow. We've got expedited clearances and falsified transponder codes, everything the budding spy needs."

"Iris?" Jeric asked, incredulous. "What the hell is the Fifth Battle Fleet doing hanging around Iris? That's in the next sector!"

"Too close for comfort," Leon agreed. If a front opened there, it would likely draw in the rest of the planets along the Alkyra, Eve and Jackal Pack included. It was unlikely that the CRN would make the first advance, but were the VSF commanders ambitious enough—no, *crazy* enough—to launch their own ships into a sawmill? Iris had a significant tactical advantage in that the gravitational fields thrown by its binary star pair and surrounding systems limited viable conduits into and out of the system.

What worked against an attacker would work against the defenders, too, should they be overwhelmed. Jackal Pack's core competency was combined-arms surface warfare, and though their naval assets were nothing to scoff at, they were intended to support ground troops. They could never hold an approach long enough to land infantry and armor in the face of a concerted defensive effort.

There was a shouted order near the fighter, and the canvas was pulled off, revealing a chunky, aggressively angular gray ship with downward-curving wings. It looked unpleasantly like a vulture. Because it was designed for covert operations, it lacked the red tiger stripes characteristic of other Jackal Pack vehicles. The *guillotine* favored speed over armor and destructive power, but it had plenty of all three. These two had been extensively modified; in addition to sensor wave-absorbing hull coating, all non-essential electronics had been replaced with mechanical parts to reduce electronic noise and signal leakage. The power plant had been fine-tuned to go completely dormant and cold in a matter of minutes and to start up again almost instantly by way of a precision-calibrated tritium injector. The sensors had been gutted and replaced with state-of-the-art surveillance equipment, the armor had been strengthened, the engines had been overpowered, and the crew quarters had been refurbished to something that passed for comfort. They could go deep, for months on the wing.

The flight crew of four, dressed in nondescript flight suits likewise devoid of any Pack markings, ran toward the ship, helmets in hand. They scrambled up the ladder, disappearing one by one. A minute or so later, a high-pitched whine filled the air as the ship powered up, shimmering heat waves gushing from its thruster ports. Her sister ship was unveiled, and the second crew boarded. Both ships were capable of vertical takeoff or landing through their Rombaldt Masses; the thrusters would take over once they were off the ground. The rear thrusters were used for maximum propulsion, but the flanks of each ship were lined with smaller maneuvering thrusters that delivered attitude adjustments in space.

"We're done here," Leon said to Jeric, and the two turned to leave as the whine from the engines grew to a rumble.

"Leon!" shouted a familiar voice. "Leon Victor!" He turned and shielded his eyes against the setting sun.

A few dozen civilians had gathered to watch the launch, unaware of the importance of the mission. A woman was pushing through to the front, with a backpack over one shoulder. Leon froze in his tracks. It couldn't be. She had gone, vanished from his life. Yet there she was, running toward him.

Second Movement:
Second Chances

9: Rachel Case

Leon's attention was firmly fixed on the woman coming toward them, so he didn't hear Jeric curse softly under his breath as the pilot turned to leave.

Rachel Case emerged from the crowd, stopping just short of Leon and gazing at him, sober and wary. He blinked at her, unsure if it was really her or perhaps just a hallucination due to lingering brain damage from the beating he had received at the hands of Marcus Keegan.

Rachel smiled uncertainly. "Hi," she said softly.

"What are you doing here?" Leon asked, too shocked to be diplomatic. Rachel's reply was lost in the shriek of the recon ships as their engines ignited, and soon they were enveloped in a cloud of dust that stung their eyes.

Brow knitted in a perplexed frown, Leon let his eyes roam over Rachel, soaking in every detail as though she might vanish again, this time into thin air. Her blue eyes, set in a face like porcelain, regarded Leon inquisitively. She had an impish smile, but she wasn't smiling now. Just a little shorter than Leon, she had a shapely body with tight curves which her fitted black-and-blue sweater and flared pants showcased splendidly. She was a graceful beauty, every movement deliberate and naturally seductive. It had been the first thing Leon had noticed about her, and it was the first thing he noticed now. What was she noticing? Her gaze seemed to brush over his wounds and make them vanish for a moment. Staring into her eyes, he wondered how he had ever pushed her away, how he had ever argued with her or dwelt on her flaws. After the shootout on Korinthe, she stood out like a diamond in the Jackal Pack coal box, as beautiful as she had been the night they had met.

But seeing her again also conjured feelings of inadequacy, resentment, and confusion. What had he done that she would leave without so much as a goodbye or even a hint that something was amiss? More importantly, what had brought her back?

"I thought you left," he said, still unable to muster anything beyond dumb surprise.

Rachel's lips, glossy and sparkling, parted, and Leon stared at them as she spoke, remembering their gentle caress and aching for it despite his anger. "I did. I'm back, though." She said it stiffly, as though she, too, was unconvinced.

Leon said nothing for a moment. He wanted nothing more than to run to her, hug her tightly, and kiss her passionately. The thought of her pressed up against him again made his heart flutter. "It's good to see you." Even to him it sounded hollow. Awkwardly, unsure of himself or what he wanted to do, he hugged her. Coldly she returned the gesture.

They parted quickly, and Leon looked for a reaction. She gave him nothing. It had hurt when he had come home to find her gone, hurt even more when days, then weeks had gone by with no word from her. Fear for her safety had turned to depression before settling into a pit of penetrating loneliness deep in his stomach. And now she had just waltzed back into his life as though nothing had changed.

That wasn't quite right though, was it? It wasn't the same. And it never would be again. Their relationship had never exactly been founded on trust, but what little there had been was gone, likely forever. "Does your mother know you're here?" Leon asked, not meaning to say it in a mocking tone.

"Oh, boy," Rachel said, speaking volumes in those two exasperated words. She managed a smile, and Leon cracked one of his own. She smelled like berries in stark contrast to the exhaust fumes of the bombers. Right now he felt more exposed than he had when Marcus Keegan had put a knife to his throat.

"So, ah, what now?" Leon asked.

"I don't know," Rachel admitted, biting her lip a little. "I've never tried a do-over. I guess it's up to you."

She had probably meant it innocently enough, but it came out as a challenge. Leon felt himself bristling, forced himself to calm down. "We should go somewhere, to talk," he said.

They started back toward the main compound, side by side. Nevertheless, the distance between them was an unspoken accusation. As they passed the Desher Vaux, Leon glimpsed Jeric and Raptor standing in the door of the pub, drinks in hand, faces locked into masks.

§

For Traxus Tachai it wasn't a bittersweet reunion but a moment to savor. She, too, was in the pub, twisting back and forth on her barstool as she watched between the shoulders of her friends. Cool evening air drifted through the door, carrying the fresh, brisk scent of Eve, mixed with just a hint of exhaust. She smiled to herself and stole a glance at the gaudy bar clock on the wall, then finished off her beer. It was a Tagean ale with nutty and fruity overtones.

She had earned a few drinks, and as she put down the empty glass, another full one appeared in front of her, courtesy of a fellow trooper. "Nice work out there, Lieutenant," he said.

"Thanks, Bryant. We all did great. You're a hell of a support gunner."

The Human blushed. "No one clears a line of advance like you, ma'am." He withdrew.

The training exercise had gone well. Better than well, in fact. Rockmore and his officers kept Jackal Pack's troops to the standards of conventional special forces, with daily physical training, coursework, maneuvers, and assault drills. Because of their mercenary nature, how much each sojier put in was up to him or her. That being said, those who got assigned to mission crews were those who trained the hardest, those who knew how to work as a cohesive unit, to take initiative, to think beyond the foxhole they were in.

Finally Captain Braeburn had given Traxus a platoon, and she had used it to capture an entire company of the opposing force while suffering only three simulated casualties. There was a big difference between a training exercise against colleagues and real combat against enemies committed to killing her; even so, she was proud of herself and her unit, and they had accepted her as a leader.

It hadn't always been so easy. She had come under immediate suspicion as little sister to the big hero, Grand Admiral Hakar himself. Few people had dared castigate her for her failings, but fewer yet had trusted in her abilities. Being one of Leon's favorites had its advantages and disadvantages, as well, but after four years, Traxus was finally beginning to feel like a real member of the team.

Although she was Hakar's sister, she looked very little like her brother. For one thing, her eyes were green where his were red-black, and her fur was a ruddy auburn where his was a faded brown. For another, she grew the hair on her head long and bleached it blond in the Terran Revival fashion. She liked the look, though her brother thought it strange that she should try to emulate such a fickle species. He was just old-fashioned.

Many young Tagean females were going to the trouble. After all, the Terran Revival extended to more than just architecture, which he admired. Human customs had influenced Coalition society in a way no one could have predicted when that young race began spreading throughout the stars. From design to sports to fashion to food, the vibrant, diverse, and exciting cultures of Humanity had become pervasive. It wasn't all superfluous, either: Humanity's love of their solar calendar had influenced the adoption of the three-hundred-and-forty-day Tagean Solar Year as the galactic metric, superseding the wildly variable agrarian lunar calendars of most species. Most worlds kept their own calendars, as well, for local simplicity. Hakar may have complained about Traxus imitating Humans, but she knew for a fact that her older brother had considered taking the Tachai surname for professional purposes, though it was forbidden for males to carry the clan name in Tagean culture.

Seeing Rachel and Leon together again had ignited a hot little ember of bliss within her, even stronger than the pride she felt from a job well done. Braeburn's company would be partying through the night, and Traxus intended to join their revelries, but first she wanted to catch up with her friends.

Raptor and Jeric reentered the bar, faces mournful. Outside the sun was almost over the horizon, yellow fading to beaten copper and finally blood red. Already one of Eve's three Sisters was visible in the sky, beginning her leisurely ballet across the heavens.

"I can't believe she's back," grumbled Jeric, incredulous. He hopped up onto the seat next to Traxus and gestured for a beer. "That stupid bitch really did a number on him."

"He was upset," agreed Raptor, sounding unsure. His tail draped to the floor, curling against the base of the stool.

Traxus reached around Raptor—no easy feat—to slap Jeric. "How can you say that? He loves her. And she loves him, or I don't think she would have come back."

"Did you have something to do with this?" Jeric asked, eying her suspiciously. Traxus said nothing. "Have you forgotten what she did to him, how fucked up he got?" he railed, pounding the bartop angrily, to the irritation of many of the other patrons. "Look, having her back here is a bad idea. When it starts to interfere with his performance as an officer—"

"Do you ever shut up? Look, Jeric, I know that you're too small for a heart to fit in your chest. Maybe you don't believe in love."

At this Jeric looked insulted, but he held his tongue, sucking instead on his beer.

"Raptor, I have a suspicion that *you're* a hopeless romantic. You know Leon and Rachel have a real shot."

"How did you have the time to bring her back here while you were out on maneuvers?" Raptor growled curiously.

"Have you two ever heard of multitasking?"

"Yeah, but come on, Trax," Jeric said, exasperated. "You know Leon's idea of love is so damn romanticized that he can't possibly find what he's looking for."

"Can I finish?" she snapped. "That may be true, but the point is that he's not one of those guys that want to be bachelors forever. He just needs to be practical about it."

"Neither of them is exactly practical," Raptor put in. "Where do you fit?" he asked suddenly, with a gleam in his amber eyes. "Do you believe in love?"

Traxus tossed her head and gave them a vague smile. "Sure I do, but I'm way too young to start thinking about settling down with anyone, especially someone like Leon."

"Wait, what does Leon have to do with *this*?" asked Jeric, suddenly sitting up.

"Oh, please, most of the women on this base are half in love with him. But he's got too much baggage."

"Tell that to Rachel," the pilot blurted, turning his bottle on the table. "Between the two of them, they must run out of space to put it all."

Traxus laughed, then stroked her long muzzle patiently. "What, are you guys mad because he won't be out drinking with you until four in the morning? So what? Grow up and be happy for the man. Besides, it's nice to have a girl around who *can't* strip and reassemble a rifle in less than a minute."

Raptor snarled through his teeth. "So, do you have any idea why she left then?"

"That part is none of my business," replied Traxus severely. "Besides, I'm not sure she knows." She took another draught of beer. "It might be nice to have something else to worry about, with … Buzz gone."

"You had to bring that up," groused Jeric

"You want to try and forget about it?" Raptor snarled. "I was there, I saw Leon kneeling in his blood."

"I'm sorry, man," Jeric said, abashed. "It just doesn't feel real yet. I still remember when he first came here."

"He was such an asshole," Traxus said with a bitter laugh.

"He really was," Jeric agreed. "Remember all that jewelry he used to wear?"

"Oh, Goddess," Raptor growled. "How the hell were we ever going to sneak up on anyone with that? He sounded like a box of empty shell casings walking around." The three of them laughed for a moment, remembering happier times with a man who was now just that: a memory.

"So," Jeric ventured, "we've got to make our peace with Rachel, huh? I guess I'm just jealous, right?"

Traxus clicked her tongue yes. "Right. You haven't gotten laid since Alexis realized what an asshole you are, right?"

Jeric's response to that was mercifully lost in the roar as the second recon bomber tore off into the sky. Even from where they sat, the sky was noticeably brighter from the afterburn, and a billowing mountain of smoke rose behind the ship as it climbed through the first winking ranks of the night stars. The three watched through the open door before returning to their drinks.

When Traxus walked out, the smoke trail was a collapsing tower of puffy gray blocks arching across the sky until it faded into the dark upper atmosphere. All three Sisters were hanging in the sky now, white crescents that reminded her of Leon's lopsided smile. Maybe they would see more of that smile now. Warmed by the thought, she wandered off in search of trouble.

§

The two of them sat in excruciating silence, almost afraid to meet one another's gaze. The courtyard in front of the officers' quarters was quiet but for the rustling of the wind through the trees and the occasional snatches of laughter and shouts from Captain Braeburn's carousing troops. Ten endless inches lay between Rachel and Leon on the bench, ten inches of burning, unspoken questions.

"I guess we should talk about things," Leon finally said.

"We should, but we don't have to. I feel terrible about the way I left, Leon, but I just couldn't stand it any longer."

"You mean you couldn't stand me." It wasn't a question.

"No, Leon, that's not it." Rachel looked away, frustrated. "I spent the whole time telling myself not to come back. And you know what I realized?"

"Hm?" he grunted.

"There are always a thousand reasons not to take a risk. It's easy to run away. It was a lot harder to convince myself to do this. I started to write to you so many times. Give me a little credit for coming back."

Leon nodded to himself, rubbing his eyes. "You're right, and I *am* glad to have you back. You don't know how much it means to me. But *Jesus*, Rachel, you certainly have a flair for the dramatic. So where do we go from here?"

"I love you, Leon. I have almost from the beginning. I want this to work." Tentatively she reached out and took his hand. Her touch was electric against his skin, warm and soft. Their hands became a corridor for passion they still weren't comfortable enough to act upon.

"This is ridiculous," Leon said aloud. How could they be so clumsy with one another after being so close before, so close he had been ready to propose marriage?

"What's ridiculous about it?" Rachel asked, sounding hurt. She pulled her hand away.

"I feel like we're on probation. I don't want that. I'm not dumb enough to think we can just pretend the last few months never happened, but...." He looked at her imploringly, asking her to finish his thought.

"Do you trust me, Leon?" There was a strange note in Rachel's voice.

"Of course," he replied defensively.

"Okay. This may seem a little weird, but I want to try something with you. It's about trust."

Immediately Leon saw where she was going with this, and he cringed. She caught his reaction and smiled sheepishly. "I know, Leon. It sounds like bullshit to me, too." Suddenly she turned on the bench, facing him directly and staring into his eyes. "At this point, I'll try anything. You say you trust me. I want proof."

Leon leaned back to get a good look at her in the moonlight. She seemed different from the carefree, spoiled rich girl slumming it with the mercenaries; that much was obvious. So who was she? Maybe it was worth finding out. After all, what did he have to lose? "All right. I'm in. What have you got in mind?"

"We take turns asking questions, whenever we want. There's only one rule: we have to answer honestly. I ask one, you ask one, until there's nothing left to hide behind."

Leon nodded. "This could backfire, you know. Put us on our guard constantly."

"I know. What have we got to lose?" she asked, echoing his thoughts.

"I don't know," he admitted. "You, uh, want to start now?"

Rachel thought for a moment, worrying her lower lip. "No," she said, sliding up against him. "No, I just want to be with you right now." She was warm in the cool evening air, and Leon propped his chin on her head, drinking in the night.

§

Aboard the *Goliath*-class cruiser *Champion*, Vice-Grand Admiral Flora Rodriguex tapped her fingers against her cheek, staring out at the objective. Once the VSF fleet had withdrawn from the border, she had willingly pulled her forces back to the fringe of the Alkyran trade sector as originally planned. The fertile green planet of Iris floated before the vessel like an agrarian dream jewel, just out of reach and masked by clouds. The green plains and towering forests were fed by enormous river deltas that looked like varicose veins spreading across the planet's surface, and two ragged polar caps like gnarled hands possessively clutched the pristine world at either end. Rodriguex could easily make out the shores of a single large sea splashed across the planet's northern hemisphere like a bucket of blue paint. Tiny cities were spread unobtrusively about the landscape. A woman could lose herself in a view like that.

She could faintly make out her reflection in the porthole, a long, angular face superimposed on the planet, exaggerated by the curve of the reinforced crystal. Eyes only marginally lighter than the space beyond the hull stared back at her. Rodriguex was not unattractive and took care with her appearance, but she knew her no-nonsense attitude had intimidated a few suitors. It was a small price to pay for the honor of her command.

The Fifth Battle Fleet command flotilla had dropped out of conduit around Iris a few days earlier, big battleships and carriers pirouetting lazily. Soon a net of warships had been thrown across the system. There they drifted, armor-plated barracuda waiting for easy prey. But they weren't after easy prey.

Rumors of another Dragon Valia armada had surfaced, indicating that one of the Valinata's enormous war fleets was skulking along the other side of the Tears of Alkyra. Rodriguex hoped her people were ready.

Upon arrival she had been welcomed by the planetary council in their ceremonial togas, frozen smiles on their faces. She had been told that while Iris was mostly progressive, gender roles were still a little antiquated, and she had expected her presence to ruffle a few feathers. The councilors' anxiety seemed due to more than just the fact that she was a woman, however.

They had to wonder if they were in danger. Rodriguex had wanted to warn them to take the colonists and flee, but a trap needed bait, after all. "Just a routine precaution," she had lied through her teeth. They had accepted her claims that the situation with the Valinata was stabilizing, that the Fifth was simply developing maneuvers for gravitationally anomalous systems. They might not have believed a word of it, but they certainly appreciated the fleet's secondary function as an insurance policy. Lying didn't come easily to Rodriguex, but orders were orders.

The price of Iris's compliance was the Planetary Defense Force's inclusion in maneuvers. In fact, Rodriguex was happy to have them. She would tap their expertise in operating in a system that was lousy with major conduits. It might be good practice if action moved to Calama where the conflicting gravity lines would play havoc with mass and navigational instruments. The PDF pilots were not many, but they had clearly trained hard out here, and they seemed genuinely honored to be included. Unlike many planets along the Outbound Arc, Iris was firmly a Coalition world both in terms of legality and loyalty, and it made sense to use it as a staging area. It was also a tempting though unlikely target, owing to the conduits. They would be a logistical boon if captured, but their destabilizing effects on an attacking fleet would exact a heavy toll.

Rodriguex yawned unexpectedly. A little embarrassed, she belatedly covered her mouth. This was hardly a routine maneuver, but even this would grow monotonous without action. She could count on the Valinata to be unreasonable. She could count on her officers and their crews to perform admirably. She could count on the vacuum of space to suck the air out of their lungs in the event of a hull breach. Really, the only unknown variable in her equation was Jackal Pack. Grand Admiral Hakar had guaranteed their performance, but Rodriguex was more than a little skeptical.

They arrived right on time—early, in fact, sliding out of a conduit just outside the system and moving rapidly toward Iris. As ordered, they were broadcasting falsified transponder registries that marked them as commercial couriers. That wouldn't fool anyone up close or even a detailed sensor sweep, but it was better than trailing a banner that read "Coalition-sponsored Ronin." That private contractors had access to such deadly ships as the two guillotine-class fighter-bombers was exactly why Rodriguex couldn't trust them.

She went down to meet them in the docking bay, expecting slovenly roughnecks, and was pleasantly surprised to find them the picture of professionalism, standing at parade rest as they waited, too courteous to react to the glares they received from her crew. They snapped crisp salutes and relaxed only when the admiral ordered them to stand at ease.

The mission was a simple one in theory, and it should be simple to execute. Knowing what was at stake, however, Rodriguex had grave reservations. Situations had a way of changing in the field, and while she wished she could have sent her own recon flights into the Valinata, she recalled one of her mother's old sayings: if wishes were wings, then beggars would take flight. Well, the Jackals could fly, and Rodriguex had no choice in the matter. The mission was to be done discreetly, and she supposed that the Jackals, if discovered, could be disavowed without too much difficulty. Denying ownership of CRN vessels with the Coalition double-prong and falcon emblazoned on their hulls would have been a little more difficult.

Rodriguex knew of Raven Blue, but she confessed to being skeptical about the existence of those mysterious, ghostly ships. The fighters would put the rumors to rest, she hoped. Moving from system to system through Valinata space, they were to passively collect comm data and, more importantly, catalogue ships in an effort to determine who, if anyone, controlled the territory. They were not to engage VSF ships directly, but their weapons would hopefully create enough noise and light for them to exfiltrate in the event of discovery.

If they could slip inside the quarantine envelope and look around, it would be an unexpected windfall, but Rodriguex didn't realistically expect them to get the opportunity. Potentially putting Coalition policy in the hands of mercenaries didn't sit well with her. *Pray they're as reliable as they claim, and pray that they aren't out to start a war to drum up business and drive up prices.*

With the fighters equipped with new sensor equipment and outbound, Rodriguex returned to the bridge. She stood before the panoramic window with her hands clasped, restlessly tweaking the academy ring on her right ring finger, watching the steady burn of the recon jets' thrusters fade into the starfield before they winked out altogether.

She wanted to be closer, *needed* to be closer. "Prepare the fleet for redeployment to the border," she said firmly. "Talriis System."

§

Hakar looked at his watch again. Its blank face still didn't contain any answers, and when he thought about it, "face" was a foolish term for a dial that was so inexpressive. The Jackal Pack mission was out of his hands, but he couldn't help obsessing over it, mapping out contingencies.

He should have been worrying about his wife, Byeri, and his son who were vacationing in the Commonwealth. As was tradition, the child spent the first sixteen years of life under the tutelage of the mother until coming of age to be named. Until then, the child was simply known as *ja-*, child of the parent of the same gender. Hakar was ashamed that he wasn't there to assist in the teaching of the child that bore his name, but his short talks with *ja*-Hakar were the highlights of his dreary days.

Byeri had decided that *ja*-Hakar was ready to see the galaxy. Hakar wasn't one to argue with his mate, but upon reflection, she couldn't have chosen a worse time.

"Hakar, are you paying attention to anything I'm saying?" Telec asked wearily, waving a folder at his colleague. Hakar snapped back to the task at hand.

"I'm sorry. I must have drifted off."

"You look exhausted."

"I feel dead." Nevertheless, Hakar picked up another page and skimmed it. Reports had been coming in from the border fleets with precise regularity, but none of them had shed any light on the situation. Leaving most of her fleet at Iris, Rodriguex had returned to a system bordering the

Calama sector, and the buildup around Calama continued, leaving most of the Outbound Arc thinly protected. Suddenly, though, few people seemed to think the Valinata were bluffing.

Communication through official channels had ceased. Repeated hails from the Coalition had gone unanswered. No threats, no demands, no accusations, and no information. Triathan comscan had dried up. It seemed as though all the Valinata systems had switched over to that mysterious droning encryption system, which was still distressingly a source of confusion for CRDF decryptors. Inquiries to the remaining Valinata consulates, diplomats, and high-ranking defectors that had been picked up over the years had produced no more information. Oddly many of them seemed reluctant to return to their home empire.

Hakar frowned, his furry brows shadowing his eyes. Involuntarily his lips pulled back over his teeth in an uncharacteristically feral expression. "It's not like them to keep silent when they could be provoking us," he said acidly.

Telec burbled a nervous, cathartic laugh. "I'm sure they're just waiting for us to wander across the border to investigate. Could they have caught your mercenaries?"

Hakar flicked his ears quickly and even shook his head to allay that particular fear. "If they had, we'd be hearing about it. In fact, we'd never hear the end of it. I don't think there's anyone home."

"It's more than just a civil war, isn't it?" Telec asked, watching his colleague carefully.

"This Raven Blue means something, I'm just not sure what. Those ships aren't like anything the Valinata have ever fielded."

Telec made a peculiar sucking sound of exasperation. "One sample and some grainy footage aren't much to go on."

"Exactly. Something doesn't add up."

Telec's tentacles splayed as he laughed. "Something did?"

§

Leon looked up from his desk and saw Rachel perched on the edge of it, reading a newsMem. Without realizing it he patted her leg affectionately, running his fingers along the smooth skin just above her knee. She looked down at him, and he jerked his hand away. "Sorry," he said.

Rachel's expression was hard to read but seemed to be composed of equal parts amusement and irritation. "It's okay, Leon. If I didn't want you to touch me, it would have been easier to stay on another planet."

"I guess it would have been." Granted, her coming back hadn't exactly made things easier. He was ecstatic to have her back, it was true, but things with Jeric had suddenly gotten rockier, as though the pilot didn't want Rachel to be there. To make things worse, Leon found it harder to focus on his work because he wanted to spend all his time with her, reigniting whatever spark had cooled between them.

Trying to concentrate, he flipped through another few applications, signing one here, tossing out another there. Almost everything was done via computer but for sensitive materials there was no substitute for hardcopy. Because a number of Jackal Pack's potential clients were requesting services that were somewhat south of legal, it was best to keep some of the information off the networks. If he had known how much paperwork was involved in being an officer, he might have reconsidered leaving university.

Without warning, Rachel rolled up the newsMem and shoved it in her purse. "Okay," she said, sliding off the desk and crouching beside him. She took hold of the armrests of Leon's chair and turned him to face her. Her face was serious. "Round one. You ready?"

Absurdly Leon felt ready to panic. Who knew what she would ask? He nodded.

"Here comes a slow pitch. The first time you said you loved me, did you mean it?"

"That's your idea of a slow pitch?" Leon asked. In fact, the answer was easy for him. "Yes, I meant it. Honestly, I hadn't planned to say it at all." They had been playing basketball on one of the base's cracked clay courts, and Rachel, a former college player, had beaten Leon handily. She had jokingly accused him of letting her win to which he had responded by trying to make a half-court basket. Like lightning she had jumped to intercept it, batted it aside easily, and stuck her tongue out at him. All he could do was say, "God, I love you."

"Yeah, I meant it," he repeated wistfully.

"I'm glad to hear it," she said, unsurprised but pleased, nonetheless. "Now you."

Why did you leave? Leon almost blurted out, but he knew the unspoken rules. The test lay not only in the answers but in the questions, as well. If he asked something so sensitive, it would show a complete lack of trust. It was why he felt safe that Rachel wouldn't ask him about Daltar or what he had done there. At the same time, he had to take it seriously. Obvious questions would lose him just as much ground. "When's the last time you spoke to your father?" Seeing her expression freeze, Leon felt the need to soften the blow. "It's just … if I still had a father, I'd talk to him all the time no matter what he did." In fact, Leon had very carefully avoided asking what Rachel's father had done to earn himself an estrangement that made Leon's own exile look positively forgiving.

Rachel rallied herself. "Good shot," she said huffily. "Maybe four years ago he contacted me. I believe my exact words were, 'Go to hell and stay there.'" The smile that touched her mouth was anything but happy. Then she called on some reserve of inner brightness. "Call it a day?"

"Okay," Leon said. Rockmore wouldn't mind if he took off early. He hit his comm, dialing over to Jackal Pack's full-time administrator and his chief of staff. "Heidi? I'm leaving for the day. Any comms here can be forwarded to me. And I left some interdiction sanctions on my desk, but I'll get to them tomorrow."

"Roger that, Colonel. Say hi to Rachel," came the effervescent reply.

Leon shut everything down, grabbed his uniform jacket and cap, and offered his arm to Rachel. She took it, and they left the office for the open air.

It was a hot day, dry and dusty, but a steady breeze blew through the compound, staving off the sense of lethargy that seemed to settle in when the air was still. It was stretching on into mid-afternoon, and half the troops and staff were finishing up lunch or loafing about the yard. An impromptu fútbol match had begun over by the barracks, officers and enlisted shedding their uniform jackets and kicking a ball around to let off steam. Raucous laughter roared out of the door of the Desher Vaux.

Leon turned his head, cracking his neck, and looked back up at the edifice of the administration building. The muscles in his back were tight from a morning hunched over his desk, but at least his injuries had healed, all but a deep cut under his right cheekbone about a half-inch long that would likely leave a scar. Rachel had mercifully not commented on his injuries or asked how Leon had come by them, though she had to be curious. "I can't believe the nerve of some of these prospective clients," he muttered, forgetting for a moment how much Rachel hated to talk about his work. "They seem to think we'll do anything for the right price."

"Won't you?" she asked, her voice innocent but her gaze pointed. Leon knew she was baiting him.

He had to check his sarcastic laugh. "Come on, Rachel. We have codes of conduct, regulations, standards." He shook his head in consternation. "We're not murderers for hire."

Rachel looked up at him, her eyes filled with contempt. "Really? You kill people all the time. I saw that sanction for a hit squad. What's one more politician?"

It's going to take more than some question-and-answer game to put us back together. It was trouble, but Leon couldn't help being defensive. "We knock off a government official who isn't *already* on his way to a war crimes tribunal, and we win ourselves a free remodeling, courtesy of a federal bombardment. We carefully screen all clients and all targets before signing a contract. I couldn't approve anything like that anyway. It would have to be the general, and somehow I doubt that he would want Jackal Pack to become associated with petty crime and murder."

"And the difference between that and your usual milieu is what exactly?" Rachel looked faintly disgusted, the expression she might wear had she bitten into an apple and found a worm. "You just explained why you wouldn't kill this guy, not why killing everyone else is okay. I mean, the man on Amalthia, when we met, what did he even *do*? Did it matter? What about the people you killed on Korinthe? Did they deserve to die?"

Leon stopped walking. "No less than Buzz," he said as the gunfight replayed itself in his mind's eye. He saw Buzz's face, blood trickling from his nostrils and the corners of his mouth as his lungs filled with it. After a moment, Buzz became Keegan, that expression of disbelief frozen on his face as Leon filled him with bullets. He shook himself back to reality, looked into her expectant eyes, and suppressed an urge to storm off. "Rachel, it's complicated."

"I'm not stupid. Explain it to me."

Leon didn't want to argue, but it seemed unavoidable. He had gone through the same arguments with his sisters, who saw a major difference between service in the CRDF and service in Jackal Pack, whatever Rockmore's lofty aspirations. "What do you want me to say? Sometimes force has to be met with force. I don't like it any more than you do. At least, we have limits. Most of the people we fight don't." He knew that this did not necessarily help his case. "Jackal Pack has done *good* work."

"Leon, I'm not disputing that. I know you think of yourselves as knights-errant, and sometimes you *do* help people like hostages or politicians trying to make a difference in bad places. But your work almost invariably creates more victims, like killing one drug dealer so another can take his territory. I know you personally ordered Asar to shoot a man in the back from over a kilometer away. Don't give me the marketing line, Leon; I'm too close to you for that."

"I don't get it then," he confessed, unable to see his way around her reasoning. "Why come back if you hate this so much?"

"Because I love you more. I followed you because of the excitement, Leon, because of the danger. And to give a big 'fuck you' to my family. I admit that, okay? But that's not why I'm here now. I fell in love with *you*, not Leon Victor the sojier, not the officer, not the *killer*. I fell in love with you because you take me to dinner for no reason at all and stay up all night talking when you know you have to get up early the next morning. I just … can't take it when you stand there and try to justify what you know is wrong."

"Someone has to do it, right? If not me, someone less wonderful might take the job," he said, flashing a grin which was only skin deep. It was childish, he knew, but he was annoyed to find himself in doubt. A trained sojier who had always believed in honor and valor, the virtues of the Coalition Rienda, he had never really doubted Rockmore, never wondered if all the talk of codes of honor was just a gaudy lacquer over what was still essentially a collection of amoral, violent men and women. "It's complicated," he said again, half-heartedly.

Rachel smiled indulgently, a little patronizingly. But was there also understanding? "I know it is. Just think about it the next time you pull the trigger."

"There's not usually enough time, but I'll try," Leon said weakly.

Rachel had tried to be sympathetic concerning Buzz's death in the days since her return, but she wasn't about to give up an opportunity to drive her point home. "I gave up a lot to come back here, Leon, you have to realize that. I won't lose you, too."

What could he say to that? He nodded and took her hand, giving it an affectionate squeeze that conveyed what he was too tongue-tied to say.

The ambush happened quickly. Before Leon knew it, he found his neck in a vise-grip as a thickly muscled arm wrapped around him. A strong, clawed hand reached around and pinched his stomach, which had admittedly lost some of its tone over the years. "How's my little walking steak doing? Plump enough to eat yet?" Raptor growled, pressing Leon into a crouch.

Standing quickly, Leon smashed Raptor in the chin with the crown of his head, and the Prross bellowed and jumped free. Leon knew that in a real fight he would have been pinned and likely dead in under a minute. One of Leon's medals had fallen into the dirt; he knelt to pick it up, then stood to regard Raptor, whose tail was flicking back and forth angrily. "Can I help you?"

"Just wanted to say hi," Raptor said with a sneer, presenting two rows of razor-sharp teeth. Crude though the gesture was, Leon understood it as a show of support from his friend. It meant almost as much as knowing that Raptor would follow him into the line of fire. Perhaps the Prross was trying to save him from what was obviously an awkward conversation.

Troops sick of sun and drilling had gathered, perhaps hoping for an actual brawl, and they dispersed, disappointed. Rachel, who had moved off to stand by herself, managed to look neither amused nor critical. While she had always considered their schoolyard scuffles somewhat prehistoric, she supposed it was a catharsis they needed for their grief and their friendship. At least, this time they hadn't used weapons or various appliances to club each other senseless.

"Traxus and I thought we might treat you two to dinner in Tesa," Raptor said. He pointed to the vehicle park. "Jeric's waiting in the car."

"Jeric's coming?" Leon asked, surprised. It wasn't exactly a secret that he was still less than thrilled about Rachel.

"I offered to pay for him." That made more sense.

§

The citizens of Tesa were used to the sight of uniformed Jackal Pack officers marching about the streets since Rockmore kept a small garrison in the city to supplement the local shields. The city made a point of tolerating the mercenaries, offering discounts in various stores as well as free parking. After all, the Pack did almost as much for the planetary economy as the subterranean cultural district of Las Serras da Estrela, paying huge sums in taxes every year as well as sponsoring various public works. Rockmore was a born marketer as well as a career sojier.

As a rule, the Jackals stayed sober and well behaved when in uniform. No one expected the mercs to be model citizens all the time, but they tried to keep the debauchery to a minimum. On weekends and nights when big sporting events were on, shouting and out-of-tune singing could be heard wherever there were bars, but Rockmore had strict policies about his sojieri's behavior around civilians. Felonies carried mandatory termination of contract, but drunken fistfights were not uncommon between Pack troops and sojieri stationed at the Coalition garrison. The CRDF outpost was a nowhere posting, and consequently no one there seemed to have a sense of humor.

Tesa was hardly a rough-and-tumble city, but as home to exiles from various territories, most of whom hailed from the Coalition and Valinata, tensions tended to run high. Serious crime was rarely a problem, but the shields were practiced in quelling riots, brawls, and other disturbances.

That afternoon the city was quieter than usual, and the Jackals seemed subdued. Traffic moved sedately down well-laid-out avenues, and shop doors stood open. The previous night had concluded the Alkyran League Rugby Finals, and half the town still seemed hung over. Eve had lost to Benez, de facto capital of the trade sector, but the game had been close. Leon guessed that news of the fleet at Iris and the breakdown of relations along the Valinata border were on everyone's mind. Things were happening behind the Emerald Veil, and it was now impossible to ignore the lack of Valinata traffic at the spaceport.

There was a squad on the march in full kit, moving down the shadowed boulevard between towering gray edifices. Kids just out of school were following them, probably to see if the sojieri of fortune had any fortune to share.

The Pack's visibility and active stance in the community had very little to do with altruism, unfortunately. Rockmore had long realized the mercenary legion's tenuous position on Eve: they were dependent on the hospitality of local politicians who, if it suited them, would chase the Jackals off the planet at a moment's notice. Becoming a load-bearing pillar of the community made them harder to extirpate. And they allowed the planetary government to bounce checks.

Rachel and her escort of four mercenaries turned off the main boulevard, Avenida de Alkyra, down a quiet side street, and passed through an unadorned doorway. The restaurant they entered was one of Tesa's best-kept secrets, catering to the culinarily adventurous. While the patrons were dressed conservatively, few of them seemed perturbed by the sight of the Jackal Pack uniforms or the holstered pistols gleaming in the light thrown by frosted-glass wall sconces. The maître d' was likewise unfazed, and he walked crisply over and told them to make themselves comfortable while he searched for a table.

Rachel looked around the entrance to the establishment with surprise. She had been expecting to find herself in a tavern only marginally better than the one on the base or, in the best-case scenario, a pizza parlor. She felt a little guilty for assuming that Traxus and Raptor had no taste, but she could hardly be blamed for such a mistake. How had she never been here before? On Amalthia, she prided herself on knowing all the best places to eat and drink. Several old and gnarled trees grew up through the floor of the hexagonal foyer in which they waited, giving visitors the illusion of being in a secluded grove. Five benches were arrayed around a fountain made of irregular, moss-covered rock, and the group sat down to wait. There was something very soothing about the gurgling of the fountain and the smell of healthy topsoil feeding the trees.

"This is a nice place," she said, rubbing a jasmine petal between her fingers and breathing in the fragrance. She put her fingers beneath Leon's nose when he wasn't looking and he jerked, startled. Then he sniffed and smiled. "What's it called?" she asked.

"It's called 'Mareghel.' It means 'gamble' in Sheff'an Kres. The chef who started the place is Sheff'an. I keep trying to get the general to hire her away." Leon looked up as the maître d' walked by but didn't stop. "They'll prepare a meal for just about any diet, cooked to order. It's the only place I know of where you can actually order H'vir food and have it done with any skill."

Rachel's face was blank. "Who are the H'vir?"

Leon twitched a thumb back at Raptor. "H'vir are about a meter taller than our buddy there. They look like big bugs, usually red or yellow. You know what a praying mantis is? On Terra?" Rachel shook her head. "Long body, big foreclaws. H'vir look pretty menacing, but they're sweeties." Leon wasn't surprised she didn't know of the H'vir. It was a big galaxy, and there were a lot of races wandering through it. Many, like the H'vir, kept to themselves. He shrugged. "They're generally not that inclined to eat in public, but they can here."

"It's too bad. You can smell that shit from two tables away," Jeric piped up, practically his first words since they had left the Luxor Plateau.

Traxus hit him. "Don't be crude. There's a H'vir lady in Serras da Estrela. I think she's a town councilor or a judge or something. Don't listen to these guys, though. Anything you order here is guaranteed to be one of the best meals you'll ever eat."

"If you survive it," Jeric added.

Rachel smiled. She was no stranger to exotic cuisine: her estranged father had long ago instilled in her a natural curiosity and a broad palate, though she had been lucky enough not to inherit his sensitive stomach. Among other things.

While they waited, she decided to ask a question that had irked her for some time. "So, Eve is neutral, right? How come there's a Coalition base here? I mean, doesn't that violate the neutrality?" The Coalition and the Commonwealth, her home, were allies, but she had still grown up seeing the CRDF as a power-hungry war machine that dominated worlds wherever it went, welcome or not.

Traxus clicked her tongue. "I said the same thing when I came here. It's kind of a long story, but basically Eve used to be a Coalition world. And since we're at kind of a crucial point along the Tears of Alkyra, defense has always been an issue. A long time ago, before the borders were defined, Eve was one of the gateways to the Coalition, so it made sense to fortify it. Now the base is gradually downsizing. In a few years, it might not be here at all. But the Coalition pays to keep them here, puts a lot toward infrastructure, so the local government doesn't complain too loudly. Hell, we could use the company."

The restaurant itself was quite small, Rachel saw, when the maître d' came to fetch them, and the naturalistic décor continued inside, with trees overhanging the delicate stone tables in a verdant canopy. There were even leaves on the floor, and Rachel found the atmosphere quite charming. A quartet played chamber music in one corner to holographic accompaniment, and swirls of projected color danced among the branches.

They were led to a booth, and Raptor took a moment to get comfortable, wriggling to adjust his long muscular tail. "I'm starved. Let's take a hostage to get some food." He pointed. "That guy looks rich."

For a moment Rachel froze, horrified, then she realized it was a joke and laughed, nervously but genuinely. Raptor looked pleased. The sommelier brought a bottle of wine, which the Prross sampled and approved, and they all toasted Rachel's return.

10: Sins of Omission

Hakar was worried, that much Rockmore could tell just from the Tagean's nervous motions: the adjusting of his jacket, the way his tongue kept running along his teeth, the flicking of his ears. The general, for his part, hid his own misgivings. He sat behind his desk, regarding the image of the grand admiral intently, but he could taste the sour fury roiling inside him.

"I'm sorry, General," Hakar was saying with uncharacteristic aloofness. "You're not cleared for the details of the mission."

Rockmore clasped his hands on his desk. "You're really telling me I can't find out what my own crews are doing?"

Hakar appeared remorseful but only for a moment. "Perhaps it's best that you don't ask. It's the cost of business, General. Look, as soon as I hear something from them that I can declassify to you, I will."

Frustrated, Rockmore ran his hands through his hair, feeling old scars beneath the carefully maintained buzz cut. "I don't think that's good enough for me right now. Those ships weren't spying on the Valinata, were they? If they had been and they *were* captured, we would have heard from the VSF by now, likely via the sharp end of the stick. Funny, that, we actually haven't heard anything from the Valinata for some time now." He watched Hakar for a reaction, knew it would be delayed in coming. "No contract offers, no inquiries. Hell, our news network feed cut out a week ago. I wonder why that is." His tone was clear: it wasn't simple curiosity. He wanted answers.

Hakar evidently wished he could give him some, but he didn't. "General, you understand what 'classified' means as well as I do. This isn't the first time the Valinata have instituted a comm blackout." That was a weak excuse, and they both knew it. The image flickered and cut out, returning a moment later. *Damned long-range transmissions.* "Old friend, I'm sorry about this. You'll have to go on faith here."

"You always call me 'old friend' when you're keeping me at arm's length. If you were anyone else, Hakar, I'd tell you to go fuck yourself. But I suppose you've earned a little credit with me. One condition, though." Rockmore leaned back and crossed his arms: this was nonnegotiable. "You put my people in a situation, you had better make sure we have the intel and the tools to get through it. Am I clear?" He waited for Hakar to click his tongue yes and was relieved when the grand admiral did so. "Hakar, throw me a lifeline here. The Fifth Battle Fleet is out there, parked right next to Iris. That's damn close to us. And the Valinata are damn close to us, too. I want to know one thing." He looked directly at the hologram, his eyes meeting Hakar's through light-eons of space. "Is Eve in the line of fire right now?" Rockmore didn't have to remind the admiral that his little sister was on the planet in question.

The Tagean grand admiral adjusted his jacket and ran his tongue along his teeth again. His ears flattened. For a Tagean, that was the nervous gesture of all nervous gestures. "I wish I knew, Jon."

§

Aboard the *Champion,* Admiral Rodriguex was drumming an elaborate beat on the armrest of her command chair. For a line officer, waiting was the hardest part of any action, and being responsible for so many lives made it harder. There were only so many plans she could draw up, so many contingencies she could predict, before she found herself going in circles. After seeing things resolved at Iris, her command flotilla had rotated back to the border, as close as she dared and in defiance of orders. She couldn't simply leave the VSF unobserved, and now they faced a new fleet, larger and more heavily armed than the last.

The mercenaries had gone deep and would send no more reports until they exited Valinata territory. *Champion*'s communication systems and sensors were top of the line, but so far they had had no luck penetrating the Valinata's communications blackout. Who knew what they were planning in there? If there had been a civil war, it scarcely seemed possible they could keep it a secret. And yet they could have been burning whole worlds, and no one would know it. Could she live with herself, knowing millions had died while she stood by?

Rodriguex licked her lips, but her tongue was almost as dry as they were. The one thing she had never liked about space travel—and she generally loved it—was the dryness of the air, which chapped her skin and left her dehydrated.

There was another possibility, she had to admit. It seemed unlikely, but in a time of strife, who knew? She couldn't ask anyone. What if the VSF was preparing for an all-out assault, total war against the Coalition? It was conceivable that if they hit hard all along the border, they could overwhelm the meager planetary defense networks and drive deep into the interior. Under such a veil of secrecy, it was possible that the Valinata would have cut off all communication to avoid tipping their hand. And the Valinata frequencies were silent, comm satellites blinking silently to themselves.

But why would the Valinata attack the Coalition alone? The Valinata Tête was many things: arrogant, belligerent, bigoted ... but stupid? The Coalition Royal Defense Forces were the largest, most powerful military in the galaxy, fielding half again as much as the Commonwealth or the Shar'dan Confederacy and twice as much materiel as the VSF, at least. Whatever they stood to gain from an attack, the Valinata would almost certainly lose it and more if they attempted to sweep the CRDF from the sector.

Rodriguex forced herself to stop chasing trouble, instead looking out the bridge windows. Far away, Valinata ships were watching them, six big battleships and a dreadnought. Space on the border was dark, speckled with distant, cold stars, exactly as it had been before Humanity or any other race had taken to the stars, exactly as it would be when they were gone. The void didn't care who claimed what part of it. It was empty, murderous nature that looked for ways into their puny little ships, to suck them out, sap their heat, and swallow their screams. What arrogance, to think they could own any of it.

"You seem on edge, Admiral," Prime Minister Somerset observed softly. He wore his sash of office diagonally across the breast of his richly tailored suit, proudly displaying the Coalition Rienda and the falcon perched upon an eleven-pointed star. He looked more than a little out of place on the warship's bridge.

"That I am, Prime Minister," Rodriguex replied. No small part of her anxiety was due to being assigned to safeguard one of the Coalition's most important leaders. It was both an honor and a chore to have him and his retinue aboard.

"Is there anything I can do?" the senior parliamentarian asked.

Rodriguex looked at him carefully. He looked honest, and he looked sincere. He also looked faintly afraid. "I don't know that there's anything either of us can do, sir." How to tell him that the Fifth would likely be decimated if the VSF attacked in force? "You should make yourself comfortable."

"And take the seat that is rightfully yours? I'm sure your crew would love that." Somerset chuckled. "Admiral, I appreciate your position. I hope you don't think I'm here because of a lack of trust."

"I'd much rather make use of your talents than those of my crews, Prime Minister. I'm just not thrilled to have you so close to danger."

"I'm not exactly thrilled myself. In fact, I'm downright terrified. But I trust you, Admiral, or I wouldn't be standing on the bridge of the most prominent target in your battle fleet. I've known Admiral Winters for some time, and he speaks very highly of you."

That vote of confidence meant a lot to Rodriguex, and she smiled thinly. At first, she had regarded the reposting to the Arc almost as an insult until the extent of the dispute became clear. They had essentially made her theater commander of CRDF forces along this sweep of border at the edge of creation.

The comm officer snapped upright. "Intercepting a priority hail from the Valinata interior."

"Try to triangulate and decrypt," Rodriguex ordered, sickly grateful to be rescued from her ruminations. "Everyone keep an eye on those VSF ships. Helm, prepare to take evasive action."

"Movement!" shouted another officer. "VSF ships coming about."

Rodriguex braced herself. "Prime Minister, you should go below."

"I'm staying, with your permission, Admiral."

"Very well. There's an observer's seat in the alcove behind my station. Can you strap in on your own?"

"I think so." Somerset went aft as Rodriguex took her seat and strapped herself in.

"Tracking, report!" Not waiting for information, Rodriguex brought up her own tactical monitor, using the console built into her command chair. From there she could access the data seen by all her officers.

"VSF formation still banking … presenting broadside, Admiral."

Rodriguex glanced at her screen to make sure all ships had their defensive grids on and fully powered. Then something strange happened. The VSF ships continued turning away, no longer aiming the bulk of their weapons at the CRDF vessels. What was this?

The first flash signaling a ship's entry into a conduit surprised Rodriguex. The second, and she knew what was happening. "They're retreating! Comms, get me a fix on that signal!"

"It appears to be coming out of the Vendran Sector, deep in Valinata space, Admiral. I'm getting a lot of interference, I'll try and scrub."

"Any luck with the content?" Rodriguex wanted to know what they were saying, but if it was that new encryption, it was easier said than done.

"Should have it in a few minutes, ma'am." That would have to do. As predicted, it wasn't long before Rodriguex was looking at a partial transcript. Even with the gaps, the message was clear. Someone was apparently attacking a Valinata foundry world, and the death toll was rising. The planet had requested immediate VSF intervention to repel the aggressor and evacuate civilians. The admiral sank back in her seat, deflated. It was the first confirmation of a civil war she had seen, and it was as bad as it could have been. Wholesale slaughter of civilians.... Who were these barbarians?

Somerset was at her elbow. "Admiral, I'm exercising my authority as senior diplomat to enter Valinata space."

"I can't let you do that, Prime Minister. It's far too dangerous, and I can't risk sending military vessels in without orders."

"I wasn't asking for an escort, Admiral. I have to go. Lives are at stake, and I can't wait for authorization from Her Majesty."

Rodriguex looked into Somerset's eyes. He was deadly serious, and she could tell there was no use arguing with him, not on this. As brave as any sojier, this politician was volunteering to risk not his reputation or his approval ratings but his very life, to help strangers. Not just strangers but enemies.

Less than an hour later as *Royal Dawn* crossed the now-undefended border and leapt into a conduit, Rodriguex felt the first treacherous tendrils of doubt snaking through her, and she knew she would not see Somerset again.

§

I earned everything I ever got, thought Joseph Winters as he stormed the defense ministry, having just arrived from Terra. He didn't like being called to Tagea unless it was important, but he absolutely hated not being called when things were this serious. And so he had come on his own. Once in his old office he started the Kaf brewing, and sat down to read the latest reports from Rodriguex.

He sat in a chair that had been given to him for his fiftieth anniversary with the Coalition Royal Navy. Had it really been that long?

Not long ago, reaching eighty years old was about as much as most Humans could have hoped for. Medical advances had extended that lifespan well beyond a century for many. Fifty years of service, more than twenty as a grand admiral. Winters had earned his crowned bars one by one; he had earned every medal on his chest; he had earned his fleets, and the office in which he sat. *I earned the right to be informed, Goddammit. They're not going over my head any more.*

The grand admiral sat back and massaged his temples. *Something's very wrong.* This refrain had repeated endlessly in his head for quite some time, a steady backbeat to his thoughts. Hakar and Telec claimed that the Valinata had initiated some sort of major consolidation, pulling back to protect their core systems. The Coalition had a similar contingency plan, called the Kyriakos Directive, if all else failed in the event of invasion. Somehow, though, Winters suspected that the situation in the Valinata was even worse than that. Even the CRDF's clandestine contacts had fallen silent.

Winters needed to speak to Hakar. He and the grizzled Tagean had been through much over the years, and while they had not always been on the same page, there was a frankness to their relationship that was refreshing. He didn't believe the Tagean admiral would ever bow to Telec's ruthless pragmatism. *Unless he's changed more than I thought.*

The clock on the wall read 0330 hours. Winters had been awake far too long to be of any use. Regardless, he got up, poured himself a cup of Kaf. He grimaced as the scalding, bitter liquid washed over his tongue and down his throat. Being a member of the Chamber had never been a nine-to-five sort of job; lately he had taken to working through the night and catching a few hours of sleep between briefings. If only he could be aboard a battleship steaming toward battle, not sifting through spreadsheets and reports. Honestly Winters had felt more like a clerk than a flag officer since his elevation to the Star Chamber.

He poured another cup and buttoned his uniform jacket. Steaming mug in hand, he strolled tiredly down the corridor past darkened offices until he came to Hakar's door. He knocked and entered. He wasn't surprised to find the Tagean admiral at work despite the late hour.

Hakar was perched on his desk, talking to an intelligence officer who held a dossier as though it was the most important thing in the world, his fingers dimpling the folder's surface. As Winters stepped in, the man's eyes slid up to him, and he pulled the folder out of view. He nodded curtly to both admirals and left.

After the door had closed, Winters turned to the man whom he had once called a friend. "What was that all about? You having a slumber party?"

The Tagean flicked his ears, looked away. "A ... slumber party?" The meaning of the English word escaped Hakar for a moment.

Winters couldn't help laughing. "Sorry, but I love it when Tageans try to speak English. So what are you doing?"

"Just getting the latest bad news," Hakar said, unamused. "Welcome back. How are things on Terra?"

Winters snorted. Of all the sentient species, Humanity had let their homeworld fall farthest into disrepair. It was going to be a long road back from the brink. "Things are progressing," he ventured. "Hakar, I came here to talk to you about this situation on the border. Did you know Prime Minister Somerset left Rodriguex's protection and took his retinue through the Emerald Veil?"

"It threw us for a loop, as well, but that was at his discretion. Rodriguex did the right thing letting him go—just about the only thing she's done right so far. Maybe there's something he can do. He's had success with similar situations in the past."

"I didn't come here to talk about the Prime Minister, though. I'm concerned that you're leaving Rodriguex out there without anyone to cover her flank. She's working with what she's got, and it's not much. I understand that Calama is important, but I think you've put all your eggs in one basket. More importantly, one of those eggs is mine."

"Joe, the Fifth is all we've got right now. It takes time to move resources, lines of supply...."

"I am aware of that. But the Fifth is a meat and potatoes fleet. Take someone else's ships. How about Admiral Telec's? Or perhaps your own? The Fifth is too much firepower for a small problem and too little for a big one. So which is it? It's no match for a Dragon Valia armada, and if one of those enters the fray, we're going to have hundreds of thousands of casualties ... and we'll be no closer to having Calama."

Middle of the night or not, Hakar seemed wide awake and ready for anything. "We're looking into our options," he said cryptically.

Iris isn't the bait, the Fifth Fleet is, Winters realized with a cold chill. He wanted to warn Rodriguex but knew that it was suddenly beyond his mandate. "Hakar, what the hell is going on in there? The Valinata's falling apart, isn't it?"

Hakar slid into his chair and began typing. Winters took the hint. "All right, Hakar, good night." He turned to leave.

"Hang on, Joe. I'm just crunching some numbers. I told you I was looking into options." Hakar waved to an empty chair. "Please, stay. I'm expecting a report, and I think you may want to see it."

"I have a feeling I'm not going to like this. What is it?"

Hakar sighed sadly. "Black box data from a mercenary recon jet."

For a moment Winters didn't make the connection. "Mercenary?... Oh, your Ronin contractors. I've heard the scuttlebutt about their mission. So they're dead. So much for that."

Hakar's expression darkened, but he held his tongue. Facts clicked into place, and Winters mentally kicked himself. "You're still hung up on that colonel, aren't you? If Her Majesty knew you were reaching your hand into the royal cookie jar and outsourcing sensitive operations to mercs based on old friendships or some misguided sense of guilt...." Winters shrugged meaningfully.

Hakar clicked his tongue thoughtfully. "It was that or reconnoiter ourselves."

Winters's smile looked more like a grimace. "I know you, Hakar, and when you reconnoiter, you send in a full expeditionary force." He sat back and tweaked his ring finger where a wedding band had once sat. A seat on the Chamber usually superseded meaningful relationships. Only Hakar and a few others had managed to preserve marriages, and even those were rocky. "Look, I know you still have contact with that colonel. What was his name? Victor?"

"That's right. You know it was our fault, what happened to him," Hakar said, a defensive edge to his voice. "He was a good officer and loyal."

"He had potential. But it was you or him, and he wasn't a grand admiral."

"He could have made a great one," Hakar said, face drawn.

It was an old argument and one Winters was not keen to revisit. "Rodriguex will make a good one, too. A better one, I'd wager, based on her ability to avoid total fucking disaster."

"How's your Kaf?" Hakar asked, taking a stab at chit chat. Winters could tell the Tagean was annoyed, but so was he.

"Hot, tastes like battery acid. You'd think they could get a better blend for the goddamn ministry of defense."

"Try this," Hakar said, reaching into a drawer and withdrawing a small pouch. "My XO, Shra, sent it."

Curious, Winters opened the pouch and sniffed. It stung his eyes immediately. It was an odd choice for a peace offering. "What the hell is this?"

"Some Tagean colonial spice mix. It'll certainly wake you up."

Winters stirred some into his Kaf, looking wary. He took a sip and was pleasantly surprised. It was as hot as he guessed it would be, searing his tongue and sparking off every taste bud. But it also had a remarkably subtle flavor that was both sweet and savory, the taste ebbing and flowing on his palate. "Not bad. Are my lips supposed to go numb?"

"I hadn't thought of that," Hakar admitted. "Joe, there aren't many people we can trust along the Outbound Arc, even among the ones who wave the Coalition flag. Especially them, actually. But I trust Leon Victor and, by extension, Jackal Pack. Their crews gave their lives for us, same as our own sojieri." Winters watched as the Tagean slipped into the swamps of his memory.

The two of them waited in strained silence until one of Hakar's adjutants knocked lightly on the door and entered. She held a foil-covered packet marked "EYES ONLY: FLAG RANK AND ABOVE." Hakar took the packet and sat back down, regarding it as though it might explode.

"No point in waiting," Winters prodded, earning himself a bemused glance.

Hakar tore the foil off and leafed through Mem screens of data, pondering one in particular. His eyes darkened, smoldering. "Well, we've got unidentified contacts along the systems bordering Calama. They defied scans and vanished before anyone got a good look. Surprise, surprise. I'm getting sick of this hide and seek bullshit. What's this?" He broke off, holding up a data key.

"Is that the black box data?" Winters leaned forward, his palms perspiring.

"Must be." Hakar slipped it into his terminal, passed several security checks, including one the computer threw up when it detected Winters's presence, and expanded the Mem screen.

The two of them listened to partial reports given by the data analyst aboard the Jackal Pack recon jet, identified as Chamber MacMillan, former fighter group captain in the Unified Commonwealth Authority. Huge swaths of Valinata territory had been sheared off by a mysterious faction, known only as Raven Blue within Coalition intel materials. The reports described terrible things: fields of wreckage millions of miles across, pulverized space stations, whole worlds nuked black. According to the penultimate report, the jet was planning to enter the Valinata quarantine zone, with the goal of assessing the invader's strength and base of operations.

Hakar had to pass another set of security checks to access the last data entry. When he did, a cascade of charts appeared on the Mem labeled as ion profiles, spectrometry and refractive index comparisons, and a host of other sensory data, none of which had a match in the Coalition databases logging ship characteristics or emission. The last file was a video feed showing a cruiser of unknown origin or type. The feed was supplemented by a computer model created by the sophisticated sensors, but the model did nothing to illuminate the mystery.

"What the fuck is that?" Winters asked, squinting at the images.

"I'll be damned if I know," Hakar murmured. "The only match we have is to the Calama sample. What are these things, and who's making them?"

The cruiser, labeled BOGEY RB-0000123, was built on fluid geometry with sweeping, organic-looking lines and bow protrusions that looked almost like tentacles. The 123 classification distressed Winters. Had there really been one hundred and twenty-two other Raven Blue bogeys?

"It's a goddamn ghost," Hakar said. "No matches, no regular sensor profile." He pointed a finger accusingly at the screen. "That recon jet was outfitted with the best sensor systems available, and it can barely tell us anything."

"At least, we know how big it is," Winters said. He had to admit that the knowledge was cold comfort, since the mystery vessel was apparently more than two kilometers in length. "I'm not seeing obvious subsystems. Where are the docking bays, the bridge? This thing is built on a whole different foundation of ship architecture."

"I agree," Hakar said gruffly, "and I'm reasonably certain the Valinata had nothing to do with its design."

"Seconded," Winters breathed. This ship ... it didn't look as though it had been built. It looked as though it had been *grown*.

They were spared further speculation when both their comms beeped loudly and simultaneously, announcing priority messages. The two grand admirals turned to their personal computers, where they had received a message from High Grand Admiral Pirsan. He was calling a meeting of the Star Chamber of Grand Admirals, presumably to draw up a comprehensive battle plan. His summons did not suggest confidence in Prime Minister Somerset's endeavor. The meeting was tentatively scheduled for one week from the following day, allowing for the travel of those admirals who were stationed abroad.

Hakar received another message less than a minute later, and to Winters's surprise, the Tagean read it aloud. It was from Telec, asking Hakar to join him for an emergency briefing. It seemed to Winters that things between his colleagues were perhaps not at their most amicable, and Hakar likely wanted him there as backup. Too worried by that thought to be insulted by his exclusion, Winters agreed to accompany Hakar but resolved to keep his own counsel.

§

"It's a conservative estimate," Telec said as the others gaped at the hologram revolving in the center of the room. The galaxy was laid out before them, the territories of the various kingdoms picked out in different colors. Present were Her Majesty, Hakar, Telec, Winters, High Grand Admiral Da-Pirsan Fon, and Admiral Doran Motayre.

Beside Hakar, Doran Motayre snorted wetly. The grand admirals were gradually trickling in from their territories, and he was the first besides Winters to reach the capital. Hakar looked up, and up, at his newly arrived colleague. Once the sight of a hulking Vodroshoyan—also known by the pejorative "Minotauri" for their resemblance to the Terran mythological beast—would have sent people screaming in terror. In fact, had the founders of the Tagean Dominion seen former enemies in the palace and a savage, tattooed Prross on the ancestral throne, they might have died of shock on the spot.

Grand admirals had not always been bureaucrats and de facto politicians. Once they had been warlords, carrying the Dominion flag and agenda to far-flung worlds, conquering or smashing all in their path. It was strange to think that a man in Hakar's position had once been a feared marauder with a massive warfleet at his disposal. Now he had to get an invoice to buy a five-talon Mem screen.

"How sure are we of this data?" asked Winters, crossing his arms. He stood across the hologram from Hakar, colored lights playing across his dark skin.

"By now you're all aware of Admiral Hakar's ... clandestine intelligence assets," Telec responded with a quick glance at Kra'al. The empress pretended to miss the look, leading Hakar to believe she was fully aware of the Jackal Pack connection. "Prior to their destruction, the crew managed to transmit an encrypted data packet through a series of open relays. It wasn't the most secure way to get the information to us, but what's important is that we got it."

"You're saying one recon crew mapped with this resolution?" Motayre asked incredulously. Hakar guessed that he was here in a similar capacity as Winters, that was to say, Telec had brought him as moral support.

"I'll get to that. This is the Valinata quarantine zone as we had originally estimated it based on comscan intercepts." Telec pointed to a sphere of red isolated from the yellow of the Valinata territories. It began near the ragged edge of colonized space. All told, it ate up almost a quarter of the Valinata's small empire. "Its nearest point is about twenty thousand light-years from our border."

Hakar clicked his tongue wearily. "And now? Could you highlight the sites of known incidents on our side of the border? Include Duuja and Vicadar." Those were the locations of the most recent sightings.

Telec entered a few commands on the console controlling the projector, and a number of blinking dots appeared along the Coalition-Valinata border from the edge of the Alkyra Trade Route to the vertex of the Amanra Crescent.

"They're probing our border," Hakar said quietly. "Looking for a way in."

"They can pick any spot they want at the moment," Doran Motayre said angrily.

Telec continued. "In addition to the black box data, our vassals in the Zoh Hegemony sent recon units to probe the Valinata, and some of them even came back." He pressed a button, and the red zone expanded. Hakar was reminded of an epidemic. "As you can see, they've come to a different conclusion."

"Well, *fuck*," Hakar said loudly. This was even worse than expected. "They're just rolling over and playing dead."

High Grand Admiral Pirsan hissed. "There's been no word from Prime Minister Somerset. Have we had any progress contacting elements of the VSF or the Tête?"

"Sources in the Shar'dan Confederacy have reported isolated distress signals and transmissions coming from the other end of the Vendran Sector, but none have been confirmed."

The high grand admiral's crimson scales rose like louvers, an expression of agitation. "I've never seen such a complete shift of power. It's a full-blown insurrection."

Telec made a gargling noise. "With all due respect, we doubt it's an internal fracture."

"Invaders have to come from *somewhere*, Telec," Pirsan snapped. The K'fallet had evolved as apex predators, and sometimes it still showed.

"Hopefully, Prime Minister Somerset will clear that up for us once he reaches Tanis Ruin," Kra'al suggested, artfully defusing the situation.

Flustered, Telec continued. "We now believe this to be the best scenario." He touched a key. Where the yellow of the Valinata and purple of the Coalition had rubbed one another abrasively for centuries, there was now a thick red wedge, and the Kingdom of the Dragon was no more. "If Raven Blue continues unopposed, we estimate six months at the most before the Valinata collapse completely."

Doran Motayre shifted his enormous bulk. "We should explore options with the Shar'dan Confederacy and the Aradon Dominion." He was referring to the other kingdoms that bordered the Emerald Veil. The Valinata had always been a strategically placed core kingdom. If the galaxy was viewed as an oblong disk, the Emerald Veil began at one compressed edge and reached into the center, also extending toward the upper reaches of the clustered stars near the core. With the enormous three-dimensional gulfs in question, it was not surprising that most of the empires in the galaxy shared borders.

Telec looked uncomfortable. "The Commonwealth may work with us on a strategic partnership, but the Aradon have refused to intervene. They've actually requested that we stand down to avoid provoking the VSF."

"Provoking the VSF," Hakar repeated, laughing at the absurdity. He slammed his fist against the base of the projector, and something inside rattled. "What VSF is that? I'm reasonably sure the last ships of the line are sitting on Calama with their thumbs up their asses."

"Lovely imagery, Admiral," said High Grand Admiral Pirsan testily. "I think we only have one course of action at the moment. First, we need to figure out a way to bolster our naval power in the region."

"But we can't call on significant CRDF assets," Telec added. It was a classic dilemma. Without a declaration of hostilities, deploying multiple fleets or armies could only be done with the approval of multiple committees of Parliament, the royal cabinet, and the governments of the region in question. Under parliamentary oversight, keeping the problem out of the public eye would become a non-issue, and the whole kingdom could panic.

Local and regional defense forces, however, operated with a certain degree of autonomy, falling under the direct control of their respective member states. By exploiting loopholes in the Coalition Charter, the CRDF could commandeer those forces without involving the reporting structure and accountants and without drawing the attention of the massive bureaucracy. The question beneath the question, however, was *whom could they count on*? "What about the Zoh Hegemony worlds?"

Telec groaned: there was no love lost between him and the Zoh Hegemony. Hakar sympathized, but while he, too, had little affection for that province or its regional defense force commanders, neither did he loathe it like so many officers in the Coalition regular military. Like many of the provinces in the empire, the Zoh had been founded by people of a unified ideology. The Zoh Hegemony was a uniquely insular and fairly impenetrable region. At times the formerly independent empire exhibited rigid socialist, autocratic, and confrontational tendencies, alienating other member states. It wasn't surprising, considering the isolationist philosophies of the founding factions, some of which had fled Terra during the great exodus. Interestingly, the Zoh had been one of the first powers to offer political representation for all species in their territory based on proportional population.

Unfortunately, even after decades as part of the Coalition, the Zoh remained apart from the rest of the member states, and that sense of mistrust was mirrored on all sides. The intolerance was only magnified by the fact that the Zoh's economy, being entirely state-controlled, was not entirely compatible with the general Coalition market, leading to a certain degree of schism on that front, as well. How could they be trusted or even convinced to help?

The five grand admirals and their empress stopped to consider. The Coalition was shaped something like a half-open pocketknife, with a wedge of Commonwealth space dividing the handle and blade. The Zoh Hegemony, the former Bason Collective, and the former Borin Dominion made up the bulk of the blade, with the Outbound Arc a narrow band along the Valinata-facing edge. A number of Zoh systems were within single-conduit range of the Valinata.

"How's Zoh comscan?" asked Pirsan.

"Adequate. The best in the region, even. They route directly into Triatha Central Communications and Tracking. Paranoia can pay off. In the event of an offensive, their comscan should be able to pull enough data from whatever's left of the Valinata network, even with the jamming fields Rodriguex has been reporting." Telec entered more commands, and a series of white lines emerged from the Zoh, intersecting with the gangrenous lines denoting Raven Blue's incursion and likely attack routes. Zoh naval forces could blunt an advance until more Royal Navy fleets could arrive if invasion occurred.

Pirsan's stubby tail twitched. "It would seem we're in agreement, then. Open a dialogue with the Zoh regional commanders."

Telec's tentacles curled inward. "It may not be that simple. We'll have to play off the bad blood between them and the Valinata." When the Valinata had last attacked the Coalition, Zoh worlds had been the first seized, and they had been brutally subjugated to prevent insurgency. "We may not be able to count on them to *not* start a shooting war. I'd be more comfortable if they acted in a support role."

"Do it, then," the empress said coldly. Kra'al was not above using a little old-fashioned manipulation to get what she wanted, ethical or not. "As long as you understand that they can still appeal and request parliamentary intervention."

Telec slowly blinked his wide, black eyes. "Yes, Highness. It's a risk we have to take."

"If you're serious about seconding Zoh units to CRDF commanders," Hakar interjected, "the Falcon Guard may provide the best alternative. They wouldn't be seen as stooges, and their own recon capabilities are second to none."

Doran Motayre grunted. "Falcon Guard won't be seen as stooges because they're former traitors to the crown. Not all of us like to run in such unreliable circles, Hakar. And if you think that you can avoid oversight while involving Falcons, you need to have your head examined."

"First of all, Chaplain Vista's Rebellion was over three hundred years ago," Hakar countered, annoyed. "Second, the Falcons *are* reliable. Chaplain Tiran is devoted to the crown, and so are his Alphas."

"They'll certainly scare the Zoh into line," Motayre allowed.

"Let it play," Empress Kra'al said. She sounded as irritated as Hakar. In the centuries before the Coalition unified, the Falcon Guard had been raiders, vicious ones, and their loyalty had always been in question. A former commander's violent rebellion and attempted coup had not endeared them to the Coalition citizenry, but as a fighting force they were unmatched, as elite as elite came.

"I'm not inclined to trust the Zoh or the Falcons either," Kra'al continued, "but neither do they trust one another. They'll watch each other, and they'll be watching the Vali, that we can count on. As long as Rodriguex doesn't have to spend all her time babysitting them."

"Let's be clear," said Pirsan through his pointed teeth, "we're not deploying actual Falcon battle groups. That would draw too much attention. My preference would be to keep the Fifth Fleet under Admiral Rodriguex as our first line of defense. I have faith in their objectivity and response. The Zoh forces should be held back in reserve under Falcon oversight."

"Do we actually have Falcon presence in the region already?" asked Motayre, puzzled.

"There's a regional base in the Outbound Arc scheduled for decommissioning as part of the demilitarization," Hakar said. "In the Alkyra, a few conduits over from the border."

"Well, we'll have to delay that decommissioning," Pirsan hissed. "A station along the Tears of Alkyra, though ... that doesn't even belong to us. Are you sure they'll receive us with open arms?"

"No," admitted Hakar, "but I think it's our best option. I can make inquiries. Discreet, to be sure."

"To be sure," Pirsan agreed skeptically. He looked to the empress, who nodded her approval. "Very well. Admiral Telec, where is it?"

Telec typed a query into the projector, and the image focused on the planet in question, the name of the system blinking. It was right along the Outbound Arc and provided ideal access to either the Amanra Crescent or Calama via a few relatively short jumps. Telec gave Hakar a pointed look. "Eve." He didn't sound surprised.

§

The Star Chamber rarely met as a group due to the cost and inconvenience of reeling in the eleven highest-ranking members of the Coalition Royal Defense Forces. What was the point when there was usually no threat greater than the Valinata's usual saber-rattling or a few ragtag bands of pirates to contend with? And so they convened now with great solemnity, all troubled by the news coming out of the Valinata, all hoping for answers.

The last full-fledged conference had taken place following the empress's coronation. Apparently no one had bothered to dust the chamber in the intervening years, and every movement sent up a cloud that gradually settled in the harsh fluorescent lights. Though they were at the pinnacle of the defense ministry tower, Pirsan had drawn the blinds, and only red slivers of light marked the passing of the day as they shifted across the wall. It had been a long time indeed, but there were no pleasantries, no hugs, no showing of family pictures.

Combined, they represented nearly seven hundred years of military experience. They numbered eleven, each standing for one of the species that had ratified the Coalition Charter and carved out an empire the likes of which the galaxy had never seen. Blue-skinned Rukadj, black-scaled Borin, black-and-white-feathered Tez'Nar, green-scaled Sheff'an, red-skinned Prross, brown-skinned Human, gray-furred Niaotl, tan-skinned Sanar, gray-furred Tagean, red-scaled K'fallet, brown-haired Vodroshoyan, all sat at the same table, breathless with anticipation. These were the best and brightest the Coalition had to offer, the men and women who had specialized not in naval warfare, not in surface warfare, but in combined-arms, mastering the art of war in every theater, in all its forms.

High Grand Admiral Da-Pirsan Fon presided from a seat at the head of the long, bare, brushed steel table. As the most senior, Telec sat to the right of the high grand admiral, with Hakar beside him. Winters sat near the far end of the table, looking impatient. Motayre loomed beside Pirsan, a giant even when seated. As commander of Her Majesty's Royal Armada, he had a place of honor to Pirsan's left, at the head of the table.

The grand admirals settled into their chairs, each built to resemble the commander's seat aboard a starcruiser, and Pirsan brought the meeting to order. Eyes flicked from Hakar to Telec and back again as the situation was explained in greater detail. The tension in the room mounted, rising volcanically.

Telec did the talking, deftly sidestepping the gaps in their knowledge in favor of emphasizing the impending mobilization of the Zoh Hegemony and Prime Minister Somerset's diplomatic fact-finding mission. Hakar objected to this tweaking of the facts, but they needed clear heads now, not zealous patriots ready to burn the galaxy down at the drop of a hat. The trouble started when Telec suggested preparing Vice-Grand Admiral Rodriguex's Fifth Battle Fleet to support a major offensive to capture Calama.

Vara Najo, the Prross with a hide the color of drying blood, raised a hand. "Relocating the fleet has already drawn attention. Shoring up the Fifth even further will be expensive and impossible to downplay." Her voice was soft. "We can't simply pull hundreds of ships of the line from their stations and toss them into the Arc, especially not after we just stepped down defenses in the region. Give *us* a little more to go on, or I can't be expected to put my signature on anything." Ever reasonable, she had delivered a perfectly reasonable ultimatum.

Murmurs and hisses of agreement greeted her words. Grand Admiral Winters leaned forward, his dark eyes flashing in the light. Though a Human much smaller in stature and younger in age than most of those present, the gray-haired man commanded an audience with the aptitude of a natural leader. Hakar respected him as did they all, and that was what worried the Tagean most. He needed Winters on his side, especially now. "It's going to be hard to explain to the taxpayers why we're launching trillions of their hard-earned talons into a conduit to the edge of the empire, especially with no direct threat from the Valinata," Winters said.

"In point of fact, the Valinata are not a threat. They have their own problems." There was a reason Pirsan had been made high grand admiral: he could make tough decisions without batting an eye. Those eyes regarded the others serenely, inviting argument. Pirsan had an elegant, long neck and a fearsome but placid visage; evolved from ambush predators, he tended to sit still and let others slip up. "Make no mistake, if our intelligence indicates an immediate threat, we *will* make the first move to protect Coalition systems from an attack, whether it originates from the Valinata or this Raven Blue."

None of them had expected the uproar that followed.

"That's *ridiculous*," Winters muttered.

"Ridiculous doesn't begin to describe it, and Parliament will never approve it. Frankly, neither will I." Najo's eyes had narrowed, and there was anger in her voice now. "When you retained your ranks, you swore—"

Motayre bellowed for silence, raising hands either one of which could have easily palmed Hakar's head and crushed it. As always, the enormous officer was willing to go on a little faith. He breathed deeply and adjusted his posture: the indolence of command had led to his gaining sixty kilos, none of it muscle, but he was still imposing. "It doesn't seem to me that we've exhausted our options for contacting and negotiating with either Vali leadership or this Raven Blue—do we *really* have nothing on them other than a callsign?" There had been a time when he would have been clamoring for action, justification or no. It was telling how much the CRDF's bureaucracy had changed the consummate warrior.

"We're still waiting on word from Prime Minister Somerset," Telec said evenly. "His last report indicated that he had made contact with a group of sympathetic Valinata governors. You all understand the difficulty in communicating with him, but we anticipate contact with Raven Blue within a week."

"As far as I can tell," Vara Najo said, refusing to let the matter rest, "Raven Blue's actions have not established a pattern of credible intent, and we still don't have confirmation from within the Valinata."

"By now you've all seen the data we have on Raven Blue's activity within the Valinata," Telec said defensively.

"*Implied* activity," Najo interjected.

"I'm sorry, but calling it 'implied' is pointless. We've had *no* contact from our sources behind the Emerald Veil. Nothing." Hakar worked hard to keep his temper under control. "Meanwhile, the VSF has either been routed, or they're preparing to attack us with the force of all their Dragon Valia armadas. I'll let you guess which one I suspect."

"Admiral Hakar, let's keep it professional." Pirsan knew when to dictate and when to be conciliatory. Hakar found himself getting tired of the bullshit already. Cryptically Pirsan added, "Regardless of *who* is staging behind the Veil, we have to prepare ourselves. You fix the roof before a storm, you don't wait until the damage is done." He steepled his clawed fingers, gazing out at his divided colleagues. "All CRDF grand fleets will assume a state of full readiness within two weeks, with the capability to mobilize all combined-arms in a maximum of one week if needed. That timetable is nonnegotiable."

This, too, garnered shocked responses from the other grand admirals. Hakar waited until everyone had quieted down to say, "We'll be implementing Strategic Directive Seven."

The grand admirals looked at one another curiously. Directive Seven had been drafted by Hakar, under Emperor Telemon, as a staggered refitting and overhaul of all line ships in the royal navy. It included provisions for intensive weapons research, development, and distribution and had been developed for a war with the Valinata that had never come. With Telemon's fall from grace, they had assumed the directive would be shelved. Apparently that was not the case.

Hakar was a member of the committee of grand admirals and parliamentary ministers who oversaw the Special Projects branch of the CRDF. It was a program tasked with developing military technologies including those of medical, sensory, and offensive interest. While Special Projects was ostensibly autonomous, most people were aware of the tenuous relationship between the branch and a variety of corporations and institutions. In exchange for granting favorable contracts and allowing them to circumvent normal development protocols, Special Projects gained a degree of control over the companies in question. These "shadow conglomerates," as they were collectively known, had grown in influence during Telemon's reign but had been seen as a necessary evil for much longer than that. Most of the grand admirals recognized that the shadows were a blight on the legitimacy of the CRDF's command and that their own authority was thereby undermined. They also recognized that their own bargaining position was a weak one.

"Is there something on the table?" inquired Tarah Charok, the Sheff'an, her emerald-green scales shining brightly. She, too, served on the Special Projects committee. Unlike most of the others, she recognized the value of back-channel work. Alone among all of them, she embraced it.

"There is," said Hakar cagily. He was reluctant to elaborate but saw from the eyes fixed upon him that he had little choice. "For the moment, we're focusing on the development of specialized sensor equipment. Across the board, we've had trouble analyzing Raven Blue ships from a distance, and we've heard of weapon lock-on problems, as well, due to the organic composite used in their hulls."

"That seems reasonable," Admiral Charok said. "What's your proposed rollout?"

"We've prioritized sensor installation for border units, but refitting will begin with the Terran Home Fleet in order to reveal any implementation challenges before pulling active fleets off the line," Pirsan explained. "*Terran Pride* and her support ships are already due for drydock and overhaul and will act as a testbed for new technologies. R&D will be working nonstop on this, as I understand, and most of the dockyards tasked with the Terran renovations will be diverted to this. Once the Terran fleet is refitted, it will rotate to the Outbound Arc for a tour of duty."

Winters was staring daggers at the high grand admiral. "And we'll need more samples if Special Projects is to develop these sensors. Is that right?"

"Perhaps Admiral Rodriguex can oblige us and provide some if she happens to find any in her crosshairs," Telec said mildly.

Winters didn't even look at him. "Are we looking for a way to meet the new members of the budgetary oversight committee? Who the hell is going to pay for *this*? I thought we were going to stop pissing away funds after Telemon."

Pirsan's eyes narrowed. "Admiral Winters, I will tolerate much, but I will not accept your insinuation that we have anything but the Coalition's interests at heart. This is a risky move, yes, but if you have a better way of containing development costs, I would hear it."

Winters was not so easily cowed. "The men and women of my command are on the Arc, and I personally don't want them put at risk because of systems developed by the lowest bidder."

Reluctantly, the high grand admiral conceded the point. "I understand your concern, Admiral, and we certainly aren't looking to cut corners. But I would remind you that time is of the essence." Winters fell silent, but it was clear he was far from appeased by Pirsan's icy response. "We still haven't addressed Raven Blue's radically different fundamental technological architecture."

"Could you define 'radically different' technology for me?" demanded Cratos Mindor without a trace of humor. The round-faced, furry Niaotl had remained silent up until this point, broad ears flat against his head, but it was clear that he resented the degree of ambiguity permeating the meeting. "How can we make an informed decision without *information?*" The other grand admirals seemed to share his sentiment, and there were signs of agreement around the table.

"At this time we are not able to do so," said Telec evenly, tentacles tucked into his face. Hakar recognized this as a sign of evasiveness, and he knew Winters, ever the armchair psychologist, picked up on it, too.

But Winters remained silent; surprisingly, it was Mindor's vexation that boiled over. "If the three of you are making all the decisions, why even bother with a conference at all? Why don't we just streamline everything and turn the Coalition over to your little junta?"

Hakar bristled. "That's uncalled for, Cratos. This is for the sake of national security. So far, the enemy—"

"We're calling them the enemy now?" hissed Charok. "So much for objectivity."

Hakar paused, giving himself time to calm down. "Let's not mince words," he said icily. "So far, Raven Blue has not made any coreward advances. That may change. Soon."

Winters's eyes were locked on Hakar, and the Tagean had to work to keep from squirming in his seat. "I would say that any incursion into Coalition space from outside our border counts as a 'coreward advance,'" he said bitterly.

"Look," said Vara Najo, doing her best to deescalate the situation, "have we considered the implications of action against both Raven Blue and the Dias Traverse dissidents? I hate to bring up thorny issues, but we haven't addressed the possible collapse of Irachan rule in our own house."

Hakar welcomed the diversion, in fact, and thought furiously as Telec fielded the question. "Direct action against Dias rebels was never viable," the Sanar said, sidestepping the real question. "We don't want to appear heavy-handed with the political opposition, so we're planning to reopen diplomatic channels and consider the removal of the planetary governor in favor of a mixed council."

Winters sat back fuming, but he didn't say anything else.

"There's something none of you mentioned," said Tarah Charok coldly, "and it's a little distressing." She eyed the rest of the table, but no one seemed to have a clue as to what she meant. The crest on her nose inflamed in frustration. "I saw a report while I was en route to Tagea that our border pickets are suddenly being overwhelmed with Valinata refugees, millions of them. I'm sure you all read the same one. We need a place to put them, and we need to process them for information. We also need to discuss options for relief efforts within the Valinata. If we don't do something, we're condoning the wholesale slaughter of civilians."

It was a sobering thought, and an oppressive silence settled over the table. It was some time before Admiral Mindor mused aloud, "If we send in the Royal Disaster Relief Fleet, they'll be slaughtered, either by the VSF or Raven Blue. But if we provide them with full CRDF escorts, send fleets in to clear the way, it might be feasible."

Pirsan made a whistling sound, his species' call for attention. "Just because we did not broach the subject here does not mean we have not considered it. In fact, Admiral Telec and I have discussed sending a relief fleet at length, and found it unworkable. We would be exposing our flanks, and we could never provide enough ships to secure the whole region. At least half the battle fleets would be required for such a push."

Hakar shifted uneasily. This was news to him. But when Winters muttered, "Here we go again," he lost his temper and lashed out uncharacteristically.

"They had to do something," he barked. "None of you were *here*. If you had been, then perhaps you could have steered strategy. We're working with what we have. We'll start shifting more resources to the Outbound Arc, but until we do, we need to hold our own border at all costs. Then, *maybe*, we can consider incursion. I'll lead the assault myself, for what it's worth."

"That won't be necessary, Hakar. Are there any further objections or concerns?" demanded Pirsan, his tone letting them all know that he did not intend to brook further argument. The Chamber members sat glumly, like sullen schoolchildren being disciplined rather than the experienced, respected leaders they were. Final details were agreed upon, orders were sent out, and the meeting was adjourned. Most of the admirals looked as though they were in a hurry to escape the ministry and its claustrophobic pall of bureaucracy.

Winters lingered by the door; on Hakar's way out, he grabbed the Tagean's arm. The dark man wore a dark expression, having brooded through the closing minutes of the meeting. His success was due largely to his uncanny ability to understand the people under, above, and all around him. Hakar had known Winters practically since the Human had joined the navy, and he had gladly endorsed his ascension in the wake of Grand Admiral Singh's resignation. It couldn't be easy to send the Fifth into a strategic question mark without sufficient support.

"Hakar, what's going on? The Dias Traverse worlds are in a precarious situation right now. The whole sector is on the verge of a political collapse, thanks to Telemon, and sending them to the back of the line is going to up the number of car bombings five hundred percent if we're *lucky*. You really think it's smart to divert our forces like this? If it turns out we're wrong, we'll lose a lot of credibility."

"I wish I could say, Joe, but I don't think we'll know until we get up close and personal. It's going to happen sooner or later, so we've got to prep. We'll get Rodriguex reinforcements as soon as we can."

"How bad is it, really? I know you bastards are playing your cards close right now, but at least let me know someone's watching the road."

"I don't know." Hakar leaned back against the wall as the last of the grand admirals walked past. None of them looked happy with the outcome of the meeting. "I'm still hoping Prime Minister Somerset will be able to reach a solution his way. If we go off half-cocked and do this wrong, we won't get a second chance. We don't even know if we need diplomacy or brute force."

Winters's mouth was a thin, pursed line. "Judging by the reports, it ain't diplomacy, Hakar. I'm as worried as you are about Raven Blue, but we can't just ignore the Dias Liberation Front. I mean, we don't even know what Raven Blue *want* or who they are. The DLF, at least, have told us exactly what they're about in no uncertain terms. We can't just ask them to 'please wait while we deal with this itty-bitty thing over here,' and you damn well know it."

Hakar clicked his tongue in the affirmative. "I know it. Her Majesty knows it, too, as do Pirsan and Telec. I am sure we're not overreacting to the Valinata issue. We can't ignore the night on the horizon just because the sun is out now."

"The sun isn't out, Hakar. It hasn't been for twenty years. Telemon was a fool, and I'm not sure Kra'al was the right choice to clean up his mess." He held up his hand and began ticking off points on his fingers. "We've got the goddamn Dias Traverse falling apart, with the Tez'Nar saying they were coerced into signing the Coalition Charter in the first place. We've got corporate malfeasance, broken infrastructure on hundreds of worlds, and now we don't know if the Valinata have been invaded, are having a civil war, or are planning on attacking *us*."

"Give her a chance. She's the right woman for the job."

"Damn, do I hope you're right," Winters said, unconvinced.

§

Jackal Pack lost sojieri all the time. It was the nature of their business. Over the years Rockmore had set up a fairly efficient process for contacting families, paying out insurance and benefit policies, and replacing lost personnel. Nevertheless, he still took each death personally.

Six men and two women were dead. They had been some of the most highly trained and specialized of Jackal Pack's combat aerospace wing. Between the two long-range fighters, Jackal Pack had lost nearly seventy-five million talons in assets. Worst of all, they had disappeared under unknown circumstances, and no one from the CRDF was talking.

Leon and Jeric stood side by side before General Rockmore's desk, watching their commander pace back and forth. "The official word is that a Valinata patrol intercepted and destroyed our ships." Rockmore's voice was like steel on stone, hard and cold. "But Coalition Star Command won't turn over the black box data." He fixed his subordinates with a baleful glare and shook his head in bewilderment. "Hakar's not telling us everything. Hell, he's not telling us anything. I guess I should be used to it." Neither of his men spoke. "We do everything they ask, fill our contract to the letter, and this is the thanks we get? Total secrecy? And now Zoh Hegemony forces are mobilizing like they're going back to war, in our fucking backyard."

He sat down on the edge of his desk and rubbed his temples. Then he looked out the window at his compound, at his troops going about their business. "I feel like I'm missing something. I'm considering recalling our field units. What do you think?" he asked over his shoulder.

Leon hesitated. He didn't like telling the general how to do his job, especially not in front of Jeric. "Sir, that contract at Rau Zeta is huge, and we stand to do long-term business."

"And if there's no one left to conduct said business?" The general turned, and the two sojieri could see that his eyes were half-lidded with fatigue. "Hakar may not be willing to go on the record, but I've still got some contacts in the UCA. They've been watching the Coalition and the VSF, and this standoff is coming to a head. Apparently the Aradon Dominion is pumping forces to their own border with the Valinata, and you know how much it takes for them to bestir themselves. The thing that concerns me the most is this quarantine zone behind the Emerald Veil. The official story is that it's a spill."

"A ... spill?" Jeric asked. "What, like antimatter or something? That doesn't make sense."

"My thoughts exactly. Then again, the Vali aren't exactly famous for making their intentions known. And with this blackout ... I mean, we're getting no comms, no traffic at all."

Leon was frowning, trying to piece it together. "Jesus, they really could be mobilizing for a big push. You don't think they're working on some major construction project in there, do you? What if they've got some sort of superweapon or secret fleet?"

"Possible, I suppose. Last report I saw indicated they were using up a lot of metal and fissile material." Rockmore tapped his chin thoughtfully. For a moment he simply looked like an old, forgetful man, but appearances were deceiving. "Do either of you still have contacts on Ti Che?"

Leon and Jeric exchanged a glance. They had led a strike team on the Valinata world of Ti Che, protecting the prime minister and his family from a rival merc company. The politician had been adamant about repaying his personal debt to the two mercenaries. "We could check into it," Jeric ventured. "It's been a few years. I don't even know if old Suec is still in power."

"I guess that'll have to do. At this point I'll take whatever information we can get," Rockmore confessed. Intel-gathering had always been a challenge as Jackal Pack relied on government contacts, not always the most forthcoming people. The general slid into his chair and unfurled his Mem screen. "Jeric, would you mind writing to the families of Chamber MacMillan and Selma Turk? You knew them pretty well." Jeric nodded. "Thanks. Alright, you two. You're dismissed. Thanks for playing sounding boards."

Outside the office, Jeric turned to his friend. "Damn, man. The general's looking pretty haggard." He blew out a sigh. "I fuckin' hate writing condolence letters."

"Sketch up a draft, send it by the office. Heidi's got a real talent for it. She can turn even your chicken scratch into poetry."

"Thanks for the vote of confidence, man. So, what do you think? Rockmore overreacting?"

"Well, something's got Hakar spooked. Hell, it's got me spooked, and I don't have a clue what's going on."

"He was right about the Zoh Hegemony," Jeric said. When Leon gave him a puzzled look, he asked offhandedly, "Have you noticed anything strange lately?"

"What do you mean?"

"Well, the CRB's been getting a lot of traffic."

Leon shrugged. The Coalition Regional Base, hidden out in the savannahs of Eve, dealt with a lot of high-level data this close to the border. With the current situation, an increase in activity was hardly surprising. "So?"

"Boy, you've just lost all interest in anything besides Rachel's tits, haven't you?" Leon shot Jeric a warning glance, and the pilot held up his hands. "Shit, I'm sorry. Anyway, I mean the CRB's been getting traffic they're trying to *hide*."

This made Leon curious but only marginally so. He was more irritated by Jeric's remark about Rachel. "How's that?"

"Yesterday on overflight I saw a group of courier ships coming into the port, standard cargo run, right? Except the couriers landed at the government VIP pad. They were Zoh ships, and the paint covering up their insignia was practically still wet. Spook ships, buddy." Jeric waved at the window in the vague direction of the cosmodrome. "I think they're running ops with the CRB, and Eve's government is letting them."

"For what? What could the Zoh gain from that?"

"I don't know, favored trade status or something." Jeric seemed eager to make his point. "Maybe they want to loot the Valinata mines when the big push happens, and they're getting in line early."

"Sure, Jerr. Next time you see one of the Zoh ships, why don't you flag it down and ask them what's up?"

The pilot glared up at his friend. "I'm right about this."

Further conversation was interrupted by Colonel Akida, who popped his head out of his office long enough to sneer and say, "Victor, I hear your girlfriend is out shopping for drapes."

They kept walking toward the lift, and Leon winked at Akida as he passed. "Some of us are cursed with beautiful women," he threw back over his shoulder, causing the smug smile on Akida's face to do a quick flip.

Jeric clapped his friend on the back after the lift doors closed. "Nice shot." Outside they were greeted by the roar of a departing fighter as it rocketed over the courtyard and disappeared into a cloud. To the east the sun was quickly setting, bathing the plains and buildings in a soft orange-pink light. They could hear the distant *thud-thud* of tanks practicing on the artillery range far below the plateau.

Rachel was sitting on one of the courtyard benches, reading. For a moment Leon's world stopped turning. A faint breeze ruffled her dark, shoulder-length hair. Her sky-blue eyes scanned left to right, left to right, and she bit her lip thoughtfully as she read. The base around her dissolved, and briefly, ever so briefly, Leon's existence achieved a much-longed-for sense of normalcy. He caught a glimpse of the future she offered him: marriage, fatherhood, peace. Leon had always wanted a child of his own; certainly not as many as his parents had had, but one or two. And he realized that in that future there probably wasn't a place for Jackal Pack. Was that the way it had to be?

Rachel glanced up, spotted Leon, and folded the Membook. She rose, straightened her skirt, and walked over to stand on tiptoe for a kiss. She tousled his hair playfully. "I've been waiting. Hi, Jeric."

"How was Tesa?" Leon asked. He knew she had been looking forward to getting into the capital and catching up with some friends.

"I have to admit, it's good to be back. I forgot how fun that place can be. The girls say hi, by the way."

"Well, hi back to them," Leon said roguishly. "I hear you bought drapes."

"What?" She looked confused, left out of the joke. "No drapes. I took the liberty of ordering us a larger bed, though. You should have seen the delivery guys' faces when I told them where I wanted it." Before Rachel had rented an apartment in the city, but when she had returned without a place to stay, Leon had insisted they share his quarters. It had been a big step and awkward at first as they explored the boundaries of their second attempt, but it was getting better. His apartment was plenty spacious, but he knew she missed the city. *A new bed, huh?*

"If there's room for it, why not?" he decided.

Jeric clapped his hands together. "Oh boy! Does this mean we can have sleepovers?"

"Not a chance in hell, buddy." Leon turned back to Rachel. "Did you check the comm?"

"Your sister Natille left a message about the wedding. It sounded like she wanted your opinion on something."

"I hope she's giving me veto rights on her fiancé." Leon hadn't met the guy yet but from the sound of it, he was sickeningly perfect. In short, he was almost good enough for Natille, who deserved the whole galaxy as far as Leon was concerned. *Maybe it's time I slipped that ring on Rachel's finger myself.* There were family men and women in the Pack whose spouses and children lived either in Tesa or the underground city at Las Serras da Estrela, the Mountains of the Star. There were even married couples who fought together. They could make it work, couldn't they? "That reminds me, I need to add you to the guest list."

"You want me to come?" Rachel seemed genuinely surprised, but her face lit up.

Leon failed to suppress a laugh. "You think I would leave you with these pirates and give up the chance to show you off there? Besides, I want to show you Crossing."

Rachel looked blank. "I thought your sister was from Old Terra."

Jeric had to cover his mouth to conceal his grin. Leon glared at him. "Crossing is a city on Terra: the provisional capital, actually. Nice place, old buildings, almost entirely renovated. I think you'll love it."

"I've never been to Terra," Rachel said wistfully. For centuries Terra had been a cesspool to be avoided, but its renaissance had turned it into a popular destination for many Humans trying to reconnect with their heritage. Leon had been born off-world, but his family had relocated when he was just a boy. He had grown up in the streets of Crossing's Normandy District, and he looked forward to showing Rachel around his old haunts. Things had changed quite a bit since the days of his youth, and it was a place to be proud of again.

Jeric hooked his thumb in the direction of the Desher Vaux. "I'm going to get our table. See you in there?"

"In a few minutes," Rachel said agreeably. It warmed Leon's heart to see the two of them making an effort. Rachel led him back to the bench where she had been reading, and the two sat down to watch the sun set over Tesa. Despite the activity of the base around them, it was quiet and peaceful, and Leon relished the moment. Soon the capital was aglow, and not long after that, twilight descended over the savannah. Three little moons hung above them, gazing down.

"Did you want to play your question game?" Leon asked after a minute or so.

"It's not a game," Rachel replied, but there was no anger in her voice. "No, let's not do it now. Just relax. You look like you've had a hard day."

Leon reflected on the conversation with Rockmore and decided not to dwell on it. "Little bit," he agreed.

They got up and walked toward the Desher Vaux, meeting Raptor and Traxus by the door. As promised, Jeric had held their seats for them as the place filled.

Before they even sat down, Raptor tilted a bottle of Tez'Nar Borro Ale back and downed it in one long swallow, ordering another from Mara even as he slid into the booth. "So what did Rockmore have to say?" he asked.

Jeric and Leon exchanged a look and shrugged simultaneously. The colonel took a swallow of Hais and put his arm around Rachel, who was splitting a bottle of South Tagean Spiced Red with Traxus. "I'm not really sure how much I should say, but he's worried about all the activity in the area."

Raptor nodded. "You don't know the half of it. I was picking up the rest of the Tilora Co. team at the 'drome with Dawson, and I saw a couple of Zoh Hegemony creepers touch down. Looked like they were unloading some heavy-duty equipment."

Jeric punched his friend, and Leon's drink sloshed all over his hand and barely missed splashing Rachel. "See?"

"Yeah, all right, I've been wrong before. Don't get too excited." Leon turned from Jeric's triumphant, grinning face and looked at Traxus. "Trax, any news?"

The young Tagean swirled her wine glass. "Some restless new recruits pissed off by the probationary period but nothing unusual." She snapped her fingers. "Oh, you may all be interested to know the betting pool on the Emperor's Cup Champions tournament is up to five grand." She took a sip. She looked like her brother, Leon reflected. Though lankier than Hakar and unmistakably feminine, she had the same noble face and the same warmth in her eyes. She was a peculiar mercenary. "I have to say, Leon, people are curious as to why we're sitting tight with the Rau Zeta contract almost up. Is there something we should know?"

And there it was, the crux of the issue. Leon had a feeling there was much they should know. Problem was, *he* didn't know much more than they did. "Nothing specific. I get the impression that the general is weighing options from a big backer. He hasn't consulted me. Chances are, if the situation on the border deteriorates any further we're going to have quite a bit to do." Leon shrugged, gave Rachel a tired smile. "Sorry, we shouldn't talk business."

She flashed her own smile. "It's okay, at least you all watch the news. Most of the people I know back home only care about celebrity gossip. Are things on the border really as bad as they say?"

Traxus leaned toward her, spicy red wine on her breath. "No one really knows. Everyone's jumping to conclusions, that it's either a sign of an impending attack or a civil war. Full disclosure isn't exactly seen as a strength these days. This close to the contested area, we don't have the option of being apathetic."

"Right," Leon added, "and the CRDF's trying to keep everything under wraps, but they're doing a terrible job. People don't like it when they know they're being lied to."

Rachel was nodding. "And if people find out that the Zoh are scared enough to put aside their differences and work with the CRDF, there's going to be trouble, right?"

Traxus clicked her tongue in the affirmative. "The Outbound planets have never been properly consolidated by the Coalition or the Valinata. Ordinarily, I don't think the Valinata would seriously consider a fight, but maybe they see a chance with all the unrest among the Coalition member states. Some Tez'Nar in the Dias systems want to defect to the Commonwealth. The DLF even called Grand Admiral Kan a traitor to the species and threatened to kill him if he sets foot on Iracha again."

"Telemon again, right?" Rachel said a little snobbishly. After all, she was from the Commonwealth where criticizing the Coalition's leadership was a national pastime. She wasn't wrong, however, and the Jackals nodded their weary agreement. Few people were proud of the deposed emperor, the instigator of much of the kingdom's recent troubles. "And what do all of you think? You keep talking about the Coalition's people, but you guys are affected, too. Don't tell me you can just separate yourselves from the equation."

Rachel was perceptive, and the Jackals shifted uneasily in response to the question. Reconciling their private philosophies and morals with their profession was far from easy. Politics was always a hot-button issue, especially in a place where people carried guns and where their fortunes, collectively and individually, rose and fell in proportion to the number of conflicts in the galaxy. They thrived on violence, inequality, and the gray areas between laws. It was easier to ignore than to face.

Raptor was the first to speak. "There's no honor in hiding the truth. The people of the Coalition deserve to know what's going on, especially if it's going to lead to war. I have a feeling the government is trying to buy time. They should know it's the one thing that can't be bought."

"You know where I stand, honey," Leon said easily. "I'm with Raptor but maybe not so fatalistically. Kra'al's claim to power is that she's not like Telemon. If it comes out that she's helped conceal information like that, she's screwed and so is the whole administration. If it happens again so soon, the way things are now, we could be looking at a civil war of our own. And while that would mean more money than we could ever spend, I'm not so bloodthirsty that I ever want to see it."

"What Leon's trying to say," Jeric chimed in, "is that he's still a loyal CRDF officer, whether they sign his paychecks or not. Personally, I think they're all a bunch of untrustworthy, ass-kissing bastards. From Kra'al on down. Same with the Valinata, for that matter."

Slowly their eyes revolved to settle on Traxus. "I hate to play devil's advocate, guys, but Hakar *is* my brother. Leon, I'm kind of surprised you didn't side with him. I know he would never want to intentionally deceive anyone, but if he does, it's because he honestly believes it's in everyone's best interests."

"And who is he to make that decision?" Raptor asked. His voice was calm and reasonable, but it was clear he disagreed vehemently. So did Leon, and Traxus's apologist viewpoint ignited an hour-long debate.

When the argument ran out of steam, they lapsed into silence, sipping their drinks, and Leon savored the moment of camaraderie. There was no denying the rush of combat or the thrill of victory, but the quiet moments were the ones he cherished. He was with his lover and his closest friends, and they were surrounded by laughter and what passed for tranquility on a base populated by warriors.

"I shouldn't have had that last glass of wine," Rachel declared, yawning. "I think I'll turn in."

Leon began sliding out of the booth to let her out, but before she could stand up, the music in the Desher Vaux stopped, and a voice blared over the public address system. "Attention all JPML personnel: As of zero-five hundred hours tomorrow, water rationing is in effect across Eve. Consult your network accounts for details."

"I guess we'll have to share the shower," Rachel said playfully, mock disgust in her voice.

"At least, Brent will stop watering down the *piss* he serves us," Jeric said loudly, throwing his voice toward the bar.

"Fuck you, shortstack! You're the only one I serve piss to!" the portly but good-natured bartender retorted. Brent had been one of Rockmore's troops when he founded the Pack, but after a blown-out eye, a severed leg, and a piece of shrapnel in his back, he had retired to do what he always did best: take bets and get people drunk.

Jeric, his idiot grin fading, turned back to the others.

Traxus was less than thrilled. "Again? I can't believe it."

Eve's long journey around its star—nearly five Terran years—brought it closer to the sun for two years at a time. During that period, the planet, never burdened with an overabundance of water to begin with, often found itself in drought. The farmers across the savannah planned for it; in addition to underground aquifers, sophisticated irrigation systems had been developed to bring water from the inland seas and polar caps to where it was needed. Eve orbited around the inner edge of the so-called Goldilocks Zone of planetary habitability, and its already marginal biosphere had been irreparably skewed by a hemisphere of strip-mined desolation.

Rachel slid out of the booth, kissing Leon on the cheek. "Good night, sweetheart. I'll join you in a bit." He was looking forward to christening the new bed.

As Rachel disappeared into the night, Leon turned and looked at his friends, who were grinning at him. "What?"

Raptor leaned back in his seat. "Wipe that simpering expression off your face, buddy."

Leon sat back down, and Traxus slid out of the seat she had been sharing with Jeric and Raptor in order to sit next to him. The Prross spread out, uncoiling his tail and getting comfortable. "Yeah," Leon said, so softly they barely heard him over the music, "I guess I feel pretty good. I'd be lying if I said it wasn't hard, but shit is it ever worth it."

Traxus leaned against his shoulder. "Good for you, Leon."

"Thanks. I just wish I knew why she left and why she came back." It had been nagging at him, but he knew he couldn't ask, at least, not directly.

"I think maybe you should take this second chance," Raptor suggested, "and not overanalyze it."

"You don't have to tell me twice," Leon agreed. After losing Buzz, he needed Rachel more than ever, and he wasn't about to blow the opportunity she had given him. He just didn't know if he was truly up to the task of being a good enough man to make her happy.

"So what, does this mean you're gonna retire, take a desk job?" Jeric acted curious rather than worried, but there was a pointed edge to his voice.

Leon was quick to shake his head. "And give up my all-expenses-paid tour of the galaxy's most exciting vacation destinations? Not while I can still pass the physical." Jeric and Raptor didn't hear the hesitation, the momentary pause, but Traxus did, and she thoughtfully sipped at her wine.

"Here's the thing, though," Leon continued. "I really want this to work out with Rachel."

"That's going to be tough, considering what a dumbass you are," Jeric said snidely.

"Uh-huh." Jeric wasn't going to make this easy. "It does mean scaling back, a little." It wasn't just Rachel, Leon had to admit to himself. Thinking of Buzz, drowning in his own blood on the floor of that palatial suite, left him with a knot in his stomach. He had lost other friends over the years, more than he wanted to count, but those he cared about the most had been able to outrun death for a long time. Being reminded so bluntly of the consequences of their lifestyle gave him real pause. If his only choice was between a bloody, brutal end and a happily-ever-after with Rachel Case, it would be easy to make, wouldn't it? And why not? A quiet life on a quiet world, with Rachel at his side, held a sort of mythical appeal.

Raptor seemed to pick up on his misgivings, and an introspective expression settled over his fearsome face. "Buzz would have been happy to see the two of you together again." The Prross spun his glass between clawed fingers. "So, when are you going to tell her about Daltar?"

Leon couldn't meet his friend's gaze. "How about never?"

"How about she's going to find out sooner or later," Traxus put in, "and if you want her to respect you after she hears it, you need to be the one to tell her."

There was movement at the door to the pub, and when Jeric's head snapped up, looking past him, Leon glanced over his shoulder. Just as quickly he returned his gaze to his drink. Akida and his crew had entered the bar and settled at a table as far away from Leon and his friends as they could get.

Brent looked over at the newcomers' table. Jackal Pack's own storied hero, he feared no one but the general. "Well, look here, everyone, it's a special occasion! The last time our glorious colonels were in here together, we had to close the place for a week to repair damages." When Akida fixed him with a withering stare, Brent simply laughed, a sound like a flooded engine sputtering to life.

The bitter rivalry between Akida and Leon was no secret on the base, and their battalions were likewise often pitted against each other. They had not actually come to blows for years, not since they had been younger and angry at the galaxy for the directions their lives had taken. Of course, the rivalry was part of Rockmore's plan to drive them to outcompete and outperform every other private army in operation.

Things had occasionally gotten out of hand. Six months into his career with the Pack, Leon had still been a borderline alcoholic coming off a bloody run as an independent Ronin. Akida had been a four-year veteran resentful of Leon and justifiably concerned that his place in the Pack was no longer secure. Akida had unwisely called Hakar an indecisive clown and an old man with an obsolete sense of nobility. The ensuing fight had cost them respect as well as money to restock drinks and repair tables and had nearly cost Brent his other eye when he tried to pull them apart. But that was a long time ago, and the two colonels now knew better.

Their subordinates were not always so restrained. Akida's crewmates were all uncannily like him: quiet, smug, and lethal. Recently three of them had tangled with Raptor in the boxing ring at the gym. What had started as a sparring match had quickly turned angry and violent. One of the men still looked a little lopsided because the Prross, in his frustration, had caved in the man's cheekbone and almost crushed his ocular orbit. He was glaring daggers at Raptor.

Leon didn't want to engage in the posturing, not tonight. Raptor, however, had his blood up and was eager to provoke. Seeing what he was about, Jeric grabbed at his jacket sleeve, but the Prross pulled free and stood up. "Hey, kids! That turning tail and running away trick you did? Really caught me off guard." He roared laughter.

"Anytime, anywhere, asshole!" hollered back one of Akida's friends.

"I'm right here, you godless coward. You want to try five on one this time?"

Akida gave the Prross a vicious glance and an even more vicious gesture which only made Raptor laugh louder. Two of Akida's friends got to their feet, chairs sliding out, but the other colonel restrained them.

"Sit the fuck back down, Raptor," Leon snapped. Grinning a grin like saw blades grating together, Raptor did as he was bid.

After that altercation, the pub crowd grew subdued, and the mercenaries quietly went back to their own conversations, but eyes kept flicking expectantly between the two tables. Leon stared into his drink for a moment while the others joked around him. Traxus noticed and nudged him. "Hey. You okay?"

It was Leon's job to be a leader, and sometimes that included putting on a brave face. With Trax, however, it just didn't seem right. "I'm just thinking about Buzz. And the recon team. They didn't sign up to die. None of us do, but somehow we just … accept it as natural. I wonder why that is." He pushed his glass away.

Traxus stood up, drink in hand, and for a moment, Akida's team bristled. She raised her glass. "Here's to giving better than we get! To Love, the Grim Reaper, Buzz Parker, and the Lost Patrol!" she called out.

Obligingly, Leon rose to his feet, and Akida did the same. The other colonel inclined his head to Leon, ever so slightly. The Desher Vaux was packed by that point, the officers elbow to elbow at the bar, and all of them echoed the sentiment wholeheartedly. *"In spite of all!"* they cheered. Glasses crashed together. Everyone drank, and many poured out a dram for fallen comrades. A cluster of them began singing an old war song Leon dimly remembered from his time in the CRDF.

Leon raised his own glass to Traxus. She smiled, and they both drank again. After the singing died down, Brent announced the weekly pub quiz, and the sojieri settled in for the first round of questions.

§

The new bed was great, the mattress soft and springy. It was quiet, too, and Rachel's cries of ecstasy had been the only sounds drifting out the window during their lovemaking. Afterwards, hair still tousled and her body covered in a fine sheen of sweat, she read while Leon snored heavily beside her.

The lamp to her left created an island of soft light around them, the rest of the apartment cast in shadow. A trail of clothing led into the darkness, but Rachel was too tired to pick it up and throw it into the hamper.

If Dad could see me now, she thought with a bitter smile, glancing from the page she was reading to the man sleeping beside her. Her father would never have approved. He might even have had a coronary if he had met Leon. Of course, as far as Rachel was concerned, the man whose sperm had conceived her had waived his rights to give her advice a long time ago. And even if he hadn't disappeared from her life, he was no better than Leon, not by a long shot.

She wondered what had happened at the pub to make Leon so tender when he got back to the apartment. He had a reputation for being a witty, easygoing guy off the battlefield, but Rachel knew him better than that, knew how intense he was, how passionate. The cynical, jocular tough guy was just an act, as much a part of his job as the uniform.

Now he looked peaceful, almost childlike, as he slept, his eyes squeezed shut and his mouth slightly open. His back was to Rachel, and she could see the constellations of scars across it, raised white-and-pink stars and lines. She could see the barcode tattooed beneath the neural jack on his neck. She was tempted to run her hands across his skin, to feel the hard curves of his muscles, but she didn't want to wake him.

Leon was handsome in a rough way, an unfinished portrait of someone more beautiful. Rachel put the book down and just looked at him for a few moments. She was still occasionally surprised by the ardent, conflicted love she felt when she looked at this man. Boyfriends had come and gone for Rachel Case—there had never been a shortage of eager men in college or the social circles she had traveled in afterwards. But she had never felt so troubled, and that was how she knew this was real. When other relationships had ended, they had ended. That was that, so to say. With Leon, she had barely been able to stand looking at him before she left, but once she was safely away, she had realized she couldn't stop thinking about him. She had gone back to her mother's lavish penthouse on Amalthia and spent her days lounging and her nights partying. She never had to wake up with the sound of sojieri drilling outside or dropships screaming into the sky, and she hadn't had to work hard to find something to do.

But it had all felt empty somehow. The time had passed excruciatingly slowly, and life had been dull and listless, shallow, as though she had been seeing the world through a filter that removed all color, all depth. Her mother had laughed off her lovesickness, and her friends had tried to help by parading before her seemingly every available rich bachelor on the planet. They had been glamour-magazine attractive, charming, wealthy. Once that would have been enough. Not anymore. She had seen the galaxy now and how everyone lived, not just her entitled friends. Friends whom she had now outgrown, just like her empty lifestyle. Leon, in addition to bringing risk and dilemma to her life, had added texture and context. And she found herself enamored of the strangely cultured way in which he went about his rough existence.

Now she felt he was really beginning to take shape before her. They had taken turns asking each other questions, easy ones at first but growing more difficult. They knew one another's childhoods, first loves, deepest insecurities, and greatest ambitions. There was so much ground left to cover, she reflected. She had to hand it to Leon; most people would have been scared off by her idea, but he had attacked it as gamely as anything else in his path.

A contented smile spread across Rachel's face as she recalled her first date with Leon. They had met by chance in the downtown shopping district of her hometown on Amalthia. He had bumped into her, spilling coffee on her brand new coat. To make it up to her, he had offered to buy her dinner. It had been a strange offer, but there had been something oddly compelling about the man in his finely tailored suit, and she had broken off another date to accept. He had been a gentleman but far more worldly than the prep school spawn she typically dated. There had been something enigmatic and disturbing about this man pouring her wine for her, as though he were wearing a thin disguise, as though he were doing a thousand things at once. The whole evening he had been strangely distracted, looking around the restaurant as though expecting someone, searching—no, *hunting*—with those restless, stormy, camera eyes. He was there on business, he had said. She had found out the hard way what that business was when another quiet dinner became a bloody firefight, and the discovery had been electrifying, exciting as well as horrifying. For someone who had led such a sheltered, carefree existence, that feeling of real danger had been a wake-up call.

I want this to last, she told herself, gently putting her hand on Leon's shoulder. He stirred and mumbled something before nestling closer against her side. Looking at him now, so incongruously peaceful, Rachel again found herself wondering what he would have been like with his virgin soul untrampled by the booted feet of vicious necessity, before his innocence was so callously torn away and replaced with a gun and a barcode tattoo. "I love you," she whispered to her sleeping lover.

Part of her wanted to recapture the magic of their first chance encounter, the spark and … her brow furrowed. Growing up the way she had, Rachel had learned not to look too closely at perfection, lest the seams show. Pushing beyond surface denial was still novel to her and led to burning questions. She feared she already knew the answer to this one. "Leon, wake up," she said, nudging him.

Years of training to be ready at a moment's notice had been only marginally dulled by age. Leon was alert in a few seconds, looking blearily at her. "Something wrong?" he mumbled.

"The night we met wasn't an accident, was it?"

Leon drew a deep breath. "No," he said after a long moment. She could tell he didn't want to elaborate further, but before she could prod him for an answer, he did. "I needed to get into that club. I knew I needed someone to vouch for me. Rachel, I'm sorry. I knew you were on the VIP list."

"You mean you knew who I was, too? Dammit, Leon, how could you never tell me? You basically used me as *bait*." Rachel didn't know how to feel about this. She was upset and knew she had every right to be. And yet somehow she knew Leon would never have allowed her to come to harm. That didn't make it right.

"You weren't supposed to be there the second night. I swear it was just for the first time. I would never have put you in the line of fire."

"So why did you?"

"I wanted to see you again." He said it sheepishly, like a schoolboy, and Rachel couldn't help forgiving him a little. "I was going to postpone the hit, but they recognized me first."

Rachel recalled him suggesting another restaurant down the strip, but her friends had wanted to meet the mysterious stranger from the night before, and Rachel had bullied him into it. It didn't absolve Leon of guilt, but it meant he had opened fire in self-defense. To protect her.

"Do you want to ask me anything?" Rachel asked. Her mind was still backpedaling through a year and a half of relationship, testing it to see if it could hold upon such a foundation.

Leon considered for a moment, his face unreadable. "I think I'll pass for tonight."

"Then I'll take your turn."

There was the faintest glimmer of a smile on his face. "Breaking your own rules, huh?" He motioned for her to go ahead and sat up straighter for what was sure to be a difficult interrogation.

Rachel paused, asked herself if she really wanted to do this, wondered if knowing would cause irreparable harm. "Have you ever enjoyed killing?"

This time Leon didn't hesitate. "Yeah. Occasionally there have been people … where it's felt like more than just work."

"Bad people," Rachel guessed.

"The worst," Leon agreed. "I'm not trying to make an excuse. I admit most of the time I don't think about it. Sometimes I even hate it. But on certain occasions," he said, making a so-so motion with his hands, "it's harder to feel guilty."

There was nothing to say to that, was there? Rachel took Leon's hand, squeezing it tightly before letting go. Her mind was racing, but she kept her own face even.

When it was clear she wasn't going to say anything else, Leon slid below the covers, rolled over, and went back to sleep. Rachel marveled that he could rest so easily after such an admission. Why wasn't he upset by it, haunted by it? How could anyone adapt to this life? She couldn't come up with an answer. Then she, too, slept, dropping off with surprising ease.

11: Escalation

Hakar and Telec chose to walk across the Plaza of Unity. They could easily have commandeered a Ministry of Defense shuttle, but Hakar wanted the fresh air, and Telec was too stubborn to complain. The first snowfall had dusted Sherata, leaving the city under a thin blanket of pristine white. It was early and had taken the capital by surprise, but it was Hakar's favorite time of year, winter turning the trees into pastries, the spires and domes crystalline. Beside him, Telec was bundled up and wearing a rebreather that covered his whole head, to keep his wet skin from freezing.

The snow muffled sound, leaving the Plaza strangely quiet and serene. This early in the morning there were few pedestrians, mostly the royal guard standing silently at their posts, only the white puffs of their breath to distinguish them from the statuary. The fountains had been turned off, but the canals were still flowing gently. Cold-looking gliders huddled in the branches of the trees, puffed up against the frigid weather.

"Well, now that we've alienated half the Chamber, what do we do?" asked the Sanar, voice muffled by his mask.

Hakar chuckled. They had alienated half the Chamber, and the other half had hated them to begin with. "You did your best to alienate me, too, or had you chosen to forget that little detail?"

"I was hoping we could move past it. God, how can you stand this weather?"

In truth, Hakar felt quite comfortable although he was reminded how difficult it must be for Her Majesty. She didn't get to go out much at the best of times, but with her lower body temperature, winter kept her isolated in the palace. Often she took Tagean winter as an opportunity to tour the rest of the kingdom. She had once confided in Hakar that she felt profoundly alien on a world where water fell, frozen, from the sky, something that never happened on her homeworld of Prrastra.

The palace loomed before them, its edifice imposing yet delicate, with airy towers and decorative sculpture erupting from every surface. They passed beneath the Peace Arch and through the less ornate doors reserved for palace personnel. Security had been tightened in response to the escalating tensions with the Valinata, but the two grand admirals passed through quickly, expedited past the majority of office workers and miscellaneous staff waiting to start the work day.

They were in the VIP cloakroom, Hakar removing his snow-dusted jacket and Telec emerging from his temperature-regulated bodysuit, when they heard a rapid thudding sound. It was getting louder, heralding the approach of Admiral Doran Motayre. They hung their cloaks and went to meet him.

The towering, broad-chested Vodroshoyan barreled around the corner, almost running down a passing dignitary, and halted before Telec and Hakar. He was panting, out of breath.

"I saw you from the control center window," he said between gasps. Evidently he had run down twelve flights of stairs to meet them at the entrance. What could have been so important?

Their Minotauri colleague ran one large, thick-fingered hand over his sweeping horns. Looming before them in the labyrinthine corridors of the palace, snorting, he certainly resembled the eponymous mythological being. And whereas the Prross loathed the pejorative "Saurian," most Vodroshoyans seemed to take pride in the connotation of "Minotaur," ignoring that it had been bestowed upon them by terrified Human explorers.

Telec and Hakar glanced at each other. "Why didn't you use the comm?" inquired the Tagean, trying to hide his knowing smile.

Motayre looked down at his shoulder where his personal computer was clipped. "In person is better," he said bluntly, unashamed. When it came to technology, Motayre was usually at a loss. Invariably preferring a greatsword and shield to a rifle, he nonetheless displayed modern, if somewhat brazen, tactical thinking. High Command could easily overlook his ignorance of etiquette and lack of technological prowess in light of his military achievements and his dedication.

Hakar started walking again. "What's going on?"

The big Vodroshoyan proceeded alongside with surprising grace, aided by the palace's other occupants, who quickly moved aside for him. "For starters, there has been another attack."

"Our side of the border?"

"Yes. A settlement on Ressa, a religious or agricultural commune. I do not remember which. It's between Calama and the Tears of Alkyra." Motayre led the way into one of the palace's many lifts, and the three ascended, turning to look through the curved glass window as the Plaza of

Unity dropped beneath them. "Black box data recovered from the wreckage indicates that their PDF scanned an intermittent contact and moved to intercept. Perhaps too aggressively."

"The same as the Myrmidon Company pickets," Hakar recalled. "It wasn't Valinata, then."

"Oh, no," Motayre said. "Raven Blue, without a doubt. We're waiting on a detailed analysis of the footage. It appears the intruders then went on to raze the colony." Motayre was clearly disgusted by the idea of ships bombarding a civilian colony, not to mention a harmless commune. It was the sort of thing to which one did not grow desensitized.

"I'm guessing their PDF wasn't very well equipped?" Telec ventured.

"It wouldn't have mattered even if they had a dreadnought," Motayre replied as the lift reached the level occupied by the Defense Council Control Center. He hunched down and passed through the door, leading the other two into the corridor. Above them skylights were frosted over, each one a lacy fractal curve. "It looks like they were up against a fair-sized armada. Eight, nine capital ships. All constructed of that thrice-damned composite. Speaking of which, we've had a breakthrough."

They passed through a security checkpoint staffed by elite armor-clad sojieri of the Falcon Guard and entered the control center, the surprisingly quiet beating heart of the Coalition's strategic command. Technicians and officers were bent over computers or huddled in discussion, moving thousands of ships and millions of sojieri across the galaxy.

"What's this breakthrough, then?" asked Telec once they were seated around the conference table in the secure briefing room.

"The report came through from Edenbridge Biotechnics." Motayre looked uncomfortable.

Hakar hid his annoyance. As the admiral in the control center, any priority traffic would naturally come to Motayre. But Kra'al had made Hakar the lead on the Raven Blue project, and anything from Edenbridge should have gone right to him. Unless, of course, Telec had ordered it rerouted. There would be time to address that later.

"The report is a little outside my area of expertise," Motayre confessed. He handed a dossier across the table. Irritably, Hakar snatched it before Telec could. The Sanar admiral graciously stayed quiet and folded his hands in his lap.

"Unfortunately," Motayre said while Hakar perused the file, "it seems Edenbridge's team was unable to decode the sample. It contained heritable genetic information, you see, but it adheres to a nonstandard configuration."

Both Telec and Hakar sat bolt upright at that. "Wait, *what*?"

"They managed to differentiate a few protein patterns but were unable to go any farther than that. Neither, I am afraid, am I." Motayre shrugged his broad shoulders in the Human fashion. "I take it you have some insight?"

That was a massive understatement. Hakar and Telec were out the door in moments, the dossier clutched in the Tagean's right hand. Telec was on the comm, his voice pitched in a tone Hakar recognized as extremely agitated. "This is Grand Admiral Telec. I need an audience with Her Majesty immediately. It's urgent, a matter of national security."

When they arrived at Kra'al's office, the empress was getting ready for a day in the throne room. She was donning an ornate blue and red halo-like ruff that attached to the back of her gown, and she looked agitated herself. When she heard them enter, without fanfare or announcement, she turned and fixed them with a calculating stare. "This had better be important." Her voice was like a pin on glass, and Hakar fought the urge to cringe like a child.

"Your Majesty," he blurted out, not waiting for Telec. "You have to recall Prime Minister Somerset right away. He's in danger."

"And you have to authorize us to scramble forces to the border," Telec added. He stood just behind his colleague, making sure Hakar took the brunt of the empress's attack, as usual letting someone else lead the charge for him.

And attack she did. "If this is a joke, it's a poorly timed one," she snapped. "I have representatives of the IREO in my audience chamber, demanding a full evaluation of Terran environmental renovations before this year's summit." She sat down, perfectly still except for her tail, which thumped rhythmically on the floor and against the desk. "Now what the hell are you two going on about?"

"We have reason to believe that Raven Blue poses an immediate danger to the Coalition," Telec said cautiously. "We can finally confirm that they're not from within the Valinata, and I can guarantee they won't stop once they're finished with their Space Force."

"Between our fleets and the VSF armadas, won't someone notice if another fleet sneaks in? The area would be rather crowded."

Hakar felt his patience slipping, "Your Highness, I know we've been playing this cautiously to bypass parliamentary oversight and avoid causing a panic. I'm willing to stake my career on this. We knew Vali communications were fragmented, but clearly none of their border forces are much better informed than we are. I'm not worried about reprisals from them. I'm worried about leaving ourselves vulnerable to invasion because we're observing the Engine Accord." It was hard to believe the once-mighty VSF had been reduced to pawns on some shadowy third party's chessboard, but there it was.

"I'm glad to hear you're considering the accord, at least, and that you recognize that we would need parliamentary intervention to overturn it." Kra'al tapped the claws of one hand against those of the other, clicking like the chamber of a machine gun with an empty clip. "So, you're willing to stake your career on this. And what about mine?"

"If we don't act soon, our careers won't be worth very much." Hakar slid the dossier across Kra'al's desk.

"You're serious," she said coolly as she picked up the folder and flipped through the Mems. "Telec, you are my defense advisor. *Advise* me."

Telec's facial tentacles twisted briefly, anxiously. *Wriggle your way out of this,* Hakar thought smugly. "I concur with Hakar. We should begin stepping up our presence in the systems adjoining Calama and make provisions for a full, rapid response. If anything happens, it will happen quickly, and we can't have it tarnish Your Majesty's reputation."

"Don't presume to frighten me by appealing to some insecurity about my popularity," Kra'al said slowly. "I'll put an emergency motion before the ministers to overturn the accord and move grand battlefleets into the region, but I'll need your full backing and the support of the rest of the Chamber. In the meantime, get the rest of the Zoh into the Arc." She looked at them for a long moment, her eyes deceptively placid. "It sounds as though you had better get to work on it," she added with finality.

§

Rockmore looked impatiently at the clock on the wall of his office. It took him a moment to figure out what time it was: Theresa had given him the timepiece when they had settled on Eve, and he would never get rid of it, but it was a bit abstract and hard to read. It was almost six in the morning, he finally decided. *Where are they?* While he waited, his gaze returned to his desk, lingering on Theresa's smiling photo, a shadow of a moment frozen in time. He couldn't remember the occasion, couldn't remember why there were snow-blanketed trees behind her. Had they been skiing? Whatever the occasion, she had been happy, smiling, full of life. That was before she fell ill and he discovered that sometimes, no matter how hard he prayed, the healing arts he had taken for granted all his life would not always succeed. If she had lasted but a few years longer, the first polymerase swarms would have been available to her; then again, he wouldn't have wished her a few more years of agony, not by a long shot. This was in hindsight, of course. He hadn't accepted it even as she passed away beside him, and he would never forgive himself for that. Involuntarily, the general's hand clenched into a fist so quickly that his knuckles cracked. Theresa had never believed in Jackal Pack, but her belief in him had been more than enough. A lonely existence was a bitter one, he reflected.

Alone, he allowed a tear to run down his cheek, fondly remembering her voice, her touch. The tear ran its course along the fissured scars on his face, the first rainfall flowing through a long-dried riverbed. There was a click at the door, and he put the picture down, hastily ran his sleeve across his cheek as it opened. *I am getting old,* he thought, embarrassed. *All my free time is spent in the past.* His orderly was showing Akida and Victor in. The two eyed each other with suspicion even as Rockmore offered them drinks.

"Kaf, please," Akida said.

"Just water for me," Victor added, looking and sounding a little hung over. Rockmore noticed that the two of them were standing as far apart as they could without making it look conspicuous.

When the door shut behind his orderly, Rockmore leaned back and steepled his fingers. "Guys, come on. You can cut the act in front of me."

The two relaxed slightly, managing to look almost at ease with each other. Sometimes Rockmore wondered if it all wasn't an act. Then again, the other night's altercation between Raptor Merikii and some of Akida's men had been real enough.

"All right," he said, blowing out a frustrated sigh. "I'm getting sick of your crews fighting in front of the troops. Sure, it's amusing for a while, and it fosters competition between your battalions, but you're setting a bad example, the both of you. You know we have some tempers on this base, and the last thing I need is for those little scuffles to spark a real brawl."

Both colonels looked chagrined. Rockmore caught the brief glance that passed between them, contemptuous and self-righteous. They were so much alike, those two, beneath their vastly different exteriors. And they were both smart enough to know the general was right. The Pack was a disciplined army but one composed of smaller groups that were used to fighting autonomously and thinking for themselves. No matter how much training and how many incentives they provided, the legion had never been able to overcome one simple problem: most of the mercenaries tended to be unpredictable, impulsive, and a little overconfident. While none of the sojieri in the Pack had a criminal record that would violate the organization's charter, many had been ejected from their respective militaries of origin for the same infractions: insubordination or conduct unbecoming. Tempers ran hot under Eve's sun, and it was only a matter of time before that heat set off the unstable mixture.

Victor found his tongue first. "You're right, sir. Is ... that why you called us?" he asked bluntly.

"I wish it were something so easy to fix." Rockmore waved his executive officers to the chairs facing his desk. "I've been getting some disturbing reports. A commune on the planet Ressa was wiped out, along with their defense picket."

Akida frowned, taking a sip of his Kaf. "Ressa's pretty close, isn't it? You think it was a Vali probe?"

"I can't think of why a VSF commander would demolish a civilian colony," Victor interjected. "Unless there were covert CRDF assets there."

"Ressa checks out clean," the general informed them. His contacts in the Unified Commonwealth Authority were confident of that, at least. Rockmore sat back, watching his executive officers think. He fancied he could hear the machinery of their minds running. Despite their colorful histories, both were officers of the highest quality and among the finest combat leaders he had ever met. Akida, once a promising black ops commander in the Shar'dan Republican Guard, had been relegated to a miserable, dead-end rotation guarding supplies at one of the kingdom's less prestigious academies. Victor had been on the fast track to becoming a Coalition Royal Defense Force grand admiral after a string of decisive campaigns under Hakar until the devastating error on Daltar that had eroded public opinion of the Telemon regime and nearly landed Leon himself before a firing squad. They were the sort of thoughtful, methodical, and courageous officers he wished he could have served with during his days in the UCA.

Akida was impassive as he ruminated, but Leon had a tell: Rockmore noticed him turning his switchblade over and over in one hand, running the pad of his thumb along the flat edge of the closed blade. "Elements of the Fifth Fleet are still hunkered around Iris," Leon said after a moment. "VSF forces could try to outflank, but they'd be taking the scenic route. It'd take months instead of days, no way to make the timetables fit for an attack." He shrugged. "It could be the reason the regional base here is running a bed and breakfast for Zoh Hegemony spies."

Akida snorted. "I'd almost guarantee the Fifth and the Zoh forces are just duplicating efforts. They won't cooperate willingly."

"Why do you say that?" Leon asked, defensive.

"Look around you. The CRDF is working at cross-purposes here. They've got forces engaging and pulling back all along the border like they don't know what to do with them. Planetary defense forces, border units, main battle fleets, none of them working cohesively. The snake has too many heads, and they're pulling the body in too many directions."

"You're wrong," Leon said quickly. "They know what they're doing."

"Please. Have you heard the term 'fall of Rome'?" Akida was sneering a little. "What's the Coalition? A huge empire composed of dozens of semi-autonomous states with their own military forces and economies ostensibly working in harmony. But look at them. The Zoh Hegemony and the Dias Traverse are just the best examples of neighbors that should never have been put together under one rule. No wonder the Coalition suffers constant threats of secession."

Rockmore's eyes flicked between the two, watching Akida's smile throughout his little tirade and Leon's mounting aggravation.

But Akida wasn't done. "I mean, come on. What kind of bureaucracy is so bloated that it strings an endless trail of prefixes to its titles just so everyone can keep getting pay raises? What the hell is a 'high grand admiral,' for that matter? Imagine an animal so big that nerve impulses from its brain take days, even weeks, to reach the rest of its body. By the time it moves to act, the situation around it has changed, and it'll always be playing catch-up, always be falling farther behind. *That*'s the Coalition Royal Defense Force, Victor, and the Coalition in general. They tried to marry different ideologies, but instead what do you have? Endless lines of overpaid figureheads controlled by a military-industrial complex that's infected the rest of the galaxy."

"You know what, Akida?" Leon snapped. "The Coalition may not be perfect, but for better or worse, they're the best protection the Outbound Arc has. You think that's easy with trillions of citizens of their own? You think I trust the *bureaucrats*? I trust in the people I know, and I know Grand Admiral Hakar. And whether you think his rank is overblown or not, he's earned every fucking letter it takes to spell it a hundred times over."

"There you go with your misguided fucking loyalty again. Why don't you try thinking for yourself rather than constantly believing the word of the asshole who sold you out?"

The general stood up. Suddenly he was weary of all this. "That's enough. You're talking about a client."

"I apologize," muttered Akida, flustered. He seemed to calm down quickly, smoothing his hair. The colonels waited for Rockmore to elaborate.

The general stood, pacing slowly before the windows. It was a cloudy morning, but there had been no rain, just gray skies. Along the rim of the plateau, batteries of condensers would be working hard to collect that moisture. "With the Rau Zeta and Tilora Co. contracts completed, seventy-five percent of our ground assets and ninety percent of our aerospace assets are here. That's the closest to full strength we've been in a long time." Rockmore wrung his hands. He had deliberated long and hard. "I want a lock on all contracts as of this moment."

His colonels reacted as though he had reached across the table and smacked them. "Sir?" they asked in unison, incredulous.

Rockmore was in no mood for either of them to question him. "Whatever's going on out there is coming to a boil. Leon, you said it yourself: the CRDF is the Outbound Arc's best defense, and they're stretched too thin. More than that, if it comes down to defending core worlds or our little free-trade zone, we'll be hung out to dry."

They saw the wisdom in his words, he was pleased to see. Even so, they looked confused and angry. Neither said anything.

Rockmore felt he owed them an explanation. "The Alkyra Trade Route has always relied on a balance of trade between the Coalition and the Valinata to keep us safe. We're worth more independent than as another vassal state for either one of them. If the VSF decides to steamroll, there's nothing we can do about it other than make Eve a less attractive target."

"Easier said than done. We've got a Coalition Regional Base here, and the VSF will want that out of the way," Leon pointed out.

"That's true," Akida agreed, "but it also means the CRDF is likely to have a more vested interest in our safety, too. Unless they just roll up the tents and pull out ahead of time."

They trusted his instincts, Rockmore saw, and they were with him in word if not spirit. Those instincts had saved him countless times in the past—he was a survivor in a line of work that didn't forgive failure or poor judgment. Those instincts had turned what should have been a failed experiment in commercialized warfare into a lucrative business endeavor with a loyal client base and a solid reputation.

"I get that you two are concerned," Rockmore conceded, "and I get why. But our retained earnings over the last few years have been steadily climbing. We should have enough to see us through this. I may have to cut base pay, depending on the length of this lock, but I'll worry about that when the time comes." Rockmore's main concern was losing some of the new investors who had been exploring opportunities with the Pack. Some, like the Insir Gamma PDF delegation who had shown interest in hiring Akida out to train their special forces division, had already jumped ship. To Rockmore, there was no question that a whole, poorer Pack was better than one unprepared and swept aside.

Active and pending contracts were to be fulfilled and expedited where possible. Arrangements were to be made for long-term contracts and clients, replacing Jackal Pack troops with competitors where necessary. Units of platoon strength or greater were to be reeled in. From then on, clients would be queued in order of revenue stream.

The colonels were far from placated. Rockmore frowned. "I know it's tough, but I want the two of you drilling your units like the end of the world is tomorrow, with a particular focus on full battalion action. I want every company to function cohesively with the others. Work on combined-arms, tactical envelopments, ordered withdrawals, all the stuff we usually skirt. And requisition surplus armament while we still can. Which reminds me...." Rockmore snapped his fingers and walked back around his desk. He rifled through a drawer of files and pulled one out. "I don't know if either of you remember Major Craf, the base commander I recruited from the Commonwealth academy on Bishar. I'm considering bringing him on long-term. What do you think?"

Leon and Akida both reached out for copies of the major's service history. "Are you kidding, General?" asked Akida after he had glanced it over. "He's a fucking staff officer."

Leon flipped through the file. "No combat duty, not a lot of leadership experience." He and Akida agreed upon little, but they were in perfect harmony regarding the quality of their officers. "Looks to me like he's just served as aide to a whole lot of generals, and now he's babysitting recruits."

Rockmore folded his arms. He should have expected this. "He's got a lot of rear-echelon experience, gentlemen. Both of you tend to micromanage your battalion headquarters staff, and I think we need to take a more practical perspective when it comes to support."

"So you're saying we're opening a financial services division? What do we need more accountants for?" Akida asked, smirking.

He might have hoped that their pasts would have humbled them, but both colonels were still so proud. "I was thinking he could take some of the pressure off the two of you and maybe serve as an instructor for crosstraining officers." Jackal Pack tended not to employ anyone without combat experience, whether they were former shields, army, navy, or even the occasional heavy hitter from the wrong side of the law. However, Rockmore insisted that all commissioned officers be crosstrained and capable when it came to administrative matters from requisition to finance. It required a lot of time, though, and mistakes were made fairly often. It would be good to have someone on board who could streamline operations.

"You take him," Leon said with a sidelong glance at Akida.

"I was about to say the same to you. If anyone needs an S-4 to help with basic math, it's you."

"I agree," Rockmore said, and that was that. "The bottom line is that I want you both to focus more on strategy, especially if the border erupts."

He eyed his colonels wearily, drumming his fingers on his desk. "One more thing before I let you go. Results from last month's drug test came back...."

Both of them were paying close attention. "Yes, sir?" asked Akida, looking a little nervous.

"Over a thousand sojieri tested positive for various narcotics. Four hundred of them were on active duty at the time and thirty of them are on missions *right now*. Five of them even tested positive for Burn. I'm sure you'll both agree that public relations has to be one of our primary concerns, and I cannot have men and women performing below spec. What if one of them was to shoot a civilian while under the influence?"

Leon and Akida had the good grace to look embarrassed.

"I've provided the roster of positives. Lucky for you, none of your own crews came up." Rockmore sighed. These were the sorts of administrative headaches he had never anticipated. "We've gone down since the last test, but I want this shit stamped out, do you understand? One of them can get others hooked, start a little pipeline here. I won't have it. Anyone who fails the next test will have their contract terminated, but for now I want you to dock pay from those people that tested positive. Make it abundantly clear, would you both?"

"Yes, sir," the colonels said reflexively.

Rockmore's attention was already elsewhere. His eyes were locked on the red sunrise crawling across the gray vault of the sky, painting the clouds and the savannahs in mirrored swaths of pink and crimson. "Give them one more day and then spread the word. That's all for now, guys. Dismissed."

§

"You know what I like about Eve?" Rachel asked. "The farms."

"Kind of a weird thing to say," responded Traxus. "You, ah, want to elaborate?"

Rachel realized how that had sounded and smiled sheepishly. Her other friends from Tesa hadn't heard—they were wandering around the apartment, opening cabinets and inspecting the bedroom. Claire was trying out the bathroom. "I think it has to do with the fact that Eve produces a lot of what it uses. Back on Amalthia, everything that isn't housing is given over to tourism. Everything has to be imported. Not everyone can afford those kinds of premiums, so a lot of people are destitute." She looked down at her own expensive Adrevani shoes and sighed. "It's one of the reasons I couldn't stay there."

"You think you could stay *here*?" Traxus asked pointedly.

"I'm going to try," Rachel said honestly. "I just wish Leon had been able to come today." At first, Rachel had been planning to keep the apartment-hunting a secret, a surprise. It didn't take her long to realize that springing something of that magnitude on Leon was not the best way to get him on board.

"I'm sure he would have liked to." Traxus walked over to join Rachel at the window. Sunlight poured into the open space of the apartment, the hardwood floors glowing. "You know he had important business."

Rachel did know that. Recently, Valinata ships crowded with refugees had flooded the Alkyra Trade Route, many of them touching down at the Eve Cosmodrome. It was strange and terrifying: everyone had suspected the Valinata Space Force was up to something over the border, and to have Valinata refugees flooding Alkyran space left them with no answers, just more questions. Rockmore had decided to be proactive and had sent Leon, Colonel Akida, Doctor Reonil and his nurse, Corporal Alexis Thorne, to the cosmodrome with an entourage of officers and sojieri. Their orders were to bring food and medical supplies to the overwhelmed port workers for distribution to the refugees and offer free medical care to those who needed it. Naturally, Leon and Akida were there to look for information, conduct interviews with anyone who might have pertinent information, and generally be on the lookout for trouble. Both of them seemed to have a knack for finding the latter. "If they wanted trouble, they should have just taken Jeric," Rachel mused aloud.

"Believe it or not, he's making himself useful," Traxus replied. "He's helping customs, running close-in scans of the refugee ships." The two of them stood silently for a moment, watching the traffic moving far below. Behind them, the other girls laughed at a joke, and Traxus looked uncomfortable. Even in civilian garb, she didn't exactly fit in with Rachel's Tesa friends. She was too much a sojier, too much a warrior.

"The view is great, Rachel. There's a lot of space, and the neighborhood is one of the best. You'd be what, two minutes from everything, right?" Claire said, walking up to them.

Traxus turned away from the vista and took Rachel's hands. Her expression was deadly serious. "Speaking of Jeric, you should be careful. There's a bar in the living room, so he may be here every night and then pass out on your floor."

Rachel laughed, giddy. The apartment was beautiful, three thousand square feet of hardwood floors, brushed steel, frosted glass, and smart walls that could change color or display custom images and artwork. There was even an option for a free-floating Rombaldt chandelier which could reconfigure its light panels by remote. It wasn't quite Rachel's taste, but she knew that Leon would like the retro-futurist look of the place. The master bedroom was lofted above the main living area and looked out onto one of Tesa's broad avenues, lined with palmas and streetlights. It was in one of the ritzier districts of the city, close to shops, restaurants, and metro stations. In the city of nearly four million people, buildings had been going up quickly to stimulate immigration and attract foreign investment, but the well-situated real estate in the center had been rising in price. The first settlers on Eve had been Human speculators from the Iberian exodus, Portuguese- and Spanish-Terrans. After arriving together, the Spanish had joined with Eastern Fego Sheff'an to found Tesa and cultivate crops, while the Portuguese had burrowed into the mountain of Las Serras da Estrela looking for ore. The building was situated between the historic Spanish-Terran and Sheff'an districts abutting Avenida de los Emperadores and had recently been renovated. The interior was trendily Terran Revival, while the exterior featured warm Sheff'an design with plenty of detailed engravings and circular motifs.

Leon seemed to understand that Rachel needed space and an identity apart from Jackal Pack. He hadn't blinked an eye when she mentioned looking for an apartment in the city, and he supported her plan to buy a new car, understanding her embarrassment at driving around in a black and red-striped Hyena.

The realtor had sensed a buyer and had left Rachel and Traxus alone to get a feel for the place. For Rachel, it had been love at first sight, but the price was a concern. Her savings were dwindling. She could always ask her mother for money, knowing that even though she had gone against her wishes by coming back to Eve, the old harridan would help. Her father would likely shower her with talons if she deigned to talk to him, but she never would. Couldn't give the bastard the satisfaction, and she wouldn't be able to sleep at night if she took his money. *Is Leon's blood money any better?*

"I don't think this can work," she said after a moment, looking up.

They meandered into the kitchen where Claire and the girls were admiring the marble-topped counters. There were rubalite flakes, and the brochure said there were also trykon veins in the stone. Somehow Rachel doubted that last part. "What do you mean?" There was genuine concern in Traxus's voice.

"I mean this place. I can't ask Leon to pay for this. I don't want to get a free ride."

"But there's already been an offer," Claire pointed out.

"Well below the asking price. The realtor gave me first bid, though." Maybe it was just a pipe dream, anyway.

"I know this probably isn't your first choice," Traxus ventured, "but would you consider working for us? With your looks, your personality, and your smile, you could go a long way," Traxus said, warming to the topic. "You've worked telecommunications before, right? I'm sure the general would pay you well, and you'd probably get to travel a lot. Damn, maybe I should ask for a transfer."

Rachel was a little embarrassed, and her cheeks flushed. "I was an engineer, not a marketing person. But actually, he already offered me a position in public relations, giving tours to investors, that sort of thing."

Gravcars were zipping by on the street below, and happy pedestrians were enjoying the unseasonably cool day. Grounds crews were watering the palmas along the sidewalks in defiance of the water rationing. "Traxus, don't take this the wrong way, but I'm not sure I could stand working for the Pack. I like the people and all, but I don't think I could wrestle with the ethics."

The Tagean gave her a knowing little smile. "I completely understand. I'm sure there are plenty of positions in your field in the city, too. Las Serras might be a little far, but I bet you could find work there if you don't mind the commute. The maglev transrapide gets there quickly, at least."

Rachel nodded and smiled. Traxus had been part of the relief/intelligence-gathering effort at the cosmodrome, but Leon had gladly parted with her, and Traxus had been delighted to take the day off. The young Tagean seemed nearly as excited as Rachel to look at apartments.

This was only the second they had visited, but it seemed perfect. Part of Rachel's reason for asking Traxus along had been because she liked the young Tagean and wanted some company, but she also felt Traxus would be able to provide some insight into Leon's mind. At times he could be remarkably hard to read. Usually frank and open, when he chose to be cryptic, he was indecipherable. Rachel didn't know whether he did it intentionally or whether it was some sort of defense mechanism. She had seen other men do it, but Leon seemed to have mastered the technique and could probably pass a polygraph test if she subjected him to it.

"I wonder if there are any good moving companies around here," Rachel wondered aloud.

Traxus's bark of laughter surprised her as it echoed in the space. "Are you kidding? The troops will take good care of Leon's stuff. Plus, it'll be an interesting way to meet your new neighbors, having a Minotauri shock trooper carry your couch up the stairs."

Rachel laughed and moved toward a white leather couch—the realtor had furnished the apartment to give potential renters an idea of how it would look, but the furniture would disappear once the lease was signed. "Can I ask you a personal question, Traxus?" The Tagean clicked her tongue, and Rachel asked. "What made you join the Pack? You don't seem like the type."

Now Traxus laughed. She joined Rachel on the couch and clasped her hands between her knees. "I'll take that as a compliment. I wish I could say it's complicated, but it really isn't. I wanted to join the military, be a sojier like my brother. Of course, this was very much against my parents' wishes, not to mention the matriarch's. They wanted me to stay and become head of the family. There's still plenty of time for that as I see it."

"If you don't get killed."

The words hung in the air. The two of them sat quietly for a few minutes, listening to the faint sounds of traffic through the floor-to-ceiling windows. *It would be a perfect place for us*, Rachel thought to herself. A nagging doubt clouded her excitement, however. "Do you think Jeric and the others will be on board? I don't want to play tug-of-war."

"That's sweet, honey, but I wouldn't give those clowns a second thought. The fact that you do care what we think is why *we* think you're perfect for Leon. Jeric just has trouble with … social situations. If he's not drunk or flying, he's usually kind of an asshole."

The truth was that Rachel understood Jeric's misgivings perfectly. Considering that she had abandoned his closest friend just a month ago, she couldn't blame him. What she couldn't risk, however, was his attitude coloring Leon's perceptions. "I just don't want him turning Leon against the idea."

"I don't think Leon usually listens to a word Jeric says. To be honest, his battalions could be run without him. He likes to think he needs to be on the base every night in case there's a disaster. Do you know the last time the base was attacked?"

"No," Rachel said. "Never?" she guessed.

"That's right. Never. Do you know the last time a battalion was scrambled for a mission?"

"Also never?"

"Correct. I'm not telling you he won't take time to consider—he will. He always does. But don't worry about Jeric or anybody else." Traxus put her hand on Rachel's arm. Her fur tickled. "If you need me to, I'll run interference, but I don't think it'll come to that."

"Traxus, thank you so much." It felt good to have a real friend again. "Tell you what, lunch is on me."

"I won't argue with that," the Tagean said with a big smile.

12: Frozen

The news of the freeze went over about as well as could be expected. The Jackals were all tuned into current events, and few of them were surprised. However, none were pleased. For enlisted Pack sojieri, base salary was only nominally above a livable wage. They were paid for going on missions, not for sitting around cleaning their weapons. The last time a contract lock was put into effect had been several years ago when the Coalition had warned the JPML to stand down during a sensitive conflict. The prospect of instituting another moratorium, again on behalf of the Coalition, was met with a less than enthusiastic response.

The last lock had meant steep pay cuts when a number of backers who had a stake in the issue had pulled out. And in spite of Leon's and Akida's assurances that pay cuts were not an immediate danger this time around, the mercenaries, wary by nature, scoffed.

Raptor took the news placidly as he prayed, scratching symbols in the dirt. He barely indicated that he had heard although the corded muscles in his neck tightened beneath his rough, mottled skin.

Perhaps because the decision meant that this new threat was genuine or because he simply wanted to convince himself, Leon felt he had to explain. "Rockmore has a feeling—*we* have a feeling—that this thing in the Valinata is going to escalate and that we're going to have to get involved. He wants all hands on deck when the shooting starts."

Traxus was next to Leon on the bench, a mug of Kaf steaming in her hands. They were sitting on the northwestern edge of the Luxor Plateau, watching the sun complete its climb over the horizon. The air was cold and crisp, the savannah stretching out below them, unbroken for miles but for stunted trees and bushes and a few forest groves erupting defiantly from the dirt and rock. "Why do I have a feeling my brother put the general up to this? Tell me."

It was entirely possible, and, in fact, Leon suspected it was so, but Rockmore would have told them if he intended for them to know. Still, it was unpalatable lying to the admiral's sister about it. "Hakar had nothing to do with this, although he hasn't been giving us any information we can use. I trust the general's instincts." His pointedly raised eyebrows forestalled any further comment. After all, he was management, and he was obligated to maintain a united front at times.

Jeric yawned, having said nothing so far. He had gotten in from an all-night patrol flight and wasn't yet responding to external stimuli. Leon had been sure that something like this would register, but then again Jeric never seemed to care about his salary as long as he got enough for booze. Whereas other mercs would wheedle and cajole, he took what he got and generally shut up. Now he just sat and drank his Kaf as if it were the only thing of importance in the world, staring bleary-eyed at the horizon. The sun was up all the way now, and the pink sky was turning golden as the sun illuminated the clouds. Back on the base, Rachel was still sleeping heavily.

Leon glanced at his watch. He hated to admit it, but facing his battalions and doling out bad news had taken a lot out of him. "Boy, it feels like the end of the day already."

Jeric muttered something into his coffee.

"Can you tell us anything about the Vali refugees?" Traxus asked, recalling his absence the day before.

Leon frowned. He had spent years training to fight the VSF. While they had worked for Valinata clients in the past, he had never been able to shake his distrust of anyone from beyond the Veil. "They're all scared, and they're all spinning wild stories. One thing they have in common is that none of them have actually been attacked."

"What do you mean?" asked Traxus, her ears perking up.

"They're all talking about this mysterious faction smashing planets. All of them got out while the getting was good. It sounds like no one escapes once the attacks start."

"So it's not just VSF lies."

Leon had seen the frightened faces of refugees and crews alike. Much as he hated to admit it, the VSF didn't seem to be the threat here. Something had prompted a mass exodus, only no one knew what it was. "I guess not," he finally admitted.

"How does this affect Natille's wedding? We still going?"

It was a nagging question that Leon had been trying to ignore. With the lock in effect and Rockmore insisting on stepped-up maneuvers, leave would be cancelled. Leave might be cancelled for quite a while, and the wedding was not that far off. "We'll have to wait and see."

"You still feel like kissing the general's ass now?" Jeric mumbled between sips from his thermos.

"Hey, come on," Traxus said. "I'm sure he'll make an exception."

"For one of his XOs, right when he needs him most? I doubt it," Raptor replied, rising from his oblations and dusting himself off.

The base was mostly quiet, with the night watch about to come off duty. A few squads were conducting early morning PT, and a maintenance crew was pruning bushes. Although it was far too early, Leon and his friends found themselves drifting toward the Desher Vaux, slipping into the startling darkness of the pub.

"Now we're talking," Jeric said, instantly perking up.

Mara approached, smiling as she wiped her hands on her apron. "A little early for Hais, isn't it, Colonel?"

Leon smiled. "Just Kaf for me, Mara. Spiced, with cream and sugar. Hey, is there a game on?"

"No signal from the Valinata national rugby championship, but I think there's fútbol on Shar'dan One."

"Great."

"Kaf for the rest of you?" Mara asked as she turned on the viewer. "By the zombie looks on your faces, I'll guess you don't want placebos." She was too cheerful for just after dawn. "So it sounds like you're all going to be getting some time off."

"I guess you could say that," grumbled Jeric.

"But I wouldn't," added Raptor.

Mara was undeterred. "If my job were getting shot at all the time, I wouldn't mind the occasional sabbatical, personally. But I appreciate your business all the same." She turned and went to fetch the coffee.

"Wait! I'll take a beer, please," Jeric amended, drawing annoyed looks from his friends. Turning to Leon, he asked, "So what are your plans for the brigades?" If he was hoping to skate by with a minimal workload, Leon was going to have a lot of fun disappointing him.

"We'll be training hard. If we're going to war we have get out of the regular routine. Small-unit tactics are out, strategic maneuvers are in. If we get a sanction, we'll probably be assigned to a support role. Combined-arms assaults, full frontal attack, the works. The general thinks we're lacking in the withdrawal department. I want each brigade functioning as a single mind and body. And since you spoke up, Jerr, I want you to work with the rest of the pilots on low-altitude precision support. Every time there's a planetary campaign, the navy seems to forget we're down there, so I want to make sure we've got some guardian angels we can trust. Raptor, I'm going to have you lead breach teams and skirmishers."

The Prross's toothy grin startled Leon.

"Bunker infiltration, boarding ops, whatever we might need on the offensive." Leon leaned back in the booth and looked at Traxus. "Trax, I want to roll you in with the armored corps."

"Typical," she bit back. "Keep me out of harm's way, is that it?"

"I read Braeburn's report, Trax." Leon understood why she might jump to that conclusion, and she was partially right. When she had enlisted in the Pack, she had been accepted on her brother's one condition: that she be kept safe. "You'll have a support platoon of your own, maybe a tank or two under your command." That mollified her for the time being. "Guys, listen up. *If* the general is right and the border goes up in flames, we're going to stick together. I'd put the Pack up against the best of the Valinata—or the CRDF—any day. But the three of you are not expendable. None of you have anything to prove. If it goes bad, get out if you get a chance, and don't look back."

For a moment, they regarded him impassively. Then Raptor and Traxus began to laugh. "You are one paranoid son of a bitch," the Prross chided him.

Leon blushed and smiled his lopsided smile. Raptor was probably right.

§

The days of the Valinata were winding down. Their government, centralized to the extreme, had ignored the danger, compounding the problem a hundredfold, and now it was too late. Too late for many things. They had wasted their efforts trying to stare down the Coalition and crushing the resistance springing up in response to the rationing efforts. Reynaldo Montoya would never say it aloud, but he had never bought into the ideologies of consolidated power and zealous militarism. As a child, he had loved the parades, the pomp and ceremony. As a young adult, he had loved the sense of belonging, purpose, and superiority. But as a man, he had begun to question the policies determining what a person did, where they could live, what they could think. It wasn't as oppressive as the Coalition media made it sound, but it wasn't that much better.

Of course, life as a VSF officer made things easier. It had opened doors, guaranteed the best schools for his children, netted him a fine country home on a quiet world. It also let him hear the whispers of real information that were denied to most of the populace. Those whispers had grown more and more disturbing over the last months. *The last months, what a fitting way to put it.* One by one, fleets had fallen silent, worlds had fallen silent. Entire sectors had gone dark. And though the Tête kept insisting that it was simply downed communication relays, closed trade routes, and travel rationing, Montoya knew that things had gone very wrong, starting at Tanis Ruin and radiating outward like an infection. Tanis Ruin, one of the Valinata's great treasures, a place that Montoya had always dreamed of visiting. Now, he would never have the chance. It was thought to have been the second seat of power for the ancient Tagean Dynasty, possibly even a second empire set up by a splinter group—and hadn't that been seen as the ultimate justification for the Valinata's refusal to submit to the Coalition? It was a glorious world dotted with crumbling alabaster ruins and hidden technological marvels, some of which still retained some semblance of function. What had it become now?

Montoya, the captain of the *Rampant*, commander of a few thousand frightened men and women, sat uneasily in his command chair. The ship's crew worked diligently as they had for the last few months. It was easy to lose track of time out here, and at this point he felt that the ship's log was the only thing tying him to a sense of normalcy. He glanced through the main porthole, eyes roving over the long bow of the ship. It wasn't long enough to suit him. He wished desperately that he were in command of some of the Coalition's new *Goliath*-class heavy cruisers and not his group of aging Valinata *Harpy*-class destroyers. His pitiful little flotilla was the only bastion of Vali strength between the Amanra and Calama, and it would barely be enough to turn away a pirate raid.

In his own mind, he and his ship were between the hammer and the anvil, obligated to remain there by an absentee ruling council. Contact had been lost with more and more colonies, and the leadership was in a state of near-panic, ordering every spare ship of the line to patrol the hastily established perimeter. The Tête had already relocated the seat of power to an undisclosed location. Montoya was no fool. He did not believe that the perimeter was so defined, and it seemed to be expanding day by day, a world here, a system there. His scanning officer had detected an unknown capital ship skirting their very patrol route a few days earlier. At first Montoya had suspected it was another Coalition spy ship, but when the computer had failed to identify the vessel by either thermal or sensor signature, the crew had gone quiet. A visual scan had shown them an odd, squid-shaped vessel; one of the invading ships had swept right through their patrol zone.

After calling in a report to his central battle group commander, Montoya had received frantic orders to fire upon anything that came within scanning range. Just having such an order piped down to him made him even more nervous. If nothing else, it showed that their leaders had no more information than he did. They were jumping at shadows.

"Sir!" shouted his scanning officer, tearing him out of his reverie. The woman's voice was cracking. For days on end, they had been at general quarters alert, and it was wearing them all down, pressure building with no way to release it. Like pipes, people would start blowing out at the seams. "Vessel approaching! Passenger liner pinging a diplomatic transponder!"

Montoya had no intention of shooting at a spaceliner full of refugees. "Get me a firing solution. And hail them." *Maybe we can avoid a bloodbath. Just this once.*

"Firing solution fixed!" shouted the fire-control officer. "Target moving approximately nine hundred klicks per hour, will pass by eighty thousand klicks on current trajectory. Course is sixteen degree differential."

Montoya nodded approvingly, and looked to the scanning officer. "Lieutenant, scan the ship. Comms, any response to hails?"

"Sweet Jesus, that's a Coalition transponder ... it's the *Royal Dawn!*"

Montoya was out of his seat in a moment, stalking among his crew. *Gracias a Dios, they made it out safely!* "Get me a full workup."

"Yes, sir. I'm getting some interference ... it's...." The officer was quiet a moment, rescanning. Montoya glimpsed the signals coming through over her shoulder. *That can't possibly be right. No puede ser verdad.* "Heat signatures are consistent with reactor damage, but I'm not reading anything from the passenger cabins." She tried again, turned in her chair, a pained expression on her face.

Montoya went rigid. "What?" He cuffed the comms officer on the shoulder. "Hail them," he repeated numbly. For several tense minutes, the young man did as he was told, calling out on the broadband, trying to elicit a response.

"Set us on an intercept course immediately." The captain tugged at his collar, which suddenly seemed far too tight. "Match their course, try to dock with them if they don't jump again first."

The big ship banked, gradually coming parallel with the liner's course. Two fighters did a flyby, looking for hull breaches or other signs of external damage. There weren't any.

Montoya swallowed as the report came through. *Un barco de fantasmas.* "A ghost ship," he mumbled to himself. The silver speck that was the *Dawn* grew in the viewport until Montoya could make out the intricate sunburst pattern on the bow, the ship's crest stenciled on the side of the hull, the Coalition Rienda emblazoned just below the bridge. The ship looked as though it had simply been abandoned and set on a course for home.

Montoya sat back down. He looked down at the comms officer, irritated. "Why aren't you hailing them?"

The young man looked up, chagrined, face shining with sweat. "Sir, they're not responding."

"I don't care. Keep pinging! I don't want to be the cause of an incident." Obediently, the young man went back to work. Maybe it would be better if the Coalition entered in force. He had never thought he would welcome those feared battle fleets.

For the next hour, like nervous lovers moving toward their first secretive tryst, the two ships slowly edged closer and closer as *Rampant* tried to move alongside. With the *Dawn* still moving at a good clip, they would have to match speed and heading perfectly. The ship's computers handled the docking, overseen by the helmsman, who jacked in using a neural interface for additional resolution.

Finally the ships were locked together in a grim embrace, segmented metal umbilicals linking airlocks. Montoya ordered a boarding party of marines to enter the other vessel and shut down her engines. What they reported shocked him beyond his wildest nightmares.

The marines were equipped with helmet cameras, and as the footage was relayed back to the bridge, the crew grew silent. Hair stood on the backs of necks, goose bumps rose, mouths went dry, eyes brimmed with tears. Stomachs churned, bile rose, sweat streamed. Montoya blinked hard, failing to blink away the grisly images. The only sounds were the rumble of the *Rampant*'s engines, the groan of her hull against the *Dawn*'s, and the terrified yammering of the boarding party washing over the speakers.

Montoya lightly touched the comms officer on the shoulder, and the young man jumped. "Send out a priority one distress signal immediately. To everyone."

"But sir, that means—"

"I know. I just hope they don't kill us all for what's been done."

§

They met quietly, five panicked leaders suddenly aware that control was slipping out of their hands. Kra'al cut out early from a meeting with her economic advisors and slipped away without a word to her adjutant. Telec left a briefing on the Coalition's Outbound supply line options in mid-discussion to the puzzlement and irritation of several junior officers who had spent the last week preparing their presentation. Hakar was embarrassed to be caught napping at his desk when the news came in. Winters, back aboard his flagship, joined them via secure comm beam while Pirsan waited for them all, a spider at the center of his web.

Epsilon Red situation cards had been distributed to all of them, instantly setting off warning bells. It was the highest priority emergency protocol used during peacetime. Kra'al's breathing was quick, and her heart hammered in her chest as she walked down the corridor that led to the comm-shielded chamber. What could possibly have happened now? Epsilon Red cards were hardly handed out casually, and two words were repeating in her mind with mounting panic, blurring together: *Royal Dawn, Royal Dawn, RoyalDawnroyaldawnroyaldawn.*

The Ministry of Defense secure comms room yawned open before her, a humming metal cave. She was the last one in, and the doors sealed behind her. Greetings were terse all around. Hakar looked exhausted and maybe a little sick, his eyes burning with fever light. The hospital-like surroundings didn't help. The room was stark white with black tiled floors and was uncomfortably quiet, aside from that infernal humming: the comm shielding and soundproofing prevented any sound from reaching them from the busy hallway outside. It felt isolated, cut off, a universe apart. With bare walls and few chairs, it also lacked creature comforts. And it was cold: Kra'al wished she had brought a shawl.

High Grand Admiral Pirsan opened his mouth to speak, his voice hoarse, leaden. "I'm not going to waste time. *Royal Dawn* has been recovered. All aboard are dead."

It was like a punch to the gut. Kra'al couldn't breathe, couldn't think, could only stare at the high grand admiral.

"Last night, at approximately twenty-three hundred hours our time, a distress call and request for aid was received by several different patrol groups along the Outbound Arc." He paused and looked at a Mem spread across the holographics projector table. "The responding ships were the light cruisers *Elri*, *Tasar*, *Illinois*, *King James*, *Orsona*, *Teshadek*, *Tigress*, and the medium carrier *Resonant*."

The faces around her were stony, strained. On his screen, Winters looked ashen. Pirsan continued. "Arriving on station outside the Valinata-controlled Gideon system, our cruisers found the VSF destroyer *Rampant* docked with *Royal Dawn*."

Are we at war? Kra'al wondered, her mind racing. Could VSF sojieri have been so stupid as to massacre Coalition diplomats? Why had she ever sent Somerset? What arrogance, to assume they could change anything.

"Majesty, are you all right?" Telec whispered, leaning over. Kra'al caught her breath and returned her attention to Pirsan

"The crew of the *Rampant* stood down immediately and submitted to boarding by marines from cruiser *Teshadek*. There were no incidents with the captives; however, as they were being transferred to *Teshadek*, a Valinata carrier group arrived in system and demanded that our ships withdraw."

"What of the *Royal Dawn*?"

"*Rampant*'s CO claims that they had nothing to do with the killings. Their boarding team recorded video which seems to corroborate his account." Pirsan stepped back and activated the projector with one click of a long, dexterous claw.

The grainy image that sprang into being before them had obviously been taken from a military issue helmet-mounted camera, an old one. The footage played, intercut between multiple camera feeds, starting at the airlock and progressing inwards. The corridors and bridge were empty. When the first images from the passenger lounge were displayed, Kra'al's lunch threatened to come back up. There was no doubt that it was the *Royal*

Dawn; she recognized the furniture, the bar, the beautiful Poral Dynasty crystal chandelier. But it was not as she had ever seen it.

Men and women in VSF uniforms could be seen in some of the shots, holding their hands to their mouths in horror or bent over vomiting. It was bad enough to see it in holo, but what they had seen firsthand must have been awful.

The lounge looked like a slaughterhouse. Blood was everywhere as though some madman had painted the bulkheads, deck, and ceiling with gore. Kra'al had to look away from the surreal abattoir. The images stayed with her.

The corpses of Somerset's entourage were everywhere, some of them mangled, sprawled about the room. More were hanging from the ceiling, swinging on barbed chains. They had been skeletonized, their clothing shredded, soaked in blood. They were unrecognizable.

All but one. The VSF marines had braved the horror and gotten close-ups of the victims. One of the bodies had been pinned against the bulkhead, arms outstretched, still wearing the tattered remnants of a prime minister's robes of office over a fine suit. Most of Somerset's skull was missing, the lower jaw gaping open, tongue lolling out.

Kra'al snarled. So this was the answer to their overtures of peace. "Turn it off."

Happy to do so, Pirsan shut off the holo, and the gruesome images vanished, but there was still a sour taste in Kra'al's mouth. The empress sat deep in thought for some time. Neither Hakar nor Telec disturbed her.

"Any thoughts?" she asked, finally.

"The prime minister ... that's a crucifixion," Winters observed, voice tinny from the speaker.

"Is that important?" Hakar asked impatiently.

"It could be. That's Christian iconography. It would be a powerful message to the right people."

"You're saying this was done by Human religious zealots?" Pirsan put in.

"Or someone who's been watching us long enough to identify the sort of imagery that we would find most disturbing." Winters's clinical detachment was useful, but Kra'al and Hakar both found it more than a little unsettling at times.

Pirsan continued, nevertheless shaken by Winters's observation. "The crew of the *Rampant* has denied responsibility. We're getting no response from the Vali leadership. The commodore of the Dragon Valia armada at Calama is demanding that the *Rampant* and her crew be returned, and that detaining them constitutes espionage and an act of war."

"Well, goddammit, we can't release them," Kra'al snarled. "What are our alternatives?"

"Put more ships into Calama because the Dragon Valia is going to come looking for them," Telec answered grimly.

"We're looking at this the wrong way," Hakar insisted. "The VSF is not the enemy. We need to open a dialogue with the commanders at Calama and put a stop to this. Get them on *our* side of the line."

Kra'al considered this. "I doubt they'll join us so easily, but it's worth trying."

"Just a moment," Winters said suddenly. They froze, looking at his face on the screen. His eyes were moving, reading something. "We have a problem," he said.

"What now?" Kra'al asked.

"Coalition Royal Navy ships have just destroyed two liners of Vali refugees." Kra'al's head sank into her hands. "Apparently they were maneuvering erratically as they approached a Coalition checkpoint," Winters elaborated. "A Captain Tucha, commanding the *Veracruz*, ordered the strike."

Kra'al held up her hand before Hakar could say anything. "Spare me your ghost stories. We now have to assume an attack is imminent." She looked up at the screen displaying Winters's drawn face. "Admiral Winters, order Admiral Rodriguex to consolidate her forces and prepare to seize Calama. I would rather risk their wrath by attacking preemptively than allow them to set fire to the interior."

Speechless, her admirals looked at her.

§

"How could I have let it come to this?" Kra'al asked as Pirsan gathered the data into a dossier. "How could I have been so naïve?"

Hakar had no answer. How could he tell her that it was not naiveté but conditioning? Even at the lowest point of Telemon's reign, violence had never spread beyond brushfires on a few worlds. Even with the Valinata's resource-burning militarization, the galaxy had become a predictable place.

Stability was the order of the day, but stability came at the cost of adaptability, and the galaxy was as susceptible to invasive species as the native Tagean flora had been. Also like those trees, the galaxy was susceptible to flame. This was going to be more than a brushfire. Hakar feared it would be an inferno. "You did the best you could," was all he could think to say. "We still have time to stop this," he tried.

"Don't, Hakar. You were right to suggest mobilization, don't get cold feet now. Parliament's dragging their feet on moving more fleets out there, and in the meantime, we have a very tangible threat at Calama. If we take it from the VSF now, we'll have a better chance of holding it against Raven Blue later. We can't afford to gamble on wait-and-see." She looked at him, her eyes zeroing in like precision lasers. "I want you on board, but I don't need you."

The weight of what Kra'al had committed them to crashed down around Hakar, and his blood rushed in his ears like pounding waves. Kra'al had taken office when the Coalition was on the verge of splintering. And what had she done then? She had demonstrated that things were going to *change*, that the corruption and the deception were ended. The Coalition's member states had long grumbled among themselves; if the CRDF could prove that it could stand against anything, *as a whole*, they would come through this. Kra'al had been an agent of change once, but now she found herself tasked with preserving the status quo. And Hakar found himself along for the ride, whether he liked it or not. They couldn't let it unravel, and they would do whatever they had to in order to keep it stitched together.

Is it possible the universe has changed so much? This mistrust, these walls we've put up between ourselves, these are the things that are going to destroy us. The Valinata have been eaten from the inside out, and they're so terrified that they'll go down shooting rather than let us help them. What kind of enemy could instill such fear that an entire kingdom would be drowned in madness?

Or do I already know?

"Joe," Hakar said, stepping before the screen. "What kind of reinforcements can Rodriguex pull from the Zoh or surrounding sectors?"

There was a momentary delay before Winters's reply reached them. "They're becoming increasingly reluctant to commit forces. Most of their available fleets have staged at the Amanra Crescent."

"The Amanra Crescent?" Kra'al said, her voice catching. "Admiral Winters, have Admiral Rodriguex make it abundantly clear that Zoh Hegemony forces are not to take unilateral action against the Valinata. They could jeopardize our entire defense. Understood?"

This time there was a noticeable delay before Winters replied. Even with the latest in resonant mass gravitational comm bursts, there were still lags as messages traveled the gulfs between the stars. Still, Hakar couldn't help wondering if Winters had slipped and was stalling. "Yes, Your Highness. As far as I know, they're only there to support border patrols trying to pick up Vali refugees."

Growing numbers of damaged and overcrowded ships had limped into Coalition and Shar'dan Confederacy border stations. The testimony of the survivors was often incoherent or useless. Even so, they could easily spread panic like a virus. Was it too late to contain it? Hakar wondered.

§

Jackal Pack's admin building was unusually quiet while Akida and most of the officers were continuing their inspection of the defenses. In anticipation of their rigorous training schedule, the general had given his mercenaries a week's unrestricted leave, provided they stayed on-planet and kept their comms on.

Leon and Rachel had planned a daytrip to drive out to one of the isolated groves that dotted the savannahs for a picnic and swimming. They had planned it, but apparently it wasn't happening. His new S-4, this Major Craf (*who also happens to be a major asshole*, Leon thought to himself), had thrown a stack of Mem files on his desk: requisition orders, inventory manifests and corrections, personnel transfers, and a surprising number of misfiled accounting forms. Craf had done a good job, and most of the Mems only required Leon's signature, but the new brigade S-4 had insisted that the colonel also review each one.

In addition to the logistical minutiae, there were plenty of contract applications that still needed rating and reviewing while they waited for the freeze to lift. Leon sipped at a hot cup of Kaf as he read over one particularly promising assignment. The Kaf was tasty: Rachel had given Leon's assistant a pouch of Sheff'an firenut-infused grounds, and they added a savory bite to the drink.

He checked a box labeled FAVORABLE near the bottom of the form and signed his name. He had decided to brave Rachel's ire and assign his crew to the job, a private security gig for four people with a payout of eight million talons or equivalent legal tender. It seemed straightforward enough, but Leon knew from experience that any corporation recruiting a "security detail" from the ranks of Jackal Pack probably had a skeleton or two in the closet. With the lock in place, there was plenty of time to investigate. Leon's most pressing concern was replacing Buzz, whose shadow still seemed to linger just behind him, with a hand resting on his shoulder. He resisted the urge to glance around, assuring himself that all he would see would be a window looking out onto a courtyard devoid of anyone but the early morning patrol.

The roster of potential replacements was long, but Leon didn't have to think hard to make his decision. Asar would make a good support gun, and a long-range marksman was always useful. Leon appended another form to the application and wrote four lines:

TEAM LEADER: VICTOR, LEON A.; COLONEL
INFIL/EXFIL/LOGISTICS: JERIC; SPECIALIST (FREELANCE)
TEAM (PRIMARY): MERIKII, RAPTOR; SPECIALIST (FREELANCE)
TEAM (PRIMARY): ABU SEIF, ASAR; SPECIALIST (SUPPORT)

Leon placed the Mem on the stack of Mems in his OUT box. Rachel would be less than thrilled, but it was his job, and the money was too good to pass up. His commission was two percent, nearly five hundred thousand talons in this case. After Pack fees and the bonus payouts he normally gave his team, that left him more than three hundred thousand, a tidy little sum. He knew Asar needed the money, too; his wife had recently given birth; unlike many Pack spouses, she had chosen to remain on her homeworld in Aradon territory.

As if on cue, Jackal Pack's resident sharpshooter walked in, hoisting a duffle over his shoulder. He wasn't in uniform. "*Sabah al-kher*, Colonel."

Leon nodded to him. "Good morning, Asar. Boy, have I got a job for you when this lock lifts."

"Funny you should mention that, sir," the other merc replied, his dark, hawkish features still, but his eyes alert and boring into Leon. "I was thinking I could go home while the freeze was still in effect."

"You want to get while the getting's good, eh?" Leon smiled and nodded understandingly. "You know that the general cancelled all off-world leave, and you're supposed to check with our new S-4."

"I thought perhaps you could grant me a dispensation, Colonel."

Leon sat back and crossed his arms, unconsciously mimicking Rockmore's posture. Leon wouldn't dare say it, but he thought the contract lock was a ridiculous idea. While he was under no illusions regarding the depth of the Coalition's disclosure of sensitive information, something as serious as Rockmore suspected would be *impossible* to hide. Especially from a group like the Jackal Pack Mercenary Legion, which had highly placed contacts in a number of militaries and governments. It was a senseless waste of time, and it would reduce their revenue for the year significantly not only from the loss of contracts during the lock itself but also the decrease in potential investors. Jackal Pack had a reputation, it was true, but people could and would go to other units: the Bloody Talons, the Sons of Mars, any of a number of decent outfits. It was a small market but a competitive one.

Leon reached out and took Asar's leave request. "Asar, as far as I'm concerned, you can go. I'll file it under medical leave, so if anyone asks, you had a toothache or something, all right?"

Asar nodded, his eyes glinting with delight.

"How long do you want?"

"A week should be sufficient, sir. I just want to spend some time with my wife and the baby. We named her Fatima."

"Cute. A week it is, plus transit. Must be some toothache." Leon edited the Mem and then turned to his own computer. "Let me just run this through the system."

Frowning his way through the labyrinth of forms and spreadsheets, he processed the request. It took a few moments, and then the words "PROCESS DENIED" appeared.

Leon grunted. "That's weird." He typed in a few commands, but the response was the same.

Asar craned his neck to see. "What is it?"

Leon turned to look at his subordinate. "Looks like the general is pretty serious about this. I think everyone but him is locked out of the system. I couldn't get you travel papers if I wanted to."

Asar shrugged, but it was obvious he was upset by the news. "Never mind, sir. I guess I'll hang around here."

"If you say so," Leon said uncertainly. "I'll check it with the boss myself when he gets back. Was there anything else you needed?"

Asar shook his head and left, deflated. Leon couldn't remember the last time the man had left Eve to visit his family. He guessed it had to have been about nine months ago.

§

Jeric glanced at the mission timer on the fighter's console. He had been stuffed into the cockpit for nearly seven hours, a trying ordeal even for his small frame. He loved flying but not like this, not following preset patrol routes that could have been flown just as easily using drones. He appreciated that Rockmore wanted to honor their contract with Eve despite withheld payments, and full security coverage was part of the package. If the Coalition decided to reach out and slap the Valinata, Eve would be in the path of the backlash. But it wasn't like there was any room for improvisation on patrol, either: the last time he had gone off on his own for some fun, Rockmore had had some choice words for him and docked him the day's pay. *"These are populated shipping lanes, Jeric, and you can't go around scaring merchants."* Yeah, right, it's the only excitement they'll ever get. They should thank me.

Jeric took a look at his sensor readout. "Hey, Hound Two, you still awake back there?" he asked tiredly into his mike.

The equally tired response came back only half-joking. "You just woke me up, One."

Jeric peered through his canopy, basking in Eve's quiet glow. It wasn't a blue-green-white jewel like Old Terra, to which Human memory still clung as the ideal. It nevertheless had a serene, native beauty and reminded him of his own homeworld. If the drought continued, however, the government in Tesa would order water reserves brought from the planet's meager polar regions, patchy grayish ice caps hardly deserving of the term. Then it would really resemble home.

He cast a look over his shoulder. A black and red shadow against the velvet field of stars, Hound Two held steady off his port wing, navigation lights blinking. "I've got a contact reading a hot ion trail. Are you picking it up?"

"Affirmative. Gotta be a Vali ship." Valinata ships were notorious for their emissions. It made them easy to locate.

"Call it in, have a customs ship meet us alongside." Jeric angled toward the new ship, waiting for his sensors to develop a more detailed profile.

Inside his helmet his head was pounding. *That's the last time I drink so much the night before a long patrol.* He took a long swallow from his water tube and knew that the resolution was an idle one. He had made the same promise hundreds of times in the nauseating grip of hundreds of hangovers.

In fact, he would have given anything for a drink at this point. Or a pillow. As it was, the snug acceleration couch of the fighter's cockpit wasn't too uncomfortable. He yawned and took another sip. His onboard computer pinged at him, and he took a look at the sensor profile of the new ship.

"Looks like a retrofitted freighter." He traced the computer-generated model. "Old design, but I recognize it. These modules look like they were taken from a space station."

"No wonder it's running hot," Two said. "Must be drawing a lot of juice to power those extra modules."

The Valinata ship's lights were flickering, and Jeric's sensors determined that its engine was cycling irregularly, probably to conserve power. Somehow it had limped across the border before putting in here. Wisely, the crew was already standing down for inspection as Jeric and his wingman angled in for a close scan before customs arrived.

"Jackal Pack ground control to Shorty. Hey, Jeric!" crackled a voice over the comm.

"You sound bored, Leon." The pilot rolled his eyes.

He could almost picture his friend grinning maliciously as he lounged in the comm room, probably sipping a pink fruity drink with an umbrella in it. "I hear they got you running a ten-hour patrol."

"Is that so? I heard *you* got me running a ten-hour patrol, you daffy bastard."

He could imagine the grin growing wider. "Now, I know how much you adore flying. Patrol flights, in particular."

"I'm gonna adore your ass with my boot when I get down there!" Jeric snapped into the comm. He almost wished Vic was with him so he could eject the smug son-of-a-bitch out of the cockpit. Out of the cockpit and into space where he could be used for target practice. "When are you going to grow out of pranks?"

A laugh floated back to him over the comm. "I'll have some coffee waiting for you when you come back down. It'll be cold."

Jeric cursed and cut Leon off while he was still laughing, viciously sweeping his hand across the comm switch to dial off the base's channel. He could hear Hound Two laughing, as well. "Hey, One? Remind me never to fly with you again."

"Who asked you?" retorted Jeric, but he had to smile. Then he turned his attention back to the listing Vali freighter and wondered what horror stories its occupants would tell.

§

Rachel awoke to the sound of a comm buzzing on the night stand. She reached over to wake Leon, but he had gone. Sunlight filtered through the blinds, spilling in thin lines across the bed. When she hit the switch to open them, the bedroom was flooded, and she shielded her eyes until they adjusted. Groggily she got up and put on a robe, then hit the button that would answer the call. She was too tired to worry about her appearance, but she smoothed her hair, wrestling it into some semblance of normalcy. *It's probably only Leon, anyway.*

The woman who appeared on the screen was young and beautiful, and it took a moment for Rachel to realize whom she was looking at: Leon's youngest sister Natille. At first glance, two people could hardly have looked more different: Leon with his rough-edged but almost quaint noble bearing, Natille with her model's good looks and instantly approachable disposition. Her dark hair tumbled artfully around her olive-skinned face. On closer inspection, though, similarities began to emerge. Her skin was a shade darker than Leon's, her face rounder, but something about her mouth and her lopsided, hair-trigger smile made her seem almost his twin. Her eyes were an emerald green, but they were lit with the same light as Leon's, taking in everything and processing it, never missing a detail.

"Rachel!" she said excitedly, managing with fair success to mask her surprise; clearly, Leon hadn't mentioned Rachel's return. "I didn't expect to see you. How are you?"

The two exchanged pleasantries; it was a little awkward initially, but Natille had an easy, disarming manner much like her brother's, making it seem as though it might just be water under the bridge. It was interesting that Natille didn't so much as comment on the border troubles, or ask if they were in any danger. Years of living in denial of her brother's lifestyle had given her a deliberate sort of blissful ignorance as a defensive mechanism, which Rachel recognized all too well. "You're looking for Leon?" Rachel asked, recalling the message from a week ago.

"I am, thanks. Is he there right now? I can never figure out what time it is on Eve."

Rachel's eyes went to the clock. She *had* slept in: it was almost midday. "I think he's at the office. Do you want me to patch you through?"

"If it's not too much trouble."

Rachel fumbled with the controls for the comm connection. Leon's associate, Heidi Eastern, appeared on the screen, all smiles, and transferred the call. Natille's image disappeared from the screen as Leon picked up the call.

Rachel yawned, ran her fingers through her hair, and almost flopped back into bed. Still sluggish, she took twenty minutes in the shower, forgetting the water rationing. She toweled off and went in search of an outfit. She was in no real hurry to get moving or begin the day, but she felt guilty for having wasted so much of it already, and she knew that a vacation could turn to indolence before long. So she sat on the edge of the bed in her underwear, her tummy folded in a little roll; she frowned at it, willing it to flatten. Perhaps she would start visiting the Pack gym or maybe get a membership in Tesa.

While she contemplated her thighs and stomach, she gazed around the apartment, quiet except for the muffled booming of distant artillery drilling. Periodically, the windows shook when large ordnance hit. It was amazing what you could get used to, she marveled. As always, her thoughts turned away from the material, from the superficial, and back to Leon. She had spent the better part of her life in luxury, insulated from the real world but, nevertheless, aware of trouble stirring beyond the carefully manicured boundaries of her upbringing. Ensuring that her clothes were all of the latest fashions, following celebrity gossip, shopping, and sharing vacuous conversations with her friends … all of those diversions were fun, but they were artifacts of her old life, fading slowly but surely into irrelevance. She wanted a future, not an easy present, and a real future took work. She had come back to Eve to work.

At least, Leon was neat. Rachel had known many men who, left to their own devices, were content to throw things haphazardly about their space. Decoration for those men typically consisted of posters or empty food containers. Not in Leon's small officer's apartment, though. The furniture was tasteful, austere in appearance, but luxurious. Rachel preferred something with a little more warmth, but she didn't mind. There were a few paintings; none were originals, save for one Leon's oldest sister had made, a vibrant and slightly surreal ink and watercolor of a cityscape she guessed was Crossing. He possessed few knick-knacks and those he had were of sentimental value. Rachel didn't care for most of them, but at least each one had meaning and a story. She consoled herself with the thought that they could just as easily have been nude models.

The shelves above Leon's desk always drew her attention, though. They were occupied by the detritus of a dozen hobbies, all false starts. There were little model ships, with little cloth sails and little cannons. There were carvings, shapes half-formed from wood or stone. The shelves themselves were an aborted attempt at carpentry. Early on, Rachel had discovered that Leon had a reverence that bordered on obsession with what he saw as a "normal" life. Somehow he translated this into picking up the most mundane hobbies he could find. Invariably, he failed to follow through, but everything was still there as a reminder, the tools neatly laid out, inviting him to try and pick them up again. It was as though they were surrogates for the life he had left behind, a life that was perhaps truly lost to him.

Even so, *this* was the real Leon, the Leon she loved. It frightened her that he could simply turn that side of him off and become a killing machine. It frightened her even more to know that he could shut away that killer when it suited him, putting him into storage until he was needed.

Rachel turned away now, feeling the first pangs of hunger in her stomach. Unfortunately, while Leon's apartment was equipped with a modest kitchen, neither of them cooked (she had never learned, and for him it was another abandoned hobby). She got dressed, slipped on a light jacket of white leather, and headed out to get breakfast in the base's mess hall.

The Pack employed members of all genders, so the sight of a woman on the base wasn't unusual. Most of the time the women of the Pack wore their uniforms, and for that reason alone, she would have stood out. With Rockmore giving them unrestricted leave, though, many had donned civilian attire, allowing her to blend in for once. Few, however, could shed their military discipline and bearing, and it was telling that so many had chosen to remain on the base. She was sure most had nowhere else to go.

Men looked her way, but she had never had to fend off the advances of a Jackal. It was refreshing to be treated with respect, especially when surrounded by such a rough-and-tumble group, but she could admit that she occasionally missed the attention. Rachel had always been a stunner, as her father (the bastard) had said, and she had learned to tune out the catcalls and pathetic pick-up lines. Noticing the absence of come-ons was like realizing the engines of a starliner had shut off after learning to ignore them over the course of a long journey.

Jackal Pack's cafeteria didn't serve the gruel she would have expected. General Rockmore hired a staff of full-time professional cooks and kitchen staff, and the base's proximity to the farms and ranches that served Tesa and provided some of Eve's modest export revenues meant it was all fresh, not frozen or synthesized from nutrient vats and chemical additives. There were fresh fruits, fresh vegetables, and even seafood from North Bay on the Lime Sea; meals were available in the buffet that stayed open throughout all thirty hours of Eve's day, except on holidays.

Even though the cafeteria served breakfast food all day to accommodate the different shift rotations, Rachel would have been embarrassed to be seen eating waffles and bacon at one in the afternoon. Instead, she picked out a salad and a vegetable soup to begin the reduction of her tummy, gladly bypassing cinnamon-baked steak, a delicacy Raptor had demanded and which was now so beloved of the sojieri that it had a permanent spot on the menu. She picked up a glass of purple juice, discovering it to be made from Sanar ocean-berries, tart and refreshing. Finding an empty spot near the corner of the room, she sat down and started to eat.

A couple of technicians she had befriended entered the mess, grabbed their own lunches, and joined her. The group passed the time complaining about the drought and speculating on league championships. They avoided any mention of the Valinata blackout with an almost superstitious fear, as though some nameless shadow lurked just over the border.

When she had first commenced her life on the base, Rachel had naturally been drawn to the female sojieri and officers, assuming they would have the most common ground. But most of the women here were of a different breed, their minds focused and mostly unconcerned with the frivolities of civilian life. It wasn't that they didn't enjoy the finer things, it was simply that such topics took a back seat to more immediate issues like war and survival. Though they certainly made time for her, there was always a distinct and almost tangible rift between them. Traxus was a close friend of Leon's, and a close friend of Rachel's, too, but it was hard to shake the feeling that she was reporting back to Leon. As a result, Rachel had found herself most welcome among the Pack's small army of noncombatant support staff: the techs and maintenance crews, the landscapers, the full-time medical staff who did what the company medics and surgeons could not. They were the people who made the base their home but did not engage in the killing. That may have been the decisive factor: they weren't killers. They didn't walk with the same heavy shoulders, they didn't seem to be permanently on alert. And they didn't cause Rachel any ethical dilemma. She liked that.

When breakfast was finished, Rachel bade farewell to her friends and headed back out into the blazing sun. It was going to be another hot, rainless day, and she felt a moment's remorse over wasting water in the shower. Several people called out greetings to her as she traversed the courtyard in the direction of the administration building. She waved and called back, embarrassed that she couldn't keep all their names straight. The captain of the guard smiled at her and waved her in.

Upstairs in the office adjoining Leon's, Heidi Eastern sat painting her nails in a vibrant and almost headache-inducing shade of lime green that matched her hair and her lipstick. She was beautiful and she was young, with large breasts and seductive, long-lashed eyes. The first time Rachel had seen her, jealousy had curled its ugly claws into her heart. It turned out that Heidi was an old colleague of Leon's who had been paralyzed while saving his life. Leon had paid for her medical care, but the damage to her spine had been too great. She couldn't fight and she didn't make much of a recruiter with such an injury, so Rockmore and Leon had bankrolled a master's degree in administration. To call her Leon's assistant was inaccurate; while she was his subordinate and nominally assigned to his battalion, she was Jackal Pack's Chief Information Officer, and she handled everything from high-level communications to client and job processing. It was loyalty that kept her in an office adjoining Leon's, not sexual attraction.

Heidi smiled at her. "Hey, sugar. Here to visit the colonel?"

Rachel nodded. "Is he busy?"

"Not too busy for you. Has he proposed yet?"

Rachel shook her head, a little embarrassed. "Not yet. I think I finally found something he's afraid of." She tried to play it off with a laugh.

"Well, if he takes too much longer, tell me, and I'll roll my chair over his throat." Heidi winked at her and waved her into the office.

The door to Leon's office was open as usual, and she could hear him conversing with the general. Rockmore was saying impatiently, "I know that, but I'm going to keep it that way."

Leon sounded flustered. "Sir, I understand, but Asar hasn't been home in a long time. There are a number of troops who could use special dispensations."

"I know about your sister's wedding, Leon, and I'll do my best to accommodate you when the time comes. At the moment, however, I'm confining our troops to Eve. That's my prerogative. If you're worried about pay cuts, don't be. I'll go into my own savings if I have to."

"It's not just money, sir. It's being stranded here that's going to have an effect on people. Look at me, I'm already getting claustrophobic. You've said yourself, tempers flare...."

Rachel paused outside the door. She didn't want to interrupt since the conversation sounded important. Instead she strolled quietly back to Heidi's desk to chat. When she came back a minute later, they were still talking. Rockmore sounded as though he was about to give ground, if not give in.

"Look, Leon, I understand your reservations, but you have to realize that unless the CRDF decides to reinforce this sector, Jackal Pack is the only real defense the Alkyra Trade Route has." Rachel knew, of course, that Eve lay along the central arc of the Alkyra Trade Route, one of the gravitational highways facilitating superluminal transit between systems. Like the other major trade routes, including the Yangtze and the Crown Road, the systems along the Alkyra channeled gravitational energy in such a way that travel was far faster even than that allowed by regular conduits. The Alkyra wasn't the largest route in the galaxy, and the worlds along it were far from the richest. However, it was perfectly located between the Coalition, the Valinata, and the central sweep of the Unified Commonwealth. It didn't take an experienced mercenary to realize it was strategically important.

"Have you heard back from Ti Che?" Rockmore asked.

"Nothing but an all-channels-closed automated response," Leon said grimly. "Based on what Akida's uncovered from his investigations at the refugee camp, I think that's the best we're going to get."

Rockmore said something else that Rachel couldn't hear and walked out. He almost bumped into her. "Good afternoon, Miss Case." Calling back over his shoulder, "You have a visitor, son!" he smiled genially and continued on down the hallway.

As she entered, Leon pushed back his chair and rose to greet her with a quick peck of a kiss. "Hi," he said.

"You busy?" Rachel asked.

"With the Pack at a standstill, I think I can afford to take off early. I was actually planning on swinging by to pick you up in a bit. Do you mind waiting a few minutes?"

"Nope," Rachel said and plopped herself down in Leon's desk chair. She spun it in a quick turn and returned to face his computer. The Mem screen was unfurled, displaying images of assassination targets. Each person had a price attached. Two Humans, a Tagean, three Sheff'an, one Borin. Rachel pretended she didn't see them. "Why does General Rockmore still insist on calling me 'Miss Case'?"

Leon simply smiled. "Who knows why he does any of the little things he does? We don't get too many women around here without ranks."

"Well, it's sweet." Rachel chewed her lip thoughtfully. "It's a little strange, though, hearing him call you son and acting all paternal."

"He means well."

"I know. But with his face all cut up like that, I'd just as soon you not follow in his footsteps."

Rachel couldn't deny being unsettled by Rockmore's scars. The first time she had seen him she had been disgusted. She had grown up in a culture of coddled perfection where the merest blemish was attacked by a legion of plastic surgeons. While the scars were unchanged, she didn't find them nearly as disconcerting anymore, aside from the one that cleaved his jaw from cheekbone to throat.

"Interested in lunch?" Leon asked, typing over her shoulder as she rested her head on his side.

"I, ah, just had breakfast," she said, chagrined.

"Working the night shift must be tough," Leon said, giving her the lopsided smile that had convinced her to board his ship in the middle of a gunfight and leave behind the sheltered world she had always known. "Are you feeling okay?"

"Yeah, I just overslept. You should have woken me up." Rachel slipped past him and wandered around the office while Leon finished up his work.

He didn't get far before something else interrupted him. Jeric stormed through the open door, his flight helmet banging against the doorframe, air hoses dangling from it like flailing arms. "You bastard!" he shouted, walking right up to the desk. He was stumbling a little bit as though his leg was numb.

Rachel stood back while the pilot vented. After a few moments, he noticed her standing against one wall and gaped at her. "You're in on this?"

"Hi, Jeric." Who even knew what he was talking about?

The pilot returned his baleful gaze to Leon, who only regarded him calmly, a small smile tugging at the corners of his mouth. "How could you? I feel like I just got out of a coma!"

"Whatever do you mean?" asked the colonel innocently, and Rachel had to suppress a laugh.

Jeric leaned over the desk and put his fist right in front of Leon's face, waving it menacingly. "What do I mean? How 'bout a ten-hour patrol flight? My ass hurts like I been sitting in that damned cockpit for a year with a hand up it!"

Leon touched a button on the comm clipped to his shoulder. "Heidi, dear, could you get me security?"

"Of course, Colonel."

Rachel hadn't seen Raptor in the hallway or even the building, but she guessed that Leon had asked him to follow Jeric after his flight in case something like this happened. Seemingly from out of nowhere, the Prross appeared, marching through the door and grabbing the little pilot. He hauled him bodily off the floor and grinned maliciously at him. "C'mon, you can play with your joystick outside." He walked off with the sputtering, swearing pilot struggling in his strong arms.

Leon returned to his work as though nothing had happened, and the office was quiet but for the clicking of the keyboard. Rachel looked around the room and quickly grew bored. Leon's apartment may have revealed some personal touches, but his office felt bland and transitory. A few family pictures, some old military awards, and the hilt of a broken saber were the only decorations. A dusty, purple tassel hung from the saber's pommel. Books on military history, leadership, basic accounting, and other information pertinent to his job lined the shelves against one wall.

Leon shut down his computer and rolled the Mem screen back into its slot in the desk. As they walked out, he related his conversation with Natille. His younger sister couldn't have known she was calling at an inconvenient time regarding Jackal Pack's fortunes, and interrogating Leon on what color boutonniere he wanted seemed to have exasperated him. It couldn't be easy to help plan a wedding he might not even be able to attend. Rachel hoped it wouldn't turn him off the idea of marriage. "So, what do you want to do?" she asked. "We could go to dinner or ... shopping. I don't know. I could get a dress for the wedding."

"I have an idea, actually." The grin that spread across Leon's face was just what she had hoped for. Unlike most men she had dated, he grew excited at the prospect of the mundane, as though shopping with his girlfriend let him pretend to be a normal person. "I do like your little fashion shows."

"You can't come in the changing stall with me," Rachel chided him. Together they exited the administrative complex and crossed the courtyard. People moved aside for Leon and sketched salutes, which he dutifully returned. His past might have been a mess, but people here respected, and even loved, him. He had an even, confident stride that she had found sexy from the first time she saw him, and she found it comforting now. He was a man in charge, if not always of himself.

Rachel changed into something more suitable for an evening on the town, and they proceeded into the shade of the vehicle park, a vast garage that extended several stories underground and that stored the Pack's cars, trucks, and light support vehicles. On the first level, Leon found a Hyena, an all-purpose military truck that looked to Rachel as though some unimaginative designer had gathered all the rectangles he could, bound them together, and set them on wheels to make a crude, vicious-looking ground vehicle. The name "Hyena" was derived from the full designation, "Hybrid-Energy, Nonfixed Assets," and referred to the multiple power sources that could be installed, as well as the almost countless configurations of equipment it could mount from communications systems to heavy machine guns or light anti-aircraft armament. Leon and the mercenaries seemed to regard the vehicles with a certain fondness. Rachel admitted that they seemed indestructible, but she suspected the name was a reverse acronym established by the same unimaginative designer who had built the ugly thing. The moniker was certainly apt on Eve where the vehicles were often seen bounding over dunes or plowing through brush. The wheels could be exchanged for Rombaldt antigravity-coils to provide a smoother ride, but most people seemed to prefer the tactile feel of dirt under the tires and the increased weight capacity of the wheeled variants.

Mercifully, the vehicle Leon chose was outfitted for transporting clients and VIPs and mounted no weapons. The seats were leather, the air conditioner worked, and even though it still displayed the Pack colors, at least it was clean. Leon put the car in gear, and they roared out of the vehicle park. Rachel looked out at the view as the road wound down the side of the plateau, eventually becoming a flat highway that split a few kilometers from the base. One branch made a beeline for the cosmodrome to the south where ships flocked around the spaceport like gulls over a shimmering sea of tarmac. The left-hand branch wound into Tesa's highway system, pointing toward bright towers that gleamed like mirages in the afternoon heat.

§

Leon was proud of himself, having surprised Rachel with tickets to a performance art exhibition. The show had been impressive and quite beautiful, but partway through, he had realized with a pang of embarrassment that he was nowhere near sophisticated enough to fully appreciate it. Seeing how engrossed Rachel was, and how obviously taken she was with the holographically augmented performers, drove the point home. She admitted to being equally surprised that such a well-reviewed tour would come to Eve. The performance had attracted many of Eve's more refined outcasts, and Leon's Jackal Pack red-on-black had drawn a few looks. As the performers had wandered through the audience, their holographic emitters turning them from people to abstractions, Leon had found himself growing nervous as though some assassin from Korinthe out to avenge Marcus Keegan might leap through the shifting, vividly colored patterns of light to plunge a knife into his heart. At least, it helped him forget that a few miles away the multitude of starving, frightened Valinata citizens was growing daily as well as the unknown reason for their exodus, which was all the more frightening for its mystery.

From there, the couple strolled through Tesa's upscale shopping district, which, while quite the place to be seen on Eve, was a shabby imitation of those in larger, more fashionable cities on worlds like Tagea or Amalthia. There was another cultural celebration in progress, this time the Cave Festival of the Borin, and they paused to watch the parade wind its way down the boulevard. While the floats and banners were drab by Leon's standards, he knew the Borin perceived a wider spectrum of light, and no doubt the decorations were positively iridescent to their intended audience. Rachel happily described her favorite parts of the performance they had seen, all but shouting over the wild syncopations of the Borin drums, and Leon listened attentively to her insights. She continued her analysis as he led her to a boutique, and he found the whole experience oddly relaxing.

He took the opportunity to look for some civilian attire for himself since Natille had made it clear she did not want him giving her away in Jackal Pack colors. The rest of the time he spent waiting in plush leather chairs as Rachel paraded first one outfit and then another before him.

The only hitch in the experience came when Rachel caught Leon looking alertly about, scanning their fellow shoppers. "Stop it, Leon. You're making *me* nervous," she snapped, and he forced himself to relax. Marcus Keegan had threatened him, yes, but it had been the idle barb of a dead man. Certainly, no one would strike at them in the midst of this store.

Finally, it was time to unveil the big surprise. Leon led Rachel down a quiet side street, away from the flashy signs and bay windows, and into a little shop. Rachel was always fashionable, but her tastes were subdued. Leon could not tell if that was because she was naturally modest or whether it was out of respect for the less affluent. Perhaps it was simply to avoid looking like a target among the rough-and-tumble mercenaries. It was one of the reasons he had decided to buy her the dress. He had brought a photograph of the two of them to the seamstress for sizing scale, and he was happy to see that the woman's keen eye and careful hands had produced a gown that fit perfectly on first trial. Rachel's gasp upon seeing it told him he had chosen well.

It was pale gray, trimmed with cascading emeralds, and it swept gracefully along Rachel's curves, revealing her shoulders and upper back, as much of her smooth alabaster skin as was appropriate for such an occasion. He knew she had grown up in a wealthy family, but still he doubted she had ever owned anything quite like this. She would never have picked out so costly a gift for herself, which was precisely why Leon was happy to buy it for her. It only saddened him a little to know that the dress would be out of fashion in a few months when the Terran Revival fad inevitably spent itself. And then Rachel would be left with an expensive reminder of a passing fashion. But for Natille's wedding she would be enchanting.

Even so, he couldn't help worrying that it was a useless gesture. If the lock continued, he wouldn't be going to the wedding. If it came to war, he might not even live long enough. He distracted himself from that thought by studying Rachel's beauty.

"You could wear it around town today," he suggested as she posed in front of a mirror, fully aware that he was staring at her ass. The shop owner made appreciative cooing sounds which Leon found grating, but for the quality of her work he could put up with it.

"I wouldn't want to risk getting it dirty yet." She turned and winked at him, just to show she knew what he was thinking. "Besides, wouldn't you feel a little underdressed?"

He caught a glimpse of himself in the mirror, standing behind her, and blushed. "You could pretend I was a pet dog or something. I mean, a pet Jackal," he added with a laugh.

"Yeah, you do enough drooling." She smiled and went back into the dressing room to change back into the dress she had worn in.

Afterwards, they went to a small restaurant for dinner. There wasn't much to see in Tesa: mainly practical and ugly apartment highrises and the stunted skyscrapers of a few corporate headquarters that had set up shop on Eve because it was cheap and offered unbeatable tax breaks. By the time they were finished walking around town and taking in the sights, the sun had set. Leon wrapped an arm around Rachel's shoulders as protection against the dropping temperature, pulling her close as they walked.

§

Rachel knew Leon was a romantic, but she had had no clue just how gallant he could be. And he understood fashion well enough to buy her a custom gown that put many of the top designers to shame. It wouldn't have looked out of place at an Adrevani show. She had dated men whose true natures showed through cracks in their superficially beautiful facades. With Leon, the opposite seemed to be the case, which she found both fascinating and confusing.

"So you're really okay with the idea of moving out to Tesa?" she probed as they joined a stream of people emerging from the Tesa Regent Cinema. They had barely talked about it since she and Traxus had gone to check out the apartment.

"I told you I am, honey." Rachel still couldn't tell if he meant it or not. Supportive was one thing, but Leon had to be enthusiastic about a change this big.

She paused and pulled him into an alcove while people passed by in a steady stream of indifference. "Is there something you want to talk about?"

"What's to talk about?" he answered blithely. Something in the way he said it pushed Rachel's buttons just so, and though she tried to catch herself, the words came tumbling out.

"The fact that you're a *murderer*, for starters." She bit the word "murderer" off as though it tasted bad.

She could tell she had struck a nerve. "For starters,..." Leon echoed. "For starters, every job I take is sanctioned."

"That wasn't always the case."

For a moment, Leon didn't say anything. He stood in the doorway, half his face in shadow. Rachel watched him wrestle with some inner conundrum until he locked onto her again with his disconcerting gaze. "Let's go somewhere and sit down."

Rachel followed him to a café where they ordered Kaf and sat by the window as evening traffic flowed by. She was blushing, embarrassed that she was ruining the evening. "You must think I'm ungrateful. I didn't mean to start this. Let's not do this."

Leon's brow was furrowed, and he licked his lips nervously. It was an oddly pathetic expression. "No, now is as good a time as any. So you want to break into the business?" he asked with a cracked grin in a complete about-face.

Rachel shot him a scathing look that killed the grin instantly. "You joke about it all the time, but it's hard for me, Leon, and it's not getting easier. It's hard for me to picture you doing this kind of work. It's hard for me to live on a military base. I keep saying it's surprising what you can get used to, and it's a way of dealing with it, I guess. But do you know how weird it is to wake up with the sound of artillery practice going on outside my bedroom window? To know that when my boyfriend is at work he isn't making spreadsheets in an office, he's putting prices on peoples' lives? You've never told me how *you* feel about what you do. What goes through your mind while you do it?"

This was a question Leon was not prepared to answer, clearly. He stammered for a few moments while Rachel waited. Finally, he explained that he had trained himself to simply *not feel* while working. He read her incredulous reaction correctly, at least. "I've trained for a long time to be this way. It's not ideal, I know, but all my friends ... I don't know if you've noticed, but I can't exactly make polite dinner conversation with people who aren't also mercenaries—"

"That's a bullshit excuse, Leon," Rachel said pithily.

"—and I don't exactly fit in when we go out, like at the performance. I've been a sojier for so long...." He trailed off, and Rachel felt as though she could see years condense upon his shoulders. "Would it help if you knew why I became a sojier?"

Rachel was taken aback. She had never known there was a story behind it; she had always assumed Leon was just a person who signed up for queen and country out of loyalty or patriotism or a desire for adventure. "It might," she said. "I'm not the same spoiled rich brat you met on Amalthia."

"You were never a brat, sweetheart," Leon assured her.

She smiled at that. "I'm not stupid, you know. I know people can make excuses for a life they would never otherwise defend. I know maybe better than you realize. I told myself when I came back that I wouldn't make this an issue, but I'm sorry, I can't let it go." She leaned forward and gazed into his eyes, demanding an explanation.

So Leon told her. He had never spoken much about his parents—she knew they had settled on Terra when Leon was very young, and she knew they had both passed away unexpectedly. It had always simply been another chapter of Leon's past that he seemed reluctant to let anyone else read.

They had been planetary engineers working for a joint venture between Crye-Locke Industries and a company called GalEco. Like many returning Humans, they had been given financial incentives to raise a large family, the better to repopulate the depleted homeworld. The oldest of six siblings, Leon had shouldered more than his share of responsibility early on, since neither his mother Maria nor his father Alex was in one place for more than a month at a time. When Leon had been just twenty-three, having finished his university studies and preparing to enter a doctoral program, his parents had been killed in an industrial accident caused by his father. A dozen of their colleagues had died, as well.

The bitterness in Leon's voice was heartbreaking. He clearly admired his parents for their ideals but resented them for their shortsightedness, which had left him and his siblings orphans with no family on Terra to turn to.

"What about benefits?"

Leon nodded wearily. "Because it was Da's fault, they refused. I would have loved to sue them. But by then GalEco was defunct, and they couldn't pay out enough to support all of us. I didn't even bother going to the Terran government."

"Why not? They could have helped."

"Back then they could barely find a building uncontaminated enough to hold session, never mind protect a bunch of orphans."

Rachel was beginning to realize that she and Leon came from fundamentally different backgrounds. He and his siblings may all have been quite well off now, but that had not always been the case, and sometimes she forgot that. Since they had almost nothing in common besides being Human, it was no wonder she had trouble wrestling with his inconsistencies. How would she be if she had come from such a mold? She shied away from the question.

"So you joined the military."

"That's right. We needed money and fast. I couldn't let my brothers and sisters wind up laboring in those polluted wastelands. I sold the house, I sold the plots of land Ma and Da had bought for farming." Leon sounded proud of his grim pragmatism. "I convinced a couple of friends to join up with me so I could get a signing bonus." For a second, his eyes grew shadowed.

"Raptor and Jeric?" Rachel guessed, but she didn't think that was right. He had met them after he left Her Majesty's service, hadn't he?

"No ... not them." He swallowed, and Rachel could tell the memory wasn't a happy one. "Anyway, we needed money, and the CRDF paid. Not well, but well enough, and it was all tax-free." He ticked off the points on his fingers as though trying to convince himself in retrospect. "Free room and board, hazardous duty bonuses.... The first few years I never took leave, pulled extra duty, whatever I could do. I made friends with the mess cooks and ran errands for them so I could send back a few contraband cans of food. People knew my situation, and most of the officers looked the other way."

Knowing Leon was a proud man, Rachel was touched by the humility on display. She refused to be embarrassed by her advantages, but she also refused to be blind to the disadvantages of others. It was yet another reason she and her mother had clashed so often.

She could see why he had never really fit in with the CRDF and that he would never truly fit in on Eve. He had always been removed from his comrades, a sojier out of necessity rather than desire. Fifteen years later, he was still fighting, only now he was a warrior without a nation to fight for. It was in his blood, though, like an infection, and Rachel suspected that in a perverse way he wanted to stay infected.

They sat in the café for a few more minutes, with nothing but dregs in their mugs. Leon jerked his head at the door. Rachel nodded, and they rose and left, making room for another couple on what was hopefully a more successful date.

At the Hyena, Leon opened the passenger door and held it for Rachel as she got in. She watched him through the windscreen as he walked around the front of the vehicle and got in. He didn't start the engine right away, instead resting his right hand atop her left on the cracked plastic of the center console.

"I owe you an apology," Rachel said, her voice a breath above a whisper. "I always mistrusted your motives."

"Understandable," Leon allowed.

"I always just … assumed you were one of those guys who can't sit still for more than five minutes, who need action to survive."

"Like Raptor?"

"Raptor's a Prross. He was born for this, bred for it. You weren't. You deserve a peaceful life."

Leon's head lowered. "I don't think I'd know what to do if I got one."

"We'll see."

Leon reflected on that possibility. Rachel wondered if he imagined scenes of tranquility with himself finally at their heart, a modest fantasy within his grasp. "Once I *did* think of war as adventure," he admitted. "The thought of reading a book on a beach was surrender, practically stasis. I kind of figured that over time I would forget the appeal of simple pleasures, that I'd need a bigger and bigger rush just to feel normal, but the opposite has happened. Now I get excited about the littlest things."

"I submit that as evidence for reform," Rachel said lightly. "It doesn't all have to be harrowing, life-or-death thrills."

A quiet pattering on the windshield alerted them to the fact that it had begun to rain lightly, barely more than a drizzling mist. It was unexpected, and the pedestrians on the sidewalk stood with their faces upturned, blinking and smiling in wonder, not one of them equipped with an umbrella.

"I may not like what you do, but I know you do it well. You know you could retire, Leon, if you wanted to. It's not like you're short of talons." It was an old argument, one they had gone over time and again. "You could even just scale back, do some recruiting or consulting."

Leon started the car and pulled away from the curb. "I've been thinking about that," he admitted.

They were quiet for a few moments, each of them following different avenues of possibility, and then Rachel spoke again. "I never really thought about what it must be like not to have a home. It's hard, isn't it?"

"Eve's my home," Leon said. "At least, that's what I tell myself. It's true, too. I love this place. I might have considered settling here, too, if...."

"If you weren't forced to be here," Rachel finished.

He gave her his rueful half-smile. "There are a lot of neutral worlds in the galaxy, but Eve is one of the nicer ones. No matter how nice it may be, though, it's still a world apart, a home for the homeless."

"Can you ... I don't know, move back?"

Leon laughed as he turned the Hyena onto the highway that would take them to the base. He activated the windshield wipers, and they flicked away the rain. "I'd have to apply for a visa and go through immigration. And I can never apply for citizenship. No, the only way to go back is as a guest."

"The Commonwealth grants citizenship through marriage," Rachel said idly. Leon didn't say anything, but he was smiling when she glanced over.

The darkened, empty highway was a black slash across the dark landscape, heading toward the flat-topped Luxor Plateau, which looked like a mountain that had had its top two thirds chopped cleanly off. Who knew, with Eve's mining history, maybe that's exactly what it was. Rachel looked over her shoulder at the mist-hazy lights of the city with their angelic coronas.

The comm crackled and clicked as it ran an encryption routine, intruding on their thoughts. Leon's personal unit had interfaced directly with the vehicle's built-in radio, patching the call through. "Victor, this is Akida."

"Go ahead," Leon said without bothering to keep the irritation from his voice.

"Is anyone besides Miss Case with you?"

Leon's eyebrows went up at that. "No, we're alone."

"All right, return to base immediately. We're going out."

"What for? It's raining."

"Gosh, I'm sorry," replied the other colonel, his voice dripping with disdain. "Customs requested our intervention with a Valinata ship. This one's military, and it's damaged. Hull breaches and what look like laser burns. The crew stood down. They're at a VIP pad at the cosmodrome right now. I've alerted your command staff, and I've cherry-picked the duty rotation. Lieutenant Tachai is heading the security detachment, so we can bring them right in."

"No shit," Leon breathed, stepping on the accelerator. "I'll be there as soon as I can. Call it forty-five minutes." The wipers whipped back and forth faster to keep up with the rain.

"It's bad?" Rachel asked after Akida had disconnected.

"Probably," Leon said. He looked over at her, and his eyes were concerned. He didn't elaborate further.

"No way, Leon. Stop trying to protect me. I know you've been interrogating Vali refugees. I want you to tell me what's going on."

Leon seemed to weigh his options for a few moments. "They don't know, and neither do we. We've been hearing some ridiculous stories. Monsters hiding behind comets, ghosts coming out of Tanis Ruin, garbage like that. The thing is, almost none of them have had any exposure to the threat. Most got out ahead of the front, long before their planets were actually at risk. Some of them still think we're—sorry, the *Coalition*—is behind it, funding some rebel faction." He snorted grimly. "You can tell how fucked they are that the average Vali citizen is less than surprised by the idea of a civil war." He lapsed into silence, chewing on his lower lip as he drove. Rachel let him think.

When they reached the Luxor Plateau, the base was floodlit as though for a fútbol match. A line of Hyenas and troop transports stood at the gate, and a line of officers and a few security troops stood at ease, smoking and checking over one another's kits in the rain. Leon pulled their Hyena into line and opened his door, half-stepping out.

Rachel reached for the door handle and was surprised when her door swung open. Colonel Akida was standing there with an umbrella, looking at her impassively. "Good evening, Rachel. Sorry to cut your date short." He handed her the umbrella. "We'll probably be a while."

She went around the vehicle and kissed Leon. The rain had gotten heavier, and it was already running down his nose and through his hair. "Be careful," she whispered. She stood aside as a sojier brought Leon a Sprawler pistol and a light flak vest. The sight sent chills down her spine.

He was turning away when she grabbed his sleeve. "Leon, I'm not trying to control your life. I'm trying to save it."

She couldn't tell if tears had joined the rain streaming down his cheeks or not. "I know, and I love you for that," he said softly, barely loud enough to be heard over the engines and chattering troops. "Don't stop."

He smiled at her reassuringly before ducking back into the vehicle. She heard Akida berating him already. "We're there to talk. I don't want you intimidating the VSF officers."

After they drove off, Rachel dropped off her shopping bags at the apartment. Too preoccupied to sit still, she went looking for Traxus. She found the Tagean by the gate, wearing full body armor and armed with a frighteningly large assault rifle. Traxus's face was a stoic mask, her eyes cold, but her expression softened when she saw Rachel. Despite her protests, Rachel waited with her in the rain as the yard turned to mud. She recognized a few of the other guards but didn't want to bother them. Even Traxus was different on duty, nearly as robotic as Rachel imagined Leon must be.

Over an hour later, the convoy returned, roaring through the main gate and skidding to a stop in the cul-de-sac before the administration building. Leon and Akida got out, accompanied by Major Dawson and

Major Da'Cir. Also with them was a man in a ragged brown uniform with green trim, who limped and had an arm in a sling. More similarly attired officers emerged from the other vehicles, some badly injured and on stretchers. Rachel knew at once that they were Valinata, and she guessed by the different uniform types that some were naval and some were infantry, but she couldn't tell which was which.

Suspicious but willing, the VSF officers followed their Jackal Pack hosts inside. At once the guards began speculating among themselves. Rachel, too, wondered what had happened. Had their ship been attacked, or had it evacuated VSF troops from a battle? One thing was certain: they would have more concrete information for Jackal Pack than the host of frightened but uninformed refugees. How bad had it gotten that a VSF battleship was looking for asylum?

Leon and his colleagues didn't have long to question their guests before a large and sinister-looking ship roared overhead and began circling. As it passed over the gate, Rachel saw deadly-looking weapons pointed at the ground. Traxus's comm came alive with chatter, and soon the ship touched down.

Rachel stood stock-still, heedless of the mud that stained her dress and splattered her heels and bare legs, as a ramp lowered in the rear. A very serious-looking group of people debarked and made a beeline for the administration building. They were met by a group of Jackal Pack officers including Leon, Akida, and General Rockmore.

Squinting through the rain, Rachel could make out the black-and-gray uniforms of CRDF Falcon Guard officers. She knew that they were the elite branch of the Coalition Royal Army Ground, or CRAG, and that their fortresses were said to be impregnable. The other group she could not identify. They wore long coats with insignia on the sleeves, and each of them seemed to be wearing some sort of cybernetic sensor unit over the left eye. They were nearly all Sheff'an, but there were a few Humans. Rachel saw that they wore purple armbands with the Coalition's double-pronged Rienda picked out in silver, marking them as allies.

The Jackals immediately adopted a subservient attitude toward the Falcons, but several of the officers, including Leon, appeared confrontational with those in the long coats. Leon pointed at one and said something, but the officer did not react. Finally, Akida took Leon aside, and when the two rejoined the negotiation, he had calmed down.

Apparently the newcomers got their way: a few minutes later, the VSF officers emerged, some looking hostile, most looking completely defeated. Doctor Reonil and some of the medical staff accompanied the injured VSF officers aboard the Falcon ship, which promptly took off and went west, its departing roar seeming loud enough to wake half of Tesa.

Rachel bade goodnight to Traxus and went to Leon where he stood with the rest of the rain-soaked and furious Jackal officers. He looked up and saw her, and his expression went carefully neutral. "Hi, Rachel. Now's not the best time."

"It's fine, son," General Rockmore said, overhearing. "Get some rest. Miss Case," he added, inclining his head.

The two of them headed for the apartment where they peeled off their wet clothes. Rachel had hoped to take his mind off whatever was upsetting him, but he paced back and forth in the nude while she sat patiently on the bed, her legs crossed. Finally, he stopped and smiled contritely at her. "Sorry, sweetheart. I guess I'm not a very good date."

"It's never boring," Rachel said, trying to sound cheerful. "We'll just have to keep at it until we get it right." She patted the bedspread, and Leon came to her.

13: A Crack in the Ivory Tower

Leon kept his sunglasses on. The grove was tranquil and verdant: most of the trees were still green, their canopies lush, but Eve's treacherous drought had done its work and the recent rainfall had done little to help. Leaves drifted to earth, golden stars and twirling bells with their stems pointed downward, almost like little parasols. Smooth trunks like veined marble had started to dry and crack. In the center of the grove stood the crumbling remains of an eons-old Tagean Dynasty explorer's marker, one of only a handful on Eve. The cracked columns and the tumbled ring of white stone they had supported were a potent reminder of the ephemeral nature of the universe. An ancient starfaring people had once set foot on this world and left a sign of their passing. Now a few ghost cities and markers like this one were all that remained of the bygone Tageans who had ruled a galaxy.

To Leon's left, Rachel's face was still, but her cheeks were hollow, her eyes brimming with tears. She held his hand tightly, her rings digging into his fingers. He found comfort in the pressure and made no effort to escape her grip.

To his right, Traxus stood in uniform, long hair pulled back in a ponytail. She held her cap in one hand against her breast and a bouquet of flowers in the other. The flowers were fresh: pink, yellow, red, with lush green and blue stems. Purple sprigs of something puffy stuck out from between them. They would be dried and shriveled in a day or two, but their fleeting beauty was reassuring. Out on maneuvers, she had missed the funeral. Paltry as the ceremony had been, she wanted to observe their friend's passing with something tangible.

The three of them stood before Buzz's marker. It was simple, obsidian with stripes etched in the left side, uncolored. The surface was glossy, reflecting some of the dappled sunlight. NICOLA "BUZZ" PARKER was engraved there, and below it the inscription IN SPITE OF ALL along with the date and location of his death. Leon found the inscription depressing in light of everything that had come to pass, but all the markers bore the same words. They stood in a field of them: black markers with names, dates, and that oft-repeated justification. There were few bodies beneath the moss and leaves, only those of the men and women who had no families to claim them. When Leon had arrived at the Pack, there had been a few dozen markers. Now there were several hundred.

"What was he before?" asked Rachel quietly.

Leon had to think for a moment. "Shooter for a criminal syndicate somewhere in the Shar'dan. Got arrested too many times, managed to back out of a dead end for something more rewarding." *Did he find it?* Leon wondered sadly. Buzz had never married, never had children, never settled down. Had he wanted to? They had been close friends for years, but Leon wondered how well he had really known the man. He had found a job offer from the Polaris Security Company as well as Buzz's half-finished letter of acceptance while going through his friend's effects.

Leon's injuries had healed and the bruises had faded, but his memories of that night had not. Sometimes when he closed his eyes, he could still see muzzle flashes and men falling, fountains of arterial blood. His dreams were loud with the thunder of guns and screams. It had been a long time since a job had affected him this much, but Buzz was still missing from the dinner table and his parts in their oft-told inside jokes and stories were spoken by no one.

He prayed that Rachel wouldn't take this opportunity to lecture him on how wrong it all was, and she didn't. She gave his hand a loving squeeze. "Buzz was a good man. And he had good friends."

Traxus stepped forward and put the flowers down, nestling them in the grass before the stone marker. It was the only marker with any flowers in front of it. The sojieri of Jackal Pack were not the most sentimental people.

Leon slid his arm around Rachel's waist, pulled her close, and inhaled her aroma, sweet in the crisp air of the grove. "It was nice of you to come down here."

"Of course, Leon. Buzz was my friend, too. It's not exactly the picnic we planned, but it's important."

"About that, I'm sorry. I wish I could just take you on a vacation."

She smiled at him. "You should try it sometime. The world can go on without you for a few days."

Leon feigned shock. "How can you suggest that? I'm the center of everything." Realistically, though, he couldn't leave. It was a sensitive time for the Pack. Rockmore had seen to their defenses, reinforcing anti-aircraft batteries, including the massive Nuclear Dispersion Cannon known as the

Skybeam. With their feelers out, they were as ready as they were ever going to be. Now all they needed was an enemy.

Traxus was still kneeling beside the marker, her head down, her long form folded before the stone. Leon got the impression she wanted to be alone with her thoughts so he guided Rachel toward the trees where they could continue talking.

He had been hoping that a visit to the grove might take his mind off the instability along the border, but that was wishful thinking. They hadn't gotten much information from the Valinata officers other than finding out the VSF had pulled back from a massive action at Sturmvaald, one of the Valinata foundry worlds. They had been routed, suffering nearly a million casualties. And after the Falcon Guard detachment from the Coalition Regional Base had intervened with their trenchcoated cronies from the Zoh Hegemony, all of the Zoh assets on Eve had packed up and left, cold-starting their engines and lighting out for points unknown. Presumably they had taken the captured Vali officers, crew, and sojieri with them. They had managed to avoid filing flight plans or declaring manifests, departing as though they wanted to get off the ground while it was still there.

Perhaps Rachel was right. Standing among the empty graves, Leon suddenly wanted to get as far away from wars and violent people as he could. With her, he might just make it. *You know it's not so simple, friend. This life has its own unavoidable inertia. It gets to a certain point, it resists slowing. You can't jump off without killing yourself.* He didn't want to believe that.

"It's so beautiful here," Rachel said, yanking him back to the present as she tilted her head back so the warm patches of light could play across her face. "I never would have pegged Rockmore as the romantic type."

"Oh, he's full of surprises," Leon said with a smile. "He feels a connection to everyone here whether he knew them or not."

"You're the same way. It's admirable. I've seen company executives who don't even acknowledge the people they see every day, but here you all make time to talk, see how things are going. And you don't forget the people who are gone."

"To be fair, company executives don't have to rely on their subordinates to provide covering fire, but I appreciate the compliment."

"I think you should know my mother has had a steady stream of friends and relatives calling and sending me emails," Rachel said suddenly.

"They want me to leave Eve and the Coalition, go back to the Commonwealth where it's safe."

Of course, "safe" was a relative term. Leon shouldn't have been surprised, but he was. "I'm inclined to agree with them," he said. It was a hard thing to admit.

"Well, like I told them, if you stay, I stay." Rachel crossed her arms, and that was that. Leon couldn't help smiling.

After a few moments, Rachel caught Leon gazing at Buzz's headstone. "He was really like your brother, huh?"

Leon chewed his lip thoughtfully. It was gradually getting easier, but it was still hard to talk about. "You know, I didn't even like him the first time I met him. He was such an arrogant little prick. Hell, I liked Akida better. So yeah, he was exactly like a brother, I guess."

"But you gave him a second chance."

Leon smiled again. "And a third, fourth, fifth, sixth … I was close to strangling him at one point."

"What changed?"

The smile widened. "Guy saved my life. That's all it takes, usually. Could have kept going, but he turned back, pulled me out under fire. After that his attitude didn't seem so bad. I even started to think his jokes were funny."

"That's important."

"Very."

Leon and Rachel were looking at each other, smiling, when Traxus approached looking refreshed. "Shall we?" she asked, straightening her uniform. "It's a nice day."

§

Over the last few days, the Coalition Ministry of Defense had locked down, turning into a paranoid enclave within the "Sunset City" of Sherata. A feeling of impending doom had settled among the cloistered generals and admirals and their various staffs. All of them were busy preparing for the opening salvos at Calama. Kra'al was spending what political currency she had to get approval for fleet redeployments, but without a full declaration of war, it was proving difficult.

Hakar and Telec, racing through the upper halls toward the tactical chamber just below the Chamber's conference room, were uninterested in the maneuverings of their colleagues and subordinates. As Hakar careened around a corner, several startled junior officers scrambled to get out of his way, paperwork fluttering across the hallway. The grand admiral stammered an apology and kept going.

Sprinting along at his heels was Telec, burbling worriedly into his comm, summoning Grand Admiral Motayre and High Grand Admiral Pirsan.

The marines guarding the door to the tactical chamber stood aside, and the two admirals entered, smoothing their jackets. They had to maintain some sort of decorum, after all.

Beside the holographics projector were two men and a woman, waiting calmly, their faces placid. They wore civilian attire, but security clearance badges were clipped to their jacket pockets. The clearances were at the highest level.

"Agents," Hakar said in greeting.

"Admirals," the lead agent said, equally deadpan. He was seated at the desk beside the projector. The man was a Human of average build, smaller than his two muscular companions.

"You sent the Epsilon Red cards?" Telec asked perfunctorily. He didn't bother to mask his agitation.

"Yes," the lead agent said blandly. Hakar was careful not to look at any of them too closely. They all looked familiar but at the same time alien. That was part of their job description, no doubt: to creep out everyone they met for no reason at all. There was something plastic and unwholesome about them. And their involvement usually meant one of two things: either the Coalition intelligence services had a handle on the situation or things were completely out of control. Hakar suspected the latter.

"The Zoh have decided to share after all," the agent said, rising from his seat. Far shorter than Hakar, shorter even than Telec, he nevertheless dominated the room, casting a larger shadow than he had any right to. He walked over to the holographics unit and fished through a briefcase standing on the base, then pulled out a folder containing several Membooks and a data key. He regarded Hakar and Telec for a moment with inscrutable gray eyes before deciding to hand the packet to Hakar. The two admirals gathered close around it, noting the stamps that declaimed various levels of secrecy.

"This is everything you'll need to start your war," the female agent said, startling Hakar and Telec.

"I would be careful, though," the lead agent said mildly. "The Vali are already claiming that the *Harridan* was ambushed and the crew taken hostage by marauding Coalition forces. They left out the bit about *Harridan* seeking asylum at Eve." He shrugged, then turned and left, his colleagues following him out.

"He's right, you know," Telec said when they were alone. "Whether we want a fight or not, what's left of the Valinata is itching for one."

"I know," Hakar said grimly, a hangdog expression on his face. It wouldn't help that the Zoh Hegemony authorities had probably tortured the captives to get the information after removing them from the Jackal Pack base. It was detestable, but Hakar was not so naïve as to think that mattered. "The VSF border fleet is about to go atomic. Can't Her Majesty talk down the Tête?"

Telec made the Sanar equivalent of a shrug. "She's tried. No one's picking up the phone. It seems to me that the VSF is operating without oversight right now."

"That makes them doubly dangerous."

"I agree."

Hakar paced, scratching his muzzle. "Someone's going to ask us about Primrose. You know that."

"I don't see why they should. I can't see a connection between that and Raven Blue."

"The similarities are piling up, Telec. And I've been having dreams."

"Dreams? Lovely, what am I supposed to say to that? Maybe we were a bit hasty when the results came back from the Edenbridge labs," the Sanar scoffed, "but the samples are different. You saw for yourself: no genetic homologies."

Still uneasy, Hakar changed the subject. "Has anyone from the *Rampant* talked?" After recovering the *Royal Dawn*, the crew of that VSF battlecruiser had seemed like the best hope for getting any sort of real information.

"No. They won't budge. Half of them still think we're behind it all, and the other half seem scared shitless because they know we're not. The end result is the same, unfortunately."

Hakar frowned. "You'd think they'd be willing to bargain for protection."

Telec snorted. "I'm about ready to use coercion of a more immediate nature."

A shadow fell across them as High Grand Admiral Pirsan ducked through the doorway, followed by the even more immense Motayre. "I felt the same way," Pirsan hissed, "but as it turns out, this Captain Montoya is a well-trained little VSF officer. He knows how to cover his ass for the inevitable backstabbing. Every priority comm was logged in his personal computer, and he didn't have a chance to wipe it before the ship was boarded. I have to tell you, it's some pretty awful stuff. The Valinata is on the run, and whoever's doing the chasing is using no restraint." Pirsan stood tall before them, and his red eyes glared down at them accusingly. "Is this what you expected?"

"What we expected?" Telec asked, puzzled.

"I'm aware that both of you reacted rather strongly to a report from Edenbridge Biotechnics. You have some information regarding these marauder fleets?"

Both Hakar and Telec made negative gestures. Motayre looked uncomfortable to be witnessing this. "I've never seen ships like these," Hakar said, frowning. "My reaction was based on a detail in the report, that the organic composite armor was made up of heritable proteins of an unfamiliar configuration. But I cross-checked it, and it was just a coincidence."

"I've read the report," Pirsan said tersely.

Hakar looked at Telec. The other grand admiral was breathing dryly, a sure sign of stress. He was likely wondering how to fulfill their duty while covering their asses. Hakar found himself wondering the same thing. "We made an erroneous conclusion," he finally said.

Pirsan's scales rose briefly. "I see." He gestured to the packet Hakar was holding. "Perhaps we should see what the Falcons and our friends in the Zoh squeezed out of the *Harridan* crew." The four grand admirals gathered around the projector that dominated the cavernous room, and Hakar inserted the data key. It was hard to believe that such an innocuous little object could be the source of so much anxiety to experienced warriors.

The program that ran from the key was a Coalition intelligence program overlaid on the Valinata code. The software graft allowed Coalition hardware to decrypt and decode the Vali programs without encountering compatibility issues. Hakar keyed through the menus until he came upon the black box data from the *Harridan*. Coalition Intelligence had generously flagged the relevant files. Hakar opened one at random.

Moments later an image burst into being above the projector's base, and Hakar frowned as he gazed at it. His face fell as the last vestige of hope that this was all a misunderstanding evaporated. The room had darkened automatically when the projector activated, bathed in an eerie half-light that reminded Hakar of pornography and nightmares. *This is what we get for sitting here and waiting, hidden in this ivory tower like so many shriveled crones. The foundations of the galaxy are going to fall away, and we'll still be sitting here waiting for Armageddon. Unless maybe* this *finally opens their eyes.*

He sat down heavily, and the four officers watched in silence as more images cycled through. Hakar forced himself to read through the Mems in that nightmare glow, his teeth bared in anger.

A VSF Dragon Valia armada was one of the most fearsome gatherings of naval might in the galaxy. A single Dragon Valia consisted of enough ships and firepower to completely sear a populated world to cinders. *Harridan*, a light troop carrier assigned to deploy sojieri under orbital cover of capital ships, had been part of just such a fleet. Based on the tag in the corner of the hologram, the footage they now watched was recorded by a bow camera. Standard battle star formations of cruisers moved purposefully toward a nondescript brown planet with an asteroid ring around its equator. Before them, floating just above the ring, lay another fleet of elongated black ships, ghostly silhouettes against the planet's cloud cover.

Within minutes the two fleets had engaged one another, silent space turning into a kaleidoscope of light and color. *Harridan* dove below the merging walls of battle, heading for the atmosphere in the company of more troop carriers.

Without more information (presumably contained in the reports), it was hard to tell exactly what happened next. Several blinding explosions went off near *Harridan*, washing out the image. When it resolved again, two of the other cruisers were gone. The image swirled as *Harridan* abandoned its initial advance, wheeling about for open space. Now the two fleets were fully entangled, and their foe was plowing through the Dragon Valia armada, heedless of their own losses as dozens of the black squid-shaped vessels burned.

Numbers were on the enemy's side: another fleet had arrived, pinning the Dragon Valia between two unbelievably massive armadas. The image shook as *Harridan* was hit again and again. Finally, the file stopped as the injured troop ship jumped to a conduit. They had never even made it to the fight.

Suddenly Hakar missed having a pistol strapped to his hip. It had always provided a sense of safety, of being in control of his destiny, no matter how bad things seemed to be. At the very bleakest, it at least provided one last bullet for himself. If something wasn't done soon, the whole rim would burn. And that would be only the start.

Pirsan was clearly thinking along the same lines. "Her Majesty is still considering a preemptive strike on Calama. I intend to endorse that decision, and I would like the three of you to sign off on it, as well." Anticipating further questioning, he held up a clawed hand. "Admirals Najo, Charok, and Daris have already put forward their support." He watched them expectantly, his expression unreadable. "Well?"

We can ride the wave of change or be drowned beneath it, Hakar thought sadly. "Very well."

§

The world is quietest before a storm, Rodriguex reminded herself. *Of course, in space even the storms are silent.*

So many times she had nearly been spurred to action, but Strategic High Command had kept a choke-chain on her. Every time she wanted to move she was halted, pulled back straining and frothing to her masters' feet. Her crews were likewise showing the strain. What had started as frenzied efficiency was dulling to frustrated complacency.

In recent days there had been nothing, not even a stray commsat. All that was about to change. She had scarcely believed it when the orders came through. In less than a week, Grand Admirals Daris and Najo would arrive to spearhead the advance on Calama. Their arrival would bring the number of CRDF ships in the sector to nearly fourteen hundred, nearly five hundred of them dreadnoughts of two kilometers long or greater. If she was being honest with herself, Rodriguex was happy to be reduced to a supporting role. She had studied the scans of the Dragon Valia armada across the border, and she knew it would be a hard fight, even for three battle fleets.

The Calama system was directly ahead, barely half a light-year away. The Fifth Fleet and its supporting local pickets hung in space just off the planet Talriis, a dusty, jagged little world with far too much ammonia in its atmosphere. Once a bustling mining world with valuable deposits, the planet now thrived as a trading hub, albeit an orbital one. Terraforming Talriis had been deemed unfeasible, and as a result, the population of sixty million lived in a constellation of space stations orbiting the planet. Old but serviceable designs, the stations contained enormous hydroponics facilities and dormitories, simulated environments, and quite a few casinos, making Talriis a popular destination at the outer edge of the Alkyra Trade Route. Being an officer responsible for all those lives, plus the more than a hundred thousand crewing her fleet, had suppressed whatever gambling urge Rodriguex might have possessed.

Far off to starboard was the Flamingo Nebula, a pink swirl which extended between the Coalition and the Valinata. Formed hundreds of years ago when two stars collided, it was still rapidly expanding and might one day engulf Talriis—and Calama, as well.

An alarm chirped, indicating an incoming priority message. Rodriguex turned her chair to face the comms officer, who was already decrypting. She waited, feeling a trickle of sweat trace its way down her temple.

"Ma'am, I'm getting a priority dispatch from the Amanra Crescent Regional Base, relayed via the Alkyra. They've received reports of possible VSF hit-and-fades along the border." The comms officer hesitated before continuing. "Four border stations destroyed, contact lost with two pickets."

Before she could react to this news, Rodriguex's thoughts were drowned out by another siren. A light was blinking over the tactical control pit. The chief tracking officer sat bolt upright in her seat. "We're reading a massive power surge in the Flamingo Nebula, Admiral."

Energy fluctuations within the nebula were to be expected as the nebula's own discharges and reactions interfered with sensors. Smugglers and illegal immigrants had long used it as a corridor to pass between the Coalition and the Valinata without encountering patrols or checkpoints. Today, however, Rodriguex was not inclined to give it the benefit of a doubt.

She was about to order the firing of a probe when one of the junior tracking officers exclaimed, "Holy shit! The Dragon Valia is moving!"

Wasting only a moment on surprise, Rodriguex quickly marshaled her thoughts and allowed years of training and protocol to guide her. So much for waiting for Daris and Najo to turn the tide. "Comms, send a priority dispatch to High Command and an alert to the Talriis PDF. Gunnery, I want solutions on all VSF ships updated. Prioritize any vessels with vectors intercepting the civilian stations." Turning to her control panel, Rodriguex opened a channel to the captains of her fleet. As she talked, she strapped her combat webbing across her chest and shoulders, to keep her in the seat in the event of impact. Around her, the officers were doing the same. "Ladies and gentlemen, we're monitoring systematic movement of the Valinata Space Force assets in the region. I have no choice but to implement Operation Eviction without the support of our fleets. Brief your crews and stand by for orders."

Another keypress patched Rodriguex through to the intercom. "This is Admiral Rodriguex. All hands report to action stations. VSF forces are currently advancing toward our position. Operation Eviction is now in effect. Prepare to engage." With that completed, she triggered an automated announcement system and alarm that would blare throughout the ship. Below her, the decks would swarm with crew stowing gear, loading weapons, and checking systems. Bulkhead doors would seal, turning each compartment into an individually pressurized environment. Marines would stand by to board enemy vessels or repel invasion should the fleets close. Armored shutters slid into place, covering vulnerable portholes in case the defensive grid was breached and sealing away the starlight. For now, the bridge portholes remained open but could close in an instant if the threat arose.

Rodriguex turned her attention back to her bridge crew. "All right, everyone. Initiate Phase One Integration to subsystems." She took a deep breath and sat back in her command chair. The chief environmental officer activated the neural interface array, and a jack rose up from the admiral's headrest, affixing itself to the matching socket at the base of her skull. Moments later discrete displays of information erupted in her field of vision, colored overlays that seemed to float before her eyes. As always, the images were disconcerting, causing momentary disorientation and tunnel vision. The benefits, however, more than made up for the temporary discomfort: she had instantaneous overviews for all ship operations, could access any hull camera or sensor readout, and could even take command of any subsystem, including gunnery or navigation, via her hardwired override with just a thought.

The entire process had taken less than a minute from decision to action. The Fifth Battle Fleet was functioning at optimum efficiency, officers and hardware in perfect harmony, crews at the ready. If it had to happen, Rodriguex was glad it was happening to her. She trusted her crews to fight hard enough and long enough to hold any VSF fleet in check until help arrived. If help arrived....

"Admiral," said the chief comms officer, "there's been no response to our hails."

Rodriguex didn't expect the VSF commander to respond, but she would rather err on the side of caution. "Keep trying. Anything you can tell me about that signature in the nebula, Miss Dufresne?" she asked the chief tracking officer.

"Unknown signatures, Ma'am. Still trying to clear it up. We can't tell if it's interference from the nebula or something else."

Rodriguex suspected it was something else, and she also suspected she was not alone in that suspicion. They had been waiting to make contact with Raven Blue since the standoff had begun. If the Vali ships had also detected the power surge, they may have assumed it was a CRDF invasion force. But how to make them understand if they wouldn't respond to hails?

An alarm blared, and red lights began flashing. Dufresne called out, "Incoming warhead cluster, Admiral. Time to impact six minutes."

The VSF had forced her hand. Jaw clenched, Rodriguex gave her orders. "Return fire and prepare AMS to knock down those missiles." At such distances, the standard procedure was to fire torpedoes at the enemy fleet and follow up with an energy beam strike to weaken defensive grids just before impact. The warheads could track the enemy, but they were slow. Conversely, plasma beams and laser bursts could flash across the distance almost instantaneously, but they were weaker and could miss a target completely if the targeting was even a fraction of a degree off.

A new sky's worth of starlight seemed to erupt from *Champion* and her attendant vessels as they launched their own missiles, tiny thrusters burning rapidly to build up speed. It was grim business, counting down the seconds until their attacks reached their targets. Nervously, Rodriguex's fingers twitched on the armrest, waiting to beat out the drum roll of a brand new war.

"Admiral, we're monitoring movement in the nebula." Chief Dufresne sent the data to Rodriguex's console, and an image of the nebula appeared before her, magnified tremendously. A bright spark of light advanced along its smoky pearlescent edge, moving at an incredible velocity. It dipped and vanished into the s-shaped cloud.

"Time to impact, four minutes, Admiral. Gunnery standing by."

"Thank you, Mister Cahill." Rodriguex watched the stars ahead as though expecting to see the distant VSF fleet or the missiles streaking toward them through the void. "Stand by to commence energy bombardment."

Beads of sweat trickled down Admiral Flora Rodriguex's forehead. She wiped them away. She could do nothing but wait, and that killed her. Then, as though the reams of data hanging before her eyes were finally allowing her to see clearly, she had an epiphany.

"Mister Cahill, can you still reprogram our own strike?"

There was a pause as her chief gunner explored options. "We're rapidly running out of time to do so, Ma'am."

"Send them into the Flamingo Nebula. Set them to fix on heat sources in the rough vicinity of that power surge." It was a tall order, and Rodriguex knew it. If her gunners could pull it off, however, they might be able to avert crushing defeat. If it failed, they might do nothing more than open a battle on two fronts. "And keep hailing the VSF commander."

The missiles had already traveled several thousand kilometers, and a minor course correction altered their trajectory enough so that they would plunge into the Flamingo Nebula, missing Valinata space.

"Valinata warheads are still inbound, Admiral," announced Dufresne. Rodriguex's stomach clenched. It was do or die, and she had gambled their lives on the hope that the VSF commanders would see what she was doing.

"All right, close the bridge shutters," Rodriguex said resignedly. With a *whoosh* the metal shutters slammed closed, and the stars vanished behind a dull steel curtain.

The crew grew tense, and Rodriguex didn't have to be psychic to know that they were all praying she was right. They didn't have time for a mutiny at this point, but if they survived and she was wrong, her credibility with the hundred thousand-plus people she commanded would be irreparably shattered. In that case, she would prefer death.

"Impact in one minute, thirty—holy shit! VSF warheads have gone dead!" A cheer went up from the tactical pit.

There was a commotion at the comm officers' station, and the chief stood up. "Ma'am, we're receiving a return signal from the Valinata commander. It's pinging a diplomatic code."

Rodriguex didn't bother to mask her relief. "Open a channel."

The exchange with the Dragon Valia commander, a male Huridet with dull yellow feathers, was terse and unpleasant. It was unlikely that there would ever be trust between Coalition and Valinata. At least, it was proof that the commander could think for himself and realized that they were better off putting aside their differences for now.

"Ma'am! I'm reading a mass coming in from Valinata space. That's a damn big profile," Dufresne interrupted.

"Get me a fix! How many contacts?" ordered Rodriguex, abandoning her discussion with the VSF.

"I'm reading.... I can't be sure at this range, but..." Dufresne trailed off, then shouted, her voice shrill. "They're coming out of the cloud! I'm reading ... I'm reading...." Words failed her. It was really happening. Raven Blue was emerging from its cloak of secrecy and in force.

Data was scrolling across Rodriguex's field of vision at an incredible rate, yet long years of practice had taught her to keep up. The ships varied in size, but they were all big. They also varied in their emissions readings from different ion profiles to spectral ranges and amounts of radiation. Whoever controlled them didn't seem to favor standardized technology. And yet, there was uniformity of design, with great, sweeping pronged bows and matte-black hulls. There were hundreds of them, the sensors picking them up erratically as they poured out of the nebula that had hidden them. How long had they watched the standoff between VSF and CRDF? How long had they waited for them to annihilate one another and leave Calama open?

Rodriguex's muscles were taut, her spine rigid. She had waited and served for years, patient, obedient. Now her trial by fire would truly begin. A new wave of sweat beaded and fell. "Range?"

"Nine million kilometers, closing rapidly. Eight million. Seven. They're decelerating."

They were too far away to see with the naked eye, but that would change. Sure enough, as Rodriguex scanned space, she could see an amorphous shadow blotting out the pink flank of the nebula in the direction of the Valinata. She felt that she could see to infinity and wondered if by chance the enemy commander was looking at her as that fleet flooded the system.

"Notify Strategic High Command of our situation and intent to join the battle, and order the Talriis PDF to scramble and assemble on us. Patch me back through to the VSF commodore. We're going to need help," ordered Rodriguex, trying to be heard over the sudden din of sirens and shouts over the comm from her captains. She could taste the excitement in her mouth, a metallic tang not unlike blood.

Slowly, surely, the massive armada drew closer, rolling across the border like an oily black wave composed of enormous ships, many of them dwarfing *Champion*. Rodriguex did a double-take, revolted, as the sensor feed displayed an enhanced image of one of the ships. Surely, no such horror drifted between the stars. *And yet I'm looking right at it.*

As the distance between the three fleets shrank to fighting range, Rodriguex tried to marshal her thoughts and come up with some sort of strategy that didn't involve sacrificing the entire Fifth Fleet. It was not quick in coming.

Third Movement:
Where Angels Prey

14: City of the Dead

Leon leaned over Heidi's desk, his vantage point giving him a clear view down her blouse. He tried not to stare, but she made it difficult, relishing his distraction by pushing her breasts together and winking up at him. Her smooth skin sparkled with the glitter-laced body lotion she used, and she had changed her hair color to a bright pink with matching nails and lipstick. Heidi had always enjoyed teasing Leon and likely always would.

"You don't think it's too much?" he asked. He reached over to press a button on her keyboard. The picture changed, showing a broad deck overlooking a golden beach and azure waters.

"Are you kidding me?" Heidi replied, laughing. "If you showed me this, I'd probably get up and walk again. Three million seems a little much, though."

"Beachfront property, Heidi. Beachfront property. It's a steal."

She snorted and reached for her tea. "I guess, but it's only that cheap because there's no one on Tamil Nadu."

Leon straightened. "That's not even true. Do you know how many celebrities have summer homes there? Like, thousands."

"And what do you do in the winter?"

He grinned at her. "There is no winter."

Heidi scrolled back through the file. "I can't believe you're really thinking of going." She gave him a sulky look.

"I'm just getting a quote, is all. No reason I can't have two places."

"No reason you can't have two girls," she said, stretching her arms provocatively over her head.

"I think not getting killed is a pretty good reason," he replied with a good-natured smile. He enjoyed bantering with Heidi—she was a good friend and a competent administrator, considering she had spent most of her adult life shooting at people. Nevertheless, it was easy to detect the bitterness beneath the surface of her constant jokes. *It must be hard to be stuck in a wheelchair while the rest of the world walks. Just remember it's because of you.*

"So it's just a vacation place? You'll stay here, maybe do some seasonal work?" She seemed genuinely anxious about the prospect of saying goodbye.

"Sure. Hey, maybe I'll franchise." It was odd to consider calling a different world "home" even if it was just another placeholder. "You know, it wouldn't be bad to have a vacation place where Jackals can go to take it easy, all expenses paid. You could use it."

"If you want to get me into a bikini, all you have to do is ask." She reached for the drink beside her comm, deftly changing course when the device buzzed for attention. "It's the general," she said, glancing at the ID. "Take it in your office?"

"Sure. Hey, thanks for everything," Leon said, putting his hand on her shoulder. She put her own over it and gave it a little squeeze.

"What are friends for, right?" Heidi picked up her comm handset. "Hi, General. Colonel Victor will be right with you." She shooed Leon away, and he walked back into his office.

Picking up his own handset, Leon slid into his high-backed chair. "Victor here."

The general's voice put an end to the good mood. He sounded strained as though he was fighting off an assailant while making the call. "Leon, things have changed. Are you busy?"

"No, sir."

"Then please come to my office. I need your opinion."

Leon was on his feet and out the door in a moment. "Heidi, before I forget, will you put Echo Company in the line for a bonus disbursement?"

"Right after I handle the garrison rotation for Tesa," she called to him as he vanished down the hallway. "See you!"

The door to Rockmore's office was open as always, but even as Leon stepped through, he could sense that something was wrong. The air seemed thicker, tenser somehow. The blinds were drawn, letting in slats of orange light that slammed across the floor and walls at crazy angles. Rockmore's desk, usually immaculate, was strewn with paperwork. Leon spotted maps, starcharts, and what looked like transcripts or comm intercepts.

He came to attention. "What's going on, sir?" Was the contract lock over? Somehow he didn't think things were as cut-and-dried as that.

The general was drinking Scotch. Judging by his breath, it wasn't his first of the day. He slammed the glass down on the desk with a loud clink. Leafing through some papers, he pulled a printout from the pile. When he picked up the glass again, it left a ring on a map of the galaxy. "I've got a job for you. It's personal."

Instantly intrigued, Leon slid into a chair facing the desk without being asked.

"Scotch?"

"No, thank you, sir." Leon wanted a clear head for this. "So, what's up?"

"You ever hear of the planet Aethaleia?" When Leon shook his head, the general continued. "It's two and a half parsecs across the Valinata border, Rebuss Sector."

Leon craned his neck to look at the star-chart. Now he saw where Rockmore had marked a route. It was roundabout, but it looked like it would avoid most of the major conduits, the systems most likely to be patrolled. "We have business there?"

"We do." He handed Leon the printout, and the colonel found himself looking into the smiling face of a woman who looked to be in her mid-forties. It was a candid photo, taken of her in a lab coat holding a liquid-filled graduated cylinder and wearing goggles. A name was scrawled beneath the photo in the general's unmistakable script: Moira Traveler. Traveler had a nice, surprised smile and looked like the sort of woman who enjoyed a good story. Leon frowned as he scanned the photo.

"We're not out to kill her, before you ask. This is a rescue mission." Rockmore stood up and walked to the window, peering between the blinds. The sunlight carved a bright beam across his tired face. "Years ago, when Theresa got sick, a doctor named Gina Redford was the one who fought hardest. She never gave up, and Redford was the one who was there for her at the end." Rockmore looked down at his shoes, the beam of light sliding up his forehead. "She helped Theresa greet death while I still refused to acknowledge it. She tried to help me understand, too, but I was in denial right up until the cremation." Leon didn't see what all this had to do with the mission, but he knew better than to interrupt. He was sure all the pieces would fall into place.

"At the time, Gina Redford was married to Moira Traveler. They divorced ten years or so back, but the other day Doctor Redford commed me out of the blue, asking if we would retrieve Doctor Traveler from Aethaleia."

"Let me guess: no contact with the planet."

"Are you surprised? With the comm blackout from the Valinata, we have zero intelligence, and none of my contacts in the VSF are responding to inquiries. I want your assessment before I proceed. What do you think?"

Leon's heart was racing. *No intel, no way.* Of course, he couldn't say that. Rockmore was asking him to analyze the feasibility of an operation. "Risky. It would have to be a small team, masquerading as civilians. Valinata security's always been pretty tight; I can only imagine what things are like now. Best bet is to file a commercial flight plan, land, and make contact. I assume there's a catch to simply getting this woman a travel permit."

"She's a researcher at the Valinata École Centrale des Sciences Appliquées de Aethaleia. Working under VSF contract, Biowarfare Division. Her departure would almost certainly be viewed as a defection."

"Well, holy shit," Leon breathed. "You certainly keep interesting company, sir."

Rockmore's face was humorless as he turned back to Leon. "I owe Doctor Redford, and I would go myself if I thought I was up to it. Moreover, I agree with your assessment. You were right about using a commercial vessel. We can't have this mission traced back to us. I'm sending the team you assigned to the Mekon Davoi job."

Leon felt his muscles tense, felt gooseflesh crawling along his arms. *No, not my crew.* Suddenly he felt sick to his stomach, so strong was the regret he felt for having written their names. "You want my team?" He wasn't able to keep the dismay from his voice.

"I'm afraid so, Leon. The purse is four hundred thousand, all to you, to pay out as you see fit. I'll make sure there are bonuses when you get back, too. It should only take three days: one to reach the objective, one on-site, and one exfil." Rockmore came around the desk and sat beside Leon. "I know you have experience extracting Vali defectors."

"Twice, General. Neither went so well."

"Unfortunately, that's the best track record we have."

"How do we even know this woman wants to leave? I don't intend to show up at her door only for her to turn us in to Vali political security." In answer to that, Rockmore handed him a comm transcript dated a few months ago. It was clear that Moira Traveler was already planning to evacuate, but she was being watched. Better and better.

"What about Raptor? The Vali don't exactly like Prross, and he'll stand out."

"That's your call. He can remain on your ship as backup. Keep in mind, we don't know the situation on Aethaleia. It could be a warzone. And I need your expertise. You still keep current on genetics, right?" Leon nodded. "You're the only one here who could possibly talk his way into and out of a research laboratory like that."

No, no, no, no. Every fiber of Leon's being was railing against the idea of this mission. If they *were* caught fleeing with a defecting military scientist, it would be the death of them. *But how can I refuse the man who's done so much for me?* He couldn't, and that was the truth of the matter. Loyalty was too deeply ingrained in Leon, the only question in this case being whether his loyalty to Rockmore outweighed his loyalty to his friends. Could he ask them to make such a journey and risk another debacle? "I need to talk it over with the crew, sir."

"Okay, Leon." Rockmore seemed to have expected that reaction, and he nodded. "Give me your answer by midnight. I've already gotten hold of a Valinata-registered freighter. One more thing: no one can know what you're doing in case we have a security breach. As far as anyone knows, you're on a recruiting trip in the Shar'dan." The general sighed, the sigh of long, weary years. "I wish it could be someone other than you, Leon. But Doctor Redford means too much to me to entrust it to anyone else. She couldn't save Theresa, but if I can save Doctor Traveler, we still won't be even."

The general seemed to be on the verge of tears; Leon didn't think he had ever seen him so emotional. "You don't know how much it pains me to ask you to do this, son, but I don't have a choice."

Neither do I, Leon realized. *After all, he called me "son."*

§

Leon brought the topic up over drinks. Raptor, Jeric, and Asar sat across from him at the table in his kitchen, each sipping his poison of choice, which was fruit juice in Asar's case. As he expected, all three were excited by the prospect of a job. At this point, anything seemed better than the battalions' brutal drilling regimen. For Raptor it was a break in the monotony, for Jeric it was a chance to prove he still had the discipline and skill. For Asar it was more money to send home to his family. "A hundred grand to each of you," Leon said.

"Even split?" Asar asked, stunned.

"Equal risk, equal reward," Leon answered. They nodded appreciatively at that. Sadly, Leon picked up his comm and gave Rockmore the answer.

§

The Jackal Pack armory was vast and surprisingly cold, Rachel reflected as she shivered in an oversized sweatshirt. Rows upon rows of weapons lockers, armor racks … it was a monument to violence, fetishizing the tools of their monstrous trade. They sat under lights as though they were museum pieces. Ordinarily, Rachel understood, the armory was staffed by the Pack's security teams, the weapons kept under lock and key. For this trip, however, Rockmore had dispatched everyone so that his prizefighters could have the run of the place.

It meant a lot to Rachel that Leon had been honest with her, going against orders to reveal the truth of their mission. Part of her wished she didn't know. Where they were going there would be no reinforcements, and no hope if they were captured. That knowledge had left her numb and unable to even raise a protest.

She walked beside Leon as he checked rifles and placed them gently on a rolling cart, along with dozens of magazines. "Are you scared?" she asked, suddenly.

Leon stopped in his tracks and laid another weapon on the pile. "Terrified," he admitted.

"But you're going anyway."

He nodded. "That's right." He reached for another rifle and paused. "Rachel, I hope you can understand."

"I understand," she said darkly.

A braying laugh drew her attention. In a far corner, Raptor and Jeric were checking armor. The pilot stood straight with his arms out while Raptor tugged on the armor plates, checking the straps. Gallows humor was not new to Rachel, but she found it unnerving when all she could be was afraid for the man she loved. "It's times like these I wish I believed in God."

"So you could pray for me," Leon guessed.

"Oh, I'll pray anyway. I just wish I believed it would help."

A few minutes later, General Rockmore entered, pushing a cart loaded with food. He gave Rachel a queer look. "It's nice to see everyone's taking the secrecy of this operation seriously." Leon didn't apologize, and the topic was dropped. "I brought you all breakfast," the general continued. "Rachel, you're welcome to it."

Rachel wrinkled her nose at that. How anyone could eat at a time like this was beyond her, and yet Leon and his team fell on the hot food as though they hadn't eaten in days.

Afterwards, Rockmore drove them all to the cosmodrome himself. Before the sun was even up, the sky still a colorless gray expanse of clouds, the mercenaries were loading their stolen ship. No one but Rachel, Akida, and the general had come to see them off in the predawn gloom. Only a handful of people knew where Leon and his team were going or even that they were going on a mission at all.

There was no point in protesting, no use in being angry, so Rachel decided to make the most of her time with Leon before he left. She couldn't help wondering, though, if her destiny was to be one of those helpless spouses who waited in anguish for their lovers to succeed or be killed. She didn't know if she could stand that. When she stood on tiptoe to kiss Leon and her hand clamped down on his wrist, an electric shock seemed to course through them.

"I love you," she whispered fiercely in his ear. "*Come back.*"

"I love you," he whispered back. "And I will."

§

Ten minutes later they were airborne, abandoning Eve's warm plains for the unforgiving chill of space, the freighter shuddering as she rose through the atmosphere. She was a small ship, more of a courier than a cargo hauler, really, only eighty-seven meters from bow to stern, built on an asymmetrical chassis with the control cabin and crew's quarters slung beneath the starboard side of the main hull. The ship was called the *Faithless Bitch*, which Jeric thought endlessly amusing but which Raptor and Asar both considered unlucky. Leon just thought it was stupid.

"Looks like you get to fly into the Valinata after all," Leon said to Jeric, who was grinning as they left Eve behind. Beneath them, the Rombaldt Radiant Masses in the deck had already been set to 40% charge, and Leon's stomach was churning.

"This wasn't exactly what I had in mind," the pilot conceded, but he couldn't mask his excitement.

"So, big deal," Raptor said, lounging in one of the seats furnishing the cramped bridge as they drifted through customs. "It sounds like a straightforward retrieval. I mean, of course, it's risky, but we're used to risk, aren't we?"

"Do you suspect we'll be in the line of fire?" Asar asked. "Otherwise we should be able to land and do our work without too much trouble."

"I have no idea what to expect," Leon admitted. "It could be all sunshine and happy smiling people or it could be a warzone. And we won't know until we're too close to get away."

"What Vic here isn't saying is that he's feeling gun-shy after that last job," Jeric chimed in from the helm. "Aren't you?"

"That's ridiculous," Leon snapped, knowing that it was far from ridiculous. "But the whole galaxy is a time bomb right now. I don't want to be responsible for a war between the VSF and the CRDF just because some friend of Rockmore's wants her ex-wife brought back."

"You're just mad 'cause you have no chance of scoring with a lesbian," Jeric chided with a clown's grin on his face.

"Don't be juvenile," Raptor growled. "You should learn to respect love in all its forms, but then again I suppose you would have no frame of reference."

That killed Jeric's smile, and the pilot turned back to plotting their jump coordinates. Leon watched him. Although Jeric's insensitivity annoyed him, he wouldn't have wanted anyone else in the pilot's seat, especially if things went wrong. These three men were among the best with whom he had ever served, brave and quick. If the job could be done, they would do it. Leon had waged war on dozens of worlds in the company of thousands or in the company of a few handpicked troops, sometimes even alone. He was not a self-deceiving optimist, thinking anything was possible. No, it was a convergence of fates, so to speak, the aggregation of all the diverse elements and variables of the equation. Occasionally, Leon still thought as a scientist, and he knew that mercenary work was far from the realm of controlled experiment, worlds removed from predictable outcome. But he had learned long ago that when the deck was stacked against him it was best to hold a few aces up his sleeve, and Jeric, Asar, and Raptor were all aces. It was his way of controlling his own destiny in the face of overwhelming odds. *Better not to be on the mission at all.* Still, there was no sense panicking about something he could not change.

Hours later, when the ship slipped across the threshold of the universe and into a conduit, the four men gradually fell silent, each of them seeing something different in the ephemeral vortex. The blue-purple light caught in their wonderstruck eyes, hypnotic. Faces seemed to drift before them and vanish; they saw shapes that might have been tricks of the light or doorways into whole new worlds. There were undulating, threatening visions, as well, and Leon felt his stomach clench despite himself. Staring into it was like staring into the face of God, something no living being was ever meant to see or comprehend. And yet civilization had managed to smash through the walls of reality and turn something incomprehensible into something mundane, something commercialized. Only it would never be mundane, as anyone who had spent time gazing upon the conduit abyss could attest. This abyss was no metaphor; it was literal, bottomless, concrete and abstract at once. Leon was grateful when sleep came, uneasy though it was.

§

Aethaleia, a trash midden if they had ever seen one, hid beneath its smoky corona off the port bow. Constellations of garbage drifted in great, impassable clouds, giving the lie to the Valinata slogan "Progress, Always." No moons orbited the gray-green world, only a pair of immense, sprawling space stations that looked like children's block forts gone out of control. The stations were dark and there were no signs of traffic.

"Oh, shit," Jeric said immediately. Without even running a systemwide scan, it was obvious that there had been trouble of some kind.

"Comscan," Leon ordered, taking comfort in the routine. Had his voice sounded panicky, or was it just his imagination?

For over a minute, the computers clicked through the available channels, searching for a live signal. There was none. Each click felt like a hammer blow to the back of Leon's skull, the static between them a wretched scream. He had never listened to a silent system before, had never heard how ominous *nothing* could sound. Even during the most secretive of covert operations, the most underground of guerilla wars, there was always some chatter, encrypted or not. This was chilling in its primitiveness as though instead of slipping into a conduit their *Faithless Bitch* had slipped back in time.

"Nothing?" he asked, disbelieving. "Are you sure you're doing it right?"

"Dude, it's automatic," Jeric snapped. Clearly he was uneasy, as well. A glance at Asar and Raptor showed that while they sat impassively, their muscles were tensed, their jaws clenched. "I'm not reading anything but bounce-back signals that are years old."

"Aethaleia has a population of almost a billion," Asar whispered. He ran a hand through his hair several times, combing it back but succeeding only in mussing it. "They *can't* have *all* gone silent. That would be ... impossible."

"Well, it's true. Nothing out here, no traffic on the scanners. The whole planet must be taking this blackout thing pretty seriously." Jeric's rationalization sounded weak, but all of them grasped at it with the desperate tenacity of a drowning man grabbing at a piece of floating debris from a wreck. They wanted to believe, had to believe. To question it was to accept the madness that the galaxy had become. "What do you want to do, Vic?" Jeric asked in a small voice.

"Take us in closer. Full scan."

"You want I should broadcast?"

"Nothing but the standard hails." Leon turned back and forth in his chair. He was at a loss, thrown off balance by the silence. They should have known something was wrong when there was no answer from the darkened border crossing station, just an automated reply. Yet they had pushed on. "Better we stay as passive as we can in case the VSF is hiding in the trash."

The four sat as silently as sailors aboard ancient submarines hiding from sonar, each man tucked into himself as Jeric brought the little ship closer, closer. Off to starboard, one of the garbage clouds resolved itself into dented containers, rusted hull plates, and all sorts of detritus emptied by ships most likely trying to avoid customs tonnage charges. Rivers of the stuff seemed to orbit the planet in lazy arcs, the individual cast-off pieces of scrap revolving slowly. They were almost beautiful, these broken halos around the dimly glowing world, rings of shattered crystal frozen in mid-fall.

But there were no ships among them, at least none whole. When they were closer, Jeric broadcast a request for landing clearance, both to the stations and the customs authority of the cosmodrome below. None of the facilities replied, and as they passed by one of the stations, with *VSG Dévouement* printed neatly along its main habitat modules, they saw the first signs of damage. The station had originally been much larger, it seemed, with dozens of ship-sized cylindrical modules linked in a network, if the build of its sister was any indication. Nearly a third of the *Dévouement*'s modules appeared to have been blown away, and one of its main habitats had been torn open as though an enormous bite had been taken out of it. As they drifted by, none of the mercenaries said a word, but they were all thinking the same thing: *Attack.*

Attack by whom? Surely the VSF wouldn't have done this, unless the rumors of a full civil war were true. That begged the question of who held the planet now, the rebels or the Valinata loyalists? There was another option so unpalatable, it almost didn't occur to Leon. What if the CRDF had done this? *But why would they attack civilians?*

"Anything yet from Lucette?" Leon asked. They still couldn't see the capital, which was obscured by the clouds, and yet there was an otherworldly, almost infernal glow pulsing through the pollution.

Reluctantly, Jeric ran another scan, and they were all surprised when the computer cued in to a station that was broadcasting. He immediately stopped the cycle and raised the volume. The signal was faint but clear: martial music, blaring defiantly into space, brassy horns and overzealous strings, belting out a call to a war that looked as though it had already been lost. There was a voice, as well, shouting over the instruments. "Citizens, your Valinata needs you! The enemy is among us, but you are not forgotten! We stand strong together! Victory through solidarity!" The banal propaganda continued, and after a few minutes, the mercenaries realized that the transmission was prerecorded, different soundbites looped randomly.

"Jesus, welcome to Paranoia City," Jeric muttered. "What's the point, Vic? We should turn around while we still can."

"Just … take us down." Leon's mouth was dry, and he felt his stomach tying itself into knots as the little freighter drifted into the haze of the atmosphere. After a few moments, an alarm blared, and Leon's heart stopped. "Missile tracking?"

Jeric reached over and flipped a switch. The beeping stopped. "No. The sensors are picking up dangerous levels of radiation below. I … think we're flying over a fallout zone."

"What's below us?" Leon hoped it was a military testing range.

Jeric checked his map. "It *was* a city. Nouveau Calais. There's nothing left down there."

There was nothing to see. Even this far up, the air was full of pollutants, hiding the ground and whatever was left of the city presumably beneath the pall. It lent the sky a sickly gray-green color and seemed to warp the clouds themselves, making it look as though the mercenaries were looking through the bottom of a green bottle. Leon feared that Lucette had suffered the same fate as Nouveau Calais, so when the tops of Lucette's buildings emerged from the fog like rocks from frothy green water, he nearly laughed with relief. He realized how much it resembled the Terra of his youth, back when air quality warnings had been as important as air raid warnings, when acid rain had deformed toys forgotten outside. It was the same sort of callous disregard for a world that he saw now, a planet allowed to drift so far from nature that it had become nearly uninhabitable. But whereas the Terran government had finally realized the impact of negligent environmental policies, the Valinata were not a member of the Inter-Regional Economics Organization and did not comply with IREO guidelines. As a result, pollution was rampant throughout the empire, making it a haven for unscrupulous manufacturing corporations. Some of those corporations appeared to have found a happy home on Aethaleia. It was peculiar to feel a pang of nostalgia for a grimy, unhealthy world such as the one beneath them.

"Anything on thermals?" Leon asked as they passed over Lucette's outskirts. Most ships were not equipped with IR scanning equipment, but Rockmore had ordered many modifications to prepare *Faithless Bitch* for her journey. Sensors were just the tip of the iceberg.

"Yeah, plenty. Just nothing I can use. It looks like the whole city's burning. I couldn't pick a herd of elephants out of this background."

"Any radar from the ground?"

"Not a ping. No missile tracking or firing solutions. Do you want me to do a flyover of the École, spot for a closer LZ?"

Leon considered for a moment. "Better not, just in case they've got triple-A on us. Stick to the air lanes, no fancy shit to attract attention."

"Vic, there's no one down there."

Leon gave Jeric a scathing look, and the pilot nodded and turned back to his controls. The ship descended farther into the swirling murk, and the cityscape became clearer, a half-remembered dream suddenly coming to life. It was catastrophic: as Jeric had said, fires burned everywhere, great raging infernos belching smoke into the sky, illuminating the dark metropolis with a sickly orange Halloween glow. They passed over squat, uniform buildings of gray brick, their sides blackened by soot and chemical deposits. Out of the ranks of shoebox structures rose ornate and magnificent government edifices, their domes and statues likewise covered in the ugly patina. And among the blocks of apartment buildings and administrative buildings, factories dominated the landscape where they had no place being. It was the factories that burned, greedily consuming whatever toxic soups remained in their chemical reservoirs.

"I think that's it," Jeric said, pointing to a campus of buildings arrayed in a sprawling manner vaguely reminiscent of the Jackal Pack base. It was the École, all right; Leon recognized the layout from the maps they had studied during their journey. It was hard to make out any details from this distance, through the gloom, but the buildings appeared cleaner than the surrounding blocks. It looked like it had been fortified; it was a good bet the academics had holed up there. "And there's the port...." Jeric trailed off. "Motherfucker," he whispered.

Asar leaned forward over Leon's shoulder, his dark eyes narrowing. "What's left of it," he said quietly.

It was a grim sight. More fires burned where ships had been destroyed on the tarmac or crashed among the surrounding buildings. A great spherical ship rested on its flattened rear section, one of the Valinata's *Odin*-class battle carriers. It looked like an enormous cracked egg, the upper section of its hull caved in. The whole thing was listing badly on its precarious-looking landing struts. Down on the tarmac were dark clusters of objects that might have been bodies. "This is a great start," Raptor growled uneasily. "I say we skip right to scenario B. We bring the guns."

"We don't want to draw attention..." Leon said weakly.

"And I'm saying we don't have to worry about shields hassling us. Look at this place. Whatever happened happened a while ago."

It took Leon a moment to weigh his options as Jeric set the ship down on a bare patch of tarmac, while white, ghostly fingers of smoke caressed the canopy. He could leave Raptor on board and proceed on foot with Asar through the city or he could take both of them and leave Jeric relatively undefended. Honestly, Leon wasn't sure they needed to worry about finding anyone down here in fighting shape, but if they did, such people were likely to be desperate. They would kill to find a working transport. One look at the ships left on the tarmac was enough to tell Leon that none were functional. An extra gun, especially a Banshee, might come in handy.

"What do you think, Colonel?" Asar asked, his voice low and even. He was not one to lose his temper or get excited.

"All right, the three of us go. Jeric, if you see *anything* out of the ordinary, dust off and worry about finding us later. We have to keep the ship safe."

"Count on that, Vic." Jeric reached beside his seat and pulled out a small, rectangular satchel. "Here, you guys take this with you."

"Is that your HotStart?" Leon asked.

"Come on, if we get caught with one of those, it'll compound our problems! We're already crossing the line here!" said Asar, a trace of exasperation creeping into his voice.

"It'll open any locked doors, decode passwords," Jeric said with a shrug, offering the satchel.

Leon took it and inspected the contents. The computer was small but heavy, housed in a dented and scratched metal enclosure. The lid was emblazoned with a bright yellow smiling face which winked up at them. "Not exactly inconspicuous, my friend." But it could come in handy. Rockmore had also asked Leon to collect information if he found any, and the École was likely to have some. He slid the computer back into its padded case and tucked in the dangling wires. "Thanks, buddy."

"If you come across a computer you can't access, just run the Untie Gordian program. You ever solve a Rubik's cube?"

"Once," Asar said.

"Nope," Leon added. "Tried to a couple times."

"This thing could solve a Rubik's cube a thousand squares to a side in less than a minute. It'll knock down any firewall with brute force as long as it's directly interfaced." Jeric smiled proudly, as though the accomplishment was his. 'Then it copies everything, so you can run programs in their native environments."

The other three nodded appreciatively. Leon stood and began strapping on his gear, beginning with his gunbelt. As he tied the holsters across his thighs, he turned back to Jeric. "Atmosphere scan?"

"It's breathable, sort of."

"What do you mean, sort of?" asked Raptor, instantly on his guard.

"I mean I wouldn't bring a pregnant girl here unless you wanted the baby to come out looking like Vic." They all laughed, but there was an edge to their merriment.

"All right, guys, let's get to it." Leon pulled on a long, black coat and strapped his TK-77 into the lining on one side and a Jackhammer autorifle on the other. Asar, dressed in a thick olive parka with a fur-trimmed hood, carried his Gauss in a black duffel bag and a Jackhammer over one shoulder. Raptor, clad all in black, likewise concealed the Banshee in an oversized bag and strapped a Domino machine gun across his back. Reluctantly, they started for the ramp.

§

As it turned out, they needn't have worried about concealing their weapons, and they gladly readied them. As the three men emerged from the *Faithless Bitch* into the gray-green smog, they saw immediately that there had been a last-ditch evacuation attempt. Barricades had been erected to channel the crowds and keep order, but they appeared only to have funneled a stampede for the last ships, turning the spaceport into a field of death. Thousands had been trampled in the mad dash, contorted bodies lying like rows of dominos atop each other, all trapped. It looked as though shield armored personnel carriers had fired into the mob, as well, either to disperse them or to kill enemies that had gotten in among them. Again, Leon wondered who could have done this, and he found his mind warily circling the possibility of CRDF involvement. *But why?* The question rose up again, insistent. Between the École and all the factories, Aethaleia doubtless made some sense as a military target, but there were certainly more tempting ones out there. Besides, wiping out a civilian population center sent the wrong message.

They didn't speak as they walked along the concrete barriers, didn't turn their heads to look at the slaughtered masses. There was a horrible stench in the air, rank and penetrating. Raptor attempted to sample the air in order to detect any nearby presence. They had to wait while he coughed and hacked onto the concrete because of the stink of the place, death and chemicals, pollutants too numerous for him to pick out any individual element. They moved on, leaving the port grounds and entering the city proper.

Puffy white flakes drifted out of the haze, and for a moment, Leon forgot the horror they were witnessing. It had been a long time since he had seen real snow, and his spirits were buoyed. Until he held out his hand to catch a flake, and it smeared gray soot across his palm. It was ash.

The city was haphazardly built. It appeared to have grown around the port, placing the landing fields dangerously close to the center of the city. The consequences of such placement were only too evident as they trekked past a block of buildings that had been flattened by a falling liner and later passed beneath a small cargo ship jutting out of another building. There were more bodies in the street, crumpled by crashed cars and in front of shattered shop windows. The causes of death appeared numerous and grisly, but the bodies were all remarkably well preserved, most likely by the chemicals in the air, which left them almost mummified.

"What, are they pumping formaldehyde into the air?" Raptor muttered as they passed a sojier whose ashen gray face, with its hollow eyes and sunken cheeks, seemed to gaze up at them accusingly. There was a bullet wound in his head, possibly self-inflicted. "Maybe we should have brought rebreathers."

Leon shushed him; it was too late to go back. Still, they paused to tie bandannas around their heads as crude dust masks before moving on. They turned a corner, following the route they had all memorized. The boulevards were broad, designed to accommodate an incredible volume of traffic. Some of them were jammed with abandoned vehicles, others were strangely empty. To the left, above a row of squat tenement houses with dark, sorrowful windows, a line of massive tapered smokestacks loomed implausibly close, vomiting smog. It was a nightmare landscape, volcanic and dim. Visibility was poor because of the haze, and Leon wondered how people could stand to live like this, how the government could so unfeelingly mash them against their industrial facilities. The highway median was lined with ghostly white flowers that looked oddly fleshy, stunted and mutated by long-term exposure to the pollutants, devoid of pigment and beauty.

"Can you imagine an uglier place?" asked Raptor sadly.

"With difficulty," Asar replied. With his bandanna covering his mouth and nose, he looked like a fierce bandit.

Leon shot them both a warning glance, and they lapsed back into silence. None of them was in the mood to joke anyway as they walked across the cracked pavement of the old sidewalks. Their footsteps didn't echo in the strangely still streets, the sound swallowed instead by the thick, suffocating fog that seemed to hang over them like a ceiling above the whole world, manmade as surely as the smokestacks that birthed it. Leon kept them to a careful pace, checking corners and advancing from cover to cover; they would have looked incredibly suspicious to anyone observing them from the dark, soot-stained windows. Such caution hardly seemed necessary, but it was too deeply ingrained to ignore.

This is too fucked up to be real, Leon thought. *Where is everybody?* The entire planet *couldn't* have been killed off. The signs of combat were everywhere, but there was little evidence of military presence. There were numerous shield vehicles and local sojieri, but no tanks, no artillery. The Vali loved tanks and artillery.

The three men froze mid-stride as a roar cut through the air, a vast rumble that seemed to have depth and texture. Leon's first thought was that it was a battleship in the atmosphere, and he looked up, searching through the ugly haze.

"Look!" called Asar, pointing. Off to the left, over the tops of the housing blocks, one of the great smokestacks, leaning precariously, had begun to collapse. Its bricks sloughed off in great pulverized sheets; gouts of smoke and flame erupted from its flanks as gaps appeared, and the whole construct became an avalanche, tumbling into itself. The ground shook with its destruction, debris rattling and the few remaining windows shaking. Leon had to steady himself, and he saw the sharpshooter go to one knee as rubble showered down around them, little chips of stonework and dust from the near buildings.

"This place is dying," Raptor said once the sound had passed and the changed skyline was still once more. "With no one to maintain it, it's all falling apart."

"Unsustainable," Asar agreed, dusting himself off.

"We'd best hurry, then," Leon suggested, and the three picked up their pace, their eyes just a little bit wider, their hearts beating just a little bit faster. How long had the planet been this way?

It wasn't long before another structure collapsed, this time a tall building that looked like it had been a corporate headquarters or an expensive private hospital before something had ripped off its front facade. It had been swaying dangerously ever since it came into view, but the mercenaries thought they could slip through before it failed. They were wrong. The top floors suddenly dropped down like a lower jaw in an expression of surprise, smacking loudly into the levels below them. Soon the building was telescoping downward, floor tumbling into floor, the whole of it pancaking before their eyes. Without warning, its downward momentum shifted outward, turning it into a vast flattened palm of dust and wreckage swinging across the avenue with outstretched claws of glass and metal.

"*Run!*" Leon bellowed over the din, throwing himself into a desperate sprint. He could feel his gear slamming against him with each long stride, could feel his lungs sucking in and expelling that horrible, noxious atmosphere, could feel his temples pounding out a tympanic rhythm. The wreckage cascaded down around them: girders folded like straw, and great cinderblocks were crushed to dust, while towering plate glass windows turned to a fine, lacerating hail and swatches of carpeting flapped like ragged pennons. Asar, sprinting bent-over, and Raptor, hurtling along with the Banshee held against his chest, vanished in the pall.

Leon threw himself forward with one more burst of frightened energy and passed out of the crashing tempest that had tried to engulf him. His left boot caught on a tumbled piece of debris, and he sprawled forward, his proton rifle leaping from his grasp as he threw his hands out. He fell, cracking his chin hard against the concrete, his breath rushing out of him in a pained *whoosh*. An upthrust piece of glass carved through his glove, leaving a neat gash in his left hand, and he saw the bright red line his palm smeared across the rubble-strewn asphalt. At last, the rush of air and the steady patter of debris came to a stop, and the city resumed its tired, labored descent into entropy, seemingly exhausted after such a frenzied seizure of destruction.

Surely, there was someone left to be drawn by such an event. Leon tried to scramble to his feet but found himself unable to move. *I'm trapped!* he thought frantically. *Fuck, something collapsed on me!* But nothing had fallen on him; he was simply paralyzed with fear. Realizing the fact didn't make it any easier, and he tried to rally his limbs to him.

Before he could panic, he felt Raptor's big hand sink into the fabric of his coat, and he was hauled from the street and dumped on to a sidewalk behind the cover of a crashed gravcar as smoke and dust billowed around them. "You okay?" the Prross growled. He was covered in dust, looking gray and corpselike. Blood trickled from a few small cuts on his face, bright red against the gray-white powder.

"I think so," Leon said, trying to slow his breathing. He checked for wounds and found nothing but a bleeding abrasion on his chin and the long cut across his palm. He dabbed at them with his bandanna before tying it around his hand. He glanced at Asar, who was limping and bleeding from a gash on his scalp. "Asar?"

"I'm all right," the sharpshooter said. He pointed. "Well, would you look at that?"

Leon glanced across the street and saw a grimy billboard advertising the Trego Renzo Band, one of the galaxy's premier jazz outfits. Jeric was a big fan of their music—possibly the only thing remotely cultured about him—but none of them had realized the group called Aethaleia home.

"Great, if we see them, we'll get an autograph for the little guy," Raptor said impatiently. "What now, Leon?"

I don't know. Leon suddenly felt inadequate to the task of leading these men. They had already nearly been killed, and they hadn't even faced the enemy yet. They didn't even know who the enemy was. The memory of Korinthe, of Buzz bleeding out in that little kitchen, suddenly rose up as freshly as though it had just happened. Jeric was alone, as Buzz had been. He was stuck on that ship with little in the way of weaponry or countermeasures. And Raptor and Asar were trapped out here with Leon in a city that had become a charnel house.

"Leon, are you all right?" Raptor was leaning over him now; Asar, scanning for activity, glanced over worriedly. "We've got to get out of here before someone comes to investigate."

Leon nodded wordlessly, feeling his mind running in panicked circles within the walls of his skull. What was this sudden overwhelming blankness? He couldn't fix on a single thought long enough to make sense of it, everything jumbled together, lost in the contrast. Had his doubts regarding Rachel somehow metastasized to his leadership, as well? *I am not fit to lead these men.*

"Man, come on!" Raptor snarled, real concern creeping into his expression. "What are you, fucking shellshocked?" He shook Leon, and the colonel's head cracked against the car door. "This is not the time to reevaluate your life!"

Somehow the crack to the back of Leon's head cleared his mind or, at least, focused his anger. "Let me go." He scrambled to his feet, took back his proton rifle, and pointed. "Come on. We've got to get to the École. We can worry about finding another route back afterwards."

"What if she's not there? I'd say that's a very real possibility at this point." Raptor's face was drawn as he voiced their collective worry.

"Then we go to her apartment, just as we planned. If she's not there either, then the mission's over. We're not going to hunt through this whole sea of corpses for one woman. Come on, the school's not far." Leon took off, with the other two close behind. They moved more quickly now as though clocks were winding down across the world and it was only a matter of time before all the buildings collapsed, turned to dust, and were reclaimed by the vengeful ecosystem of ghostly white plants. *We're close.*

Senses sharpened by their brush with death and warier than ever, the lonely trio continued through empty and silent streets past buildings that had become the tombs of millions. The true impact was hard to quantify, but it shook the very foundations of each sojier's psyche. Confronted with such complete and utter destruction, they shut out their emotions, trying to maintain distance from what they were experiencing.

After a time the squat buildings of the École Centrale emerged from the gloom, a cluster of thick structures that looked more like a fortress than an academy. This impression was enhanced by the presence of barricades and wrecked shield vehicles that had attempted—futilely, that much was clear—to defend the place. Dead, grasping trees with almost translucent trunks dotted the quad, once decorative but now only a potent reminder of how far this world had fallen. A number of the buildings had been flattened, not collapsed as the smokestack and the skyscraper were but *flattened*, as though some malevolent god had simply stepped on them. Spars of wreckage jabbed out like grave markers.

"The bioengineering building is across the campus," Asar said, pointing the way. He took point, scrambling over barricades and picking a route through the overturned vehicles. Here the stench was even more overpowering; shield officers had been cooked alive in their APCs like cans of meat thrown on a campfire, and the fumes of the burnt fuel were acrid, searing.

"Well, I guess we trek back to the cosmodrome, after all," Raptor said when they came to the open quad at the center of campus. They had intended for Jeric to come pick them up there in the event of a hasty retreat, but that plan was now out the window. A military dropship lay twisted in the brittle, skeleton-white grass, its back broken. It looked tragic, this great, fallen ship, swatted down like a bug.

Leon stopped dead, chewing his lip. He felt panic creeping over him again, at the edges of perception, blurring the world around him. *Keep it together, dumbass. Don't let them see you lose it.*

"What is it?" Raptor asked. He whistled, and Asar, up ahead, paused and crouched, his eagle's eyes restless, hunting.

"Just thinking," Leon said curtly. "What could have done this?"

"Let's leave the analysis for the after-party, okay?" Raptor sounded frightened and looked nauseated, possibly by the airborne chemicals which were gradually affecting him.

They found the bioengineering building mercifully intact, a great glass-sided cube ridged with balconies along its top three levels. They passed between a great archway shaped like a double helix of DNA wrought in white steel and entered. The lobby was quiet, a grandiose hall full of art celebrating dominance over nature. There were cots and crates of equipment everywhere, crudely partitioned when the building had been turned into a shelter. They could hear the sighing of the wind outside and the steady *drip, drip* of water from broken pipes. A bronze statue of a stylized Humanoid stood in the center of the space, bathed in the pallid shaft of light spilling into the building's atrium, a strand of DNA in its hand. Leon felt a pang of envy at the sight, realizing how much he lamented his own truncated past. *I could have been someone.*

You are someone, Mourning Star.

The lift banks were dark and dead, so the three of them climbed eight flights of stairs past classrooms and laboratories filled with empty chairs and silent equipment. They emerged into a dark gray hallway full of dust, great motes of it drifting through the silent air. Aethaleia had been like this for months, at least. Again Leon's mind strained in its traces, begging, *Who did this?*

They stopped before an office door. It was closed, and when Leon tried the handle, he found it locked. There was a plaque on the door that read:

MOIRA TRAVELER, PhD
BIOINFORMATICS & GENOMICS
SENIOR RESEARCHER, ASSOCIATE PROFESSOR

Beneath the plaque a paper was pinned, listing Dr. Traveler's office hours.

"Raptor, do the honors." Leon stepped aside, and the Prross punched the door inwards with a crash. The three passed through the swirling dust into the dark, silent office. There was dust everywhere; with revulsion, they looked at its source.

Leon fished the printed photo out of his pocket and held it up. "Well," he sighed, "I guess that's the end of that."

15: In the Wake of Abaddon

It felt good to get out of uniform and enjoy some of the high-end civvies she so rarely got to wear, Traxus reflected. She and Rachel were seated in Altitude's cocktail lounge by a window overlooking Tesa. The exclusive club and restaurant sat atop one of the city's tallest skyscrapers, giving it an unparalleled view of what was, ultimately, a pretty drab skyline.

Despite the suspicious circumstances of Leon's departure, Rachel Case was doing a remarkable job of keeping it together. It couldn't have been easy, not with the rumor mill on full power, grinding out stories ranging from Leon's and his team's dismissal from the Pack to their being selected to go behind enemy lines and assassinate the leader of the enemy force (although just who comprised this enemy force remained unclear). One thing was certain: no one bought the story that they had been sent to recruit troops.

"How's the duck?" Traxus asked after a sip of wine.

"I don't know," Rachel said glumly. "I can barely taste it."

"I know it must be hard on you." Traxus ate some of her own meal, locally caught fish from the Lime Sea's North Bay. It did seem wasteful to eat such a delicious meal when they were too stressed to enjoy it. The aroma of the golden, crisp duck would normally have been heavenly, but Traxus found it nauseating at the moment.

"Are you upset you didn't go with them?" Rachel asked.

Traxus studied her companion before answering. Somehow she suspected that Rachel knew more than she was letting on. "I don't know if we should be discussing this."

"How does it feel when they pass you over for jobs?"

In truth, this issue had rankled Traxus for a long time. "I don't blame Leon for that. It's my brother's fault. His relationship with Leon and Rockmore puts them both in an awkward position. But yes, it's frustrating."

"Hmm," Rachel said and picked at her food. She seemed oddly at peace, all things considered. "I've been thinking about Leon's past a lot lately."

"What part do you mean?" Traxus asked warily. After all, she didn't know how much Leon had shared, and it wasn't her place to discuss Daltar and how he had become the Mourning Star.

"I know it's bad … but how bad do *you* think it is? I mean, on a scale of one to ten."

Neutrally, Traxus said, "I guess that depends."

"On what?"

"On how much he means to you."

Rachel nodded, accepting this. "I thought he was some bored kid who decided to become a sojier to have adventures, and that one day he just went out of control. I don't want to be rude, but there are a lot of people in the Pack who give that impression. I thought, 'Maybe the whole conflicted thing is an act.' But he's just lost perspective after so long in this career, hasn't he? Like he put up walls to partition the different parts of his life." Rachel screwed up her face at Traxus. "Does that sound crazy?"

Traxus flicked her ears and reflexively ate another piece of fish. She wasn't surprised that Rachel would try to reconcile the opposing aspects of Leon's life. There were few people Traxus admired more than Leon—and few as insecure as he was. He dwelt on the past almost obsessively, studying it as though he could change it. Admittedly, he didn't exhibit most of the symptoms of those downward-spiraling sojieri who couldn't adjust to a life outside of service, but his persona was a fragile one with numerous fractures, in need of validation.

"I know how much the Pack means to him," Rachel was saying. "I just hope it doesn't rule his life. Heidi seems to have taken well to retirement."

"First of all, Heidi puts on a hell of an act, but she misses fighting with Leon and Raptor. She tried to kill herself when she found out she would never walk again." It had been Leon who had helped Heidi through her depression, feeling responsible for all of it. "As for Leon," Traxus continued, "he's spent half his life as a sojier. It's hard to let go of something like that."

"I understand that," Rachel admitted unhappily. She picked at her food but made no move to eat any more. "Sometimes he acts like he's waived his right to free will. I love him, Traxus, you know that. But it's so damn *frustrating*."

Everything Traxus thought to say would have sounded like her mother, patronizing, so she considered hard before she spoke. "You know I'm not a religious person, but the Tageans have a saying, that no one can change their destiny until they accept the path that led to their present." She shrugged and smiled sheepishly. "It's a dumb saying, but the point is that most of us have never had to make such difficult choices as he has, as a brother, as a sojier, as a leader." She smiled and waved, taking in their meal. "Deciding to get the fish or the duck is as hard a choice as some people ever have to make."

"I get why everyone acts like Leon's past is sub rosa," Rachel mused. Her eyes were like lasers, her pretty face flushed with wine or tension, Traxus wasn't sure which. "It's kind of sweet of the troops to be so protective, it's like they walk on eggshells around me."

"It's not our place," Traxus said, hoping Rachel wouldn't put her in a tough position by probing further.

Rachel sat quietly for a long moment, weighing her words carefully. "Thing is, Traxus, not everyone here seems to feel the same way. I've been … wrestling with this for a while, but I have to tell someone. I *know* about Leon."

Traxus drew in a deep breath. "I don't…."

"Someone on the base slipped me an article. I didn't know what it was, and I read part of it."

"That's why you left," Traxus realized. *But why did you come back?*

"That's part of it. I needed time to get my head together, to wrap my mind around what Leon did on Daltar. The nukes, the war crimes tribunal, the mutiny, fighting his own people…. He clearly made some serious, horrible mistakes and some awful decisions. I can see how much it eats at him. It's incredible he's managed to go on with his life at all. But I know he wouldn't have done it if he saw another way. What I *don't* get, and what I'm having trouble with, is his trying to hide it from me and making you all complicit in that lie."

Traxus found herself almost wishing she had gone on the secret mission with Leon. She would rather have taken her chances with the Valinata than sit here in Rachel's crosshairs. "I'm not going to make excuses for him, Rachel. He's been a coward for not telling you sooner. But you do know he's only delaying because he can't stand the idea of losing you."

"That's why I came back. That and the fact that I want the *why*. The article told me the how. I never thought Leon was a willing butcher, and now I see that he's trying to atone for what he did, like his actions are out of penance, like he won't allow himself a happy life because of it. I came back to figure him out."

"So you could decide if he deserves love." Traxus took a bite, but the meal had lost its flavor. "I've been wrong a lot, but you were right to come back."

§

The withered body of Moira Traveler, PhD, Bioinformatics and Genomics Senior Researcher and Associate Professor, ex-wife of Gina Redford, sat at her desk, shrunken within a finely tailored suit. Long blond hair hung to her shoulders in stringy clumps, and her lips were pulled back in a rueful, desiccated smile. She had come to the place that mattered most to her to die.

Raptor and his companions stood looking at her with unsurprised regret. *A fool's errand*, the Prross thought bitterly. Asar removed a camera from his pack and took several photographs as evidence that they had located their objective and not simply gone off for a sandwich somewhere. Clearly, she had been dead for some time, long before they had been given the mission, in fact. She had slit her wrists all the way to the elbows, and her shriveled, skeletal arms lay on her desk amid dark patches of flaking, dried blood, palms upward in a supplicant's pose of beseechment. *I hope she found the peace she was looking for.* Her sleeves were rolled up.

They had come prepared for this. Raptor drew one of his *khura*, the long, curved warblades he wore at his hips, and neatly chopped off a dried finger. He slipped it into a vial to take back for DNA testing. It was distasteful work to disturb the dead, but it had to be done.

Leon was chewing his lip again, and Raptor left him to his thoughts, beginning to search the office and adjoining lab for valuable intelligence. He found a diary beside one of her hands and gently picked it up in his claws. Some blood had stained it, turning the first dozen or so white pages a dark brown. He dropped it into his satchel beside the vial and opened the drawers of Dr. Traveler's desk, careful not to jostle her corpse. Academic forms, graded papers, correspondence. Raptor straightened up. "Find anything?" he growled to Asar.

The sharpshooter was tossing the office closet, pulling open file cabinet drawers. "Nothing but school papers. I think everything of importance is likely to be on her hard drive. Colonel?"

Leon nodded, looking distant. He slid the satchel containing the HotStart off his shoulder and handed it to Asar, then went over to the balcony. He opened the sliding doors, and a gust of Aethaleia's poisoned air whistled in, blowing papers off the shelves.

Raptor turned back to Asar with a questioning look on his face. The Human only shrugged and crouched by the doctor's computer, pulling out the little hacker's device. There was no power in the city, so he ran both computers off the HotStart's internal power cell, and soon they were up and running. Jeric's computer made short work of the security software, and within a minute Asar was downloading.

"It's a damn shame about Traveler," he said, frowning in concentration as he worked to figure out the program's interface.

"Yes," Raptor replied, glancing at the sad little mummy. They had come all this way to rescue her, but there had never been any chance at all. What must her final days have been like? Cowering in terror as the VSF lost control of the city block by block, ceding it to a mysterious enemy that appeared to have vanished, as well? What would they learn from her diary and computer files? With any luck, there would be useful data there, valuable data. Data they could sell to the CRDF or another high-bidder, but not before they learned what it could teach them.

"Well, that should do it. Now we just wait while it duplicates everything." Asar stood up, snatching his Gauss rifle off the dusty floor. They turned in the dark office, eyes drawn to Leon, who stood morosely on the balcony. The sickly green wind whipped around him, snapping his longcoat. As he gazed out upon the burning, dying city all around them, his eyes took on the aspect of a stormy sea: deadly, fathomless, and cold. His proton rifle protruded from his coat as the tails flapped up high, appearing for a moment as darkened angel wings.

"He looks at home here, doesn't he?" Raptor asked, awed and saddened.

"Like the devil in Hell," Asar muttered.

It was true. Leon seemed frighteningly in his element, calmly surveying the wreckage of a civilization, those bottomless eyes drinking in sights which would have unhinged more delicate psyches. His jaw was clenched, grinding back and forth, his right hand tight on the stock of his rifle. Few things scared Raptor, but in this moment, this brief fragment of time, Leon did. It was the way he seemed to own the entirety of this cataclysm. Not for the first time, the Prross comprehended how his friend could have destroyed a city. And yet, there was something pitiful about Leon's expression, too, a lonely melancholy that there was no one left for him to fight.

Raptor was grateful when Asar announced that the HotStart had copied Moira Traveler's computer files successfully. He left the sharpshooter to pack up and stepped onto the balcony. The structure felt as though it could collapse at any moment. He put a hand on Leon's shoulder, and the colonel's eyes snapped to him. "We ready?"

"Ready," Raptor confirmed. "You all right?"

"Stop asking me that," Leon said tersely. His shoulders were hunched, the collar of his coat turned up against the wind. "I'm just trying to get a handle on the situation. Wondering how, why, and who."

"Yes, I am, too. And I'm not coming to any satisfactory conclusions." The two of them stood in the swirling green soup and watched as a distant tower crumbled, its death rattle rumbling across the cityscape. It was the death knell of Aethaleia. "Come on, let's go. We have to find another way back to the port."

They left the building as quickly as they could, skipping steps on the way down. Back in the dead streets they half-ran, every sense attuned to the slightest change, the smallest sign that something was not as it should be. *Nothing here is as it should be*, Raptor reminded himself as he stepped over another corpse that had been cut neatly in two at the waist. The stench was overpowering, nearly enough to bring him to his knees.

And then Raptor knew what it felt like to have his heart stop. All three of them froze in their tracks, statuesque parodies of themselves, as a deafening trumpeting sound filled the thick air, followed by a thunderous crunch only a few streets over.

"*What the fuck was that?*" hissed Asar, his eyes looking as though they had suddenly doubled in size.

"Shut up," whispered Leon, quickly throwing himself into a darkened doorway. His two companions followed. They waited, hardly daring to breathe, listening for another sound like the first.

None came, but they felt rather than heard another crash as something massive fell to earth. *More buildings collapsing*, Raptor told himself, knowing even as he did so that it was nothing so simple.

A few seconds later there was another crash, and Raptor felt his teeth snap together from the impact. He began to count. Six seconds later came another tremor. He counted again. There was another six seconds after that. Too regular to be collapsing buildings. No, something was *walking*.

"It's a mechana," Leon said, arriving at the same conclusion. "Has to be."

"Whose?" Asar asked in a small voice.

"I don't think we should stay to find out." The colonel waved them forward, and the trio ran from cover, hurdling wreckage as they crossed the street.

Raptor was breathing heavily, cursing the weight of his Banshee. For a long, time such weapons had been impractical for infantry use due to the weight of the ammunition and the power supply, as well as the recoil that could throw a man off his feet. Advances in kinetic recoil absorption and power cell technology had made the Gatling infantry-portable, but the damn things were still heavy.

Leon stopped so quickly that Asar slammed into him from behind, and the two stumbled. Raptor stopped, too, wrenching his ankle as he tried to keep his balance with the big gun. Turning to see what had brought them to a halt, he saw Leon standing with his mouth open, dumbstruck.

The thing moving between the buildings disappeared from view in an instant before Raptor managed more than a fleeting glimpse of it. All he got was an impression of black oil, glistening and viscous, poured over a hulking, curvaceous monstrosity. It was enough. As Raptor looked at the rows of windows where it had been, he was stunned to realize that he counted thirty stories to where the bulbous dome of a head had reached. Nearly a hundred meters! He had also seen the edge of a great, curved limb built like a scythe before it, too, disappeared. *That was no mechana*, he realized with a jolt of fear.

No, it's the air, it's making us see things. As if to refute that, another blatting roar echoed off the rooftops, long and loud. *No mechana ever made a sound like* that.

"Run," Leon said quietly, wonderstruck. The three of them broke into a full-on sprint, hunting for a side street that would take them around the fallen skyscraper and put them back on the path to the cosmodrome. They had to reach the ship before that thing did. Thankfully, whatever it was selected another route, and its pounding, leisurely footfalls gradually faded behind them. The last thing they heard was a strangely mournful roar, almost a howl, filling the sky.

§

After the titan had receded, Leon and his friends searched for a route that would take them around the fallen skyscraper. It was easier said than done, and making their way through the rubble was treacherous, slow going. The dust and smog were even thicker where the building had toppled, and Leon had to pause for breath at the top of a mountain of concrete and steel that had spilled through an apartment building like a jagged mudslide. Far from being able to see from his vantage point, he found his view obscured by the thick haze.

When the bullets hit the twisted girder beside him, Leon's instincts kicked in, and he dove prone, setting off a minor avalanche of debris. Below and ahead of him, Raptor and Asar were likewise going for cover behind the skeletonized upthrust of tenement. *We're not alone. Not sure it's a good thing, though.*

"You smell anything?" Leon whispered into his comm as he scrambled for defilade that would protect him from more incoming fire. Another bullet rang off a steel plate, pealing like a bell.

"Are you kidding?" growled his friend. Leon looked at Raptor, spotted a trickle of blood coming from one nostril, and wondered how bad this atmosphere really was for them.

"You see anything?" he tried.

Asar gestured with his left hand, to nine o'clock, and held up five fingers, twice, before waving his hand uncertainly. *Ten contacts, give or take.* Leon squinted into the smog but could see nothing beyond the vague shapes of buildings and cars. He raised his TK-77. The grip was slick with the blood from his injured palm. Below, Asar had readied his own weapon. The three mercenaries stayed absolutely still. *Is this the enemy?* Leon wondered. Having seen the destruction, he felt cold fury rising within him. If these were the people responsible, he would make them pay.

When the assailants finally emerged from the smog, whooping and hollering, Leon's rage ebbed. These were not the ones who had emptied Aethaleia, but the lingering ghosts of its victims. Armored in odds and ends cobbled together from the gear of slain shield officers and kitchen pot racks alike, the people that ran from cover were the sad remnant of Lucette's population. In a short time, amidst the ruins of their planet, they had reverted to a desperate, barbaric state. There were twelve of them, eight Humans and four Tageans. Four of them were armed with shield carbines, the rest with crude clubs, wrenches, and blades. Peering from between the broken cinderblocks, Leon was overcome with pity. How many more were there like these, cowering in the wreckage, scavenging their own dead?

"Hold your fire," Leon whispered. If possible, they would take these people with them. In any case, they didn't appear to have seen Raptor or Asar.

Still whooping, perhaps thinking they had killed Leon, the survivors began scrambling up the wreckage, cutting their hands and arms on broken glass and jagged metal. He could hear a woman's voice, giving orders. The gunners had slung their weapons, and Leon decided this was his moment to attempt a bloodless solution. He rose, dust and debris tumbling off his coat, his hands up, TK-77 dangling at his waist but within easy reach. "Don't shoot! We're here to help!"

The survivors froze, their eyes bright in their grimy, soot-stained faces. They hardly looked like people anymore, and there was little comprehension in their eyes. *Bad idea*, Leon realized a moment too late.

The gunners went for their carbines, and Leon dropped back again as they opened fire, raising his own weapon. With a shrill scream, the club-wielders charged.

"Drop them!" Leon barked into his comm as bullets snapped around him. The survivors were exposed on the slope of the mountain of debris and had no hope. It was regrettable but necessary.

Asar's first shot went right through the chest of the nearest club-wielder, a Human woman with wild, tangled hair, the one who had been shouting orders to her companions. She was wearing scrap metal plates as armor, but the Gauss round punched right through it and out her back. For an instant, Leon could see through the smoking, fist-sized hole in her torso as she tumbled. She was silent as she fell aside, the club, a pipe with barbed wire wrapped around it, slipping from her slackened grip.

Crazed and starved though they might be, the gunners weren't stupid, and they went for cover themselves as Raptor opened fire on them from behind a cluster of bent girders. The Banshee's energy bursts sent up fountains of debris and kept the gunners pinned.

The people with the clubs were unbelievably fast, and they had closed quickly. Leon fell back as two came screaming in at him, their weapons raised above their heads. Leon fired his TK-77 from the hip, and a lucky cluster blew off the head of the nearest man in a red mist and a bright flash. As the body toppled, smoking, Leon shifted his aim.

The second attacker slammed his club into the proton rifle, knocking it aside. Leon let it fall and grabbed the club with his gloved hands. A nail bit into the tender flesh between his thumb and forefinger, but he did little more than grimace. Yanking hard, he pulled the scavenger toward him and brought his knee up into the man's abdomen. As his attacker doubled over, Leon drew one of his Sprawlers and shot the man twice in the chest.

He dropped the smoking pistol back into its holster and raised his rifle again, finding that its strap had gotten tangled with his sleeve. The Banshee was still screaming. Leon moved forward to the lip of the depression in which he stood, TK-77 tucked against his shoulder.

Raptor had managed to kill one of the gunners and had turned his fire on the running scavengers. Below and to Leon's left, Asar stood before a half-circle of collapsed bodies, but one of the Tageans managed to close with him, swinging his crude cleaver. Leon's eyes went wide as the metal buried itself in the sharpshooter's shoulder. Asar screamed, dropping his rifle as he fell.

Leon shot off the man's arm, and the smoking limb dropped into the wreckage. Letting out a feral scream, the Tagean tried to run away. Feeling no remorse, Leon shot him in the back, and the man's torso came apart. *He would have gone for help,* he told himself.

The gunners saw that they had no chance, and they tried to make a break for it. A woman wearing the tattered remnants of a shield uniform popped out of cover first, and she jerked as Raptor turned the Banshee on her. Smoking holes appeared all over her body, and she dropped like a rag doll. Leon joined in, and together they cut down the remaining scavengers.

One of them was still moaning, and Raptor dispatched him with his *khura,* jamming the blade deep into the scavenger's chest. In the silence afterwards, he and Leon made their way to Asar, who lay still behind a tumbled wall. The cleaver, which appeared to have simply been cut from dented scrap metal, one end wrapped in cloth to make a handle, was still embedded inches deep in his shoulder, and blood pulsed slowly out around the blade.

Leon's mind was racing; they might as well have been back on Korinthe. A look at Raptor, and he knew the Prross was thinking the same thing. They stood over their friend, trying to determine the severity of the wound.

Asar was looking up at them, his eyes glazed over with pain, expectant. His blood-covered hands were up by his head, hanging limply, and it was clear that he didn't want to look at the wound. "Am I going to be okay?"

Leon slung his rifle and crouched down beside the sharpshooter. "I don't know, buddy," he said, trying to keep his own fear out of his voice. Who knew what infection could set in in this cesspool? "I have to pull it out." He snapped his fingers. "Raptor, hold him down."

The Prross looked over, nodded, and put down his Banshee. "We need to hurry. No telling who'll be drawn by the gunfire. I would rather not see our big friend again."

"I concur," Asar mumbled.

As Raptor held the man's shoulders flat against the carpet of rubble, Leon took hold of the cleaver's handle and yanked hard. It came free in a spray of dark blood, and Asar cried out and kicked him violently, knocking him back. Blood was pumping freely now, flowing over the bone that had been briefly visible, so Raptor tore a strip from Leon's coat and, after peeling away the bloodsoaked parka and flak vest, pressed it into the wound. Leon looked at the blade. It hadn't cut as deeply as they thought, most of the attack having been blocked by the vest, but Asar had lost a lot of blood.

His eyes were squeezed shut, and when he opened them, they were filled with tears. Leon understood how painful it had to be, but he was so relieved that the sniper hadn't been killed that he almost laughed in his face. "Can you walk?"

"I guess ... I have to, unless you have a ... limo service."

"That's the spirit," Raptor said, and he and Leon pulled Asar to his feet. Their wounded friend's face was ashen. He stumbled several times as they descended the wreckage. *At least he's alive, no thanks to us.*

After the din of the gunfight, the hazy boulevard was startlingly quiet, and they limped along, struggling with their burdens. All three were listening for the sounds of more survivors, all knowing that they couldn't hope to evade pursuit with Asar hanging between them, all trying to avoid facing the grim likelihood that if they did come across more people, they would have to kill them, too.

They didn't talk, simply moved as quickly as they could, trying to rejoin the main route to the cosmodrome. They were nearly there when Raptor quickly let go of Asar and dropped to one knee with his Gatling.

Leon, unprepared to take all of Asar's weight, stumbled and fell on top of the sniper, who cried out again but quickly clamped his mouth shut. Leon hastily regained his feet. "What is it?"

"I heard something," Raptor hissed. He hacked up blood onto the street and resumed scanning.

Leon paused, listened. All he could hear was the groaning of the sagging buildings and the disappointed sigh of the wind. "Are you sure? Come on."

"*Wait.*"

Glancing over his shoulder, Leon could see the vague outline of the spherical *Odin* cruiser looming out of the gloom. They were so close. What was Raptor doing? "Stop wasting time!" Leon said quietly. "We have to move."

"Just a—" Raptor went silent, and Leon squinted into the fog. "Oh, *fuck me.*"

"What is it?" Asar asked in distress.

Leon couldn't be sure. "Sojieri. Let's move. *Now.*" They were spilling out of a side street a few hundred meters away. Leon could barely pick them out against the drab cityscape, but there was something wrong about them. Even from this distance, using abandoned cars as a frame of reference, Leon could see that they were tall, nearly three meters, if he had to guess. While he could not make out any details, it was clear that they were sojieri, for they moved in perfect synchronization in a staggered formation.

What the fuck am I looking at? Leon shook his head, squinted again, trying to clear his vision. They weren't bipeds but insect-like, like the H'vir. *Could it be...?* But the H'vir were pacifists! Weren't they? Clad in blue-black armor, these things looked far from peaceful.

"It's a kilometer to the ship from here," Leon guessed. "Can we make it?"

"I don't know," Raptor whispered back.

"Then we better go now." Leon was turning back to Asar when something green flashed by, less than five meters away. He looked up quickly, his eyes fixing on a patch of burning asphalt. The flame was pale green in color, giving off a greasy smoke. Another one burst behind them, toward the cosmodrome. "They're firing! Move!"

"Take Asar!" Raptor bellowed, standing up. He depressed the trigger of the Banshee, and the barrels spun up and began spitting red darts of energy into the oncoming mass. More green fire flashed past them, hissing and spitting.

Leon knelt over his injured comrade, pulled him up to a standing position, and threw him over his shoulder. Grunting, he rose, the weight of the sharpshooter and their combined gear crushing. Another burst splashed against a nearby car, and Leon felt the heat on his face. He walked as quickly as he could—which was not very—toward the ramp that led past the barricades and bodies and onto the cracked tarmac. Asar's rifle banged against his right leg with each step, on several occasions threatening to trip him. By the time he had gone a few hundred meters, he was panting, drenched in sweat, and exhausted. Asar's blood was soaking into his coat, and the sniper continued to moan weakly.

Off to the right, Raptor was walking backward, picking his way over rubble and corpses, firing into the enemy formation. The Banshee's characteristic wail was comforting in a sick way, and the weapon seemed to be suppressing their pursuers.

"*Ah, ya Allah!*" Asar moaned. "Fatima! Don't let me die here, Colonel!"

"Don't be afraid!" Leon screamed through gritted teeth, the weight of the man compressing his spine, each footfall sending spasms through his legs, his muscles suffocating as his lungs fought to draw breath from the choking atmosphere. "Trust me, Asar, I'll get you home. I swear on my soul." A burst of the green fire hit nearby, and Leon turned, nearly losing his footing, to rattle off an ineffectual volley, holding the TK-77 one-handed. *I'm not leaving this man here. Better to die with him than abandon another friend.* The thought was loud in his head, and Leon redoubled his efforts, though his body cried for respite. But he had to get back to Rachel, no matter what.

When the Banshee stopped firing, Leon's first thought was that Raptor had been hit, but when he looked over, the Prross was struggling with the Gatling as heat radiated off it in shimmering waves. "It's down! Overheated!" he roared, running over. "Give me Asar!" He shouldered their friend as though he weighed nothing, freeing Leon to provide covering fire.

The colonel dropped to one knee and fired into the formation as it drew closer but grew no clearer. At this distance, through the haze, it was difficult to tell if he'd hit anything, and the enemy was moving with a peculiar, almost skipping gait that made them hard to lead.

It was too much, this fight. There was something almost supernatural in the air that terrified Leon, and fighting first those crazed scavengers and now.... Whatever these things were, it was taking its toll. And he didn't even know if the ship would be there when they got to it.

He stood and ran to catch up with Raptor, who was struggling with both Asar and his Gatling. The Prross's tail swung from side to side like a pendulum, keeping his balance. Up ahead, the *Odin* battlecruiser seemed to have drawn no nearer, and Leon couldn't see the *Faithless Bitch*, either. He turned once more, dropped to his knee, and fired a flurry of shots. The power cell clicked, drained, and he threw it aside and loaded another. On impulse, he held his fire, dropped the TK-77, and raised Asar's Gauss, which he still carried. The rifle was heavy and cumbersome. He wanted to get a better look at their attackers through the scope, but before he could get more than the briefest glance, another dart of green fire crashed into the ground a few meters in front of him, nearly knocking him flat. He scrambled backward in a crab-walk and struggled to his feet, breaking into a mad dash, as another volley of greasy green plasma crashed down around him.

One thing was certain: this was no Valinata splinter group. They advanced like that, Raptor jogging with the Banshee and the injured man in his arms, Leon sprinting to catch up, pausing to return fire. He burned through three more power cells and all the magazines for the Jackhammer autorifle, and still their marching, wraithlike pursuers refused to give up.

When *Faithless Bitch* materialized out of the gloom, Leon was so relieved he almost sank to his knees then and there. He forced himself to sprint the final hundred yards, past the flattened ranks of bodies. They were laid out in orderly, overlapping rows behind the barricades, forever waiting to board ships that had never come. He pounded up the ramp, saw Asar lying on the deck, bleeding profusely. Raptor's Banshee was beside him, still steaming. *"Jeric, go for sky!"* Leon shrieked at the top of his lungs. *"Now!"*

The ramp was already closing, and the ship leapt into the air as Leon and Asar fought to hold on and ended up sliding across the deck into a bulkhead. They were glad to be rid of Aethaleia, and Leon gratefully watched the broken world recede through the smudged porthole.

16: Layover

The great spaceborne horde would not stop. They had spilled out of the Flamingo Nebula like a great black wave of vacuum, blotting out the pink and red gases. They had swept down upon the Fifth Fleet and Talriis with stunning ferocity and upon the Dragon Valia armada, as well. In mere minutes, foes on the verge of war became tentative allies, if only for one bloody battle.

"Status on Talriis evacuation?" Rodriguex demanded. Strapped into her command chair, she felt powerless despite knowing that she was in command of a state-of-the-art warship and its fleet. Her neural interface flooded her with data from all the ships, but there was little she could do to act on the information.

One of the comm officers responded, "Stations *Kent* and *Bengal* have been fully cleared. Most of the other smaller platforms have been evacuated, as well. Enemy forces are preventing us from reaching the rest of the survivors on *Cydonia*."

"How many are left?"

"About two-thirds, maybe twenty-five million people."

Rodriguex clenched her fists. She couldn't accept that those people, those *civilians*, were beyond help. She was here to protect them, and she would. She would bet any of her warships against any five of the enemy's unshielded vessels, but there were just so many, pinning down her transports and overwhelming point defenses. Their fighters, swarming like flies over a carcass, were unbelievably fast and incredibly agile; individually, they could hardly hope to damage one of the Fifth's cruisers, but their constant stings were gradually wearing down the defensive grids.

At first, the enemy had concentrated on taking out the space installations, allowing the Fifth Fleet to chew up their flanks. They destroyed the planet's primary gateway station first. It had exploded in a great spiral of burning modules, most of which fell into planetary orbit and were even now decorating the sky with fiery trails. Rodriguex had lost ten vessels of her own getting between them and the other stations, including a troop carrier full of marines, brave men and women incinerated or sucked out through the hull. No wonder they called space the Deeps. A person could fall forever out here, frozen in a hellish suspended animation if their blood didn't boil upon decompression first.

They had breathed brief sighs of relief when the enemy fleet had withdrawn the previous day, limping out of the system and leaving a third of their ships burning and drifting in their wake. What force could sustain such heavy losses and not be deterred? It had been a ruse, of course, designed to draw Rodriguex out so she would spread her fleet too thin. She had been unsurprised but despairing when the enemy reinforcements arrived, in greater numbers, and resumed their onslaught.

It wasn't enough to secure Talriis, Rodriguex knew: they had to drive the enemy away from Calama. For good.

"Enemy ships closing in, Admiral," Dufresne said nervously. "Range two thousand kilometers." That was close enough that the slow speed of the enemy's plasma-based weaponry would no longer be a limitation, and the CRN would lose its range advantage. Unfortunately, Rodriguex had her back to Talriis, and retreating was not an option. Going on the offensive was.

She opened the channel to her commanders. "All battle groups stand by to come about. Cross the T and expend light ordnance to keep their vanguard contained. Then split off and hit their flanks. Chop the head off that advance." Rodriguex forced herself to sit back, stilling her fingers in their restless drumming. Her ships formed into a rough wall ahead of the enemy vanguard, facing in two different directions. Space was filled with bolts of energy and beams of coherent particles, flickering off into the far distance, into that faceless, voiceless fleet of ships, ships that flew no flag, bore no insignia, had no names.

A ragged cheer went up from the tactical pit. A gunnery officer pumped his fist in the air, a gesture of fleeting triumph. "Confirming hits, multiple targets damaged. Two, three, four destroyed," announced the chief gunnery officer.

Rodriguex watched her opponents for a change in tactics. With singular drive, they continued on their course, plowing toward the center of the Fifth's main line. "Follow up with warheads. Antimatter and low-rads. Full spread."

Champion shuddered as rockets ignited, launching from tubes along the great ship's flank. The stars ahead shifted to the left as the big vessel banked to starboard, rolling over. Other ships in the formation were doing the same, rolling to deliver fire from their leeward sides while the windward batteries reloaded and recharged.

The salvo did significant damage to the advancing black ships, due in large part to the massing of their ships. *Safety in numbers, how quaint*, Rodriguex thought to herself as enemy vessels disintegrated before her. The trick wouldn't work twice: quickly they put distance between themselves, dispersing their attack along Rodriguex's main line.

A retaliatory blast slammed hard into the bridge, and Rodriguez flinched even as the defensive grid dissipated the blast in a flickering green curtain that seemed to shimmer across the camera feed. She called up information on the Dragon Valia armada and saw that, although their numbers were far greater than her own, they were still badly outnumbered, the Raven Blue ships in and among them. Ships were not meant to get so close, and the VSF vessels were struggling to consolidate their lines.

"More incoming contacts!" shouted the tracking officer, and the triumphant mood that had threatened to break over the bridge like a wave vanished. As though they weren't badly outnumbered already. "Seventy, eighty signatures!"

Rodriguex felt her heart clench within her chest even as her nails dug grooves into the rubberized armrests of the command chair. "Identify bandits, task a fighter wing to harry them until—"

"Wait, Admiral! They're hailing. Transponder readings identify them as Zoh Hegemony ships."

It was the Armada Tertius, commanded by a rear admiral named Agoston Szabo. Rodriguex had never trusted the Zoh to do more than shove a knife in her back if worse came to worst. She couldn't believe they were actually coming to her rescue. They fell on the enemy ships with reckless abandon, waves of old but serviceable fighters loaded down with heavy armor and more torpedoes than they knew what to do with. The lead elements of the enemy advance shattered and broke off their attack, at least for the moment. The Fifth Fleet and the Dragon Valia began moving inward, two arms of a vise crushing the Raven Blue fleet between them. There was butcher's work yet to be done.

Still, Rodriguex did not for one moment delude herself that this was over. She knew it was only beginning.

§

Faithless Bitch was a good ship, having been well maintained by her previous owners, whoever they might have been. But she betrayed her Valinata manufacture at the Karano Shipyards with an exceptionally rough ride through the conduit, hull crackling with barely contained gravitic discharges and giving the four men aboard a rough impression of what it might have been like to fling themselves into the dark halls of time and space during the dawn of empires.

They were used to rough rides, however, and after the horrors they had witnessed among the ruins of the city of Lucette, one of the great wyrms could have materialized from the vortex and they likely would not have batted an eye. Jeric watched his instruments and downed beer after beer, Raptor slept, Asar sat with his prayer beads in hand, reading from the Qur'an as he nursed his wounds, and Leon found himself completely absorbed in the writings of Dr. Moira Traveler.

Sagittarian 15, VNI 1123:

The naval garrison under High Commander Ketoff departed early this morning. The attaché informed us that the fleet was only going out on maneuvers but we all know better. Signals have been getting through despite the comm blackout and the jamming fields that have popped up between the systems. I never trusted the attaché anyway. Such a little weasel, always spouting whatever propaganda comes down from the council.

I couldn't care less what the garrison does. The École has been functioning more or less as usual, even though students and faculty alike continually look up, all of us trying to see if we can spot our doom before it lands on us. Security has been monumentally tightened since the samples came through but what good can we do with what we have? If only they would let us see the entirety of the data perhaps we could make more progress. I'm almost sure that Roubideau and Mellan have received similar samples but the integrity of the cells has been compromised. It's taken me months to isolate the chromosomes ... but I digress.

Those of us who know what's happening—not that I delude myself that I know anything—may be looking up, but the rest of the world is looking firmly down at their shoes, as always. Look down, nod when spoken to, watch the nightlies, buy the latest fashions. We've become a nation of sheep and I fear that our shepherds are asleep. There are wolves outside, the fascists of the CRDF and the exploiters of the Commonwealth, but more, as well I think. I wonder at the wisdom of their leaving us to fend for ourselves.

Sagittarian 27, VNI 1123:
I think I've made a breakthrough! I sent a secure missive to Roubideau asking after an old colleague, trying to test the waters, and in his reply he inquired whether or not I had received any secure samples from the VSF. While he and I have never gotten along, his theories on gravitational effects on mitosis and the impact of artificial chromosomes in germ line cells have always been sound. I shouldn't even be writing this. I suppose a journal would be the least of my concerns if my secret collaboration with Roubideau is discovered. I couldn't understand the full beauty of the genome until he forwarded some of his data on the totipotent cell lines. And to think I believed the samples were bacterial in origin! If only Gina were here to see this she would have been struck dumb. I am exhausted, more when I get a chance.

Sagittarian 40, VNI 1123:
All my research is for nothing. The fools, the damn fools! We heard the offers of assistance on the comm snoopers, heard the CRDF <u>offering</u> <u>assistance to us!!!!</u> And our own navy scoffed and threatened to attack! We had a chance, a real chance, and our research could have made a difference. They did not even provide us with a garrison in the end, and now those great leviathans have arrived, dropping out of the comet trail, carrying the minions of the Dragon. They are come to punish us, I understand, but I can't get past the knowledge that it could have been different. It all could have been different.
Now they've jammed our comms—we can't even contact Nouveau Calais twenty kilometers away—and we saw an explosion in the sky last night, possibly from the <u>Dévouement.</u> I'm afraid we squandered our last chance. I only hope that someone, somewhere else is working along the same lines. I only wish I could give some hope to the students but I think it's too late for that anyway. Classes have been cancelled and we are under martial law. A shield captain has turned the École into a makeshift fortress, trying to rally us and protect our base of knowledge. I wonder when he'll

give up and flee with his officers. I have already decided that if the beasts enter Lucette and we still have not heard from the fleets I will take my life. I don't think the École will ever open its doors again. I will miss everything. As these are likely to be my last words I feel like I should write something poignant, something meaningful, but nothing springs to mind. I am so afraid of being in a universe where suicide has become socially acceptable, that I don't think I want to live in it any longer.

Leon put down the diary with its blood-stiffened pages and heaved a sad sigh. The clinical rationality of Dr. Traveler's last words was heartrending. As he read through her diary, he felt as though he had gotten to know the woman whom he had only seen as a smiling snapshot or a dried husk of a corpse. Her last days on Aethaleia must have been a nightmare as this mysterious enemy seized the whole planet. Had people dived from roofs and windows, embracing death? Had they mobbed the ships and been shot by their own police? What kind of enemy was this that people would rather kill themselves than be occupied by it? Was the Valinata propaganda machine so effective that the populace saw the CRDF as monsters?

But it wasn't the CRDF. After all, Moira Traveler's journal had speculated that there were other enemies out there, worse even than the Coalition or the Commonwealth. Somehow he didn't think she was referring to the Shar'dan. What were those things they had seen on Aethaleia, obscured by the haze?

"Hey, Jerr."

The pilot looked over, lowered his beer. "Yo."

"Will your HotStart open the files we downloaded?"

"No reason it shouldn't. It copies the whole hard drive, operating interface included." He pulled it out of its case and handed it to Leon. "Be my guest."

"Thanks." Leon opened its smiling lid and switched it on. The little machine was full of surprises. He had seen Jeric use it for many things, but never had he expected to use it to unlock the research of a dead woman.

The metal keys clicked as he hunted through the various files and folders in the computer. Again, most of it was academic or administrative. The files pertaining to her research were partitioned off from the rest and isolated with their own passwords. The HotStart plowed through them like a truck through a pile of dried leaves, and her last project, her life's work, lay open before him.

The bulk of her research was concerned with cross-species gene therapy, using viral vectors to deliver artificial chromosomes coding for xenoform proteins. It was hardly revolutionary, but she had experimented with more complex gene arrays than were typical.

She had also dabbled in molecular physics, he saw, coauthoring several papers with the same Roubideau mentioned in her diary. The studies had focused on protein-to-protein interactions and the effects of different planetary conditions on degradation of immune function across generations of colonists. *Most likely it would have been suppressed by the Academic Council if it made the Vali look bad*, Leon thought with a derisive snort.

Most interesting of all, however, was the latest twist her career had taken. She had been researching the genetics of telepathy, attempting to find markers that might explain or at least help to identify various empathic and telepathic sensitivities in research candidates. "The Gift," as it was called, was more of a curse as far as Leon was concerned. Readers were rare, Senders even rarer, yet the CRDF had developed a rigorous screening process to weed out telepaths who could jeopardize security by reading officers' minds. Of course, there had to be a specific division where the most promising candidates were used as psychic operatives, but Leon had never met any as far as he was aware. One in every ten million Tageans exhibited some degree of the Gift, apparently, one in every forty million Humans. It was almost unheard of in Prross and Sanar but was most common among the avian Tez'Nar, who claimed one in every four million. The reclusive Talqai Gardeners were all powerful telepaths, but their numbers were so few and their colonies so isolated that they had little interaction with the rest of the galaxy.

The implications of a robust telepathic study were not hard to grasp. If Traveler had been able to identify the genes coding for telepathy in any one species—if, in fact, the trait was genetically linked and not some mystical fluke as many thought—the potential existed to clone more, to create a psychic army and train them from birth. It was a frightening thought.

That seemed to be the reason she had been chosen to take part in the mysterious Project Abaddon, just one among likely hundreds of researchers, none of whom were supposed to be aware of the others, none of whom were intended to have the full picture. His first thought was that perhaps the Valinata had dabbled in something they shouldn't have and had inadvertently released a weapon that had destroyed them all, but that was ludicrous.

Moira Traveler had been given a sample of tissue consisting of several hundred cells—a tiny sample, by most standards—in deep cryogenic stasis, and her task was to isolate the genes. While the specific base composition of gene molecules differed from species to species, the coding units were roughly homologous. Nature's variability was limited by practicality, and there were only so many ways to pass genetic information.

The source of Traveler's sample tissue had not been identified, and the genetic information in the cells had begun to degrade very rapidly on thaw. Apparently the good doctor had perfected a method for stimulating dead cells to enter stasis at room temperature, giving her time to engage a polymerase chain reaction to amplify the gene sample. And yet she had assumed—completely understandably—that her sample was bacterial in origin. Either that or the degradation had destroyed much of the genetic material before it was put into stasis as there was very little to work with. The Human genome was made up of three billion nucleotide base pairs and contained a little under thirty thousand coding genes as well as a large amount of redundant and vestigial DNA. By comparison, the Tagean genome, the closest Human analog, was made up of two billion base pairs coding for thirty-five thousand genes, far more efficiently packed in. The Rukadj, also relatively close to Humans, possessed a genome of four billion base pairs coding thirty-five thousand genes, although using six bases instead of four.

The sentient organisms of the galaxy fell into three genomic configurations, based on the evolution of life on their worlds. The first were those whose cells replicated by reading the helical strands of chromosomes, known as heliconomic, and included Humans, Tageans, and Tez'Nar. The species in the second, and most common, category were known as tubulonomic organisms, replicating their genes from unwinding tubular sheets which were unspooled by proteins in similar fashion to those of the heliconomic species, and included the Rukadj and Sheff'an, among others. The third and least common type was the spironomic genome, which was typified by a long, single-stranded spiral of genetic information. All of the sentient species belonged to one of the three primary configurations. On and on it went, different dialects of the same language, one of the unifying factors that had brought the races together.

At least, that *had* been the case, Leon supposed. Looking at the data, which were at first maddening in the flurry of uncertainties, he saw that something very different had emerged onto the galactic stage. Tentatively categorized as "spheronomic" by Doctor Traveler and her colleagues, this new chromosomal configuration was unlike any Leon had come across, and it was unsurprising that at first scientists had assumed it came from a microorganism. In its size and structure, it was deceptively simple. A hollow sphere, a single superdense chromosome without a nucleus, compressed and wrinkled inwards almost like the cortex of a brain, contained the species' entire series of heritable information on its surface. Like the pins of a music box's rotating cylinder, the loop-shaped bases interacted with a comblike protein that read them as it passed over the sphere. Expanded, the spherical chromosome would have been far larger than the cell it occupied, but it compensated by stretching out only a tiny portion at a time. Leon wondered how an organism could progress to sentient levels with such a small and exposed genome and assumed there must be some protective mechanism as yet undiscovered. And to think this creature's incredibly complex biology coded off the equivalent of an eight-hundred-million-base-pair helix!

Traveler had also elaborated on the difficulty of obtaining viable genetic information. Apparently, once she had established a protein mix which could successfully approximate a basic stem cell, using modified Tagean macropolymerases, she had found that small variations in vitro yielded radically different protein chains. The variety had confused the proteomics sequencers and set Traveler back months as she tried to figure out if there were any contaminants. In the end, she discovered that minor differences in the non-native polymerase chirality (the directionality of the proteins) was enough to throw off replication, something which presumably did not happen under normal conditions. When she finally cleaned it up ... Leon scanned downward and paused, shocked. "Holy *fuck*," he breathed.

Jeric turned to him, draining his bottle of beer and tossing it onto the deck. "What's up?"

Raptor, too, had stirred, slowly opening one amber eye. Asar closed his Qur'an.

"This genome ... it's impossible."

"What is it, Colonel?" asked Asar, his face ashen. "The data?"

"Damn right the data." Leon reread it, scanning quickly through the charts and renderings. *This is amazing.* "This organism, whatever it is, has the most complex and efficiently packed genome I've ever seen. It's less than a third the length of a Human's, but it has sixty *thousand* genes encoded in it. Sixty thousand genes in a genome only a little bigger than a prokaryote's."

"That's a lot, is it?" Jeric asked disinterestedly.

"*Yeah,* that's a lot. There are almost no redundancies, almost no junk genes. Look, most heliconomic chromosomes can be read in multiple ways by shifting the reading frame—that's the number of gene bases that correspond to RNA and then protein—but this is just crazy. I've never seen an organism code so efficiently."

Asar's brow was creased. "What does that mean?"

"It could mean a couple of things. The first one that jumps out at me is that the genome has been engineered or at least cleaned up."

"You're saying it's an artificial organism?" Raptor seemed disturbed by the thought of a life form engineered from scratch.

"I don't know. It doesn't seem likely because there are no recorded sequence homologies with other species. She didn't have time to really compare the bases themselves, but I'm impressed at what she managed in the time she had. The nucleotide bases don't match up, and no one would take the time to develop a whole new molecular language. This ... this is revolutionary, whatever it is. Because it's a sphere, the reading protein has three hundred and sixty degrees of freedom, so it can code functional proteins in any direction along the source and even code across wrinkles in the chromosome surface, skipping bases. *And* it looks like the complement can code functional proteins, too. That's the mirror version of the original.... But there are no noncoding sections, that doesn't make any sense. Where are the buffers to protect against mutation or degradation? Either this organism is very susceptible to mutations or something in its cells is an unbeatable goalie."

Leon looked at his friends, saw only blank faces. *They don't understand ... this is a new organism, something more complex and capable than anything we know. A perfect organism, so economical in its construction, so flexible, full of possibilities. Perfect. And wrong.*

Something tickled the back of Leon's mind: he wanted to see what kind of lifeform these genes would produce. Suddenly he sat bolt upright. "This is the enemy. This is what destroyed Aethaleia. What the Valinata was fighting."

"Bacteria?" asked Jeric, sounding sluggish.

"Maybe, but I don't think so. I mean, it *could* be a biological agent, but there's so much more going on here. A creature with a genome so perfectly evolved, so beautifully assembled, that it's almost godlike." He looked at their blank stares, their uncomprehending faces. "I had a professor once, Doctor Roja Bryku, Sheff'an. Brilliant guy, really inspired me. He said that every genome, of every organism, was a catalog of trial and error, a map of genetic encounters from the dawn of its formation as a possibility. *This*, this is an organism with *no mistakes*. Professor Bryku said that an organism with no mistakes was an angel. Shit, if only he could see this."

"Could these be the ... things we saw?" asked Asar uncertainly.

Leon froze, his mouth open, as he was about to reply. It *was* possible. He had assumed ... but now he didn't know what to think. It was all so jumbled in his mind, the memories foggy. Something dripped onto his hand, and he realized his nose was bleeding.

"Vic, you look sick," Jeric said, concerned. The ship's console beeped at him. "Oh, shit. Gotta readjust." He flipped a few switches and pulled a lever. The ship lurched and the staring eye of the conduit vanished, scattering into countless pinpoints of stars. They were in empty space. "Duraj Sector," Jeric said by way of explanation. "Gotta switch conduits for the final leg across the border. It'll just take a few minutes."

Leon sat in silence, dabbing at the blood coming from his nose and marveling at the data scrolling across his screen. How understated Moira Traveler's writings had been. Her discoveries and those of the other scientists of Project Abaddon were nothing short of seminal. It was a tragedy that she had died before being recognized, before sharing her discovery with the galaxy. She had shotgun sequenced and partially mapped a completely unknown genome configuration in record time. *She should be a hero, not forgotten.* Leon wondered if any of the other researchers were still alive.

The siren surprised him so much that he nearly dropped the HotStart. Raptor, whose eyes had closed again, snapped upright in his seat with terrifying speed, his dorsal spines extending.

"Shit, we've got a contact," Jeric said, turning to the sensors.

I don't want to meet the owner of this genome, was Leon's only thought. "Conduit, now. Nearest one."

"Not that easy, Vic. The solar sail deployed." Jeric's voice was chagrined.

"The *what?*" Asar demanded. He had risen in his seat, and if possible, his face seemed even more drained of color.

"I told you guys before, the main cells on this bucket run hot and bleed off ten percent faster than they should. This ship drains its cores like hell in cond—"

"Retract it, now!" Leon tossed the HotStart aside, its monumental contents forgotten. He looked through the viewport, and now he could see the umbrella-shaped black expanse of the solar sail, designed to absorb and store solar energy. *What was he thinking? We were almost home!*

"It was automatic!" pleaded Jeric as though he had read Leon's thoughts or, more likely, his seething expression. "I think it's all that sensor equipment and shielding Rockmore had loaded. This ship's power supply was never meant to sustain this kind of operation. I'm guessing they never had time to upgrade the power cells."

"Solutions?" Leon asked through gritted teeth.

"I don't know," Jeric cried out, studying the controls. "Maybe … maybe we could speed it up by precooking the primer plates for the next jump. But Vic, we can't open a conduit without enough charge. If we do, it could destabilize while we're still inside."

Raptor pointed to the console. "Looks like they're hailing us." He leaned forward and pressed a button on the comm panel. A furious voice was shouting in the Zetzoy tongue of the Tez'Nar.

"This is the VSF battleship *Fidelitas* to the unknown aggressor. Stand down immediately and prepare to be boarded or we will fire on you. This is your only warning."

We can't outrun them, not with the fucking sail hanging out in front of us. "Jeric, comm them back. Do what they say."

"Are you *crazy?*" Asar blurted. "Those VSF lunatics are going to dump us into space!"

"Look, I'll bet you they're terrified. If we can get on that ship, we can do more talking in the brig than we can as tiny particles floating in space. We're standing down." Leon injected his voice with as much authority as he could, and Jeric nodded.

"*Fidelitas*, this is the *Faithless Bitch*." He nearly laughed at the irony of this encounter between two ships whose names could not have been more diametrically opposed. "We're a trading vessel out of Aethaleia, bound for Naritrea."

Jesus, I hope our flight plan checks out. Their falsified records had been prepared in a hurry; more than a cursory inspection would be enough for even the thickest VSF officer to figure out they weren't who they said they were. Leon wasn't sure how detailed the Valinata's ship registry was, especially given the current omniarchy of their empire.

The ship that came around their port side in attack position was fearsome-looking with a divided hull, the larger dorsal section curved and smooth, the ventral section blocky and irregular. Its engines were massive, leaving glowing trails of incandescent gaseous byproducts. Like everything else about the Valinata, this ship was inefficient in the extreme. Tubes jutted out of its hull at regular intervals, venting reactor waste and making it look as though it were smoking. Every cannon on its hull was pointed in the direction of the *Faithless Bitch*, a hundred black, emotionless eyes. There was a great tear along the ship's starboard side, revealing decks that had been exposed to the vacuum. The faded green and silver paint and the emerald dragon on the ship's prow sent a sudden jolt of irrational hatred through Leon. All those years he had spent preparing to fight the VSF were hard to ignore. *They're not the enemy here, I'm sure of it.*

An umbilical emerged from the belly of the great battle cruiser, snaking toward the *Faithless Bitch*. There was a loud clang followed by a groaning sound as the flexible corridor affixed itself to the ship's main hatch. Leon stood up and calmly took his Sprawlers from their holsters. He pulled out the power packs and laid them on his seat. Looking pitiful, his companions did the same. Unarmed but still plenty deadly, the quartet proceeded to the airlock.

§

Jeric spat blood onto the grimy deck. *This fucking ship smells as bad as Aethaleia*, he thought, kneeling with his hands planted on the vibrating metal plates. The marine who had hit him slammed the butt of his gun into Jeric's back, nearly knocking him flat.

The VSF was taking no chances with them. A full squad of marines in green and silver battle armor, their faces hidden behind reflective orange visors, stood pointing their guns at the mercenaries while their comrades searched the ship, top to bottom. The Tez'Nar sergeant leading them had removed his helmet, and his bright blue plumage gleamed in the harsh lights, feathers ruffled in the cold rush of air coming from the vents.

"I'll ask again. Who sent you to Aethaleia?" His voice was quiet, even, venomous.

Jeric pointed at Leon. "That asshole's in charge. Ask him."

Leon shot him a look. "We were just passing through, to pick up supplies for our next run. We found the planet in ruins and fled."

"How unlikely," the officer said, clicking his broad beak. His large, round eyes were full of contempt. "Empty holds, exotic weapons. And Coalition registry logs."

"We bought those weapons for protection! We were over the border in the Alkyra," Asar interjected. He was rewarded with a rifle butt to the stomach, and he grunted in pain. For a moment, he looked as though he might pass out.

"Can you explain the military-grade sensor equipment? Or this?" the Tez'Nar asked, holding Jeric's HotStart by its connector wires. "You think we ignorant Valinata sojieri don't know what this is?"

Great.

"This is a professional thief's tool. And if you're thieves, you're enemies of the Valinata. Now, on your feet."

Jeric glanced at Leon as did Asar and Raptor. The colonel nodded slightly, and they began to rise. The officer wasn't blind, however, and saw whose orders they were following, which only infuriated him further. A rapid clicking came from his beak, naked rage, and he grabbed Leon by the collar.

"What's this?" he shrieked. One of his delicate-looking, long-fingered hands yanked down on Vic's collar, exposing the interface jack and the unmistakable barcode tattoo beneath it. "CRDF *scum!*" he warbled. All around them, rounds were chambered in rifles.

Great, Vic. Once again your fucking ink gets us in trouble. Jeric squeezed his eyes shut, wondering if they would be shot immediately or thrown back into the airlock without the benefit of the umbilical to get them back to the *Faithless Bitch*. Odds were the Vs would toss them into the void to see how long they could hold their breath. *And we were so close to home.*

"On your *feet!*" The Tez'Nar shrieked again, and the mercenaries rose. He pointed a graceful, feathered hand at Raptor. "Is your barbarian tame?" he asked Leon.

"No," Raptor growled. Lightning-quick, he snatched the rifle of the nearest marine and snapped it over his knee. A moment later, he was blocked from view as five of the sojieri beat him down with their weapons. There was a loud *zap!* and a bright flash, followed by the unmistakable scent of charred flesh. Shocked nearly unconscious, Raptor thudded to the deck. The guards set about clamping manacles on his wrists and ankles. Soon the groggy Prross was hauled to his feet in chains, but he still looked more than capable of ripping his captors into fillets.

"If anything like that happens again, you'll be treading the eternal sea," the VSF officer said icily. Jeric believed him.

They had been thoroughly searched. Asar's Qur'an had been confiscated and his prayer beads broken and scattered. Jeric had forgotten to hand over a little push dagger in one of his pockets, which had earned him the broken nose. He had seen sojieri afraid before, reduced to an animal state. There was no mistaking that these troops were frightened of something, but a curious phenomenon appeared to have taken hold here. These marines had turned their fear into a driving force, a *raison d'etre*. They had probably been wandering the stars in search of friend or foe, anything definite. And they had found something they could label, categorize, something on which they could focus their fear. It was just too bad that Jeric had been there when it happened.

Bound and with guns pointed at them the whole way, the four were led to the bridge of the *Fidelitas*, where a crew of junior officers little better than huddled refugees went about the thankless task of keeping the lonely ship functioning. In the captain's seat sat a young Human man who looked too inexperienced to be carrying the weight of such a command. In fact, he was, as he wore a lieutenant's insignia. It took Jeric only a moment to spot the bloodstain across the seat's headrest, a stain which meant one of two things: the captain had committed suicide or there had been a violent mutiny.

"Sergeant Matiti informs me that you four are Coalition spies," the young man said in a quavering voice.

Jeric looked to Leon. Vic would know what to do, somehow he always knew what to do. But Leon said nothing, only stood there with his head raised defiantly. Jeric saw a familiar cold regard in those stony eyes and felt himself overcome with a secret loathing for his friend. *That ain't my pal Vic, that's Victor the logical fucking officer, Leon the planet-burner.* Jeric's friend Leon was predictable and easy to deal with, but the Mourning Star was not to be misjudged. Friendship had no place in the equation. Jeric knew this, but he wondered if the young lieutenant had any inkling what sort of man he was dealing with.

"Silence equals consent," the promoted-by-blood officer said with a decisiveness he couldn't quite manage. "Our good ship *Fidelitas* patrols this sector. We guard against the enemies of the Valinata."

"And who might they be?" Leon asked, his emotionless voice startling on the quiet bridge. "Do any of you even know?"

There was a moment's hesitation, and in that moment, barely half a second, Jeric saw confusion and fear flicker through the Valinata officer's eyes, a dangerous current. "You are not of the VSF. That means you have appropriated your vessel. As foreign operatives in *our* sovereign territ'ry without authorization, *you* are the enemy."

"Where was the Aethaleia garrison?" Leon asked. It was not the voice of a prisoner, but the voice of an impatient teacher prodding a student for an answer. "Why wasn't anyone guarding the planet?"

The lieutenant seemed on the verge of answering. He stammered, then clamped his mouth shut. Leon, however, plowed onward. "You still don't know what you're fighting, do you? You just got called out on the hunt and followed your torch-wielding mob into the dark forest, didn't you? And let me guess, something was waiting in the trees. You got away because you were in the back, fled back to the village only to find it burned down." There was a smugness in Leon's voice that Jeric didn't like. Neither did the Tez'Nar sergeant whose dexterous hands clenched into fists. *Careful, Vic.*

"And what business did *you* have on Aethaleia?"

"Trying to find one of your scientists," Leon answered simply and surprisingly. *Now what the fuck are you playing at?* His abrupt change in tone shocked everyone present, even Jeric. Now he was conciliatory, wanting to help. "She was already dead when we arrived. Listen, the CRDF may offer you all asylum."

"*Bullshit!*" screamed the lieutenant, half-rising from his seat. He was a scrawny kid, not meant for such a position, not by a long shot. "You want us to surrender to your bloody fleet so you can interrogate us!"

Leon's smile was cruel, a curved knife. "What information could you possibly have?"

"Careful, *spy*," the sergeant hissed, his beak snapping on the end of the last word. He poked his rifle into Leon's back, but the colonel barely flinched.

"You should all be very careful. Whatever force destroyed Aethaleia is unlikely to shy away from a single, damaged *Iliad*-class ship like this. I don't want to meet up with them any more than you do. We're carrying valuable intelligence, and we intend to get it to the people who can use it. Your leaders have betrayed you, all of you, by keeping these terrible secrets, and now it's too late. But it's not too late for the rest of the galaxy, and if you help us, we'll promise you safe haven."

"Who are you to make such a promise, spy?"

Leon sighed and did something Jeric would never have expected. He turned around. The sergeant, startled by the movement, backed away. *They're afraid of us*, Jeric realized. It was almost hilarious. Then Vic pulled down his collar, exposing the barcode beneath the jack. "Check this."

Moments passed as Leon stood, holding his collar aside. His companions were like statues, and Jeric tried to get a reading from Asar and Raptor. The sharpshooter was an enigma, his features still, his dark eyes molten, and Jeric couldn't even tell what the man was looking at. Even swaying on his feet, seemingly close to passing out, he looked capable of anything. Raptor, on the other hand, could barely contain his fury. *He's just waiting for a word from Vic, and he'll tear the bridge apart.* Jeric shuddered. He wasn't cut out for this. There was a reason he sought out the comfort of a fighter cockpit.

Finally, an officer came forward and read the number into a computer in a perfunctory manner. The machine announced a "positive ident" and read out Leon's ID in a tinny voice. Jeric knew it by heart: ACQ373-716T-XRK, the number of the beast. Coalition Royal Defense Forces, attached to Second Fleet's Battalion 603 Drop Division: Information Operations, Reconnaissance, and Strategic Intervention

Regulatory Activities Detachment, IORSIRAD. Unit Disengaged. Status: Deactivated. The eyes of the officer holding the computer had gone wide.

"The Mourning Star," she breathed.

Jeric was satisfied to see that the face of the young lieutenant had gone markedly pale. *So great to pal around with a celebrity. Now's probably when they shoot us.*

"Hailing," announced the comms officer, breaking the tense silence.

"Who?" demanded the lieutenant.

There was a pregnant pause, then, "It's a Zoh Hegemony ship. The *Volgograd.*"

"You've led them here!" the lieutenant screamed, pointing at Leon.

The transmission was piped over the speakers, a woman's voice in Russian. "This is *Kapitan-Puruchik* Natasha Semyonova of the Zoh Armada Octus. You will be boarded. Stand down."

"Tag, you're it," Leon said. "Think quickly, Lieutenant. I don't think they're apt to be any more understanding than you."

"But—but this is *our* territ'ry!" the young officer blurted out as though explaining himself to Leon. Even now a number of glittering specks were visible in the far distance, close enough to fire.

"I don't think that's true anymore," Leon said evenly, placating. "Do the smart thing, kid, and we can all get out of here."

The lieutenant would not be so easily cowed, however. It seemed he had a spine, after all. "This is Lieutenant Vaughn Baker to *Volgograd*. You are in violation of sovereign Valinata space, and your actions are in aid of espionage and, therefore, an act of war."

"Explain," the impatient voice said.

"We have captured CRDF spies who claim to be trafficking valuable intelligence. They are unlawful combatants and will be executed as such. Return to your space, or we will fire on you."

Whatever the Zoh commander said in reply was lost in the mayhem that followed. "I don't have time for this," Leon snapped in Xhosa, resignedly, Jeric thought. With the officers and marines distracted by the standoff with the Zoh vessel, this would be their only opportunity. In an instant, he had turned back to the Tez'Nar and knocked the officer's hand away. The barrel of the rifle snapped to the side, and when the sergeant reflexively tightened his finger on the trigger, he sent a bullet through the back of the captain's seat. Yet another officer died sitting in that chair, and the young lieutenant fell to the deck with a childlike expression of surprise on his face.

Raptor bellowed and swung his manacled arms around in a great double-fisted punch that flattened three marines. In their bulky armor they had trouble maneuvering, and the Prross bowled into them, crushing half the squad against the blast door. Asar, though his left arm was pinned in a crude sling made from his belt, jabbed a man in the throat and seized his rifle. While the marine sank to the deck clawing at his collapsed windpipe, the dark-eyed sharpshooter turned the weapon on the other marines, cradling its barrel in his slung arm.

Jeric went for the HotStart, wrenching it from the grip of another sojier before pulling the surprised man's sidearm from its holster and shooting him in the leg and arm. He cradled the computer against his chest lovingly, aiming the pistol at the stunned officers. Half of them looked relieved to have had their decision made for them.

Leon had finally succeeded in getting his handcuff chain around the sergeant's neck and had him in a lethal choke hold. The marine officer's rifle lay on the deck, out of reach. The colonel's face was red from the exertion, but he refused to relinquish his stranglehold until the Tez'Nar gave up. "Shut down your engines," he ordered. "And allow yourselves to be boarded. We just saved your lives."

§

Leon didn't blame the Zoh captain for ordering them locked up and was thankful she had the presence of mind to separate them from the Vali crew. Once they were back in Coalition space and a priority message had been sent to High Command, the mercenaries' identities were confirmed. As Jackal Pack was still under a rough contract, they were released, although their weapons were held in storage aboard the *Faithless Bitch*. After the industrial squalor of the Valinata vessel, the worn but relatively clean interior of the Zoh ship was welcome.

The four of them still looked and smelled horrible after their time on Aethaleia. Captain Semyonova granted them a shower and a meal before their debriefing and sent them to the infirmary to be examined by the ship's doctor and a team of diligent corpsmen and -women. Asar would be all right, and he would keep the use of his arm although the cleaver had gone straight into the bone. None of them appeared to have been permanently affected by their time in Aethaleia's toxic soup though both Leon and

Raptor were now suffering from bloody noses, and Jeric was coughing uncontrollably. Captain Semyonova was younger than Leon would have expected and would have been attractive if not for her downturned, scowling mouth and dead eyes. She wore a black leather jacket and a floppy cap that looked almost like a train engineer's hat, but it was clear from the way she proudly wore her red shield insignia, polished to a sheen, that she was a card-carrying Zoh loyalist. And while Leon had inherited Hakar's distrust of Zoh ideologues—and all ideologues, for that matter—he wasn't about to spit in the face of his savior for her beliefs.

"You see, *Polkovnik*—" it took Leon a moment to recognize the Russian word for *colonel*—"Victor, we have been patrolling this sector for a week now. One of our scouts spotted your ship entering Valinata space. The circumstances of your incursion were … suspicious, so we held position to monitor for any subsequent activity."

"It's lucky that you did," Leon said, his fingers wrapped around a hot cup of bitter coffee.

"Luck has little to do with it. You and your *strelitzi* were spying on this world Aethaleia, were you not?"

Leon had already decided that the best tack with this woman was full disclosure. "Our mission was actually to rescue a potential defector from one of their academies. The purpose of the mission was not intelligence-related."

"But you collected intelligence."

"We did."

"I would see this. Now." Semyanova held out her hand. *Surprise, surprise,* Leon thought as he withdrew the data key from Jeric's HotStart from his pocket. She took it. *"Spasibo, Polkovnik."* She popped the key into the briefing room computer and looked over the streaming data with that steely, unfeeling gaze. After a few moments, she turned away. "This will go to High Command. I pray it will prove useful."

The other mercenaries stirred. "We were planning—"

"On selling this information to us, I do not doubt. Let me assure you, *Polkovnik*, that you will be paid with your freedom. I suggest, however, that you *not* pursue further compensation for this particular information. You have already stated that your mission was not intelligence-related. That is a good thing. I am sorry you did not find the person you searched for, but I fear there are more people missing, including many among our own population. Our concern is with their defense, not the Valinata's."

"What will you do with the Valinata crew?"

"That's not for me to decide." Semyanova shrugged as if to say *I couldn't care less.* "If they provide useful information, I do not doubt they will be given asylum of some kind. I do not think their information will be as good as yours, but we shall see." She leaned back, twisting in her chair. "It is good for you that you have friends in the High Command. In fact, Grand Admiral Hakar wishes to speak with you at your earliest convenience." Was that a note of awe in the *kapitan*'s voice? Leon allowed himself a weary smile.

As Captain Semyonova stood and led them to the hatch with her arm outstretched, Leon noticed the black armband just below her Zoh Naval crest. In the corridor he saw more armbands on the crew. How had he missed them before? When he asked what was going on, the captain's face became even unfriendlier. "This may come as a shock, but Prime Minister Somerset is dead."

Leon had to pause to catch his breath, while his companions swore. Some of the nearby crew lowered their eyes at the sound of the late prime minister's name. "How did it happen?"

"Apparently, he was spending time alone at his vacation home, and he slipped and fell down the stairs." The captain sighed sadly. "It is a sad end for a great man. He was always a true friend of the Zoh."

When Leon sat down in the secure comms room at the rear of the bridge, Hakar was waiting for him. The grand admiral's face, displayed in miniature on the screen, registered relief at seeing Leon in one piece. He came right to the point. "I'm glad you and your men are all right."

"Thank you, sir. Is it true? I heard that the prime minister is dead."

When Hakar's response bounced back to him, the grand admiral's face fell. "I'm afraid it is. It was a stupid, avoidable accident, but sometimes the universe gives us results we don't want. He always liked to get away to write."

It was too much for Leon to process. Instead, he turned to the immediate concerns. "Should we be looking forward to prison?"

"Don't worry, I've dealt with High Command. As far as we're concerned, your team was never on Aethaleia." Hakar's voice took on a serious, anxious tone. "What did you see, Leon?"

Leon had to pause to collect his thoughts. He had expected the question, had even tried to formulate an answer, but it didn't come easily. "I'm … not sure, sir. They looked like H'vir. They moved on four legs, and it looked like they had more limbs. But I can't say for certain. It sure as hell wasn't any Valinata separatist group."

When Hakar's response came back, it was startlingly abrupt. "Leon, please stay on the band." He vanished, and Leon stared, open-mouthed, at the screen where his mentor's face had been. When he reappeared a minute later, Hakar looked and sounded distressed. "There may be another factor. The Valinata—or the splinter group, whichever it was—may have deployed a new nerve agent on Aethaleia. We're not sure, but one of the symptoms of short-term exposure appears to be potent hallucinatory episodes."

Leon chewed his lip. The corpsmen aboard the *Volgograd* hadn't found any trace of a nerve agent. "Wait, sir, I know what I saw—"

"No one's disputing your perception of events, Leon. And I don't doubt that there *was* someone down there with you. I'm simply suggesting that the chemicals in the air distorted what you saw."

"But the bodies, they were cut to pieces, and the shields shot *hundreds* of people at the spaceport. And Raptor saw the same things Asar and I did. How could it work the same on Prross physiology?"

"That's a good question. I'm not sure, but again, this agent is a powerful one. Maybe you *did* see people cut apart, but it could have been a hallucination, or maybe the people were hallucinating when they rioted, thinking they were fighting monsters when they were really killing each other."

"What the fuck kind of bioweapon is this? Could it have come out of Aethaleia's École?"

"We're still working on that. It's called Raven Blue, and it seems that the Valinata have deployed it to … pacify urban uprisings."

All of this was too confusing for Leon, who was still exhausted, still disoriented, still frightened. And now he was being told there might be a deadly nerve gas in his system? Something didn't add up, but what was it? Hakar wouldn't lie to him, would he?

"One more thing, Leon. Did you encounter any naval assets? Did Jeric record any tactical data from the ship?"

"No, the only ship we encountered was the *Fidelitas*. Why?"

"I was hoping you could shed some light on the aggressor," Hakar said, but there was an odd relief in his voice. "But listen, you need to—"

"What about the data we found? The genome?"

"Yes, Captain Semyonova told me you recovered information. That's what it was? genes?"

"Yes, but not like yours or mine. Something I've never seen before."

Hakar couldn't quite hide his reaction, but Leon had trouble figuring out just what that reaction was. He recovered quickly. "Okay, well, don't say too much on this band. I'll make sure you're compensated, I'm just not sure how. And I'll see that the data goes straight to CRDRIG, to see if there's a possible connection to those things you fought." CRDRIG was the Coalition Royal Defense Research Institute for Genetics, Leon knew. There was an element in Hakar's voice that he found strange. It was as though the admiral was prodding him, leading him.

Leon's mind was sluggish, but he picked up on the inconsistency. "Wait, I thought you said it was a nerve gas, not—"

"Of course. Listen, son, I promise you we'll get it to the right people. I hate to do this to you, but you understand discretion." Leon understood discretion all too well, and his blood boiled as Hakar brought this up. "I need you to avoid discussing this with anyone. We don't want to start a panic."

"I don't mind telling you that I'm panicking here, sir."

"I understand, but I'm talking epsilon levels of secrecy here. I know that doesn't sit well with you, and it doesn't sit well with me, either. Can I count on you to make sure Raptor, Jeric, and ... what was his name?"

"Asar."

"Asar, right. Can I trust them?"

"As far as you can trust me," Leon said coldly.

"Good. Give my love to Traxus. But listen, Leon...." Again Hakar's voice had changed, and this time Leon thought he detected a trace of fear. "Keep one eye on the sky." The transmission ended.

Leon sat in the darkness for a few moments, bewildered. It was as though he had been speaking to someone else, not Hakar, not the man he had trusted from the moment he had met him. In fact, it had been as though someone *else* had been speaking *through* Hakar. When he emerged onto the bridge, Captain Semyonova was waiting for him. "Captain," he said wearily. "What now?"

"Now? Now you may take your ship and go home. But I do not need to remind you not to return to Valinata space. There is nothing for you there."

Leon nodded. That was indisputable. He began walking toward the lift bank that would take him back to the hangars, his friends, and his ship. He could feel the eyes of the bridge crew on him the whole way. At the hatch he turned. "One last thing, Captain. Do you have any idea what "Abaddon" is? It's the name of the Valinata project, and it's familiar, but I couldn't place it."

Semyanova nodded sharply. "It's biblical. Abaddon is the Angel of the Abyss."

§

On Tagea in the defense ministry's secure comm room, Grand Admiral Hakar turned to Grand Admiral Telec, his coal eyes burning angrily. "Deeps take you, Telec."

"What would you tell him otherwise? And thank you *very* much for slipping up and feeding him 'Raven Blue.' Are you *trying* to violate the epsilon protocols? You are, aren't you?"

"That's the least of our problems. We've got millions of witnesses to the battle over Talriis, not to mention two billion Vali refugees. We're running out of space in the refugee camps, and we're running out of people to police them. More and more ships are slipping through every day." Hakar locked his gaze on Telec's. "Word will get out."

"What scares me is that there aren't more of them," Telec confided. "As for Talriis, we're spinning it as a joint training exercise to strengthen relations between the Valinata and the Coalition."

Hakar laughed, despite himself. "Who the hell is going to buy that?"

"You'd be surprised. At times like these, people are desperate for good news. Speaking of which, Admiral Rodriguex's mop-up operations are going smoothly. Our visitors were apparently bloodied enough by her defense that they've vanished."

"We need samples."

"Oh, we'll get them. Apparently, three tenders full of recovered wreckage are on their way to Triatha right now." Telec looked smug, his facial tendrils pulsing happily. "Once Daris and Najo secure Calama, I think we can safely say the only easy way through will be the Arc."

"I'll kindly remind you that my *sister* is on the Outbound Arc, along with billions of other people. And you heard Leon. He said they looked like H'vir. That sounds familiar, doesn't it?"

Telec ignored that, offering neither assurances nor condolences. Instead, he asked, "Will Victor follow your orders?"

"Oh, yes," Hakar answered, regretful certainty in his voice. "He's always followed my orders. Too well."

17: Homecoming

Faithless Bitch resumed her journey to Eve, gravitational energy whipping against the hull in crackling waves. With each burst, the Rombaldt Masses seemed to slacken, and Leon's stomach would lurch as the gravity within the ship fluctuated. The four mercenaries had retired to the galley and had withdrawn into themselves, drinking hot Kaf while Leon explained the situation as Hakar had explained it to him.

"That's absolute bullshit," Raptor snarled, not bothering to hide his contempt. The atmosphere aboard the *Faithless Bitch* was distinctly cold, and it had nothing to do with the climate control.

"Please, shut up. I don't think Hakar would lie to me." Leon couldn't help the defensive edge to his voice.

"Oh no?" Jeric asked with a sardonic smile.

"We all saw the bodies, Leon," Asar said quietly.

"Well, maybe there's more to it than that."

"You," Jeric began exasperatedly, "are one in a million." He looked around. "Am I the one who has to say what we're all thinking?" He snorted. "I'll bet ten to one that your man Hakar is really the one behind all this. Think about it: we're sent on a mission behind Vali lines to extract a defector who just *happens* to be highly placed and working on something of vital interest? Hakar hired us, not Traveler's ex-wife."

Leon didn't say anything. He found himself reminded of his fall from grace; being in *Faithless Bitch*'s rusty little galley was akin to being back in the cell where they had put him upon his unceremonious removal from command. It had been a little room with a little window, his only company a frightened, disoriented deserter and an unrepentant rapist. It had been as though High Command wanted to remind of him how far he had fallen in their eyes. Leon Victor had taught himself long ago how to sleep through artillery bombardments with shells falling around him, with the bright, neat lines of laser cannon discharge flickering over his head. But that first night he had lain awake until the sun rose, punching a shaft of brightness through the gloom of that little concrete room with the water stains on the walls. It was Grand Admiral Hakar who had come to see him then, to throw the first handful of dirt on his buried career.

"Look, there's something out there, obviously. But it's not our business."

"Are you *kidding* me?" Jeric cried out, incredulous. "If it's war, it is *exactly* our business."

Leon sat quietly for a moment, realized that he didn't know how to say what he was thinking. "Well … maybe it's not *my* business anymore, then."

§

Atyre Kra'al awoke with a start and would have tumbled from her divan had her tail not been more awake than she was. Reflexively, she regained her balance and lay in the half-dark, breathing heavily. Her dream had been vivid, replaying events more clearly than she could actually remember, and she wondered how much of that had been true recall and how much had simply been her mind filling in the gaps with whatever took its fancy. Had it really been almost a decade? Eight years had passed, yet she felt as though she had aged a hundred since that day. She looked through the window of her office to see if it was the sun's rays that woke her. But no, it was still dark outside, and most of Sherata slumbered beneath a peaceful blanket of clouds and snow.

The dream had been vivid, all right. She could still taste the Tagean *daba* wine, a carbonated orange drink not unlike the champagne Humans seemed to favor for their own special occasions. The first time Kra'al had tasted *daba* had been on her acceptance to the parliament as the Prrastran representative. It had not been nearly as spicy as Kra'al was accustomed to, for Prross *khumbrin* was served hot and laced with pepper powder. She had reflected then on the omen of imbibing such a bland drink to mark such a momentous occasion.

But in her dream the *daba* had been like sweet ambrosia flowing down her throat. Usually she didn't remember even drinking it though she knew she must have, for it was custom to celebrate with a vintage that reflected the rising monarch. And *daba* was the wine of emperors as it had been since the Young Wolf claimed his throne.

As Kra'al gradually shook off the last vestiges of sleep, she wondered idly what the Young Wolf would have thought had he seen a Prross holding what had once been a hereditary office reserved exclusively for his progeny. The legends painted him as a singularly noble and open-minded figure, the only person who could convince the Terran Unity to lay down their arms and join his growing Tagean Dominion. People had a way of failing to live up to their legends, but even if the Young Wolf had, Kra'al doubted his mother, the Iron Queen, would have been thrilled. As in most things Tagean, the female had been the true driving force behind the ascension and the Dawn War, and historians rarely claimed that she was anything but ambitious and ruthless.

But it had been a changing universe then, and it would have been unthinkable for the Tageans to select a male leader at any other time in their history. And though the vast majority of his dynastic successors had been women, Kra'al had ascended after a long string of male emperors that culminated—or rather, reached its nadir—with Franz Telemon, the man with the golden tongue and the black heart.

Yes, the *daba* wine had been sweet, but the taste of victory had been even sweeter. In her dream, Kra'al had seen many faces. She had seen the face of her clan's high priest, who had never before left the soil of Prrastra. He had looked uneasy in the company of the galaxy's leaders, but he had been more commanding a presence in his simple robes and headdress than any head of state. She had seen the face of Horus Duraneth, Chancellor of the Unified Commonwealth, and Terrista Jos, Prima of the Shar'dan Confederacy, with her scales the color of gold. Behind them had stood the two senior members of the Valinata Tête, Labarulin and Osspan, who had emphatically joined the incoming empress in promising that a new day was dawning. And there had been the knot of disgraced grand admirals, the Star Chamber reduced to a handful, their leader and their colleagues locked away in the dark recesses of the Vault where they could forever reflect on their complicity and their guilt. Those who remained—Hakar, Telec, Pirsan, and Najo—had not been free of guilt, but they had honorably admitted it where their colleagues had denied it. They had also called for Telemon's ouster and Kra'al's ascension long before it became a popular notion. Near them had stood the uneasy cluster of newly minted grand admirals, taken from the ranks of vice-grand admirals or lower, when the vice-grand admirals, too, had been removed. They had been led by Doran Motayre, the imposing Vodroshoyan with the enormous horns, terrifying but guileless.

Well, those admirals had gotten what they wanted. Despite plans to the contrary, Rodriguex had held Talriis and seemed to have repelled the enemy. Somehow, she had managed to make a tentative peace with remnants of the Valinata Space Force. Perhaps they had managed to force their new adversary into an early stalemate. Kra'al could only hope.

Kra'al had risen as the first Prross monarch and the first female monarch in nearly a hundred years, promising that the universe was changing again. How many people had she disappointed? With a sigh that was nearly a growl, she rose from the divan and went to the window. Past her haggard reflection, Sherata's Plaza of Unity was still, like a photograph of itself. All she had now was memory, like a collection of photographs, for her past was so full of hope and potential, while her future at this point appeared uncertain, at best. She knew that their denial of what was happening along the Arc was unsustainable, that it was going to erupt, and soon. She had never thought she would see it, but war was coming. It was one thing to know it and quite another to see it gathering on the horizon like a great storm, to feel the first gusts of its wind on her face.

She looked out over the sleeping city again and felt a stab of sorrow. It could just as easily have been abandoned, lifeless, with nothing but a veneer of dust and the lace of cobwebs to decorate its crumbling splendor. Had she worked so hard and climbed so high only to become the caretaker of a dying age?

§

The dingy little Valinata freighter touched down before them, and Rachel pulled her jacket closed against the gust of wind kicked up by its braking thrusters. The sad backdrop for this homecoming was the growing Valinata refugee camp. The dropoff in traffic from the Emerald Veil had left almost half of the cosmodrome's tarmac empty. And so, with nowhere else to put them, the planetary government had allowed the refugees to erect a sprawling tent city. The fluid perimeter was guarded by Jackal Pack and shield officers who quickly removed any Valinata military personnel they found for interrogation by the Zoh officers who arrived like clockwork as though picking up dry cleaning. Uncomfortably, Rachel watched the Vali civilians swarming around a food truck, begging. Elsewhere, the Coalition Rienda flew at half-mast in honor of the fallen prime minister.

When the ramp at the front of the ship opened with a hiss of pressure seals and groaned downwards, Rachel caught a glimpse of her man that sent a shiver up her spine. *What happened to them?* The four mercenaries looked like the survivors of some great catastrophe as they stumbled, exhausted, out of the ship, and the celebratory mood at the pad turned somber in an instant. Asar, Raptor, and Jeric all looked as though they had been injured. The short pilot's nose was broken, and one of his eyes was surrounded by a broad, purple bruise. The Prross looked as though he had been tenderized: one of his eyes was swollen shut, and his head and arms were covered in dark welts and thin cuts. Asar looked worst of all, his left arm in a sling, his shoulder bandaged and bloody. He was supported by Raptor as he walked weakly down the ramp. All of them looked positively demoralized, drained of energy.

What did they do? Rachel wondered; her conscience screamed at her and would not be silenced. *Leon, what did you do?* She had seen pictures of shell-shocked sojieri, and her boyfriend and his companions fit those images to a T, from their hollow eyes to their weary, hanging limbs. They seemed barely able to lift their heads. Rachel wanted to run to Leon more than anything in the world, but she held herself back, standing between Traxus and Major Dawson.

Glancing to her right, Rachel saw surprise register on Liam Dawson's expressive, open face. He quickly flushed his shock, and his long, handsome features took on their professional, distant countenance again. He had always seemed young for his rank, partially because he shared none of his superior's world-weary and haggard character. He looked up to Leon, followed him, and lived happily in his shadow. And he was a little afraid of him, Rachel thought. She saw that fear now beneath Dawson's calm exterior.

General Rockmore met the mercenaries at the base of the ramp. He returned their salutes and then shook each man's hand, murmuring words of encouragement. His eyes were gentle, sympathetic, but Rachel didn't think Leon and his friends even noticed. They nodded dumbly at his words and continued on in a little knot while the assembled sojieri looked on.

When Leon came to Rachel, his eyes lit up a little, and he embraced her, tightly, desperately. She hugged him back, immediately aware of his stiffened joints and tensed muscles. One of his pistols pressed coldly against her thigh. "Are you all right?" she asked, whispering into his ear.

"More or less," he said. "I think I need a shower." When he said that, Rachel became aware of the chemical smell rising off him in waves. It was acrid, and she wrinkled her nose.

Sliding her arm through Leon's, she led him from the landing pad toward his apartment. The day was fine, the sun shining, and Leon seemed stunned by the sky. "So beautiful," he said, sounding haunted. "I forget sometimes." When Rachel glanced at him again, she saw that he was now gazing fixedly at her.

She felt a thrill run through her at the unrestrained passion in his stormy eyes, the revelation of what he had nearly lost. What had he seen to make him look at her so? Whatever it was, it was likely beyond her reckoning, and she was glad he had escaped it. There was something else in those eyes, too, besides the emotions so clearly directed at her. There was something wounded and unsure clouding them as though he had had a particularly nasty trick played upon him by a trusted friend.

In an instant, his detachment slid over his eyes like a blast shield as General Rockmore approached. "Why don't you take a break, son? Hakar briefed me already." Rockmore looked and sounded uncertain, too, as though he was embarrassed at having sent Leon and his friends on the mission. Tentatively, he laid a fatherly hand on Leon's shoulder.

There was an uncomfortable silence before Rockmore withdrew, leaving Rachel and Leon alone, or as alone as they could be amidst the mercenaries and technicians crowding around the ship. "I want to get out of here," Leon said softly but urgently. He was looking at Rachel again, and the remoteness had fallen away once more.

Seeing how battered Leon was, Rachel was happy to seize the opportunity. "Whatever you want."

His eyes seemed to regain some of their spark, and he managed a half-smile. "I love you, Rachel." They began walking together toward a waiting Hyena.

"What the fuck, man?" Jeric's words were slurred behind them. He had been drinking aboard the ship, Rachel could tell immediately. "Where you going?"

"I've got things to take care of," Leon cast back over his shoulder without turning around.

"No, you've got *us* to take care of. We just risked our fucking—"

"That's enough, Jerr," Leon said sharply.

"So you're just going to walk off with that bitch and leave us stranded?" A murmur cut through the crowd at that.

Rachel wished she could feel surprise at this outburst. Far from it, she felt relief that it was finally out in the open. She didn't want a fight between Leon and Jeric, but she wanted the bad blood dealt with. She just wished it could have waited.

Leon was turning in slow motion, the weariness having fled from his face, replaced with a sort of confused fury. He walked toward Jeric, looking like a hungry wolf. Raptor and Asar had begun drifting away, but now they stopped and started back toward their friends.

Leon towered over the pilot, but Jeric refused to shrink from him. Rachel felt incredibly awkward, hoping that this wouldn't turn bloody as seemed likely. *It's because of me.* They had been through too much together for their friendship to end like this or, at least, that was what she hoped.

She couldn't hear what Leon said to Jeric, but there was unmistakable anger between the two. Rachel felt a flush creep across her cheeks, felt eyes boring into her.

General Rockmore intervened before the two could come to blows. "You're all exhausted, I know. Jeric, why don't you come with me? A new bottle of fifty-year-old Gaidhlig Cairdeas just arrived. We'll take care of the bonus situation in my office."

"Scotch?" the pilot asked, blinking. He seemed temporarily mollified, but before he could leave, Leon put his hands on Jeric's shoulders, mirroring what Rockmore had done to him, and pulled him aside with Asar and Raptor. The ragged quartet stood apart, seemingly untouchable amidst the uneasy ranks of officers in their red-on-black uniforms, and Rachel waited while they huddled, their heads almost touching. Asar with his slack jaw, barely able to hold himself up, Jeric with his broken nose and black eye, and Raptor with his innumerable cuts and bruises, they all stood and listened.

Beside Rachel, Traxus was stiff, and, she could tell, a little hurt at being left out, but Rachel thought she should have felt lucky not to have seen what they had seen. She went to the Tagean and put an arm around her shoulders, which was awkward because she had to reach up. Traxus returned the gesture, and together the two waited.

Long moments passed as the wind blew across the landing pad, until the returning mercenaries straightened. Raptor looked pleased, and he embraced Leon quickly, followed by Asar. Jeric was the last to move, and he seemed reluctant, but finally, he wrapped his arms around his friend, and they stood like that for a moment that seemed to go on forever. When they parted, Leon said something, and Jeric nodded. He turned away with Raptor, helping the Prross lead Asar toward the clinic.

"Is everything okay?" Rachel asked, not wanting to intrude.

The color seemed to have returned to Leon's face, and he nodded, then wiped at some blood trickling from his nostril. "I think they understand. It's like Raptor always said. Nothing escapes change. It's absolute."

JP Ishaq

Intermezzo

The inland Lime Sea was named for its greenish-white waters and was normally a haven for visitors; today, though, the shore of its North Bay was far from crowded. Though the beach would seem a natural place for people to congregate during the drought, tourism was depressed. The threat of war, combined with the news of a great battle at a world called Talriis and the arrival of more Coalition fleets, had eroded people's spirits. So Leon and Rachel had the beach to themselves for long stretches, walking its length while gentle waves lapped around their ankles. The bulk of the sand and rock in the area were limestone, giving the water its milky appearance, but scattered black upthrusts of stone jutted from the water a kilometer or so beyond the beach, standing out against the pale, placid surface. It was serene, peaceful, beautiful. Rachel just wished Leon was in the mood to enjoy it. He almost aggressively stalked the shallow dunes and splashed through the water as though hunting for a way to have fun. It was painful to watch him.

"Sweetheart, why don't you slow down?" Rachel called out. With a fleeting look of childlike shame, Leon hurried back to her. His slim, muscular torso gleamed in the sun, his chest toned beneath fine curls of dark hair. Rachel didn't even mind the scars—at least, there didn't seem to be any new ones beyond some minor cuts on his hand and chin. She had vowed not to press him on what had happened as something had clearly cut him to the core.

One of her sandals, dangling from her fingertips, dropped into the water and was almost swept away in the receding wave, but Leon dashed over and snatched it up. Shaking water from the shoe, he handed it back to her. "I'm glad we came out here," he said. "Thanks for being so supportive."

"Are you kidding? I figured we'd be sitting in the pub all night, and you'd be throwing up tomorrow. A walk on the beach? Are you the same guy who left four days ago?"

"Not exactly." Leon smiled, but Rachel sensed a bit of regret in his expression. He got down on one knee in front of her, and her heart skipped a beat. For one selfish moment, Rachel hoped that whatever terrible thing had happened to him might have convinced him to propose marriage, to put all the violence behind him.

But Leon did not ask her to marry him. Still on his knees, he hugged her to him, pushing his face against her belly. After a few moments, he pulled her down beside him onto the warm, white sand. Rachel's disappointment passed quickly.

"Listen, Rachel, I wish I could tell you what I saw out there ... but I can't."

"I understand. I'm just glad you're back." She turned to look out over the sea so he wouldn't see her eyes brimming with tears. Finally, she rolled over to look at him lying on the sand. "God, it's beautiful here. I feel like we have the whole world to ourselves."

"No, it's a much nicer feeling than that," Leon said, his face suddenly shadowed despite the sunlight pouring across it. The same sunlight shone off the water, turning it into a rippling sheet of gold. "You know, the universe is a scary place. Somehow seeing you ... makes it all bearable."

"I feel the same way, Leon."

"It's just that there are so many things we don't know about and can't understand." He chewed his lip, and they sat in silence, watching the sun slide across the sky, listening to the friendly whisper of the water. A gull was running along the wet strand at the tide line, hunting for a tasty morsel.

Rachel let herself fall back into the sand, felt it yield against her bare back. She squeezed a clump of it in her hand and felt its abrasive particles sliding between her fingers. It was so hot, as though it had just been baked. The sky above was a blinding blue dome, crystal clear. One of the Two Brothers drifted overhead, a great white potato of a moon. It almost looked as though it had a face, benevolent but disinterested in the trials of the people beneath it.

The moon disappeared as Leon leaned over her, his face in shadow. Much of the tension had melted from it, but still he looked troubled. "You look like an angel."

She laughed up at him. "That's sweet." Then she pulled him down to her, and he gladly rested his head on her bosom. His stubble on the tops of her breasts was scratchy but not unpleasant. For a man who looked so deadly—and whom she knew to be just as deadly as he looked—he was surprisingly tender. One of his fingers began tracing the line of her collarbone, and she shivered a little. It tickled. "It's a long drive back to the base."

"It is," he replied.

"The sun will be down soon. You don't want to drive in the dark, do you?"

"I don't mind that much," Leon said, not taking the hint.

"Well, you still look tired." *Wherever you went.* "I think it would be safer if we just got a hotel room for the night, played tourist tomorrow."

She felt his lips split in a smile against her chest. "We could do that."

And so they sprawled on the warm sand as the sun slipped down to the east. Eventually, the tide made its way to their toes, and they got up, startled and laughing. Holding hands, they made their way back into the town of North Bay, past the trawlers coming in with the day's catch, past families pulling their little day sailers up to the slip. The streets were lit with lanterns that hung on cords between the buildings. Eve was a beautiful place once you got used to it, beautiful enough to call home.

That night they ate local shellfish and climbed up to a quiet room in a quiet hotel where they made love with the balcony doors open and the wind carrying the sound of the sea in to them. Rachel wanted to tell Leon that she knew about Daltar, had known for some time the truth of the Mourning Star and the terrible wrongs he was trying to right. But she knew that truth would break him now, and so she said nothing. It would keep, she decided.

As they sprawled on the soft hotel sheets, drifting off to sleep, Rachel's mind tumbled through the layers of her memory. A year ago, she had received a painful and very unsettling wake-up call from her dream of luxury. While she never would have expected to fall in love with a man such as Leon, here he was, lying beside her in a room overlooking a tranquil, deserted strand of beach on a world she had never heard of until he had brought her to it. Their relationship had been ignited in a blaze of gunfire and spilled blood. She had been afraid that it would flare out and nothing but smoke would remain when the novelty wore off. It wasn't so, and Rachel knew they had a chance. Leon had given her a new perspective on the universe, though it wasn't always a pleasant one. The least she could do in return was to give him peace. Their differences were still great—she could hardly deny them—but they could be overcome. Just looking at Leon was proof that adversity could be overcome. *We're here, together. The whole galaxy could fall apart around us, and we'd still be here.*

Acknowledgements

The following people were instrumental in getting this story to you, and these words will never be enough to properly express my gratitude. My parents, Mousa and Kristin, supported my passion from a young age, and my mother, Kristin, provided invaluable editing expertise from first draft to last.

Allison Miller, software engineering Voodoo queen and drinking buddy, got www.jpishaq.com up and running and kept my ego in check.

Kristina Drobny Bond, marketing guru and gourmet, lent her photography skills and offered plenty of constructive criticism on the book ... and everything else.

Many friends, relatives, and colleagues supported me from start to finish. Chief among them have always been Chris G. and Naim, Nesreen, and John Q. And back in the day Christina L., Sunder B., and Kim S. told me to "put it in the book," so I did. Cheers to all of them.

The Jackal Pack crest depicted on the cover was designed by the author and produced by the team at Quality Embroidered Patches.

Last but certainly not least, I must thank the giants on whose shoulders I've stood to get a better look at the stars: Isaac Asimov, Orson Scott Card, John Scalzi, George R. R. Martin, Frank Herbert, Robert Heinlein, Douglas Adams, Walter Miller, and the other legendary writers of science fiction and all other forms of literature.

About the Author

JP Ishaq grew up visiting farflung relatives and historical sites, cultivating a love of adventure and culture as well as a healthy disdain for airports. He learned the art of storytelling from his grandfather's tales of genies and bandits and began writing at a young age, first as a hobby and then as a passion. He attended the University of Vermont, where he studied molecular genetics. Vermont is still his base of operations.

Made in the USA
San Bernardino, CA
26 December 2017